INTO DARKNESS

Blood of
the Durit

Book 2

Into Darkness

Angie Caedis

For Karisa—

Not only did you let me yap endlessly about this story for months, but you never once met me with anything other than constant hype. You kept me sane during this book's creation. Thank you for being its #1 fan (and Hassan's).

PRONUNCIATION GUIDE

Names

Ren / Serehna	*wren / sir - wren - ah*
Mikel	*mick - el*
Hassan	*huh - san*
Savi	*saw - vee*
Tariq	*tar - ique*
Vish	*vih - ssh (like fish)*
Riat	*rye - at*
Kai	*ka - i (like my)*
Malachi	*mal - uh - ka - i*
Quin	*coo - win*
Ivar	*eye - var*
Tofá	*toe - fa*
Chani	*chaun - e*
Lorik	*lore - ick*
Roel	*roe - el (like noel)*

PRONUNCIATION GUIDE

Names (cont'd)

Asha	*ah - ssh - ah*
Bair	*bear*

Daemons, Creatures, + Things

Daemon	*day - mon*
Hekkriti	*heck - cret - e*
Turiden	*tur - eh - den*
Durit	*dur - it*
Hesha Mol	*hesh - ah mole*
Yenti	*yen - tea*
Pehmi	*peh - me*
Hutri	*who - tree*

Gods

Hael	*hay - el*
Veles	*vell (like hell) - iss*

PRONUNCIATION GUIDE

Places

Jahaer	*ja - hare*
Caen	*kay - en*
Letka	*let - kah*
Hira	*hear - a*
Tol Dena	*toll den - a*
Artolen	*are - toll - en*
Kohe	*co - hey*
Raulik	*raw - lick*
Tilket	*til - ket*
Weshí	*weh - shh - e*
Rikyir	*rick - year*
Fála	*fall - la*
Gahven	*gah - ven*
Sefti	*sef - tea*
Denheir	*den - ear*

Hael-blessed Daemons

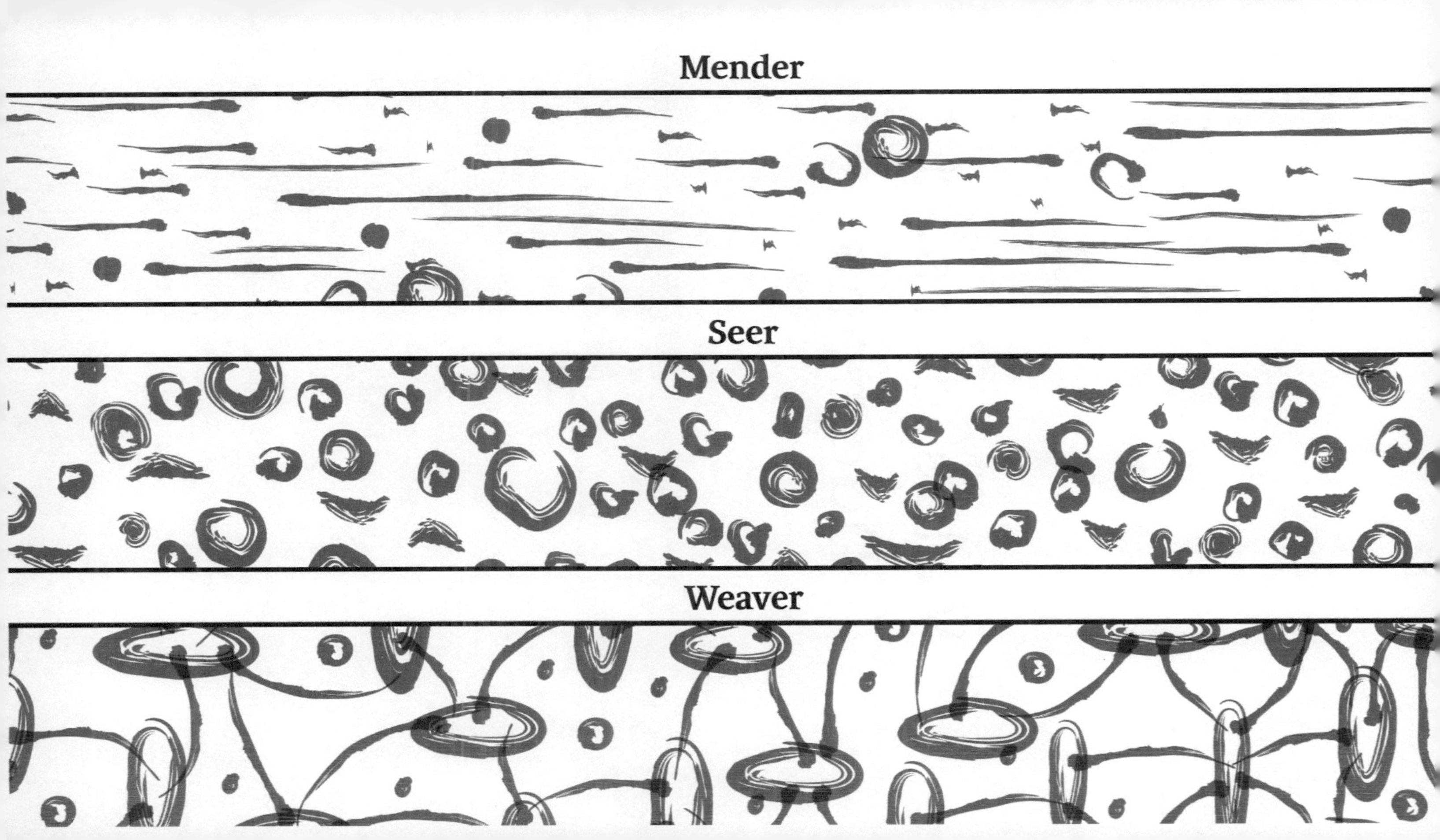

Mender
Seer
Weaver

Veles-cursed Daemons

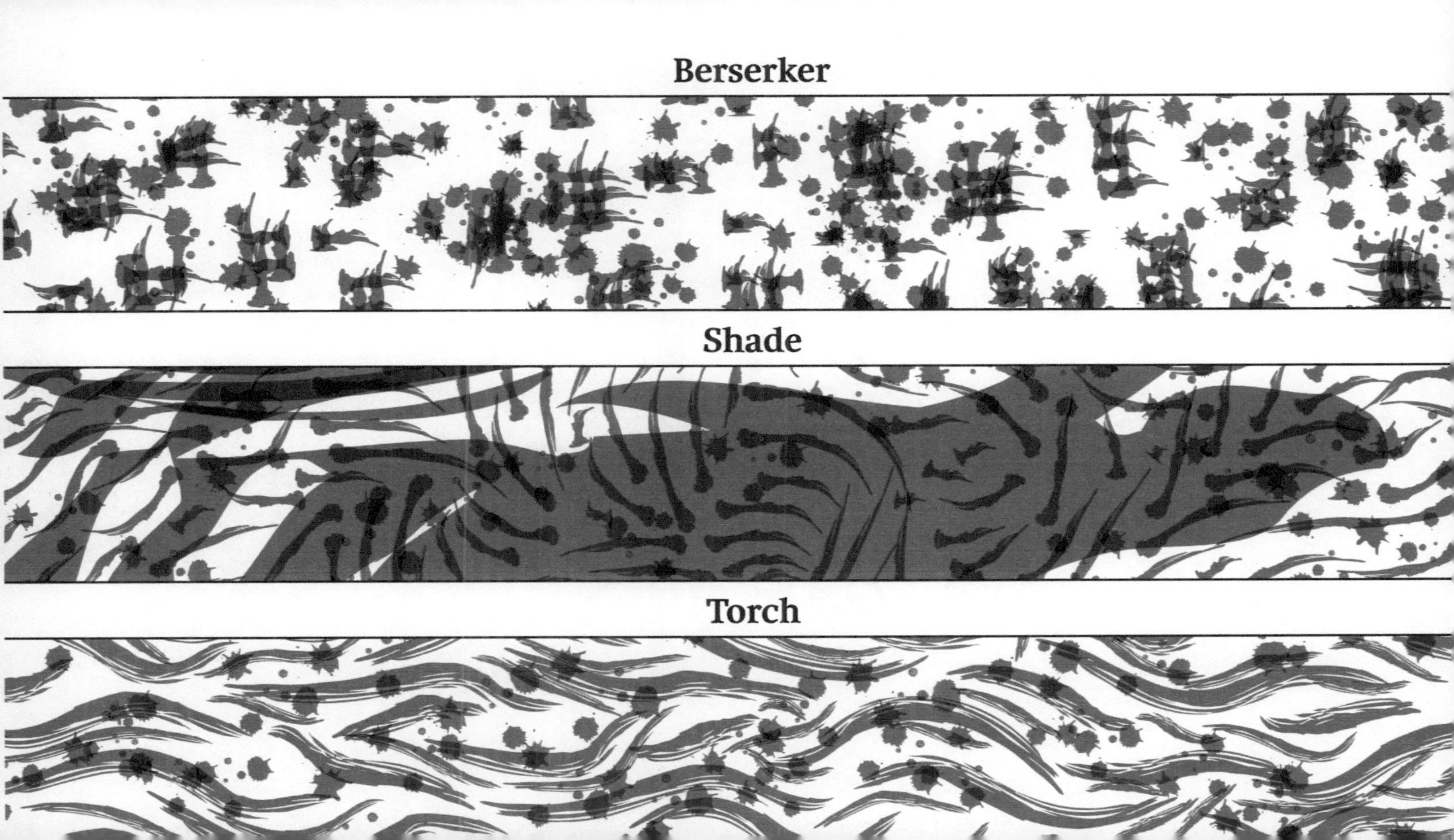
Berserker
Shade
Torch

Bair's
Prophecies

The Seeker
The Durit
The Born

Death would have been kinder.

gods-drenched north
may the gods watch over you
Jahaer Desert
Kanti
Gah
Bosin
Asho
Deshi
Monole
Varhi
Ricten
Tol Dena
Kohe Mountains
Piro
Denheir
Pála
Weshi
Kypor
Fiöl
Hanta
Lehro

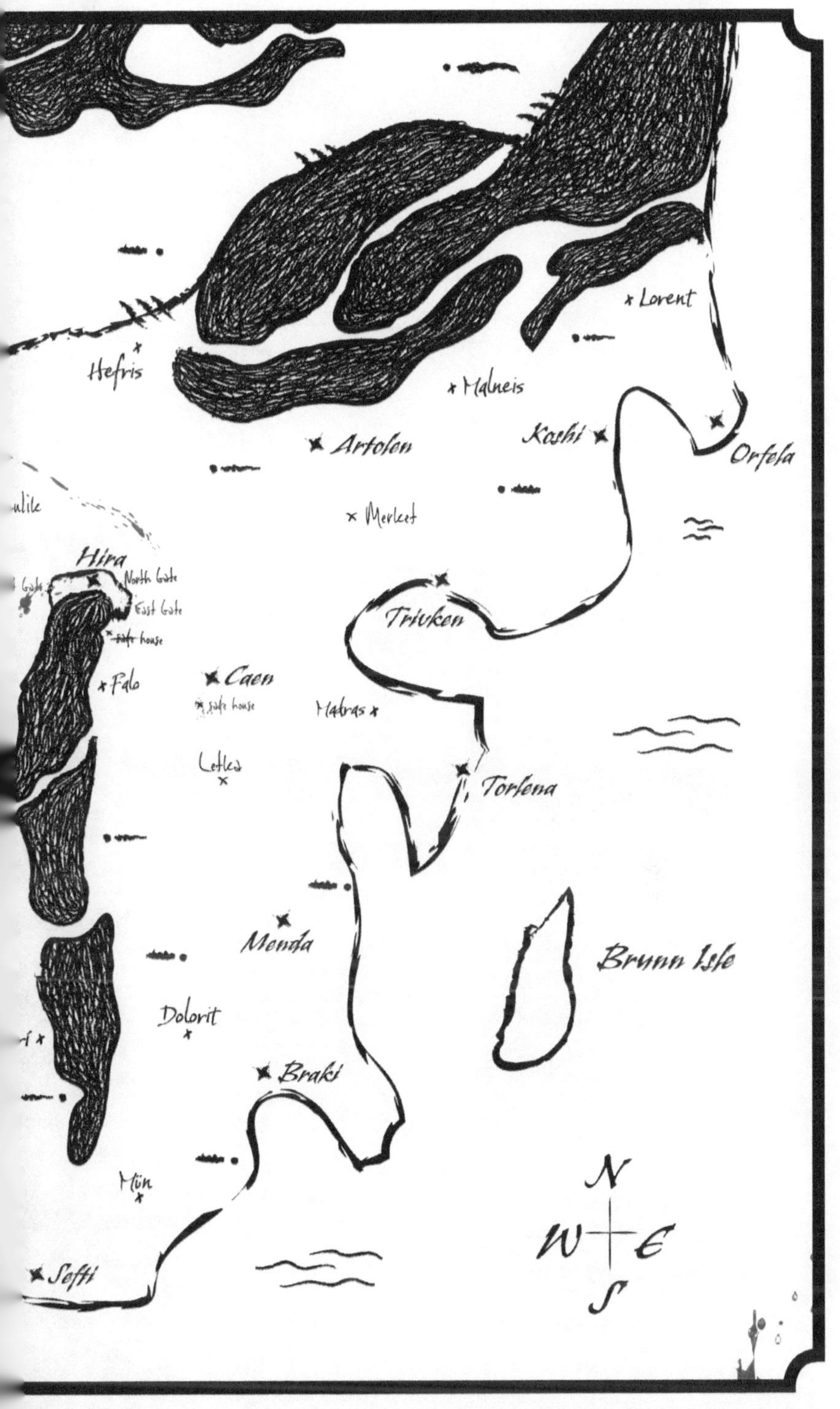

Lorent
Hefris
Malneis
Artolen
Koshi
Orfela
Merket
Hira
North Gate
East Gate
safe house
Triuken
Caen
safe house
Madras
Palo
Letka
Torlena
Menda
Brunn Isle
Dolorit
Brakt
Mün
Sefti
N
W E
S

PROLOGUE

My eyelids flutter open, stifled by a heaviness I can't seem to shake. I've gone in and out of this moment so many times, I'm not sure if it even exists. The pitch black is a muddled haze around me—a sweeping lush of shadows and bleariness that all but makes me blind. It's cold here, too, wherever here is. Or maybe, it's me that's cold.

There's a damp slipping across my skin and into my bones, raising my flesh in goosebumps. It feels like water running down my neck, seeping into the fabric of my tunic. I try to shiver, but my muscles are locked down tight, clamped like I've been turned to stone. I fear if I move, I might break. Exhaustion mixes with something foul in my gut—an awareness that only hastens every shuddering, shallow breath I take.

This is not the darkness the gods promised.

The hairs on the back of my neck raise against a slick of sweat. It pools on my forehead, too, dripping down my brow and into my eyes. I don't blink the drops away; I don't have the energy for such things anymore. Rather, I let it sting and blur my vision. My lids grow heavy as sleep beckons me back once more. It's a tempting lullaby, a siren's call into depths darker than those I already face. My head lulls to the side, but before I can slip back into the oblivion my body craves, I'm yanked by the steady grip of steel.

Panic eats through my last lick of sanity as I thrash without concern for the clutch around my throat. More rivets of water drip down my neck, like the gods themselves weep for what I have become. I cough and gasp until a scream tears through my lungs with an agony I simply don't have the strength for. My body is consumed by a pain I cannot fathom; every new tear in my flesh is a vicious reminder that, somehow, I'm still alive. Though as each moment of this suffering seeks to burrow into my very soul, I know death would have been kinder.

I raise my hands to free myself, but before I can find relief, pain shoots through my arm like the touch of a hot poker. I cry out, though nothing but a strangled rasp chokes from my throat. My left arm is on fire, searing with a type of pain that doesn't seem possible. Dizziness overtakes me, followed by a nausea that rocks my aching stomach. My vision wavers, but it's not the darkness I crave that overtakes me. No—it's a flash of gray, and that sight alone threatens to pull another scream from my lips. Though I know he's not truly here—rather, lost to another darkness—he's come for me all the same.

Silas looks at me steadily. Solemnly. I blink, but there's no escaping this. No escaping *him*. The world spins. My gaze grows bleary and weak. But still, through it all, he persists like a ghost behind my lids.

It seems the gods are relentless in their punishment.

I find no playful gleam in those light irises of his. No mischievous quirk resting in the corner of his mouth. There is only a cold severity, a dead emptiness. He looks at me with an unwavering certainty. A knowing. *A damnation.* My eyes scour his face, searching for absolution, but I deserve none, so none is given. Every flicker of those gray eyes is a stake in my heart—a torture driven by my own hand.

I blink the illusion away, not able to face what I've done, only to find a harsher reminder of it. My gaze drops from his face, past the markings, to the swirl of shadow wrapped around his throat. The darkness wavers, as if frozen in time—*like it's waiting.* I open my mouth to scream, to call back the rage I unknowingly unleashed, but it's too late. The black cuts across his skin in a slow, torturous sweep. Though I know it happened quick that day, the darkness takes its time now. It savors the moment, cutting rivers of red into his flesh, one after the other. I watch every drop of blood fall, watch it seep out of his chest and stain the fabric of his tunic. I know it isn't real, not this time, but it steals the breath from my lungs all the same. As tears brim my eyes, I can't help but glance to the one place I know will wreck me further.

His eyes are wide—the horror unmistakable. Shock turns to pain. Pain to acceptance. I watch his life dwindle before me, and somehow, it's even worse than the first time. I lunge for him, but he slips through my fingers like the very shadows that burdened me with this pain. I tear through the dark, desperately grasping for the warmth of his flesh, but it's too late. He's truly lost to me now.

Instead, I'm falling—crashing into a pool of red. I slip under the hot slick of his life to find the hell I crave at last. Silas's blood coats every inch of my skin, slides inside every crevice. I'm flailing, sinking, drowning in it. I fall deeper, choking on the coppery tang as it pours down my throat and fills my lungs. Red overwhelms my vision until everything else ceases to exist.

This must be true death.

Then, nothing.

Once again, the dark is all that greets me. There is no blood. No abyss to drown in for eternity. I'm left with only an emptiness that creeps over my shoulder and curls around my throat like a cat. It hums. It settles. But all too soon, that emptiness comes for me. Like an errant wave, it yanks me under just when I reach for shore. I'm thrashing against it. Begging for it not to take me. Choking on its endlessness. Shadows reach for me in the dark like hands—eager to take me where I belong. Down, down, and down I go. Darkness rakes across my skin like cut glass, eager to deliver me to the depths of eternal suffering. Though fear curdles my stomach, I know it's what I deserve.

I take my final breath, though the gods toss me back to this world like a doll flung from the highest window.

My body shudders and drops as consciousness slams into me. Vomit spills from my chapped lips as I heave with every ounce of energy I have left. My skin pulls against the metal cuffed around my neck, desperate for any slack, though I'm quickly punished for the effort. There's a nip—a bite of the smallest torture—then a cool trickle down my skin. I scream, though soon relent, giving in to the pain I cannot escape. My eyes flicker heavily as I glance over my shoulder to the wall and the chain that connects me to it. It strains against the pressure, pulled taut with nothing left to give.

How many times have I awoken like this? And how much more must I endure?

My shoulders slump, head dipping as far as it can go. Tears spill from my eyes as a shuddering chill ripples across my skin. I shake uncontrollably, though it only spikes that intangible pain and prompts the slick, wet flow across my skin.

Gods, help me.

Though I know what I will find, I force my eyes open. I stare into the dark, and the dark stares back. It thrums like a living thing, and I know better than to think it anything but. Past the dark, I strain my ears for something more. There's the distant *creak* of a door. Then, the muffled *shush* of sand somewhere further. Rats scurry in the distant corner, feet pitter-pattering along the stone. But the thrumming comes back too quickly, like it never even left. Something tells me it never will.

My stomach lurches, fighting the ever-present swell of nausea. The darkness spins. I pull my bound arms closer, tucking them against my body as the world teeters. The effort costs me greatly, but I let pain ground me amidst these horrors. There's an itching in my veins, a pressure that feels ready to pop. Stronger than that is the twinging scorch of poison that courses through my blood like it belongs there. I know its sway all too well now. My body quakes and retches. The world around me is a shuddering whirl, a dizzying expanse of nothing. I wait for death, but death never comes for me.

I'm slipping deeper and deeper into the dark when, against my better judgment, I think of him. But not of shadows and death. No, I think of things I know better than to. These memories are a fleeting comfort—ones I don't deserve. I snatch them with greedy hands all the same.

I think of what it was like to be curled up in his embrace, even if only for a night. I think of his lips on my skin, the way his hands molded to my waist. But my mind is quick to betray me, just as he did. I think of the way Silas held me down in the sand, how he handed me over like nothing more than a reward to be collected.

Rage warms my chest, and I welcome it. I think of those shadows, how they sliced into his chest like a blade through parchment. How righteous it had seemed. How much I had craved that moment.

He deserved it. I thought he deserved it. *He did, didn't he?*

My brow furrows as a lump of emotion grows in the back of my throat. I try to swallow it down, but it won't budge. It stays there, churning memories and regret alike. It was all out of my hands. It wasn't my fault—wasn't real. Though that violence had felt good, though it felt like that darkness answered to my very call, it wasn't my own.

Right?

My hands shake. A flicker of grief rises up in me like a deadly tide. *No.* I'm shaking my head, thrashing against the chain holding me in place. My flesh screams in protest, but neither it nor the cold bite of metal against my throat settles my frenzy.

No. I didn't. I couldn't.

I feel an unholy pressure under my veins, an incessant itch in my very blood. It swells with a wicked glee, a certainty that begs no doubt. My gaze grows hazy as tears flood my waterline. I manage to glimpse it among the dark—a soft swirl of shadows along the stone floor. My eyes widen, and my blood thrums in turn. It's then that I realize there is no sweet release of death waiting for me on the other side of this agony. What I face now is true perdition—more harrowing than being dragged down to the underworld to wallow in eternal darkness. These are the real hells the poets speak of, the ones made of our own suffering.

I let out one final scream as unconsciousness claims me too late—for there is no denying what I now know. The gods have decided my fate, and it's worse than I could have imagined.

CHAPTER 1

Finally, night has fallen. My fingers splay against the hilt of my sword, almost twitching in anticipation. I look to my left and search my cousin's face for any sign of hesitation. There is none—only determination in the taut grooves of her face that tells me we're really doing this. She looks like a force of nature, and I'm glad, because I need her to be. There's a firm tension in her jaw, and a readiness set in her crouching figure. But her eyes. Her eyes give her away.

As she glances my way, she can't hide her worry from me. The gaze that meets mine swims with unspoken questions. She doesn't need to voice them; I know her fears all too well. As we've watched this day fade to night, I've harbored the same ones. I think about offering her some sort of reassurance, but I can't. There are no guarantees in this life. Anything I could say to alleviate her worries would be a carefully crafted lie. She doesn't need that, and I promised. *No more secrets.*

Savi swallows harshly. "You sure about this?"

I grit my teeth and tear my gaze away from my cousin. "No."

The snicker to my right does little to ease the tension riding my shoulders.

"Oh, come on." Riat grins. "It'll be a piece of cake." He throws an arm over my shoulder—a gesture I'm quick to brush off. "How do you think she'll repay me after we rescue her?" he yaps. "A kiss?"

Riat taps his chin with one of his throwing knives before his face lights up with mischief. "I guess you could just drop us off at the closest inn and we'll see what—"

My fist finds his gut before I can stop myself. "Enough," I grunt. "I need you to focus."

Riat coughs quietly as he pulls a full breath back into his lungs. "*Bollocks*," he croaks. "I was just trying to lighten the mood."

"Don't," I snap. "We need to be ready for whatever we find in there."

My jaw locks as I think back to what we already know. Vish had been right. The Berserker took her to Letka—the same city whose shadows we currently hide in. Even without the tracker by my side, it didn't take long to find a familiar, ghostly-white mare in front of one of the inns. A pack was secured to the saddle, but the witch was nowhere in sight. The three of us staked out the inn for hours, and as each passed, my unease grew. I know Vish's worries; he's been whispering them in my ear for the past week. Every day she remained in our presence, he only grew more certain of what she was. And, though I didn't want to believe in such things, the evidence is getting harder to ignore.

Vish was given a name: Serehna. There was a description, too—mere fragments of what to look for. A scar from a knife wound that should have killed her. A trail of Seer's marks down her neck. Two cities she once called home, both of which left her abandoned. And there were other things, too; things I couldn't understand for myself. Vish said his gift was different—*fabled*. It worked in ways others couldn't comprehend. He knew things; not everything, but if he asked the right questions, the world would simply unravel for him. He said it was like the gods were whispering in his ear—slipping knowledge into his mind. It was there. Tangible, but not. Known, but unproven. *A Seeker*, he calls himself.

The word tastes bitter, even as I think it now. Over six years of friendship, tainted by a single omission. He said it was for his safety—and ours—but an omission is still a lie.

I shake my head, shoving away things I haven't yet come to terms with. There's only one thing that matters now. Vish asked me to get the witch back, and though I had a million reasons to say no, I couldn't bring myself to. Even before we scoured this city and tracked those men here—loud mouthed and drunk—I knew I couldn't leave her to rot. I knew it in the desert after she'd come for my head when it was that traitorous daemon's she should have sought. *Hells*, I'd known it when she tackled that bounty whose capture she had no stake in. There was no fate that didn't lead to this path; Savi has called me foolish to deny it, though part of me still wants to try.

Vish told me the witch was important from the moment I carried her into our camp. She was the one he'd been looking for—though Vish had been sure to leave me in the dark until it was much too late. Not an omission this time. A lie. I knew he was looking for a weapon; he'd been tracking it down for years now. And while I had offered my help long ago to make sure his mythical weapon didn't fall into Rohan's grasp, I never expected it to be her. I should have left Vish to deal with his own problems the moment I found out. Daemons and prophecies aren't my business to get involved in; but yet, here I am.

As I stare into the night's black, I can't help but let my mind wander. The pain in her amber eyes as she'd hoisted her dagger high, ready to strike me down, is a memory I haven't been able to shake for days. Part of me wonders if she did manage to bury that blade in my chest, because I surely feel the ache of it now. She had been so sure I was the one to betray her, and in the moment, I wasn't convinced she was wrong. *What would have happened if I'd only told her the truth? Would the Berserker have killed us like Vish assumed? Or would I have spared the witch the fate she now faces?*

My hand clenches around my sword. It doesn't matter. Those answers will solve nothing.

"Savi. Riat," I utter, my voice so low it all but melts into the night's hum. "Do what you must. Honor what you can't."

Savi takes a deep breath before rising from my side. She saunters casually toward the southern edge of the house, bow draped across her back. Her hips sway in a way that almost cracks a smile onto my sullen face. She's really playing it up. Though it makes me want to roll my eyes, it works.

The two men we followed here perk up at the sight of my cousin. Time has left them sober, making this part of the plan much more delicate. They speak in low, mumbled tones as their eyes roam over Savi in a way I should gut them for. I don't care to hear the conversation that passes between them now—I heard enough before.

Insufferable bitch was what they'd called the woman that ordered them from the tavern hours earlier—a woman Savi quickly identified as a Torch by the white flurry of markings on her dark skin. After hours of searching the city for any sign of the witch, it seemed our luck had finally won out. The men were anything but discrete, despite the way the Torch had snapped at them to keep quiet. From behind the rims of barely-touched pints of ale, we watched, and we listened. But even before the woman had mentioned a problem that left all of her men wounded or dead, there was one word that made my ears burn. *Rohan.* The mere mention of his name brought back everything I hoped to keep buried. Rage. Hate. Grief. In the blink of an eye, I was twenty-something, barely a man and faced with a devastation I had never known. Hearing his name was like stepping foot into that outpost again, seeing the land scorched and left to rot. Bodies strewn about the sand. Ash and blood coloring the desert in its sick decay. I had never known true hatred until that day. The overwhelming pull of malice that came over me felt like it had belonged to the dark god himself. I would have been lost to that righteous pull of violence if not for Savi.

It was the look on her face that grounded me every day—her caring, bright light the only thing that kept me from razing the Continent to the ground in search of those who caused her harm. I withstood those urges for years until I could no longer bear it. Though when the blood finally coated my hands, I realized nothing had changed. I was still angry, and my dear cousin still scarred. Worst of all, the one who had sent his men into my cousin's home for no purpose other than greed still lived. I realized long ago that until my blade pierces Rohan's heart, I will never be sated.

Today, it's the same devil who sparks that old, vengeful fire within me. Though the Torch told her men that Rohan was waiting for his prize in Denheir, the lack of his presence does nothing to calm the simmering rage I feel. I'm far from the man I once was, but my hand still twitches eagerly around the hilt of my sword. I fear the witch is the only thing keeping me from slipping into reckless habits I've far outgrown. If there wasn't more at stake here I would have barged into that house hours ago, impatient and eager for the slick of blood on my blade. But the mere thought of her—somewhere behind those walls—is a gnawing reminder as to why I'm here mixed up in things I barely understand. Rohan wants the witch, and I'll be damned if another person suffers at his hand. Revenge can wait. Some things are far more important. Some people, too.

I snap back to reality as Riat slinks against the eastern wall of the house, having slipped from my side long before thoughts clouded my focus. The plan runs through my head like it has countless times since we hunkered down in these shadows. I search for a flaw—any misstep that could fuck this up. There's about a hundred different ways we could fail tonight. A hundred different ways I could leave without the witch, only to find myself and my crew broken and bloody. Though I want to, I know better than to ask the gods for help; if anything, they'd see fit to test me.

My fist tightens at my side as I watch Savi flirt with the two men. They laugh too brazenly, forget their duty too easily. I should be thankful their vigilance is so pathetic, but I can only simmer in my contempt. They pay no mind to the weapon strapped to Savi's back, much too interested in the front of her. The tension loosens from my shoulders at the realization that this may prove easier than I expected, though only slightly.

Riat's shadow dances against stone, separated from Savi and the men by a corner of the house. I hold my breath and balance on bent legs. Watching. Waiting. My muscles twitch in anticipation— itching for the moment I allow them to spring forward. But for now, I don't dare move a hair. Instead, I sink deeper into the shadows and watch Savi step to the left. She sashays closer to the shorter man, the one who rests furthest from the house—furthest from the encroaching shadow of my knife-throwing idiot.

Riat is making wild faces, gesturing to the men before rolling his eyes playfully. His expressions, though silent, are too loud. I can practically hear him taunting the men, berating them for being so easily swayed by a pretty face. My gaze grows dark, eyes tightened in what I hope he sees as a threat. He merely winks before slinking closer to his target, and my lips curl in response.

Veles damn him. If he ruins this, I'll well and truly kill him.

But the men who guard the most dangerous thing on the Continent continue their chatter, oblivious and easily distracted by Savi like I knew they would be. My eyes dart from left to right, searching this desolate street for any flicker of life. Nothing. No one. The night is calm. I take a deep, steadying breath as I watch it all play out according to plan.

Savi leans against her man, wrapping an arm around his neck flirtatiously. She all but dwarfs him, and the sight would be amusing if not for why it's necessary. Just as Savi's lips graze the shell of his ear, and his companion is distracted by the scene unfolding before him, a knife whips silently through the air. Practiced. Steady. It plunges deep into its target, and I all but sigh in relief. The leering man's eyes go wide, and his hands dart to where the blade pierces his jugular. But before his choked gasps can reveal us all, Savi thrusts a dagger into the supple flesh of her own man's neck. My stomach drops as I watch it all play out, but now is not the time to doubt my cousin. The man under her blade wheezes, eyes bugging as he thrashes. Savi quickly muzzles his sputtering groans with the palm of her hand, and too quickly— too easily—it's done.

With a harsh grasp, Savi withdraws her blade and lets the man's body drop with a *thud*. Riat is at her side in an instant, silencing his man with a final slice. For a moment, I'm stunned, but soon remember myself. I'm propelled into action, helping Riat drag the bodies out of sight behind a stack of open crates. Once it's done I plant my hands on Savi's shoulders and force her to face me. I search her expression for signs of regret—any flicker of hesitation. She's never taken a life, and though she made her own choice, I can't help but feel responsible if that choice haunts her now.

Her teeth are clamped down, as if biting back the words she wishes to keep inside. There's a slight shake in her hands and a quiver in her bottom lip that makes my chest grow tight.

"Are you—"

"They were bragging about it," she utters with a steadiness that shocks me. "Told me they worked for someone important. That they were hand-picked to guard his most prized possession."

Though it's nothing we didn't already know—aside from their boastful embellishments—dread fills my stomach.

"She..." Savi's voice shakes, but as I study the violent flare in her eyes—the vibrant hazel we both get from our fathers—I know she harbors no guilt for what she's done. Something else has spooked her, something that awaits us in this very house.

"They looked inside, couldn't help themselves," she grits out. As she takes a deep breath, I hold mine. "They thought it was funny, that they were tasked to guard such a thing."

"Is she—" Riat asks uneasily, though Savi doesn't let him get the words out.

"Alive," she finishes. Her gaze wanders off until she's staring at the house—at the worn wooden door that'll lead us inside. Her next words as no more than a whisper. *"Merely a lamb for slaughter."*

I don't dare look at Riat, already feeling his eyes on me. Instead, I steel all emotion from my face and tighten the grip on my sword. The jagged, broken blade not only reminds me of what we faced in the canyon, but also what we might face inside.

"We don't know what or who we'll find in the house," I state as flatly as I can. "There's no telling how many men rest behind that door or where they're keeping her." My gaze tightens on the solid wood that stands between me and that which I'm not ready for. "Riat," I command, finally turning toward him. "Savi and I will clear the way for you, but once we find wherever they're keeping her, it's on you to set her free."

He nods quickly, expression resolved of any ill-attempted humor he might have offered to ease the tension. There's nothing there but a callous stare and a brutal acceptance of what we're doing. The sight lessens the weight in my chest by a fraction. *Good.* I need him to be focused. Our lives depend on it, and so does hers.

"Savi—" I start.

"Move quickly, and take out anyone I see. In and out." She looks at me steadily, though I spy the worry that flickers through her gaze. "I know the plan, cousin," she utters. "Let's just get her out of there."

I grunt in affirmation, though I hesitate. Something rests heavy on the tip of my tongue, but I keep my words silent. None of my men, nor my cousin, have ever followed me blindly. They always have a choice, and tonight they made theirs. We all agreed—we need to do this, regardless of the consequences. If what Vish says is true, the significance of failing is far greater than we can imagine. But it's not fear for the Continent's future that propels me forward. And I don't think that's what drives my companions either.

An earlier survey of the perimeter told us that this house—situated in a deserted part of the city and surrounded by a maze of alleyways—has only one way in and out. Wide windows pepper the western walls, and though I wanted nothing more than to peer inside earlier, it was too risky in the daylight. What had me more intrigued, then and now, is the northern and eastern sides of the house. No windows grace the walls. There are no cracks or gaps in the stone—nothing to let even a flicker of light inside. Those walls tell me everything I need to know about where they're keeping her. Leave it to Rohan to inflict the most basic of cruelties.

One nod of my head is all it takes for Riat to slink his way toward the door. He's prepared to pick the lock, but it isn't necessary. The cocky bastards left it open. As my eyes sweep the alleyways, looking for trouble, Riat shimmies the knob and pulls at the door. The hinges creak open with a whine that sounds like a yell in the night.

Savi and I act on impulse, flattening ourselves against the exterior walls and silencing the breath in our lungs. Seconds tick by. No one stirs from inside the house. Nothing comes to greet us except a thick silence that worries me more than it should. Riat snakes his head around the door, peering into the dark interior. I wait with unused adrenaline twitching my limbs.

After a moment that feels much too long, the silence is broken.

"Empty," Riat utters with a sigh.

I slip past him and into the house without a word. My gaze snaps through the space, searching each and every corner for threats. I feel Savi and Riat at my back, buzzing with the same frenzied anticipation I harbor.

The room is deep and dark. A kitchen flanks the left side, dusty and unused. Moonlight pours in from western windows, cutting swaths of milky light through the shadows. On the right side rests a large table and chairs, as empty and untouched as the kitchen. Clearly, they don't use this house often, which is good. No one will be stopping by for a meal and a pint of ale. It means no surprises—at least, I hope it does.

I take careful, soundless steps through the room. There's a door on the far back wall, and to the left, behind the kitchen, is a hallway. The sight of both is bittersweet. Each could lead me to her—or reveal whether or not this house truly rests unguarded.

My jaw muscles feather under strain as I look back at Savi. "Whatever we find—"

"Don't let it distract me," she breathes. "I know, Hassan." Her throat bobs uneasily before she hardens her face. "Let's go."

I nod to her curtly and take a deep breath. The moment I step forward, my gaze flickers to the left. The hallway is empty. I'm greeted by nothing but stone walls and wispy glimmers of the moon through faraway windows. I swallow harshly, gripping my sword tightly in hand as I turn back to the door in front of me. Something heavy coils in my stomach, preparing me for what I might find once I turn the knob. I know she's alive, but some things are worse than death. Before my thoughts can sway me from the task, I push the door open.

Nothing. A lone bed rests against the wall, sheets soiled with dirt and eaten by moths. My eyes sweep from corner to corner before I take a step back and close the door. A shake of my head is all I can muster before we move on.

Savi's breath is a saw against my eardrums as we venture down the hallway. Her anxiety seems to grow with every step we take; I can feel it tainting the air as if it's my own. Maybe it is. I grit my teeth and slow as we come to a corner. The hallway takes a sharp right, revealing a bank of windows that illuminates the tight space in an eerie, waning glow. I search every inch, eyes flickering wildly as they fight to adjust to the dim moonlight. A doorknob rests further down on the right, and though the worn brass is within reach after a few steps, my hand takes too long to grasp it. One deep breath is all I can manage before I tug the door open. My heart lurches before settling. Broken crates litter the space. I eye a few dusty bottles peeking out from wooden slates before I close the door. *Empty.*

As I step back into the hallway, something foul slithers up from my stomach and perches at the base of my throat. It's an inevitable, inescapable dread that waits with bated breath to strike. Our footsteps pound quietly against the stone floor. There's a chill in the house that nips at my skin like blood-hungry insects. All is quiet except for the frantic pounding of my heart in my ears. I'm almost certain that—aside from the men we struck dead—no one guards this place. My chest tightens painfully and unease compounds with every press of my boots against the floor.

The words Savi spoke earlier echo through my mind with a vicious throb.

A lamb for slaughter.

I clench my jaw and force my legs to guide me further. Though I don't want to witness how she's been tamed, I can't bear to let the witch endure this fate for even a second longer.

Up ahead, the hallway ends, leaving nothing in my path but a solid stone wall. My eyes dart to the right, and suddenly, the hallway feels a little darker—like Veles has snapped his fingers and snuffed out the moon. At first, I only see the door. Dark wood. Worn, but sturdy. Then I force myself to see what I, at first, chose not to.

There's a large iron bar resting across the door, locking away whatever rests within its confines. There's no intricate lock for Riat to pick. No key for us to find. The sight chills me, rattles me more than it should. I step forward, hand hovering mere inches from the only thing separating me from her. My boots scuffle against the floor as I stop myself from going any further. This is why we're here, but for some reason, I can't find the strength to face what comes next.

Savi takes a deep, wavering breath and rests her hand on my shoulder. It's the only encouragement I need. I grip the iron bar and shove it away with a renewed impatience. It groans against the casing, but slides free nonetheless. When I finally pull the door open and let the moonlight touch the darkness inside, my every fear is confirmed.

CHAPTER 2

I can't move. Can't breathe.

A sharp gasp tears into Savi's lungs, and somehow, it makes things worse. It makes things *real*. She steps inside the room, bow strung across her back and hand covering her mouth.

"*Fuck*," Riat mutters next to me.

Somehow the curse shakes me from my stupor. It alights every nerve and sends my heart rate into overdrive. "Riat," I growl. "Get that off her. *Now*."

He scrambles forward, quickly pulling tools from his belt.

Savi backs up slowly until she's standing next to me again. There's a slight shake in her hands, one she probably doesn't even notice. "I knew he was cruel, but—"

"I know," I grit out. "Go watch the door. This isn't over yet."

"Hassan—"

"Do as you're told, Savi!" I snap.

She reels back like I've struck her. Her gaze drifts toward the far side of the room—to the place I can't bear to face again—before nodding. Her fingers tighten against my shoulder, a squeeze of understanding I know I don't deserve. Then, she leaves.

I stay where I am, feet rooted to the floor, as Riat fumbles with the collar. He stares at it for too long as if he doesn't even know where to begin. Tools clank. Curses spill from his mouth with every heavy breath he takes. But soon, I hear him mumbling softly as he works. Though we both know she can't hear him, Riat doesn't stop trying to soothe the witch with his words.

With dread swimming in my veins and my jaw clenched roughly, I force myself to look at her. She rests in the corner, head lulled to the side, body crumpled beneath her. Her clothes are stained with blood, and—by the gods—though I wish it wasn't hers, most of it clearly is. Rivers of red taint her skin, trailing out beneath the collar that's fitted around her neck. The dried blood is cracked and flaking, but quickly brought to life by a fresh flow as her body strains and pulls against the iron's savage grip. Anger shudders through me at the sight.

"Careful!" I seethe at Riat.

Though I don't want to, I force myself to get closer until there's no mistaking what I see. Tiny metal spikes line the inside of the iron collar, like thorns that draw blood at the slightest touch. They pierce into her flesh, welling rivets of red like payment called forth by the gods. Her knees dig into the dirty stone floor as her unconscious body leans forward, held up by a single chain rooted to the wall. Riat does his best to keep the collar from tugging, but she's deadweight in his grasp. As my gaze sears into the restraint clamped around her neck, I vow to make Rohan suffer.

More blood trickles free before Riat manages to ease the burden of the collar's strain. He leans her slumped form against his knee while his tools chip and pry. Rage heats the back of my neck with every bead of blood that slips down her pale skin.

Though I want nothing more than to look away, I study every detail—commit the worst to memory. Her limbs hang limply in front of her, wrists bound tight with rope. There's something wrong with her left arm, and as I step closer, my stomach roils. Even in the dark, the sight of her so battered is too much. Her arm looks unnatural—nothing more than a boneless sack of flesh. Nausea curdles my stomach as I eye the splinter of bone pressing against her skin, eager to break free.

I'm so close now, I'm all but looming over Riat. He swears under his breath, fumbling with his tools as he works to weaken the collar's hinge. The shuddering cry of metal on metal blasts through the room. I cringe back against it, worrying someone will hear, but the limp figure in front of me is a far greater worry.

The witch is too still, unfazed as Riat hammers his tools mere inches from her face. I wait for her to wake. I wait for her to startle at the ungodly racket and flash me a look that's pure challenge. I wait, but she doesn't so much as flinch. It's only by the slow, lethargic rise and fall of her chest that I can tell she's even alive.

The incessant *clank, clank, clank* of metal becomes a background to my thoughts as I stare at her. There's a bruise marring her cheek. The skin is swollen and angry, splotched with reds and faint purples. Death clings to her like a warning. Flecks of blood coat her face and chest, and I can only hope she gave her captors a taste of the retaliation I know she's capable of. I spot two long cuts—one on her arm and another on her shoulder. And, while the bleeding has stopped, the split flesh is bright with irritation. Her complexion is ashen, void of any of its normal spark or heat. She's a shell of herself. A broken fragment of the woman who pointed a blade at me so many times.

I shake my head to clear it and step away to let Riat continue his work. Every *shriek* of metal makes my teeth grind against each other. I pace the room with heavy footfalls, no longer caring about the noise that may give us away.

Let them come.

My fingers tingle against the hilt of my sword, eager to put it to use. As my boots carry me back and forth across the floor, I imagine what it would feel like to thrust my blade through Rohan's chest. The fantasy is one I've pictured a thousand times, but right now, it isn't enough. Instead, I picture the Berserker and how that cocky smile might slip from his face when my blade runs him through. I don't need to know exactly what role he played in this, just that he's as guilty as the rest of them.

A trill whistle instantly pulls my focus. It's a call I've heard before, but one I'm always hoping never to. Two chirps—short and strained. *We have company.*

Riat and I lock eyes, and one look is all it takes to send the metallic hacking of his task into a frenzied pace. He hammers at the collar, straining his fingers to keep the tool steady against the hinge. Another whistle cuts through the house, and just as I step toward the hallway to buy us more time, I hear the tell-tale sound of metal clattering to the floor.

Riat barely has enough time to peel the collar off her neck before I'm scooping the witch up into my arms. I don't dare look at the fresh puncture wounds that mar her flesh, only clutch her more tightly. My sword hangs limply in my grip as I try to hoist her higher. I yell at Riat, ordering him to loop her bound hands around my neck. It's a clumsy process, and one that causes me to roar at Riat numerous times, urging him to be careful of the witch's broken arm while simultaneously berating him to be quick about it.

The pounding of footsteps in the hallway instantly yanks my focus.

Savi's face is panicked as she joins us. "We need to go," she pants. "*Now.*"

I cradle the witch tightly to my chest with one arm while the other sloppily brandishes my sword. We're dead to the gods if the others need me to fight.

Just as we round the first corner, the deadweight in my arms slips lower. I grunt, struggling to hoist her higher without dropping my weapon. My heart is a frantic beast in my chest, overtaking the control I worked years to harness. It's nothing but panic I feel now—a helpless, frantic fear.

I have to get her out of here.

As I hike her up against my chest, the sound of her voice stills me. Her lips are moving, but the words she speaks are too soft to hear. Blood pounds in my eardrums as I lean in close, only to be met with delirious mutterings I can't make out.

I grit my teeth and press my lips to her ear. "Hang on, *witch*," I utter. "You're not rid of me yet."

She nuzzles her face against my tunic before slipping into unconsciousness once again. I know she'd be mortified to see herself now, snuggling against me like a cat. The sight is something to behold. I'd be grinning like a fool if it weren't for the bruises and blood—evidence of a torment I all but lead her to. Anger heats my chest, and cold focus returns to me with a quickness.

I'm tearing through the house now, oblivious to the world around me. As I round the last corner, I bump right into Savi's back. A figure hovers in the doorway ahead, blocking our escape. There's an all-too eager smile perched on her face, but the sight brings me no ease. Even in the moonlit shadows of the room, she's unmistakable.

Long, white braids hang down to her waist. She's still wearing the same black trousers and tunic from earlier, the fabric rumpled and crusted with old, dried blood. Her arms are bare, revealing her in a way I could have never deciphered if not for Savi's help. The design that marks her as one of the gods' own is a flurry of curved lines and flaring ink-like splatters. But the chaotic white markings on her skin don't hold my focus for long. My eyes widen at the deep scar slashed across her forearm. I hadn't noticed it before. It's fresh. *New.* The skin is healed, but the sight of decayed flesh around its edges makes my heart seize in my chest.

There's no mistaking what caused the damage. A Shade. My only question now is: *who?*

I look down at the woman in my arms, and my heart beats a little faster.

"I knew Dehran and Kirk weren't right for this job."

My gaze snaps up to the Torch. I watch her fingertips turn blacker than night as she calls her gift forward. Fire erupts in the palm of her hand a moment later.

"Something told me they'd fuck this up when I found them three pints deep at midday," she utters. "But *she* left me with little option..." Her lips curl as she eyes the woman in my arms. "Quite a shock to discover Silas's plaything was the Durit."

I grit my teeth to contain the curse that threatens to burst free, but it's too late. The Torch notices the way I scowl and hold the witch close.

"Good thing he's not here to see this." She laughs bitterly before a wicked smile slithers across her face. "He was never one to keep his nature in check. I can only imagine after their romp at the inn, he's all but laid claim to her."

My blood boils under my skin, but I hold my ire behind a tight mask. Riat mumbles something violent next to me, fingers twitching at his sides. I know he's eager for blood, just the same as I.

The Torch saunters closer, gaining ground while still blocking the front door. I firm my stance, but as I clutch the witch tighter, our enemy quirks a brow.

"Seems Silas isn't the only one with attachments…" Her eyes roam across me before regarding the woman in my grasp once more. "She killed one of ours," the Torch bites. "Though Rohan cares only to get her back to Denheir, I'm not so quick to forgive and forget." Her bright eyes flash in challenge. "Guess I'll have to take it out on you instead."

Just as I move to step forward and bear the brunt of this threat, Riat beats me to it.

"Get Ren out of here," he urges. "I'll take care of this bastard."

The woman turns to him, noting the way he plucks his throwing knives from their holsters. She laughs, voice airy and dry as she toys with the fire in her grasp. The flames roll across her knuckles as she turns her hand over.

Suddenly she stops, and her eyes grow wide in delight. "We've met," she recalls, a smile stretching across her face.

"South of Weshí," Riat says through gritted teeth. "Four years ago." He uses the tip of his blade to raise his tunic, revealing a patch of fire-scarred flesh on his side. "Been wanting to return the favor."

The Torch's laughter fills the dark room, only stifled when Riat takes a step forward, blades gripped tightly.

"You really want to play, boy?" she chides, eyeing him up and down. "You must have liked the taste of my flames on your skin."

Unbeknownst to the Torch, Savi has quietly drifted further away. Out of the corner of my eye, I see her unsheathe a small dagger.

"As I recall, you're pretty good with those knives," the Torch continues. She looks Riat over once more, grinning smugly. "But not good enough."

The Torch raises her hand, but before she can spray fire across the room, a dagger flies through the dimly lit space. It doesn't hit its mark, but it serves its purpose. The distraction has the woman flustered, reeling toward Savi with a violent burst of flames. Savi ducks and rolls under the kitchen table seconds before fire consumes the place where she once stood. Riat wastes no time. He chucks his knives one after the other, advancing on the Torch with a brutality that soothes the vengeful ache in my chest.

The woman screams as two blades bury deep into her stomach. Her eyes grow wide and fevered, and as she raises both hands toward Riat, all hope dies in my heart. It happens too quickly, and I'm left helpless. The Torch thrusts a wall of fire at Riat just as he chucks the last knife in his grip. His aim is rushed, and the blade falls to the stone floor the moment he does. But he's not quick enough. Fire blazes forth like the breath of ungodly beasts, barreling over Riat. His chest hits the ground with a heavy *thud* as flames scorch the air, devouring the room. The back of Riat's tunic catches ablaze, and I can only watch as the fire licks at his skin. He rolls feverishly, trying to dampen the flames as they bake fabric into flesh. His bellowing screams echo through the house, finding a home so deep in my ears I'm afraid I'll never be rid of the memory.

Before the Torch can even think to turn that violence on me, she's in my sights. I drop my sword and rip the dagger free from my belt. It leaves my hand with a vicious precision I've honed for decades. Worry floods her face for a mere instant, and in it I only find delight. The fire dies in her calloused palm as she reels back to swat at the blade. She yells in frustration, and the sound stirs the smoke-filled air around us. She's seething, eyes alight with fury as she looks to the gash of vibrant red cut across her palm. The blood drips quickly, hitting the stone floor in heavy splatters.

I take a moment to catch my breath, though it feels much too heavy in my lungs. I adjust my grip on the witch, holding her tightly to me. The curtains have caught on fire, and smoke pools against the ceiling, tainting the air. My eyes snap across the room, finding Savi still holds her position against the far wall. But Riat... Riat writhes on the floor, and guilt floods my chest for what has befallen one of my men.

Through the chaos of it all, the Torch stares at me with murder alight in her gaze. "Leave the girl," she snarls, "and I'll let your friends live."

Her hand firmly clutches her stomach, trying to staunch the wound. She dares not rip Riat's knives free; it would only make things worse. She's badly hurt, but I am no fool. She could roast me like a hunk of meat, could char me where I stand. But for some reason, she doesn't. Her gaze shifts to the witch, then back to me. She steps closer, and it's then that I see the resentment in her eyes. She wants to kill me, but she can't—not while a certain woman rests in my arms.

The realization has me drifting closer. My eyes don't waver from the Torch, though my hand—the one clenched at my side—motions straight ahead, then flicks right. The movement is too quiet and quick for the Torch to notice, but I didn't do it for her.

"What is she to you anyway?" the woman hisses. "Do you even know what you're taking? Who you're stealing from?"

Her voice wavers as the words screech through her teeth. She's losing blood; I don't miss the way she winces as she steps forward. If the witch wasn't deathly still and cradled in my arms,

I would finish this here and now. I would gladly do it for her—and for Riat. And *gods*, do I want to.

My eyes don't leave the Torch, but the urge to check on Riat claws at my sanity. He's finally stopped screaming, though he's panting much too hard against the floor for my liking. I clench my jaw as I take another step forward. The Torch is grinning like she's convinced I'll give up the woman I came for—like I would be such a fool as to let her slip away twice. When the Torch lets out a cocky laugh and steps closer, I stifle the urge to take a blade and slam it through her. But I don't have to, because Savi does it for me.

The subtle hum of a bowstring and resulting *whoosh* of air makes me hold my breath. I track the arrow from the corner of my eye—watching as it sails through the room on a whisper before lodging deep in the Torch's throat. The room stills. Savi exhales just as the Torch gasps. Blood trickles free, staining the arrow's wooden shaft. I almost sigh in relief, but as the Torch's eyes go wide, I see her pain as a promise for violence. The room is thrust back into chaos before I can even blink.

Her hands raise quickly, and though the gesture wavers in strength, her frenzy does not. I throw myself to the floor, barricading my body on top of the witch's just as fire blasts through the room. The heat is suffocating, baring down with such force that I'm not sure if it's the air or flames that lap at my skin. I crawl forward, dragging the witch underneath me, knowing I'm bound to do more damage to her. Sweat beads on my brow. Panic eats my heart.

I have to keep her safe.

The smoke is stifling, choking the air from my lungs as the inferno rages on. Flames light the room in an orange glow, banishing every shadow and lingering touch of night. The Torch is too consumed by her rage to notice my approach, nor Savi's. As I watch my cousin crawl toward her task, I seek my own. I clutch the witch tightly to me, dragging us just a few feet further. My fingers reach across the floor, desperate for purchase. Though I don't want to, I loosen my hold on the one thing I never wish to lose again, and stretch some more. When I feel the smooth touch of metal against my fingertips, determination chases fear away. Just as quickly as I found it, I shove Riat's throwing knife away from me. I watch it spin across the floor, grating against stone. I don't have time to watch a familiar hand curl around its hilt, I just have to trust that it does.

The flames spit and churn above my head, violent and eager. I press myself lower, desperate to cover every inch of the woman underneath me. My weight drives a choked breath from her lungs, and the sound all but cuts me down. *Fuck*! I try to move off her, but the threat is too great. The air sizzles and blares with a violent storm of fire—a thing set to devour and end. It's too much. Too inescapable. The heat rises to an unbearable level, sucking the life from the room. My skin is red, growing swollen, and close to blistering. I don't dare think of the woman underneath me—can only hope that my pain is preventing her own. My body envelopes her, desperate to spare the life I told myself meant nothing. It's a lie, and one I could never fully swallow. I close my eyes—bracing for the agony of it all, wishing I'd made a different decision in the Jahaer. Then, I hear it.

She gasps. The Torch pulls in a sharp breath, and the fire around me chokes. Savi staggers where she stands, but doesn't relent. She presses the blade deeper, teasing the delicate space where muscle gives way to arteries until, at last, the Torch drops. She collapses into a heap, blood pouring from her chest. I watch as her eyes grow dim, then settle into empty stillness. It's only when the last fleck of light has left those turquoise irises that my thoughts snap back to the witch.

I immediately drop my face to hers, pressing so close that her lips brush my cheek. The touch is bittersweet. I hover against her and wait. My heart hammers through my ears, striking so loud it muffles every other sound. One moment ticks by, then another. Dread pools in my stomach and sends renewed panic through me. Finally, I feel it. The tickle of her breath is faint, but it's there.

I lean back, giving her some space. My fingers press roughly into my temples as I close my eyes. "*Fucking hells*," I growl.

My lungs immediately seize with a harsh intake of smoke. I stutter and hack and hack some more before I manage to get control of myself. Once the fit has passed, I pull the witch toward me—hands desperate like she might slip away—before taking stock of the rest of my people.

Riat is on his knees, coughing violently. The back of his tunic is in tatters, burned away and melted against his flesh. He breathes in and out, wincing at the blistering pain I know he must feel. He pulls himself to his feet slowly and takes in the room, same as I do. It's in shambles. The curtains have all but burned away. The cabinets are nothing but splinters of charred wood. Some of the furniture is still on fire, while others merely emit smoke.

Riat shakes his head and dares to shoot me a toothy grin, though he winces through it. "And you were worried something bad would happen."

I pull in a tight breath and sigh. *Hael give me strength.* My eyes lift to Savi who is leaning out the open door, heaving in bouts of fresh air. I rise from the floor, taking the witch with me as I make my way across the ravaged room. Her arms are still looped around my neck, and I pull her body against me until there's no space left between us. Though I tell myself the proximity is merely for her safety, I can't ignore how it loosens the ache in my chest. I can feel her heartbeat against my own. It thumps softly, yet steadily. She's strong—a fighter. *She'll be fine. She has to be.*

Everything feels too heavy—my lungs, my heart, my limbs—and yet, for the first time in days, it feels like I can finally breathe. I take a deep inhale and immediately regret it. I cough and sputter once more. The lingering smoke burns, but I pay it no mind. My focus is locked on the unmoving Torch as Riat collects his throwing knives. The daemon's lifeless gaze stares up at the ceiling, and the turquoise of it is as dark as an empty well.

As Riat reclaims the last blade from her stomach, he moves with a stiff hesitancy that tells me he's in pain. He sheathes the knife in its holster and grunts a parting retort at the dead woman before shuffling away. Even as he slips from the house, I can't take my eyes off the slayed daemon. But it's not the arrow in her throat or the wound in her chest that I stare at. It's the black scar on her arm that holds my focus and reminds me what I've gotten myself into.

I swallow harshly before looking down at the woman in my arms. The markings on her skin make her the very thing I've avoided my entire life, but for some reason, running is the last thing I want to do now.

"Hey, boss," Riat calls, popping his head into the doorway. "We going? Or do you wanna wait for the next daemon with an attitude problem to show up?"

Savi stands behind him, eyes everywhere but me. Her head swivels left to right, checking the perimeter like I taught her to so long ago. "He's right," she states. "We need to go before someone else comes to pay a visit."

Though she tries to temper it, her eyes widen as she catches sight of the roasted flesh on Riat's back. She says nothing, but

I can see her worry. My cousin cares more deeply than anyone I know, despite what this life has done to her. And though she yelled at me the entire way to Letka, berating me for letting the witch go, I know she doesn't blame me. Though, I wish she would.

As Savi loops the bow across her back, I catch a glimmer of something nasty. I reach the doorway in two quick strides, keeping the witch securely in my grasp. My hand snatches Savi's wrist before she can pull away.

"Were you going to mention this?" I ask gruffly.

She scoffs as she pulls out of reach, hiding the violent burn streaked across her arm. "Now is not the time for show and tell," she quips. Her jaw ticks as she stares me down. "Ren's not safe yet. We have a long night ahead of us, and you've hit your threshold for being a dick today. So shut up and get moving."

My mouth gapes open, leaving me silent as she turns to leave.

Riat looses a chuckle before patting me on the shoulder. "She has a point."

The searing look I give him earns me another laugh. He quickly grows bored with me though, preferring to focus on the witch.

Riat brushes the hair out of her face, smiling softly to himself. "I'm glad she's back." He stares quietly—content—before looking up at me with mischief arching his brow. "Don't worry," he teases. "As much as I want it to be, I'm fairly certain I won't be the one she hopes to repay for this." He smirks, flashing his eyes at me. "The real question is—now that she's back—are you going to tell her?"

My upper lip curls into a scowl, though my quickly beating heart betrays me. "Tell her what?"

Riat merely rolls his eyes before slipping through the doorway. "Best do it quick," he tosses back. "I'll only wait so long before

I deem it fair to steal her from you." His laugh remains to taunt me even as he disappears from view.

I stare down at the woman bundled against my chest and feel the tension leave my shoulders for the first time since we stepped into this city. But in its place, something unwanted and infuriatingly warm spreads through me like the sun over a new day. It's the kind of hope I haven't allowed myself to feel in years, and the brush of its tempting claws makes me grit my teeth.

A grumble leaves my throat as I shake my head. "What are you doing to me, *witch*?"

With her wrapped up in my arms, I step into the night before more trouble can find us.

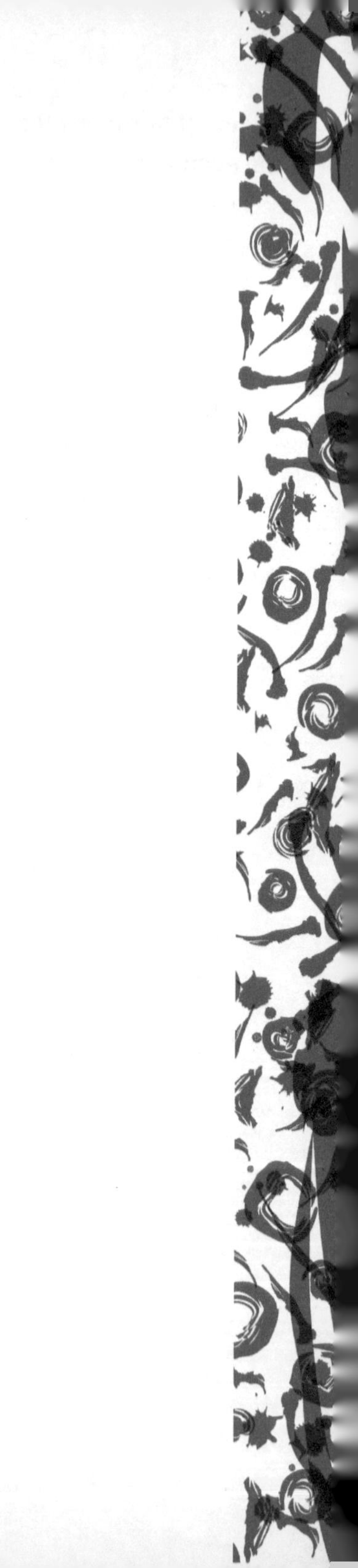

CHAPTER 3

It's hot—too hot. I flail against the weight on top of me, desperate to be free of it. I wince and curse under my breath as pain splits down my arm, but I don't relent until I've shrugged off the pile of blankets cocooning me. Only then do I look down to discover what agony pulses through my skin. My left arm is bandaged, wrapped in a tight sling and pressed against my chest. Lines furrow between my brows, growing deeper as I rouse from sleep's foggy haze.

What in the gods—

I wiggle my fingers only to have pain shoot straight up my arm. *Shit!* I press my tongue against the roof of my mouth, eyes clenching shut as I wait for the blinding fire of it to wane. After a while, it lulls to a dull throb, though I don't dare flex a muscle. As I sit there unmoving, I force myself to feel every uncomfortable pang that ripples through me. There's a pounding in my skull— each drum of it violent and unforgiving. I try to summon a mere memory as to how I came to be like this, but the effort only works to squeeze my mind like a vise. Saliva coats my throat thick with dehydration, and my stomach is as empty as a barren tomb. It feels like I've been asleep for centuries, and the heavy ache in my back only seeks to prove me right. But worse than the constant pain I feel is the realization that, as hard as I try to remember how I got here, I cannot.

I look around, eyes blinking against the senseless dark until everything comes into focus. There's a fireplace next to me, and though the flames went out long ago, the wood stacked in the corner is well-stocked. The room I find myself in is sparse of furnishings, offering little but the bed underneath me. No drawers to check for blades. No lavish fabrics draped across the walls. Only barren stone floors and a cluttered collection of books that feels personal. Nothing is familiar, and the room unveils no clues. Save for one. *This is no inn.*

I take a deep breath, eyes still flickering about in search of answers. The air fills my lungs in desperate pulls, like I haven't tasted it for ages. Hunger is a gnashing beast in my belly. The pangs are strong, yet reassuringly familiar. It's been days since I last ate. I'm certain of that, at least. I close my eyes and press the fingertips of my good arm against my temple. Memories hold strong behind walls of black. It's all blank—clouded by whatever troubles brought me here. I grit my teeth and squeeze my eyes tighter, willing the gods to spare me this small torment. I *need* to remember.

There's a sheen of sweat on the back of my neck, and as I press my fingers harder against my skin, I feel the lingering flush there. My head drums in my skull, and my jaw grinds against the pressure. Through it all, I feel the twisting ache in my stomach— the remnants of a sickening purge. My eyes snap open as I try to shift atop the bed and accidentally jostle my arm. Pain is quickly becoming second nature. I stare at the sling—at the boneless heap within it—until, at last, I remember.

The memories come too quickly, and as they begin to slip through my mind, I almost wish they'd stayed forgotten.

A city guarded by monoliths. An inn with a heavenly bed.

Letka. The alley. Olen.

Silas.

I can all but see him wide-eyed, clutching his throat with desperate hands. The shadows dance around my mind, eager and satisfied. They remind me of things I'd rather forget. Taunt me. I see Silas in a memory I wish had been lost to time. He's choking. Gasping. *Dying.* And it was all my fault.

My fingernails dig into my skin.

No, not a memory. A nightmare. It was only a nightmare.

I shut down the thought before I can convince myself otherwise. Another pops up in its place, though it brings me no comfort.

Poison.

The breath sucks into my lungs in a harsh gasp as the realization hits. I look myself over, confirming what I already know to be true. Though the cuts Rohan inflicted in Denheir are now scars, I find new ones have broken flesh. Two, to be precise. The first runs across my forearm, sliced the length of two fingers and crusted with dark blood. *Fresh*—though the damage looks days old by now. I count fifteen stitches before my gaze creeps higher. My left shoulder bears a slice of its own. Though small, this one is deeper. The skin around it is red and angry—fighting infection. Nine stitches hold it together, and already I can feel the uncomfortable itch of cording against my irritated flesh. I sit silently on the bed for far too long as I try to piece together what I know.

The last thing I remember is the Torch—*Asha*. There she was, her heartless gaze blazing into me. Then, the cut of a blade. I look back to the cut on my shoulder and feel my empty stomach ache with dread. Though I should be eager to determine what poison I've been dosed with, a single thought loops through my mind, drowning out all others.

How long has it been since that day?

My mind is nothing but a swirl of intangible chaos as I try to remember something—*anything*—about how I got here.

Did they take me back to Denheir? Am I still in Letka?

The only thing that creeps from the recesses of my mind is that darkness. That never-ending abyss. Nausea slithers through me as I recall how it swallowed me time and time again. I remember coming and going, slipping away to only fall deeper into oblivion. Gasping. Shaking. Delirious. There was nothing but eternal suffering in that place, and, somehow, it seems the gods found pity and delivered me from it.

My eyes sweep across the room yet again as worry takes hold. I can't help but wonder if this isn't salvation at all, but a fresh, new hell.

My throat clenches roughly at the thought. I don't remember traveling, let alone being placed in this bed, but I'm wise to Rohan's games now. His kindness is not to be mistaken for anything other than a promise that his cruelty is close at hand. He'll use everything he has to break me; he won't make the same mistake twice. That leaves me with only one option. *Escape.*

I sit up, and though it takes me a while, manage to pull myself from the bed. The pounding throb in my skull has me swaying, worsened by the stiffness in my joints. The room teeters until a deep breath helps me find equilibrium. It's with the clench of my jaw that I fight the desire to lie back down. It would be too easy to admit defeat now. But gods, would it bring relief. Instead, I grit my teeth and take a staggering step. My legs almost buckle underneath me, the unused muscles weak and unsteady as I lurch forward. I cling to the wall, fingers digging roughly into stone, until feeling slips back into my legs with a tingling jolt. As my body shakes off the last ebbing waves of disorientation, noises from the other side of the door still me dead.

Low voices hum and dishes clank. My heart patters with a desperate ache as I frantically search for something to arm myself with. I stumble across the room, legs trembling as if I were a newborn foal. A murmured curse leaves my mouth the moment my foot collides with a wooden crate. The smack sends pain throbbing through my toe, but worse than that is the deafening sound of it scraping across the floor. It's too loud to ignore.

The house goes silent. I hold my breath, and every muscle in my body quakes in anticipation. My eyes flicker around in fretful search before I spot the only thing of use. I slink over, quickly grabbing the object as heavy footfalls break the silence. I brace myself for anything, clutching my makeshift weapon in a white-knuckled grip. The door flies open, and I swing.

"*Gods above*," Hassan hollers, ducking just before I have a chance to smash the tome against his temple. "How is it you're still trying to kill me, witch?"

The breath catches in my lungs. All I can do is stare at him. I look into those stern, hazel eyes and all at once—like a storm whipping across the Jahaer—relief crashes into me. The book drops from my hand, landing with a heavy *clunk*. I stare. I stare, and I stare, but the longer I do the more I feel that relief turning into something frightful and feral. All too quickly it grow fangs and claws.

How did he find me?

The question stays trapped on the tip of my tongue. Chills rake across my fire-warmed skin as he steps into the room. I stagger backward on instinct alone and nearly trip in my haste.

"You're awake."

He says it matter-of-factly, but there's something almost choking his words. I stare at him, at the hesitant expression muddling his face, and find my panic stirring.

This isn't right.

His focus hovers too long on my neck before he swallows thickly. My mind spins wild tales as it tries to catch up with the reality in front of me. I search his face for deception—proof that I was right all along and Silas wasn't the only betrayer lying in wait. But the longer the silence builds between us, the more I notice the pain in Hassan's eyes. It swims there among the hazel, looking as battered and trapped as I feel. He puts his hands up cautiously and appeases me by taking a step back. The distance between us settles the panic fluttering in my chest for a brief moment before it comes back stronger than ever.

"What are you doing here?" I demand to know. "Where am I?"

If Hassan dislikes my biting tone, he doesn't show it. He merely stares at me, his gaze devouring my face with an unnerving focus. He looks at me like I might disappear at any moment, like I'm nothing more than an illusion. Or maybe he thinks I'll run if given the chance.

"We found you in Letka," he finally utters.

"Where?" I prod. "How?"

He takes a deep breath before answering. "In a house... *though prison cell is more fitting*," he comments, more to himself than me. Before I can press further, he continues. "Vish tracked you to the city. We didn't trust the Berserker, so Savi, Riat, and I followed. By the time we arrived..." His words grow choked again. "It was already done. He'd already made the trade, and I couldn't—" He stops himself abruptly, pressing his mouth into a firm line.

Though there are about a hundred questions whipping through my head in fast succession, I hold my tongue. My silence seems to grate Hassan's nerves, because his jaw ticks, and then he's speaking again.

"I don't give a damn what name Vish calls you," he rumbles. "I believe in prophecies like I believe the gods are kind." His upper lip twitches, and he shakes his head. "I had to get you out of there. No one deserves to endure what you would have suffered at his hands."

When his gaze snaps back to mine, my brow is a fuddled mess. I chew on his words, though nothing about them settles the gnawing anxiety in my gut. This doesn't make sense, and yet, here I am.

I replay every conversation, every vision, everything I've been told, and everything I've seen. None of it helps. There are too many unanswered questions—too many unknowns. I grit my teeth as I step toward him. There's only one thing that feels certain now.

"I want to speak to Vish."

Hassan lets out a rumbling scoff. "I bet you do."

As I open my mouth to argue, he stops me.

"Vish left days ago. Headed to Caen to find a Mender for you. He's due back today." Hassan crosses his arms over his chest as he leans against the doorframe. "He'll answer whatever you ask of him. I'll make sure of it."

All I can manage is a curt nod. I watch Hassan carefully, my body tensed for a fight. My gaze sweeps across him, searching for a threat even though I know good and well he already is one. Tightly coiled muscles spread across his daunting build.

There's a dagger holstered at his hip, and I'm already thinking of ways I could lift it off him. He holds himself with the same rigidity he did in the desert, guarded against the most trivial of vulnerabilities. Always on the defense. Always ready for anything. There's a heaviness in the set of his jaw, a tension bunched in his shoulders. As usual, he's frowning. But when my gaze finds his, the certainty I feel wavers.

The harsh hazel I'm used to holds something deeper now. I bristle against the attention as Hassan's eyes trail from my face, to my neck, down to my broken arm, then back up again. He takes his time with me. Each pass is painstakingly slow, like he's committing the details to memory. I shift where I stand, feeling all but bare under the scrutiny.

My cheeks flush, but I'm quick to stifle the reaction the only way I can think to. A smirk as fake as the steadiness in my voice slips across my face. "Easy, *hunter*," I taunt. "Stare at me any longer and I might think you like what you see."

His eyes darken as he takes a step closer. "Don't call me that," he snarls. I watch his fists curl at his sides, watch the way he drags in an unsteady breath. That brutal glare is back like it never left. "Unless you want me to think of *him* every time I look at you."

My stomach drops, and all of my bravado fades in an instant. I dart my gaze to the floor before Hassan can see what it reveals. "You shouldn't think of him at all," I utter.

"And why's that?" Hassan asks through gritted teeth.

Something uneasy ripples under my skin, like fresh poison has flooded my veins. I let the world go numb and lose myself to the violent pull of things best forgotten. His gray eyes find me, like they always seem to now. Desperate. Beseeching. The shadows are on him before I can stop it. Swirling. Slicing. They steal his breath, rip his flesh. I know he's not really here, but I can practically see the blood pooling at my feet. My veins itch. There's a hum under my skin, a satisfied purr. I blink, but all I can see are shadows. Caressing my skin. Swirling in the dark. They want to consume me. It feels like they already have.

A faraway voice snaps me out of the agony I deserve to fester in. Hassan's gaze is too sharp, too knowing. I stagger back toward the wall to steady myself. My hands are shaking. Blood thrumming. I close my eyes and beg the gods to free me of this torment. *It's not true. It can't be.* But it is.

"He's dead." My voice cracks as my throat grows hollow and achy.

Hassan's boots scuff the floor as he stills. My gaze snaps up to his, finding his eyes flicking across me like he can see the panic soaking my bones. I open my mouth, but can't find the words. It's silent. Too silent. Though I want to feel nothing, I feel everything. I look at Hassan and see Silas's eyes in place of hazel ones. I see the blood I was eager to spill. See the pain in the eyes of someone I thought could make me so happy. Back in the room, Hassan swallows harshly. I know he has questions, same as me, but if he wants the burdens I carry, he'll have to ask for them by name.

He gives me one last look before breaking eye contact. "Come and eat something." He sighs. "It's been days since you've had a meal."

He begins to leave, but I don't budge. My mind is filled with darkness and shadows, with pangs of regret and a gnawing dread I don't want to face. *But what if I did—*

I push the thought away, bury it too deep to reach. I tell myself it's the leftover poison that torments me so, unraveling my mind like a loose spool, nothing more. Yet the further I force the lie, the harsher its roots twist around my heart. It's a brutal ache, one that threatens to kill me from the inside. But the agony of the lie is kinder than the devastation the truth promises. So, like always, I endure.

When I finally look up, Hassan is lingering in the doorway.

"You need to eat, *witch*," he stresses. "Or are you content to grow weaker than you already are?"

The taunt does as intended. I roll my eyes, at once yanked from my thoughts and back into the room. Hassan leads, and I follow. Though feigning my reluctance to do so, the savory whiff of food drifting through the house quickens my pace. Hassan guides us down a short hallway that opens up into another room, and I immediately step back. It's bright, painfully so. Faded drapings frame the large windows, pulled back to reveal the desert around us. I blink away the onslaught of light as the sun shines in hotly.

Gods, I almost forgot what it felt like.

Before I can step any closer, I'm tackled in an embrace that nearly knocks me off my feet.

"She's alive!" Kai laughs, squeezing me so tightly I think I might pop.

For a moment, I'm lost to the relief that floods me. It loosens my chest until warmth is all I feel there. It's joy. Belonging. *Safety.* But nothing and no one is truly safe on the Continent, and I'd be wise to remember that.

I quickly blink the traitorous tears from my eyes and groan as Kai hugs me tighter. "Fuck. *Ow!* You're crushing my arm," I half laugh, half wince against his chest.

He immediately pulls back and stares at me with wide eyes. "*Shit.* Sorry," he offers meekly before delight pulls up the corners of his mouth once more. "*Gods above*, I was sure you were a goner."

"She's too much of a fighter for the gods to take her so easily."

I look over to greet the source of that deep, warm voice I didn't know I was desperate to hear until now. My waterline grows misty as Tariq smiles at me from across the room.

"You look better," he states. "Stronger."

His large hands have dropped what they're doing, leaving a whittled piece of wood and a short blade resting on the kitchen table in front of him. As I eye the object with more scrutiny, I swear there's a goat carved into the soft wood. Once more, my chest feels funny, like all that dread has been drenched in something kinder. My lips wobble, quivering into a smile as I meet Tariq's gaze.

His dimples pop against his cheeks, and he takes a deep breath as if he, too, feels the same relief I do. "I'm honored to have you join us once more, Ren," he states. "It seems fate wasn't done with this thread just yet."

My brow arches high on my face. "Don't tell me you actually missed me?" I prod.

"*Hael cleave and damn me,*" Kai whines. "It's been so boring without you." He slumps himself down next to Tariq and groans. "After Tariq, Vish, and I dropped the bounties off in Falo, we came here. Waited days for the others to show. And when they did?" He shoots Hassan a peeved look. "It was clear we'd missed all the fun. Boss here shows up grumpy as ever, carrying you like a corpse. Wouldn't leave your side. Wouldn't shut the fuck up about going back to Letka and kil—"

"Silence your yapping, *please*," Hassan rumbles. "And make her a bowl. She's starving."

Kai groans quietly, getting up and heading to the stove. As he does, Hassan's gaze flickers to me, hot with renewed irritation.

"Sit down, *witch*," he orders. "Before you fall over."

I sneer at him but find my seat just as Kai places a bowl of stew in front of me.

"See what I mean?" Kai whispers in my ear. "*Grumpy*."

I stifle my laugh with a cough, careful not to look up and face the wrath of Hassan's glare. Instead, I eat. As the first bite of stew hits my tongue, it's hard to remember to breathe. I spoon mouthful after mouthful, devouring every last drop. My stomach is in knots, desperate and empty, and I don't stop until it's all but bursting. Once I've drained the bowl, I sit back and take a breath.

Kai grins at me from across the table. "Seconds?"

I shake my head and push the bowl away, already feeling too full. Unease twinges in my chest as my gaze drifts out the window. The desert spans for as far as I can see, but it's not the Jahaer. The earth is less vibrant here, nothing but dry sand covering hardened clay that's been baked under the sun for too long. Weeds peek through the cracks, sparse and drought-stricken.

"Where are we?"

"Northwest of Letka," Hassan offers gruffly.

I don't turn from the window to respond; I stand up and wander closer. Each step is a reminder of what brought me here. Every ache and twinge grounds me with an unsettling certainty that, somehow, things have changed. My hip presses up against the ledge, hands digging into the rough stone of the open window. I close my eyes and feel the heat of a passing breeze drift against my cheek. For a moment, it feels like I'm back in the Jahaer. If I still my thoughts enough, the silence is a comforting lull—a breath of hesitation I can pretend will soon be broken by familiar things.

Mikel calling me to join him at the back of the caravan, no doubt wanting to rant about something Kiara did.

Kora chatting away with anyone in earshot.

The soothing shift of sand beneath our camels as Zoah leads us away from all pasts that trouble us.

I can imagine it all so easily, but memory of that calm life I'll never live again merely adds to the weight in my chest.

I take in a deep breath and stare across the barren landscape before me. "Why am I here?"

Silence.

I turn to face Hassan slowly, but his rigid expression only seeks to stoke my irritation. "Why—" I try to repeat.

"Because it wasn't safe to travel any further. Not with you—" He clears his throat. "Not in your condition."

I scoff. I can't help it. "And my safety is of concern to you now?"

His lips draw together tightly, and his brow furrows. I watch him bite back the words he's so reluctant to speak, until finally he lets them slip. "It wasn't just your safety I was worried about."

Something deep inside me recoils at that. It's a knowing that rests just out of reach—eager to slither free in hopes of discovery. I swallow harshly, shoving it back as quickly as it came. There's a twinge in my blood, a thrumming that feels more familiar than I'd like it to. I don't want to think about what it means.

Suddenly, I can't bear to look at Hassan. As I wander through the room, I take in the small kitchen with feigned interest and tight lungs. My fingers shake as they drift along a bookshelf, pretending to admire its contents.

"How long was I out?" I ask as casually as I can.

"Since you got here, or since we found you?"

That makes me pause. His question is a rock on my chest, heavy and unmovable. It feels like another breath—another moment of this uncertainty—might crush me. I turn toward him slowly, mouth agape, but can't seem to find the words.

"You've been unconscious for five days." Hassan states it plainly, though I see the way his jaw clenches.

Five days. Almost a week has passed without my knowledge. Anything could have happened between those final moments in the alley and now. The past is lost to me, and its clues are buried in an agony I'm not ready to wade through. Until I am, all I have is the word of the man in front of me, and I don't know if I can trust it.

"Where did you find me?"

"In a house. In Letka."

I wait for him to say more, but he doesn't.

"What kind of poison did they use?"

"We don't know."

I raise my brow at that and wander back toward the kitchen table. His eyes track me the entire way, though I can't read the emotions seeping from his intense gaze.

"And my arm?" I ask.

He looses a strained sigh. "Too badly broken for us to do anything but bandage it," he replies. "We have a Mender coming."

I nod, though my focus doesn't waver from him. He's holding back. I can see it in the pinched look on his face. He's too guarded— more so than usual. He's cold and quick with his answers, like he's eager to spit them out and be done with it. But when I look at him, I feel the weight of his stare ten times back. He's watching me, waiting for something to happen. That unrelenting focus chews at me like hutri fleas, making me all the more restless.

"So my arm is shattered, and I've been close to dead for all but a week." I try to laugh, but it falls flat. "Anything else I should know?"

"Well, there's the obvious—" Kai starts, but a sharp look from Hassan shuts him right up.

The young hunter winces and looks away, careful not to meet my gaze as he shovels stew into his mouth. My focus whips to Tariq, and while he has the guts to hold my stare, the concern I see etched around his eyes churns something nervous and scared in me. I look to the only person who's left and pray he gives me the answers I seek.

"What aren't you telling me?"

Hassan stands there, arms folded across his chest, and remains utterly silent. His focus keeps drifting away; he can't hold my gaze for more than a moment before it wanders elsewhere. My hands. My arms. My neck. His brow is a furrowed mess, only seeming to pinch more roughly the longer I watch. Apprehension floods his eyes as he sweeps his gaze over me one last time.

"Hassan—"

"You say the Berserker is dead," he utters. "How?"

My face blanches. I try to stop it, but all too quickly memories of Silas flare to life. First, it's his eyes I remember. That unholy black had faded to reveal a gray I will never forget. The sight alone had almost swayed me. *Almost.* It's his voice that comes to me next. Desperate. Rasping. He begged me to stop.

I didn't stop. Why didn't I stop?

I shut my eyes, but the darkness only pulls me deeper into my own suffering. It's too much. Too real. My blood is alive with the memory of it all. That thing I've felt since I woke up—that thrum I pretended was no more than poison's waning pull—it's unmistakable now. I feel it twitch under my skin, feel it swell as my heart rate picks up. It lies in wait, untamable and eager to be set free. It wants out—wants to slip from its prison and embrace its divine nature. It seeks its purpose.

Fighting the truth is foolish; you can't fight what you already know. But *gods*, do I fight it. I squeeze my eyes tighter, desperate for this to be nothing more than another nightmare.

"Ren," Tariq calls out gently.

My eyes rip open as I come back to the room.

"Are you okay?"

I follow his gaze down to my hands and notice I'm shaking, but worse than that is the black I see slithering through my veins. My back slams against the wall as I reel away. It's pointless. *For how can you escape yourself?*

That thing inside of me quakes and rages, slipping through my blood like fire ready to catch. It's calling me—taunting me. It's an agony worse than anything physical. It's a knowing that makes my mind scream and my chest tighten like bindings.

Hassan takes a step toward me, and I flinch. He slows, boots pressing carefully against the floor as he makes his way across the room. I don't dare move. I search Hassan's eyes for a flicker of fear or a flurry of hate, but all I find among the hazel is a steady caution.

"You say he's dead," he repeats, taking yet another step closer. "But by whose hand?"

Fear steals my heart, churning the blood like a roiling pot. I shake my head, unable to meet Hassan's gaze. As he steps closer I feel my eyes fill with tears I refuse to shed.

"Tell me," he utters. "It wasn't a blade that killed the daemon, was it?"

The thrumming in my blood rises, answering in a way only I can understand. I stare at Hassan, blinking against wet lashes as my mouth grows dry. My lips move, but nothing comes out. I can't form the words. Self-preservation scurries after lies like a horde of beetles. *He's wrong*, I tell myself. They were only nightmares.

Hallucinations. Vivid imaginings constructed by poison's hold. *There was a Shade in that alley. Yes. Someone else who—*

"*Witch.*" Hassan's voice is almost pleading. "I need to know," he presses. "I need to know you can control it."

I'm gutted, carved to the edges by things left unsaid. "You're wrong," I utter, staggering back until I'm flush with the wall once more. "It's not true. I didn't... I couldn't—" Panic wags my tongue, and the words bleed together as my throat grows tight.

My hands tremble. I shake my head again and again, denying the very thing that hums in my veins. Tears spill silently down my cheeks. Hassan looks at me, eyes wide and uncertain, and dares to close the distance between us.

I instantly slip from reach, ducking around him and staggering into the kitchen. Breath tears in and out of my lungs, spurring panic. My heart pounds, and the room starts to spin. I'm teetering, grasping at denial's frayed strings, searching for something to tether me. Every excuse I can muster slips through my fingers until I'm left with only the truth. My mind floods with visions of Silas. I picture how his eyes shuttered closed, and my world shatters.

My knees give out, but before I can fall, I'm snagged by strong hands. Tariq wraps his arms around me tightly, caging me in. As soon as his fingers start drawing soothing circles against my back, I break.

Silent tears turn into gut-wrenching sobs. The wail that leaves my lips is feral and desperate. It shakes my whole body, and I can only endure it as I quake against Tariq's chest. He says nothing, merely pulls me closer and lets me lose myself to the turmoil I feel.

"Please, I never meant to—" I shudder. "I didn't realize—"

It's then that those final moments in the alley come back to me; but this time, I remember it for what it was, not what I wished it had been.

The shadows had lashed out with purpose. Thrashing. Strangling. *Killing.* Though the poison tossed me within its hazy swell, there was one thing amidst that chaos to ground me. *Rage.* It kept me in the world, alive and kicking, because I beckoned its spite with every breath. I had watched those shadows strike true—had stoked their power, had felt them purr in delight. And it had felt good. Righteous, even. But then...

His lips turned blue. My delight turned to anguish. Regret flooded my chest. His life had faded, and now I'm left with an ache I fear will never ease. Silas's blood spilled in Letka, and I watched it happen. I *made* it happen.

"No one blames you for fighting back—"

Hassan's voice drags me back to reality sooner than I'm ready. I lurch out of Tariq's embrace, removing myself from the comfort I know I don't deserve.

"He begged me to stop," I bite through tears. "But I was so *angry.* I wanted him to realize what he'd done to me. How he'd hurt—" I'm shaking, choking on violent sobs. His eyes come to me like pools of silver, and, though I can't, I wish I could drown in them. "I didn't know—"

My voice cracks, and the sound stirs something violent inside me. I'm weak. *Pathetic.* I wipe my cheek roughly before loosing a yell that shakes the room. "I didn't ask for this!"

I feel it then—the thrumming. That burning in my veins. My knees hit the floor as I drop. I dig my fingers into my hair, desperate to stop this newfound chaos from consuming me. The darkness is there before I know it. It whips around me, tearing through the kitchen in its reckless fury. Voices yell. Things crash and break against the floor. I drag my nails down both arms, embracing the screeching agony of broken bones and the sting of newly cut flesh. I will the pain to ease me—to end this curse and free me from burdens I never wanted. My eyes blur with tears, blinding me to the whipping whirl of shadows as they snap through the air. It's only when I fall to the floor and let the weight of what I've done crush me that everything stills.

Pain wracks my body, making me shake. My chest heaves as breaths spill out frantically. I close my eyes and pray I'm still unconscious, floating in that endless dark. The slinking pressure in my veins tells me I'm more awake than I've ever been, and that there is no escaping this.

When I finally open my eyes, daylight streams in harshly. The ringing in my ears muffles all other noise, distorting my senses. I don't hear Kai and Tariq whispering, though I watch how their mouths move. I don't notice that the others have arrived until I see their camels pass the windows. All I hear is the thrum of the cursed blood pumping through my veins, reminding me of the monster I've become—one it seems I've always been.

"Look at me."

I jump slightly. As I turn my gaze, I realize Hassan has dropped to the ground in front of me. His knees rest against the hard stone floor, brushing against my own. Tension lines his face, creasing the corners of his eyes. He reaches out, but quickly stops himself. His throat bobs. I think he might touch me as his hand hovers above my own, but he clenches it tight and pulls away. I prepare myself for the fear I expect to see darkening his expression, but what I find in the rich hazel of his eyes isn't so simple.

"You're safe," he assures me, though I've never heard him sound so shaken. "I'm going to keep you safe."

My stomach clenches when I see that look on Hassan's face for what it is. *Worry.* It eats at his usual stoicism, making his gaze unsteady as it flickers back and forth between my eyes. He reaches for me again, and though I'm overcome with the urge to seek his comfort, I can't allow it.

I reel away from his touch, scurrying across the floor until I'm back up against the wall. With my knees tucked to my chest, I stare at the ground, unable to meet the hazel gaze that watches me so intensely. Voices drift in through the open windows, chittering with a joy that now sounds foreign and bitter to my ears. Camels groan. Laughter taints the air. The others have returned; none of that matters, for my mind is trapped in the dark.

There's a knowing deep in my bones, a certainty where there was once only doubt. I close my eyes and, for the first time, allow myself to feel it. It's a heaviness. A violent thrum under my skin. It's unsteady—wild like an animal snapping at an old, rusted trap. It courses through my veins, eager to be let off its leash.

Though I thought I knew the suffering this life promised me, it seems I was wrong. Hael is not the only god tainting my blood. He never was.

CHAPTER 4

I don't move from my place against the wall as they put the room back together. The damage isn't too bad, considering what it could have been—considering what I am.

Tariq and Kai move about the kitchen quickly: righting chairs that toppled in the wake of my shadows, sweeping up ceramic bowls that shattered across the floor. There's a large gash across one of the cabinets, a beastly claw mark that reminds me what havoc currently sleeps under my skin. As if I needed a reminder. I let my eyes stare at the damage until everything glazes over.

Hassan stands in the corner, watching me. He hasn't stopped. His focus is unrelenting as he buzzes with quiet anxiety. *Is he so worried I'll kill everyone?* I wouldn't know. He hasn't spoken to me since I found this spot against the wall, and I'm glad. I don't need to be coddled and soothed like a child. Don't need his false reassurances. My moment of weakness has passed, and I deserve no relief. So let him be silent, and let me stew in what I have become. Any comfort he could offer would be a waste and a lie. I prefer the silence, for at least it's honest.

Still, his eyes pierce into me like daggers. I can't bear to meet his gaze, so instead I stare at the chaos my blood so easily wrecked. A shard of ceramic rests by my feet, another remnant of the violence I unknowingly unleashed. Its edges are rough and unforgiving, and, for a moment, I'm overcome with the urge to pick it up. It would be easy to spill this curse from my veins. Simple. One brush, a glancing sweep against the inside of my wrist. I could fade back into darkness without much thought.

There's where I belong, isn't it?

I can't help but yearn for that abyss now. *Would I find Silas there? Would death be kinder than this?*

My fingers twitch for a chance at relief. The lump in my throat grows heavy and my throat too dry. I stare at the shard, mind filled with nothing but the memory of gray eyes and the constant thrum of cursed blood to haunt me. I could be rid of both so easily.

I flinch as the front door shimmies open with a startling *creak*. It pulls me from dark thoughts before I can act on them. I can't tell if the ache in my chest is relief or disappointment.

"We're back," a voice sings through the small space. "Kai, you better not have eaten all the—"

As the voice chokes with shock, the urge to slither out of my skin and hide overtakes me. I'm pushing up from the floor, desperate to slink away before I'm noticed, when she does just that.

"*Hael above,*" Savi whispers. She rushes toward me, ignoring the broken ceramic littering the floor. It crunches under her boots as she quickly crosses the room and pulls me against her. "You're awake."

The words hit my ear with a sigh of relief. She holds me tightly, and though I want nothing more than to wrap my arms around her and return the compassion she so freely gives, I go limp in her embrace. Tears brim my eyes, but I've cried enough today.

I swallow harshly as Savi pulls away to hold me at arm's length. "*Gods*, I'm careless," she frets. Her eyes drift down to my sling before she shoots me an apologetic look. "I should do better to remember that. I wrapped it after all."

Her brow muddles, ridges deep with worry, as my silence infects the room. I know she's waiting for me to say something, *but what is there to say?* Savi looks to her cousin, and, finally, so do I. Hassan's mouth is set in a firm line, gaze heavy with things unspoken. He doesn't speak, and, for a moment, I wonder whether it's anger or fear that holds his tongue.

As Savi turns her focus toward the rest of the room, I fix my gaze to the floor. I can't handle seeing her reaction to the destruction I caused. After how happy she was to see me, any reminder of why she shouldn't be is too much.

"I take it she knows."

My eyes snap up, locking onto the only person I wish to speak to as he slips inside the house. Vish's body seems to slump in relief as soon as he crosses the threshold. He drops his pack by the door and takes a long, deep breath. The bags under his eyes make his thin face look gaunt and weary. Though it's only been a week since I last saw him, the man looks like he's aged years. As he shrugs off the scarves draped across his body, I finally see what I had been so blind to all this time.

His sleeves ride up his forearms, revealing a mess of markings I've only ever read about. Harsh lines, all pointing together as if signaling some direction, smudged like ink and dense in design.

Something feral lurches in me at the sight. The numbing ache inside me is gone in a flash, replaced by a seething rage.

I push past Savi and snatch the small man by the collar of his tunic. "The Seeker?" I roar, feeling the cursed blood under my skin grow hotter. "All this time... You've been the godsfucking Seeker?"

My battered body shrieks in protest as I try to hold Vish up by the strength of one arm. I snarl and grimace, putting every ounce of pain and fury I have into smashing him against the wall. Before I have time to smite the tracker where he stands, the hairs on the back of my neck bristle.

Vish shakes his head subtly, but it's not me his eyes are locked on. One look over my shoulder confirms what instinct already told me. Hassan stands at my back, hand tightened around the hilt of his dagger. I watch hesitation flicker in his eyes. A war seems to wage within him as he looks from me to Vish. I don't bother seeing what he decides—don't care if he has any faith left in his friend, or in me. As I spin back around to face the man in my grasp, I'm met with the last thing I wish to see. Vish is calm, not at all concerned I have him bunched by the tunic. I'm teeming with the ability to destroy him—churning with a violence so potent I'm not sure I could stop it—and yet, Vish merely sighs before putting his hand on top of mine.

"Sit down, Serehna," he advises. "We have much to discuss."

I lurch back at the name, snatching my hand from his. Hasty panic has me bumping into the firm chest at my back. Hassan's hand curls around my waist, steadying me before I can tumble further. The touch is fleeting and must startle him just as much as it does me, because no sooner does my gaze snap to him than does he retract his hand. Still, the heat of his touch lingers, cracking memories wide open and forcing me to remember the last man who got so close.

Some feeble, distant part of me craves that touch—craves a second chance to go back to the inn with Silas and never leave. But I can't. There's no one to go back to. Silas is dead, and I killed him.

The confession ignites a panic so visceral that I'm afraid it'll welcome Veles with open arms. My blood thrums. My heart beats riotously in my chest. I can no longer remember who stands around me, only know that my presence is not safe. I shove them out of my way, fumbling toward the wall. I don't stop until my back hits stone. The thrum of my gift is there. Itching. Begging to come out. I look down and nearly shriek. Black swims through my veins, and I can all but feel its sluggish flow. Before those shadows have the chance to slip free, I dig my fingers into the tender flesh of my broken arm. As the pain cuts through me, I feel my blood simmer to a discontented hum. It lulls, then quiets. I try to pull in a full breath, but it shudders through me.

I survey the room like a snared animal would. My eyes devour every threat, but I don't see them clearly. They're blurs and nothing more. Adrenaline has my heart racing, has my sight growing foggy. I can't focus on the shock ringed around Kai's mouth, nor the concern widening Savi's eyes. I can only manage a quick glance before distress pulls my focus inward.

My body shivers as I feel it again—the presence of Veles in my veins. It's a reckless power, a devouring itch that demands to be set free. I'm unnerved—a cornered predator, at best. I squeeze my eyelids shut, clenching my fists in a desperate attempt to stop myself from slipping into a dark frenzy. It's through the heave of my panting breath and the blood thrumming in my ears that I hear it—the one thing that reaches through the madness to ground me.

"*Witch.*"

It spills from his lips so softly that I almost don't recognize his voice. My eyes snap open to find Hassan daring to take a step closer. It's foolish. Stupid. And he knows it. He's wary; I can see it in his eyes, but he's determined, too. He covers the distance between us in a handful of strides, and though I want to back away, I have nowhere to go. His hands are raised peacefully as he approaches, free of the weapons I know he carries.

"Remember what I said."

His voice is soothing, like he wants it to calm me. I almost let it.

"Answers," he states firmly. He nods toward the table, trying to coax me away from the wall I've backed against. "He'll tell you everything you want to know. We won't leave this room until he does."

My eyes narrow as I look at Hassan. He was willing to protect Vish from me, regardless of whatever still muddies their friendship. And yet, he's treating me like I'm his to protect, too. My brow furrows as I consider what it must have taken to get me here—what it must have cost to get me out of Rohan's grasp. That dark place flashes through my mind, and I suppress a shudder. Whatever happened in Letka, it changed things for Hassan; I can see it in his eyes. Though I can't help but wonder if that's for the better or the worse.

My throat bobs uneasily as I struggle to swallow my doubt. I want to trust him, but I've felt the cutting bite of trust's deception once before. I won't be foolish enough to welcome it back so soon. But still, I'm not naive to the fate the gods have dealt me here. I have a broken arm and no sense of where I am. I'd be a fool to fight my way out of this house and face whatever awaits me in the desert. Even with this gift—this curse—it's too much of a risk.

I dig my teeth into my tongue, biting back every accusation and threat I wish to spew. There's no time for that now—no benefit in exposing myself for the fearful creature I've become.

With the coppery tang of defeat melding on my tongue, I take a seat. The room teeters in unsteady silence as Vish takes the one across from me. I can't help the shake in my hands, nor the way my chest grows tighter with every breath. Anxiety latches around my heart. My fingers *rap rap rap* against the tabletop, and my teeth clench. All the while, Vish watches me like he always has. Silently observing. Picking apart every flicker of my expression. His dark green eyes are no less critical than I remember, yet they hold something more now. There's a quiet surrender riddled in his thick brows, almost as if he's accepted things that have or will come to pass. He's not looking at me like I'm a problem to be solved anymore—he's looking at me like I'm the solution.

"You're correct in your observation," he starts. "I am a Seeker."

My jaw grinds, and though I try to soften its clench, it's no use. "*The* Seeker," I correct him. "There is only one, as there is only one of me, it seems."

He nods, yet says nothing more. Silence permeates the room like a rotting carcass. Hassan shifts uncomfortably where he stands to my right, though I don't pull my focus from the man in front of me. Vish sits perfectly still, meeting my gaze stoically, waiting for whatever comes next.

"I have questions," I state plainly, more than a hint of malice in my tone.

The corner of Vish's mouth perks up, just slightly, before he masks the emotion from his face. "I have answers," he offers.

I stare at him, wishing I could see through him as easily as he's seen through me. "How long have you known I'm the—" The word gets stuck in my throat, and I stop myself to keep from choking on the truth. "How long have you known what I am?"

Vish watches me for a minute, drifting his eyes across my face, then down to my markings where his focus lingers far longer than I'm comfortable with. I pull my hair in front of my shoulder, covering my neck with the tangled mess as casually as I can. Vish's gaze wanders back to mine slowly as I break his focus.

"I had my suspicions the day Hassan brought you to camp. Though, I wasn't certain until later."

"Explain," I grit through my teeth.

He hums quietly as he leans forward until his elbows rest on the table. "What do you know about my gift?"

I all but scoff. "I only know what Bair and his madness told me and the rest of the Continent." I pull in a frustrated breath and dig my nails into the soft flesh of my palm. "The Seeker is one born of Hael—blessed with so much of the god's blood that nothing is unknown to them. Whatever they seek, they know."

Disquiet hovers thick in the room. The tension between us is palpable, almost oppressive. But Vish does nothing to ease it. He merely sits and waits. All the while, I feel fate growing heavier on my shoulders. Every twinge in my veins is a reminder of what has become of me, and even worse is the knowledge that Vish knew all along. That truth only works to stir my ire for the Seeker.

"So tell me," I snipe, leaning forward as my gaze burns hot. "What did you know?"

"Very little," he confesses.

His eyes wander over me again, but this time they latch onto the left side of my neck—the bare place that holds no Seer's marks. My brow furrows.

"My gift is not without its challenges," Vish admits. "I get fragments of the truth—an understanding of what is and what isn't. It's like placing the ripe flesh of a jenip berry on your tongue. You can taste what it is, instantly sense its rich tang and fizzy crispness. It's uncomplicated. Easy to understand. But bake those berries into a loaf of bread and it's harder to pinpoint where one thing ends and the other begins."

He steeples his hands in front of him, eyes settling on me sharply. "The greatest knowledge in this life is cloaked in questions we don't even know to ask. When it comes to my gift, simple questions lead to effortless answers. And you, Serehna, are anything but simple."

I bristle before leaning further across the table. "Spare me the poetics," I spit. "Whether or not you find me complicated is of little concern to me. All this time, you knew what I was, and yet—" I pause, feeling something sick twist through my stomach.

He knew. He knew, and yet...

Closing my eyes, I try to settle myself with a deep breath. The anger itching through my blood doesn't lessen, only seeming to heat like boiling water under my skin. My teeth grind down against each other, but even the ache of my jaw doesn't relieve the madness within. It would be so easy to give in—so easy to surrender to the darkness Veles promises. But I can't. The dead can't speak, and I'm due answers.

My eyes snap open and lock on Vish with a hate I hope he can feel. "You knew Silas would be the one to hand me over to Rohan, didn't you?"

He gives me a hesitant nod. "Yes. After asking the right questions, it was clear to me what his motives were."

Whether or not he feels any regret, he doesn't show it. However, I can't seem to keep my emotions from spilling into every groove and curve on my face. My heart has dropped deep into the cavernous depths of my chest, empty and aching.

"You knew he was taking me to Rohan, and yet you let me go." The words slip out in a whisper.

My throat aches against emotions I refuse to acknowledge, and I can only stare blankly ahead as my mind spins. When I pull my focus from Vish and look to the others, those emotions get harder to ignore. Savi leans up against the stove, arms crossed over her chest. But it's the way she meets my gaze—with devastation etched into her face—that shakes me. The sight brings stillness when all I wanted was to yell at her. It's betrayal I feel when I think of how they let me walk away—hurt that, yet again, one I considered a friend could abandon me so easily. But I can't even garner an ounce of rage, not when I spot the swath of deformed skin blemishing Savi's forearm. Though it's healed, the patch of rough flesh makes my stomach turn. I don't know what happened in Letka, but I do know one thing—Savi didn't used to bear a Torch's scar.

My breath turns shallow; I try to swallow my budding panic, but it sticks to the walls of my throat like wet sand. I dart my gaze away from Savi only to find Riat's focus locked on me. When our eyes meet, he shifts. I rake my gaze over every inch of him, dreading the slightest change. He looks the same as before, even curls his lips into that mischievous smile of his. But, for a fleeting moment, I see through it. And as I catch that flash of worry in his eyes, I beg the gods that he, too, didn't earn any scars in my name.

Though I should ask what befell them all in Letka, I can't. I know enough; anything that happened there is my doing. But just like this godsblood running through my veins, I was never given a choice—though I'll bear all the burden.

My anger flares once more, potent and untamable. "Why let him take me only to fight to get me back?" I snap. I swivel my gaze toward Vish, teeth all but gnashing. "Why risk your people—"

"There was a greater risk in telling you what we knew."

Vish's words all but punch the breath from my lungs. I look at him, then to Kai who leans up against the door, looking more somber than I've ever seen him. I turn to look over my shoulder at Tariq who now sits in a large wooden chair by the fireplace. His soft eyes hold pain—pain I can't bear to see. Thoughts rip through me like shards of glass as I face what's in front of me; the truth would have been easy to spot if only I had known what to look for. It wasn't just Vish who knew what I was. *They all knew.*

My hands shake, and the movement jars my broken arm. I wince and curse this stupid sling for keeping me so weak and on display. I have so many questions, so many emotions bubbling up inside of me. Pain. Fear. Shock. Shame. I'm desperate to scream from the top of my lungs, to rid myself of it all, but all I can manage to do is hold Vish's steady gaze.

He takes a deep, resigned breath as if pitying the turmoil he sees etched across my face. "The Berserker didn't know what you were and alerting him to your nature was an unfathomable risk. I knew where he was taking you. I trusted that, once the others got to Letka, they would be able to get you away from the Berserker. But..." Vish offers me a small smile, one full of sympathy I won't accept. "... things are never so simple."

His eyes shift to where Hassan rests against the wall. "Though I cannot see the future, I knew Hassan had the strength to bring you back. And so he did." Vish dips his head to the man behind me in thanks. "A sacrifice I am most grateful for."

Riat lets out a breathy laugh. "Oh, come on. All he did was carry her out of there."

As my eyes find his, he shoots me a wicked grin that almost rids me of the unrest I feel.

"It was Savi and me who took down that bitch of a Torch and saved our pretty little daemon." Riat dares to wink at me, and I laugh.

The noise shocks me and those around me. It breaks the tension clinging to my chest, and for a moment, I'm taken back to a time before all of this.

"Remember what happened last time you made me feel like a sweet, gentle thing..." I lean back in my chair, eyes raking up and down Riat's muscular frame. "I would hate to see you flat on your back with a blade at your throat again," I coo. "One would think you incapable of learning lessons."

Riat's eyes sparkle dangerously as he takes a step closer. "I would be happy to learn any lesson from you. *Over and over and over again.*" He emphasizes every word, pressing his fingers into his belt loops as he does. Once he's done, he drags his tongue across his bottom lip, drawing my attention to that scar of his.

Something rumbles from deep in Hassan's chest as he steps up to the back of my chair. "Control yourself," he growls. "Now is not the time to seduce the witch."

"Oh shit." Riat laughs. His eyes go wide in delight as he looks from me to Hassan. "I totally forgot about giving you the credit for—"

"Quiet," Hassan snaps.

Riat says no more, merely leans up against the kitchen cabinets and conceals his smile between tightly pulled lips. I glance over my shoulder, brow arching high in question. Though I want to prod, I don't. The vexed expression on Hassan's face tells me not to poke the beast. Instead, I turn back to Vish and let a familiar ire warm my chest.

"Any more secrets you wish to share?" I push. "Or maybe you could finally tell me why it is I'm here?" A bitter scoff leaves my lips as I look Vish up and down. "I doubt it was out of the goodness of your heart that you stole me from Rohan." I lean forward, ignoring the roaring pain in my arm as I get as close to Vish as possible without rising from my seat. "Tell me, *Seeker,*" I bite. "What's in this for you?"

Vish forces a deep breath, but reveals nothing. He watches me, assessing me with that critical gaze of his, before he addresses the room. "Please give us a moment. Sereh—"

I visibly tense, and he stops himself. His gaze slides to me for a brief moment before it slips back to the others.

"*Ren* and I have some things to discuss in private."

There's a long pause—as if time has stopped entirely—before the house empties. Boots scuff against the floor, crossing the room and slipping over the threshold. No one offers so much as a word or glance in my direction. No one, that is, except Hassan. He hovers next to the kitchen table, brow furrowed as he eats up every ounce of fire and unease in my expression.

"Hassan," Vish says quietly, his gaze still never swaying from me. "It will only be a moment."

The tall man's jaw ripples with tension before he turns to leave. When he shuts the door behind him, it's only the Seeker and I who remain.

"I'm sorry I've kept you in the dark," Vish offers, folding his hands in his lap. "Please know it was necessary."

The look he gives me is almost sincere. I wish I could believe it.

"Save your apologies," I grit out. "Why am I here?"

"To keep you safe," he simply says.

"Safe?" I loose a bitter laugh. "I've lived on the Continent my entire life. I don't need your protection, or anyone else's for that matter." Vish goes to object, but I stop him. "I've *always* been in danger. *Always* been alone with no one to trust.

So what if the gods cursed me with yet another gift?" I scoff. "This changes nothing."

Vish reels up, sending his chair crashing to the floor. "This changes *everything*," he urges. His eyes are huge, coursing with a kind of urgent fear I've never seen disrupt his stoic face. "You're a fool not to see it."

I snatch a broken shard of ceramic from the table, clutching it tightly as I rise. "Then I'm a fool," I rasp. "But I can still recognize when I'm being used as someone else's pawn."

Hassan barges through the door, breath heavy in his lungs. He takes one look at the overturned chair and my weapon and stiffens.

"What's going on—"

Vish holds a hand up, silencing him. "I mean you no harm," Vish addresses me. He rights the chair before sitting back down. The entire time, his eyes never leave mine. "I want to help you, Serehna."

"Stop saying that name," I spit. I feel a rush of emotions, ones I quickly tamp down before they can drop me to my knees. The jagged shard of ceramic digs into my palm, and, before I know it, hot globs of blood are sliding down my wrist. I can't help but watch as they fall onto the tabletop, seeping into the wood's dense grains and marring the surface like a stain on the earth. I stare at the blood for too long before finally finding the strength to speak again.

"What do you want from me?" I breathe, my words no more than a raspy plea.

"I want to help you avoid the fate others have written for you."

My eyes flash up to Vish, gaze unsteady and waterlogged. "And what do you know of my fate?" I utter.

"The Durit is—"

"Damned," I finish impatiently.

"A weapon," he continues. "The very one prophesied to drag the Continent into chaos if used by those who seek it for their own gain." Vish lets out a deep sigh and slowly twists the gold ring on his left hand. "Which is why I'm set to keep you from the person who desires your gift more than anything."

Time ticks by slowly as it all slips into place. "Rohan," I say softly. "He wants to be the Born."

Vish nods. "He's wanted nothing more for over a decade. He's combed every inch of the Continent—except those places none dare go—for every Shade and Seer, hoping one day he'll find the one who is marked by both gods."

I swallow heavily before dropping the shard on the table. "Fine. Then I'll go. Far from here, far from where he can find me."

Vish lets out a deep, aggravated breath. His gaze is weary, void of the heat it briefly held not moments ago. It looks like he hasn't slept in days. "There is no outrunning him. Not by yourself. Rohan will hunt these lands, use every resource he has to find you. And when he does, he'll drain every drop of your blood to gain what he seeks." Vish gives me a beseeching look. "No matter what you think of me, no matter if you trust me, you're as good as dead on your own."

I go to protest, but reminders of the past hold my tongue. I think of Olen and his men raiding Zoah's camp. I think of the cellar and the torture inflicted upon me there. I think of Silas and how easily I was guided to slaughter. And then I think of that place—that dark, endless hell where I couldn't tell where consciousness bled into nightmare.

What awaits me next if I fight this fate further?

There's a sinking feeling in my gut as I realize my best chance is the one I'm most eager to avoid. I have no choice but to trust, to once again follow the lead of others, and pray I don't come to regret it.

I slump back in my chair, almost savoring the agonizing sting of my broken arm as it bumps into the table. It reminds me I'm still here, that somehow against all odds, I'm alive and out of Rohan's reach. For now.

"What's to happen?" I relent, every ounce of fire drained from me.

I look at Vish, really look at him, and try to see him as my salvation and not my demise. He turns to the door, to where Hassan has been watching us silently.

"Have you spoken to the others?" Vish asks him.

Hassan almost misses the question entirely. His eyes are glued to where my hands rest on the table. His brow furrows, but as his gaze lifts to find mine, he's shaken from his thoughts.

"They decided days ago," he utters. "A unanimous vote in favor of it."

A rare smile flits across Vish's face. "And you?" he presses. "What have you decided?" He tilts his head curiously. "Still fighting the fate the gods have dealt you?"

I don't miss the subtle teasing in his tone, nor the way Hassan stiffens. He shoots his tracker a sharp, biting sneer, but that defiance wavers when he looks at me. As he holds my gaze, he seems to get lost in something. Those hazel eyes seep deep into my own, taking root before I have a chance to look away.

"I go where my crew goes," Hassan finally mumbles, breaking eye contact.

"Hm. Good," Vish hums. My gaze flashes to him just in time to see the shell of a smirk gracing the corners of his lips. "Tell them to get ready. We leave in the morning."

"Where are we going?" I press, panic already beginning to chew through this newfound trust.

"Caen. You need to see the Mender there," he states, gesturing to my arm. "My hope was to bring him here, but he refused to travel back with us." At the raise of my brow, Vish *tuts*, then actually chuckles. "He said I was stupid to think he'd follow a stranger into the desert, especially a stranger with two bounty hunters by his side."

I can't help the breathy laugh that leaves my throat. "Wise man. I like him already."

Vish holds back a smile as he gets up from the table. "I have a feeling you will."

Just as he reaches the door, my stomach lurches. "And after that?" I press. "Caen, I mean. Where will we go then?"

Vish stops in the open threshold. The sinking light of day peeks in, washing him in rays of heat. For a moment, he almost looks peaceful. His tired eyes close as the sun graces his face. But as soon as he opens them, the dark green irises cloud with unspoken burdens once more.

"There's something you need to find," he tells me. "Something that we must obtain before Rohan does."

My mouth opens instantly, eager to press him for more, but he's quick to stop me.

"A problem for tomorrow," he offers. "For now, you need rest."

Though I want to argue that I've gotten nothing but rest for days, I merely press my lips into a firm line and nod. Vish casts me one final look. It's guarded, yet drenched in a raw kind of worry. I can't suppress the way it makes my stomach churn.

As he slips from the house, I feel the heat of Hassan's gaze on me. The bounty hunter steps forward, and I tense instinctively. He stills, brows muddling together roughly.

"Your hand," he mutters.

I look down to see my cut palm pooling with blood. It's dripped over my wrist, and stained my cream, billowy pants with splotches of red. I stare at that blood for too long—waiting for it to change, waiting for it to reveal itself for the chaos it is. I wait to feel different. After a while, I realize it's foolish. My blood hasn't changed. It's always harbored this curse, this beast within. I grit my teeth and tear my focus from it.

"I'll get Savi" —Hassan gestures to my hand— "to bandage it."

He stares at me for a long while before seeming to remember himself. Just as he starts to leave, something in me grows desperate to stop him.

"Hassan."

He comes to an abrupt halt, hand wrapped around the doorframe. As his eyes flash to mine, the attention traps the words in my throat. That harsh gaze of his catches the setting sun, and I swear his eyes turn a warm gold. For some reason, the sight leaves me speechless. The words I'm desperate to speak settle on the tip of my tongue, but I can't utter them. Their burden weighs me down—unnerves me with the most foolish of fears. It's so simple, yet something about the man in front of me strips my heart of its courage.

Hassan's gaze is fixed upon me intently, eating up every ounce of my hesitation. It kicks my heart rate up and drives heat across my skin. I swear his eyes drop to my lips before slipping back up to meet my gaze. He swallows harshly, and just as he takes a step toward me, I panic.

"Witch—"

"It's nothing," I utter, dropping my gaze to the broken flesh of my palm. "Never mind."

He grunts, as if annoyed I wasted his time. "I'll send Savi in."

As I watch him walk out the door—watch his muscular back tense and bunch as the distance between us grows—I finally utter those two small words.

"Thank you."

CHAPTER 5

I shift uncomfortably in the saddle, gripping the reins one-handed while trying not to jostle my sling. Turns out, riding a horse with a broken arm is harder than expected. I teeter slightly before shifting my hips back into the leather seat. *Gods*. I'll never forgive myself if I fall off this horse.

It was embarrassing enough that I had to ask Tariq to hoist me up onto Mirage's back this morning. Of course, Hassan had offered first. The very thought of him sliding his hands along my hips had stirred something wild and panicked inside me. After cursing him out for thinking me so incapable, I spent countless minutes attempting to mount my horse, to no avail. I moped like a dog with a tail between its legs before finally asking Tariq for help. Hassan watched the whole thing, and I swear I caught him scowl when Tariq lifted me up. Whether Hassan found my stubbornness annoying or was merely hoping I'd fall on my ass, I don't know. But that dark flare in his gaze lingered long after we set off.

He still watches me now, tracking me from the corner of his eye. I make a point to straighten and look like the competent rider I am; though, Mirage isn't making things any easier.

When I emerged from the house this morning to find not only Mirage but my pack tied to her saddle, I was finally able to loose a deep breath. There was a flicker of relief at the sight of things known—a lick of normalcy in this ever changing world of mine. But as soon as I stepped up to load onto the saddle, I knew something was wrong. My mare's typically calm nature had shifted to a skittish one. Something had changed since the last time I rode her, and, with a gut-wrenching awareness, I realized that thing was me.

Though I'd hoped she would settle after a while, she hasn't. Every moment atop her saddle shows me the depth of her agitation. Mirage can sense the danger I now harbor; I'm not foolish enough to deny it. The dark thrum of Veles lives within me—an ever-present and unmistakable violence I don't know how to control. Even now I sense it like a dull ache.

Every time Mirage chuffs and stomps, I'm reminded just what I am and just how much she fears me now. I wish that knowledge didn't feel like knives in my chest.

I swallow the throbbing ache in the back of my throat and continue onward. The landscape ahead burns hot under the late morning sun, hazy with its heat. The baked earth is barren and dry, and a scratching wind grates along its surface to stir up sand. It's dusty. Desolate. This place isn't fit for much life, though I occasionally spy a small lizard lazing atop the rocks, soaking up as much of the sun's warmth as it can. My hands run over my leathers absentmindedly, feeling the smooth, strong scales against my fingertips. All too quickly, thoughts of hekkriti lizards shift to darker ones, and I'm reminded of the last time I wore these pants.

The shake starts in my hands, making me grip the reins tighter. I close my eyes, willing myself to push his face from my mind, but it's no use. Silas is there before I know it. Sometimes it feels like I'll never be rid of him.

My heart plunges into my stomach as I envision the tempting heat in his gray eyes fade to something dull. I see the life seep from him, see him try to form words against the air I denied.

It's my fault.

I replay the moment over and over again, torturing myself for no other reason than I deserve it. I've earned this pain. Every ache. Every biting cut. It's only the loud groan of a camel that yanks me back from the suffering I'm due. I pull in a sharp breath, eyes shooting open. The day greets me with a brutal rush, but it's darkness I crave.

I mask my face of all distress as Vish sidles up next to me. There was little time to discuss anything this morning, and my mind itches with things unanswered. It seems the more time passes, the more questions I have. There's little I know of this journey, but what I do know for certain fails to settle my nerves. Vish said it won't be more than half a day's ride to the small town of Caen. Though the distance is short, he made sure we all knew the risks. Letka is a mere three days from the safe house Hassan brought me to, which barely puts Caen any further. I'm no longer in the middle of the Jahaer with endless sands to hide among. This is the east of the Continent, littered with trading posts, bustling towns, and hordes of travelers. There is nowhere to run. No hiding for long. Vish didn't have to say it outright; his point was made clear enough. Sooner or later, someone will come for me, and the distance we've put between us and Letka is not distance enough.

"You said there was something we needed to find." My gaze tightens on Vish. "What is it?"

He doesn't bother looking my way, and my hand clenches against the reins as I prepare for him to dismiss me. Silence follows. His camel carries him forward, groaning as Mirage nips at its flank.

Vish holds the silent tension between us for a moment longer before speaking. "A dagger."

Confusion pinches my face. "A dagger?" I loose a breathy laugh. "How is a dagger going to help me hide from Rohan?"

"It isn't." He turns his focus on me, giving me that unnervingly calculated gaze of his. "If anything, it puts you directly in his path."

My mouth pops open, arguments ready to fly from my tongue.

"But obtaining it will ensure he doesn't become the Born. In your lifetime, or the next," he finishes.

I watch him steadily, waiting for him to elaborate, but like always, he never does. Instead, he goes back to ignoring me. Vish takes out his journal, flipping through page after page. What I wouldn't give to snatch the damn thing away from him and read its contents front to back.

What secrets does he keep in there? And of them, how many pertain to me?

I grumble, trying to get into a more comfortable position on the saddle without losing my balance. Just as I move to snap the reins and escape his presence, he speaks.

"Have you heard of the Hesha Mol?"

My body shudders as the words leave his thin lips. Something in my blood lurches, like it's trying to rip free from the vein. I dig my teeth into my tongue to keep the thrumming violence at bay.

"Yes," I admit.

He almost looks surprised, but the Hesha Mol is known to anyone who's read the Book. Its legend is forever marked upon the parchment of that large tome, depicting just what use the gods put it to. I read those pages more times than I could count. It was my only connection to my fate—the only answers the world provided an abandoned child with markings. Each and every word sucked me in. It's why I can recite most of the Book's contents from memory, why mention of the Hesha Mol stirs something fearful in me now. Because I know what it is, and I know its purpose.

"You want to kill a god?"

"No." Vish lets out a deep breath, like the weight of it is too much to bear anymore. "But Rohan does."

I jerk the reins, halting Mirage instantly. As Vish wanders ahead, I feel panic like a fist around my lungs. Like it knows just what Vish speaks of, my blood shudders wildly. My mouth has gone dry, skin flushed with chills despite the oppressive heat. When Vish finally turns around, realizing I've stopped, I force myself to speak.

"I am no god," I utter.

As he guides his camel back toward me, concern etches the taut grooves framing his mouth. "No, but their blood flows through your veins. And it's more than any daemon has ever been gifted."

That pressure within me hums in agreement.

"Bair's Prophecies speak of how the Born must be created by the Durit" —Vish brings his camel around until we're side by side again— "Born of their blood. The blood of the brother gods."

I can't find the words. All I can do is recite passages from the Book in my head, searching for something I must have missed.

A godless man created by the blood of the two.

One blade, older than old, to seal the land's fate.

Godsblood spilled to challenge the will of all.

My stomach turns sour. It was there all along, but how was I supposed to see it?

How was I supposed to know that fate was my own?

Vish's voice stirs me from my thoughts. "No one knows the depths of the Prophecies, nor how much blood it will take for man to become god." He offers me a solemn look, like he might actually give a shit we're talking about my death here. "But I have known Rohan for many years..." Vish looses an unsteady breath. "He will leave nothing to chance, waste not a drop."

A sickly laugh spills from my throat. "So this is the plan?" I sputter. "Find the Hesha Mol before he guts me with it? Then what?" I shake my head, trying to make sense of it all. "What's to stop you from using that blade for your own gain? Or from selling it to the highest bidder?" My teeth grit together. "You really expect me to help find the blade that promises my end?"

Vish lets out an exasperated sigh. "I do not wish to *kill you*, Serehna," he urges. "Nor do I wish anyone else to." He shakes his head. "The Born is not something the Continent can survive. No man should have that kind of power over others."

He presses his fingers against the bridge of his nose, as if my rational questions vex him. He forces another deep breath, though this one seems to calm his mounting frustration. "I merely wish to keep the Hesha Mol from Rohan and anyone else who foolishly seeks to use it," he states. "There are rumors it can be broken. That will be our first hope. And if that proves fruitless..." He snaps his journal shut and stuffs it into his pack. "Then I will make sure you and it are far from the reach of those who wish you harm."

My gaze tightens on him. I can only stare—stare and hope this isn't another one of those moments I come to regret. Because for some reason, I believe him.

"Fine," I grit out. "I'll help you find the godkiller." I eye him up and down. "For now."

I urge Mirage forward, back to where the rest of the group is waiting up ahead. They watch me with worried eyes and soft smiles. When I woke up, I knew things were different. It was more than the unsettled slinking under my skin or the way my horse feared me. No, it was the realization that despite the danger it poses them, these people have decided it's their duty to keep me safe.

I pried information out of Kai and Riat this morning, eager to have some sense of what transpired over the past week. After Riat showed me his new scars with pride, I almost refused to go on this foolish journey. The gnarled tissue marring the entirety of his back is seared into my mind forever, and—as much as he tried to flash me a playful grin and play it off as a hero's errand—I saw the pain shadowed in his eyes. But still, he smiled and taunted me, suggesting all the ways I could repay him for his bravery. Always the reckless bastard, he was excited for what might await us. Kai seemed no less eager to face the dangers we all know are coming. A little more prying revealed that, days ago, Hassan had posed a question to his crew. *Did they wish to help Vish keep me far from Rohan's reach? Or would they rather head to the nearest city and track their next bounty like none of this happened?*

According to Kai, the decision was made in the span of a heartbeat. No one so much as uttered a word of dissension. They gave up everything to be here, riding alongside me toward the unknown. And I can't understand why.

I would be grateful if I didn't resent such foolishness. This will end badly for the lot of us. But for now, and against my better judgment, I feel safe.

As much as I want to push them away and argue that my safety is only of concern to protect their own, I know better. Because they didn't have to patch me up when they found me in the desert weeks ago. They didn't have to rescue me from Rohan or tell me the truth now. They could have prevented the Prophecies a long time ago. A wound left to fester. A slit throat in the night. It would have been easy to kill me—to send my cursed blood back into the ground where it belongs. But for some reason, they didn't.

I dig my teeth against the inside of my cheek hard enough to draw blood. There's a flurry of something overwhelmingly warm in my chest, something I wish to quiet but cannot. I decide to drown it out with answers.

"Where is the Hesha Mol?" I prod Vish as he joins my side once more.

"West," he offers. "Or at least, that is where we'll find the person who knows where it is hidden."

"*What?*" I grumble. "You don't even know where it is?" I *tut* and shoot him a sidelong glare. "Some Seeker you are."

He looses a huff, and I swear I catch him rolling his eyes. "It's as I told you," he says. "Most knowledge is clouded in obscurity. Like the future, we don't know what's important until we realize we asked the wrong questions, too late." He raises a brow. "You should know that."

My upper lip twitches, but I manage to keep the scowl off my face. Yes, I know that all too well.

I bite back my indignation and sigh. "So we go see this person and they lead us to the Hesha Mol." I shrug. "Sounds simple enough."

Vish lets out a shaky laugh. "I wish it were so." He pauses, words clearly stuck on his tongue. His eyes drift to mine before quickly slipping back to the horizon. "Though before we can even think about what comes next, we need to get you and Hassan healed."

My brow furrows, but before I can pester Vish with more questions, he urges his camel toward the front of the group. I watch him go, noticing how Tariq welcomes him with a warm smile. Vish pats the large man on the shoulder in return, and they quickly fall into conversation. It's not the sight of their easy friendship that I find surprising, but the sneer I catch from Hassan. He watches Vish like he watched me those first few days in the desert—like Vish is just some daemon he can't trust. I stiffen as he sweeps that harsh gaze to me. My eyes dart away, but it's too late. Hassan is already guiding his horse over to mine.

I keep my eyes forward as he joins me; I dare not offer even the tiniest glance. It's cowardly, I know, but there's something off between us. It's not like we didn't have our fair share of problems before, but it's different now. Heightened. Every time he gets close to me, the very air seems to churn between us. Heavy and erratic. It makes the hair on my arms stand up, makes my stomach flutter nervously. Even now, I fight the urge to put as much distance between us as possible—if only to avoid the feeling his presence brings. I'm not afraid of him, hardly. That day in the desert proved I can hold my own. My aim had been focused, my strike nearly made. It was only the lingering threat of those around us that had stopped me. I would have struck him dead if given the chance. *Right?*

My hand tightens around the reins, fidgeting restlessly. I feel Hassan's eyes on me—like I always do. Even when he thinks I'm not paying attention, I know he's watching. But the question I can't seem to answer is: *why?*

I shake away thoughts of Hassan; he is of little concern. It would be best to ignore the bounty hunter. He'll only be a distraction. All that matters now is getting the Hesha Mol.

My heart patters uneasily at the reminder. As much as I always wished to hold the greatest blade in history, I never truly believed it to be real. *For how could such a myth exist?* A heavy scoff leaves my throat at the irony of it all. I hadn't believed in the Durit either, and look where that got me. The gods must find this amusing.

I loose a sigh and stare vacantly ahead. I don't know if it's playing fate's fool to acquire the one thing that can be my undoing, but I fear I have little choice in the matter. Until I'm healed, I need to rely on the safety the others say they'll provide. *And if that safety proves fleeting?* Well, I can always forsake this journey and disappear into the desert, just as I've always done.

Hassan's horse pulls my focus as it nips at Mirage. I scoff at the stallion, but before I can send its rider a sour glance, all irritation slips from my face. My head swims with a heavy pressure, but it's not the high sun that licks at my skin. No, the heat is of no concern to me now. What I see chills me to the very bone. I can't help but stare. I'm seeing everything through sharp eyes, though my mind is hazy. It's uncanny and unsettling, yet I know what this feeling is. I've felt it far too many times before—though I've tried not to.

That preternatural feeling of things already seen tightens my lungs. Trepidation torments me, and that panic leads to a familiar pressure building in my veins. I've stoked its fire before I realize it. Mirage huffs underneath me. Her head rears up, tugging on the reins with a force that almost tears them from my grip. I don't need to ask myself if it's me who's causing her this distress; I know it is. But the thrum of my blood and the unease it brings my horse fades into the background as my eyes shift back to the stoic figure riding next to me. Hassan doesn't say anything, though I know he knows I've spotted it. The clench in his jaw and the flighty flicker in his gaze tells me as much. My throat grows dry. My breath turns ragged. I stare at the marred flesh on his forearm and pray it's not true, pray that what I see in front of me is only a trick of the light. It's not. For Hael has shown this to me before.

The cut is bigger than my thumb, and the damage is deep. As much as I want to, I can't look away. I count twenty-two stitches in his tan skin. They're sewn more tightly than my own, like whoever placed them was desperate to undo what had already been done. Though the cording is pulled taunt against the wound, it gapes open as if fighting its own healing. My eyes latch onto the black, sickly curl of decayed flesh. I know what it is, but that doesn't stop my mouth from moving.

"What is that?"

Hassan stiffens. "It's nothing."

He moves his arm away, trying to hide it from my sight, but I'm quick to stop him. I drop the reins, biting back the blinding surge of pain as I reach for him. My sling bumps against his arm as I push up his sleeve to reveal what I already know to be true. I stare at his skin, now drenched in sunlight, and my stomach turns so sour I think I may be sick. My eyes flicker from his arm to his face and back again before I finally find the strength to speak.

"When—"

He shakes me off. "It's nothing," he repeats. "You were barely conscious. You didn't know what you were doing."

I grasp for the reins as I feel my world teeter. Nausea rolls through me like an unruly tide. I swallow it down, tasting the bitter tang of my own resentment.

"Is that to be my excuse now?" I balk. "Oh, don't blame Ren. She has no control—doesn't know how to temper the violence she—" Panic crawls up my throat, choking the words.

The wind whips my tunic, slapping the fabric against my skin. Everything feels too loud—the world too alive. My hand curls into a fist, eager to smother all anxiety, but it dies out quicker than it came. In its place, a new terror emerges. That unruly tug makes the breath leave my lungs. My gift swims in my veins, humming with power. It's feral, and it's itching to be free. *It wants out.*

I shake my head, but it's too late. Panic has taken root in me like a tree desperate to survive rising tides. My muscles tense, coiled like loaded springs. Mirage feels it too—that unwelcome thrum in my blood. I know she does. She huffs and stomps wildly underneath me, sliding me to the back of the saddle. My body rocks violently and before I know it, I've lost the reins and any hope of regaining the control I so desperately need.

"How did—?" I jabber. "When did I—?"

I can't find the words, can't even find a breath. Hassan simply stares. He sears those hazel eyes into mine, gaze growing fearful as Mirage bucks underneath me. His hand reaches out to steady me, like he's afraid I might break. It spurs forth a sick feeling, a twist in my gut that almost has me expelling a desperate laugh. He should not be afraid of how my body will break, but for how it will do the breaking. The intensity of his focus is too dizzying, as is the panicked horse beneath me. My heart hammers in my chest, but it's too late. I can feel it stirring. I'm feeding it with every ounce of panic, every prick of guilt that floods my chest when I look at what I've done to Hassan.

One final look at the Shade's cut on his forearm is all it takes to cement my shame. Hassan opens his mouth to offer worthless excuses in my defense, but I'm lost before he can name them.

My body flinches as shadows erupt from me. They lash out like a violent storm, sucking all sound from the world. For a moment, day becomes night. My vision spins as the chaos surges. I can hear Hassan shouting. Mirage bucks wildly, knocking my hips into the front of the saddle, then sending my body backward with a jolt. The darkness wraps me like a cloak—suffocating in its embrace.

As Mirage plants her hooves, I'm lurched forward. I feel nothing, and yet I feel everything. The heat in the air slaps across my face. My ears flood with that unholy thrum. Breath chokes from my lungs as my body connects roughly with what lies below. But it's not the depths of the underworld I plummet to like I deserve. No, I'm face down in the sand, broken arm screaming underneath me as Mirage panics further.

The shadows whip around me like tiny gales. Sand sprays as my horse stomps the earth. The world seems to still as I watch the next moment pass by too slowly. Mirage's hoof connects with my wrist, pushing a scream from my lips. The pain stipples my vision with black as I desperately clutch my hand to my chest. The dry earth is nothing but a cloud of haze around me as my horse continues to fret. I curl into myself, praying I'll wake up in my tent to find Kora watching me with worried, brown eyes. I wait for her to ask me about this nightmare—for her wide smile to give me the reassurance that the waking world is not as dark as the one I visit in my sleep. But I'm given no such respite.

The chaos around me has ceased, but the shame the daylight brings with its return is as heavy as the fading thrum in my veins. My body heaves with wild breaths as I desperately bite back the sobs I wish to sputter against the dirt. A hand grazes my shoulder, and I flinch. I scramble away from Hassan, eyes wide like the animal I fear I am. I'm breathless, choking back every emotion that's tearing through me as I look up at him. His eyes are just as wide, breath just as labored. He reaches another hand out to me, but I can't bear the touch—not when I've already spilled his blood and marked his flesh. I swallow harshly, oblivious to the pain roaring through my wrist, my arm, and my side that took the brunt of the fall. All I can do is stare at him from where I'm crouched.

My breath catches in my throat as he takes another step closer. "Stay. Away," I rasp.

He slowly retracts his hand, but—like the arrogant fool he is—he makes no move to back off. My eyes dart around, taking in the aftermath of the havoc I alone caused. Savi holds Mirage's reins, stroking her nose reassuringly. Riat, Kai, and Tariq are off their animals, too, gazing at me with worry set deep in their expressions. *Vish*—Vish looks at me like I've razed the Continent to the ground. His brow is furrowed tightly, but it's under that brow that I see it happen for the first time. Or, at least, it's the first time I understand what it is that I see. For a fleeting moment, Vish's pupils narrow into slits. They're back to normal in an instant, but I don't dismiss what I now know to be true. Vish's tell—the distinct thing that gives all different kinds of daemons away—is his eyes. Just as my gaze floods white like every other Seer and how Shade's veins flood black, Vish's eyes reveal him for what he truly is.

I gulp in a rush of air, eager to find my resolve before I lose it for good. I dig my nails into the earth and stare at Vish with unflinching brutality. He can't hide from me anymore. He's asking questions, questions about me, and whether he wants to or not, he's going to tell me what answers the gods give.

CHAPTER 6

I drape my headscarf tightly around my face and slip off the saddle before anyone can stop me. It's a steep drop—more than difficult with only one arm—but I grit my teeth through it.

The camel groans as I yank my pack free and toss it over my shoulder. One look at Vish riding Mirage into the stables is all it takes for my heart to turn more brittle and cold than it already feels. The mare wouldn't let me ride her after what happened. Savi had managed to settle the horse, but, by the time I staggered up from the ground and quelled the shakiness I felt, Mirage panicked once more. There was no recognition when my horse looked at me; fear was the only thing I saw bleeding into her pale, ghostly eyes.

I didn't want it to hurt, didn't want to care, but it was yet another cut that ripped my chest wide open. In the end, Vish had offered me his camel and taken Mirage in its place.

No one spoke of my shadows after they tore out from me like a violent swell. The rest of the journey here was filled with subdued small talk and polite smiles. Anyone passing by would think nothing of it, but the nonchalance my companions perform is a lie. I know it. They know it. Whether they keep playing pretend or not, it won't be long before the truth is impossible to ignore.

The Durit rides among them. I'm touched by Veles, and I have no control over these shadows.

The others dismount, but I'm already far ahead. There is no idle chatter to be had between us; Vish already shared where we needed to go. There's an inn at the center of town. *The Scabbard.* It's where we are to stay for the night—where he plans to bring the Mender later. The faster I make it there, the better. The others let me keep my distance during the remaining hours it took to get here, but I know soon enough they'll forget just what it is I can do. They'll forget the danger I pose, and they'll wander too close.

I bite down and savor the vicious sting of teeth against my tongue. *Gods, another city.* It doesn't matter how small this one is or what they seek to call this mound of civilization. Outpost. City. Town. It's all the same to me. My eyes dart about quickly, taking in my surroundings as my boots stomp down the street. The small town of Caen is brimming with people. *Too many people.* I ignore the hot twinge of pain that pulses through my wrist and skim my fingers along the fabric covering my neck—just to make sure it's still there. There is no telling who here is friend or foe, so I've given them little to identify me with. Every inch of my face is covered, save for my eyes. Those I hide from no one. As I look out at the faces that rise to meet my gaze, I make sure they regret the glance. My eyes burn darkly—cruel and unflinching. I catch a few women staring at my arms before they drop their gazes to the dirt.

I haven't bothered covering my scars. *Why should I?*

The message they offer the world is potent. I am no longer that wandering woman who seeks solace amidst Jahaer's sands. I am a force of violence—a beast carved by the brutalist of measures. *They should know to keep their fucking distance.*

The further I get from the stables, the more crowded the streets grow. My boots scuff the barren earth as I weave my way in and out of the masses. The air is hot and dry around me, and the bodies seem to steal any drifting breeze that might grant me relief. Overhead, the sun blares down, baking in the last of its heat before the day submits to night.

A bead of sweat trickles out from under my face coverings. It slips over my brow before my fingers have a chance to wipe it away. My scalp itches, hot and uncomfortable, and I hasten my steps. I can see the inn ahead. An old wooden sign sways in the breeze, hanging by a rusted chain that emits a shrill *groan* as it swings back and forth. While worn and faded, *The Scabbard* is too prominent to miss. The name is carved roughly into wood and underlined by the depiction of a long blade. The sandstone building itself stands two stories tall, its windows covered in drapings that have long since been faded by the sun.

I tense the closer I get, feeling myself being sucked into the busy foot traffic as it overwhelms the street. Bodies jostle me as they pass, leaving a slick of sweat on my bare arms in their wake. Hot breath huffs around me. Street vendors yell. Men grumble and rake their eyes down my body as they pass. I feel my heart patter heavily in my chest, feel my adrenaline spike too quickly. But among it all, a familiar feeling rises, dropping my stomach into the deepest dregs of panic. *No.*

I'm pushing past people now, shoving bodies out of my way as I feel myself going under. The world starts getting fuzzy and all too-bright at the edges. I trip, stuttering forward on uneasy legs as I reach the inn. My hand slaps roughly against its stone facade. I take in deep gulps of air and curl myself tightly to the wall, hiding under the canopy that shades the inn's entrance from the desert sun and those around me.

My heart is beating so hard I can feel it in my throat. I press my forehead against the warm stone and pray for it to stop. A moment's peace. A day without the gods taunting me. That's all I ask. My murmured pleas are nothing but wasted breath. It takes me as swiftly and carelessly as it has time and time again. The chaos of the street dies around me. A frustrated moan spills from my lips as my eyes flood with white, and I fade from this world.

Heat flares all around me. I can barely take in a breath. The flames reach up into the air, vicious tongues that stretch and wag as if hoping to reach the sky and burn Hael from his throne. Through the spitting fire, I see him. Shaggy black hair pools around his shoulders and frames him in shadow. A Shade's cut twists down his face, disfiguring everything from his left brow to the cheek that rests beneath. The eye in its path is void of life. Dead. Ruined. Black decay swallows the pupil, cutting through it like a cavernous void.

Fear weighs heavy on my tongue as he watches me. He looks like a devil—but it's more than the excitement flooding his good eye or the way he fidgets with the black blade in his hand like he's dying to use it. It's the smile on his face, wide and eager. His sharp teeth seem to gleam against the high sun like a monster waiting to tear flesh.

He stalks back and forth. Slowly. Patiently. He makes no move for me; there's no reason to. Not yet. The circle of flames burning atop the sand is a prison fit for the underworld and one I cannot escape without consequence.

He watches.

He waits.

It's only when the flames behind me flicker and die that I understand what's coming. He's a predator—a beast eager to hunt—and I have no choice but to allow him his fill. As he takes a step closer, I run.

I gasp, choking on nothing but air as I come back to this world only to find myself curled against the harsh ground. The noise flitters back to life around me in a raucous wave, barreling down with all its force. I'm shaking despite the heat that's thick in the air. As I look up, shame eclipses panic.

Hassan kneels before me, brow furrowed deeply and eyes holding mine with a heavy stillness. I watch his jaw tick, watch the slight twitch in his hand. The shift of his body springs me into action. I lurch away before he can foolishly offer his help.

I press myself against the stone wall, biting back twinges of pain as my broken wrist flexes and aches. My arm is no better. Somewhere amidst the time Hael pulled me under, I landed right on top of it. It throbs incessantly, despite now being relieved of my body's full weight. I'm a battered thing—both from my vision and the last few weeks of my life. Suffering feels like an old friend, one who has no intention of parting ways. I groan as I pull myself up to standing.

Gods, I really need that Mender.

Hassan is still there when I right myself. His eyes rake over my body, accessing the state of me. He opens his mouth to say something, but I push past him to get to the inn. I don't need his help, nor his pity. None of it will change what has become of me.

The others are close behind. Whether they saw the state of me, they don't say. Instead, they spread out among the inn's front room, keeping busy best they can. I do the same, if only to avoid their questions.

Like the town itself, the inn is simple. Large sandstone walls surround us, draped in fabrics woven in faded shades of red. The stone floor is covered in a thin layer of sand and dried clay that's been discarded by the endless trample of boots. There's a rumbling of voices and a clacking of dishes down the hall where I know I'll find the tavern. And as much as I'd like to fall into a bottle of rum, I want to be alone more. That and a bath.

A loud sigh fills the room as Tariq eases himself down onto a large bench. "*Hael bless the end of a day's journey,*" he utters.

The wood creaks under his burly frame, but as he leans his head back against the wall, he looks more content than I've seen him all day. He stretches his long legs out in front of him and, with another sigh, closes his eyes. I'm almost envious of the ease drawn across his face.

Kai is already wandering around the corner, no doubt in search of the cooked meat whose smoky char wafts through the inn. To no surprise, Vish has disappeared. I can only hope his retreat is in search of the Mender he promised me.

I roll my shoulders to try to lessen the tension buried there, only to suck in a sharp breath. It seems I can do nothing without jolting my arm in this sling. I bite back a groan before catching Hassan's eyes on me. He looks away quickly, and his cowardice makes me scowl.

He hovers nearby, and though I know he's supposed to be paying attention to Savi as she pays for our stay, he isn't. His gaze keeps flickering to mine. I don't know what bothers me more: the thought of him watching to make sure I don't pass out again or waiting for me to tear this place apart with shadows. As it stands, I wouldn't put either past me. Though, acknowledgment of that fact doesn't help temper my resentment for the hunter.

I ignore Hassan and instead focus on the short man in deep discussions with Savi. He looks weathered, tired from countless days behind his rickety wooden desk. There's a pinch of irritation clenched in the corners of his eyes, but it doesn't last long. I watch as Savi's bright smile draws a grin from his grouchy face—even if it is only fleeting. The man shakes his head, summoning back his crotchety grimace before handing her a multitude of keys. My stomach clenches at the sight. As I watch Savi assign rooms, panic buds like a rising sun in my throat. While my gaze tracks her efforts, a presence slinks up next to me.

Riat slings his arm over my shoulder, tucking his body against me tightly. "Want to share a room?" he asks, voice laced with all kinds of possibilities. "I've been told sleeping with me is as close to being with the gods as it gets."

He gives me a devious smile, one that threatens to drag a playful retort to my lips. The temporarily warmth I feel is smothered by an icy bitterness as reality sets in. He nudges my side like nothing has changed—like I didn't just unleash the fury of Veles a few hours ago. That kind of blind faith is going to get him killed. It's going to make this gift kill him.

I shove him off roughly and glare. "Stay the fuck away from me, Riat," I growl. "Unless you want a scar to match your leader's."

The smirk drops from his face instantly. He stares at me, brow muddled with something I tell myself isn't worry. His full lips pout before he simply shrugs. "Your loss, goddess. Though don't worry" —he steps closer and drags his fingers through my hair before I can stop him— "the offer always stands."

I'm frozen in place, lost to moments that broke me long before this one. Riat sends me a wink, oblivious to the memories he called forth to haunt me. I can still feel Rohan's fingers in my hair. Gripping. Yanking. My heart beats too fast as I watch Riat saunter over to where Kai has returned with food. The long-haired hunter clutches the plate in his hand, hoisting it out of reach as his friend tries to steal a bite. I try to ground myself in the sight of two grown men wrestling over a hunk of bread like mere children. It's ridiculous, but panic has already claimed me. I'm lost in the in-between, still tiptoeing through past horrors when a set of soft, hazel eyes appears before me. My heart jumps in my chest as I'm pitched out of my thoughts.

"And this one" —Savi dangles a large brass key in front of me — "is yours."

I swallow thickly as I take it from her. "Is anyone els—"

"You have the room to yourself." She offers me a smile, though I notice concern creases the corners. "Down the hall, up a floor," she says, nodding to my left. "It's the door with the scorpion on it."

My fingers gently curl around the key, but even the small movement sends a burst of pain through my wrist. It's white-hot fire and splitting ache. I dig my teeth into my cheek to stifle as much of it as I can. It doesn't work well enough. Tears well in my eyes, though I don't give Savi the chance to see the suffering I bear. She has enough to deal with, as does everyone else. I'm slipping down the hall and into the tavern before she can utter a word.

As I round the corner, I'm greeted by a boisterous uproar that has me shrinking back into myself. Card games carry on noisily as bets are made and cheats are called out. Drinks slosh over rims, and hands slap coins onto the bar top. Men eye me, snickering to themselves before turning back to the women resting on their laps. The air is thick with ripe, warm bodies and the pungent smells that drift from the kitchen. It's nauseating, roiling my already uneasy stomach as I push through the fray toward the carved stone staircase.

It's with heavy legs that can't seem to carry me quick enough that I rush up the stairs and cross the landing. My boots stumble against the worn rug that spans the dark hallway, all but tripping in my haste. The stench of ale follows me even as I seek to escape it. Memories I hoped to forget keep my chest tight and my breath shallow. The cellar flashes in my mind—dark, empty. I think of being trapped behind that massive door. No noise. No daylight to help me count the hours. But even worse is the memory of that other place. I still don't remember much after Asha caught me, but what I do remember floods me with anxiety.

The scurry of rats. Distant voices and the *shush* of sand. Steel against skin. The feeling of it pinching and piercing my flesh. I now know it had been mere hours, but it felt like I spent days in that darkness. An eternity endured in silent suffering. Weaving in and out of poison's haze, not knowing when that door would open, just that it would. That, eventually, Rohan would come for me.

Sweat coats the back of my neck as I push the memories away. I fight every urge to rip off the fabric covering my face if only to suck in a full breath. It's stifling. Suffocating. Panic clashes with pain, and my hand shakes as I clutch the key tighter. Small brass plates decorate the front of each door, but none bear the mark I'm desperate to see. Lizard. Camel. Donkey. *Finally.*

I let out a shuddering breath and head straight for the wooden door with a scorpion carved into its metal nameplate. Voices flitter through the hall, quickly heading my way. My fingers twitch in their rush. I can't open the door fast enough. The key slips from my hand, and I swear under my breath as I scramble for the thing. Finally, I manage to unlock the godsdamn door.

I shove myself inside and flip the lock just as a group of men drift past. Their booming, drunk voices all but pound in my ears.

Though they aren't for me, their words feel like a muffled taunt through the door. I fall to the floor, sucking in desperate breaths as I rip the scarves from my face. Tears line my eyes, but I bite my lip to stave them off. I shrug my pack from my shoulder, chucking it away as I let out a frustrated yell.

This can't be who I am now.

I dip my head low and rake my hand through the sweat-dampened strands of my hair. Pain explodes through my wrist, but I weather it with clenched teeth. After a period of drawing in deep, uneasy breaths, I pull myself up.

Fuck the gods for this fate.

I snatch my pack off the floor and head for the bathroom. It rests behind a small door, though as soon as I pry it open, a jolt of pain spears my chest. I pull my gaze from the copper tub quickly, but not quick enough. I tell myself it's nothing, that this inn is far different from the last, but thoughts of Silas aren't so easily dismissed. He's everywhere I look. As I yank at the faucet, I picture him leaning against the wall, watching me. Over the roar of the tub filling, I can all but imagine how his voice would taunt and pry. Steam heats the air, and my thoughts grow as foggy as the mirror. It's his gaze I feel on me as I strip from my clothes. I squeeze my eyes shut roughly, but it doesn't help. Silas is a ghost I'll never shake.

With a huff, I toss my sling to the stone floor. I try to lower myself into the tub without using my hands, but as soon as my feet greet the slick surface, I'm grasping for the rim. My broken wrist alights with the kind of pain I'll never numb to. Unforgiving. Shearing. I bite back a roar and quickly force myself into the scalding water—if only to temper my pain with a different sort. But not even when I sink below the surface and close my eyes am I free of torment.

Again, it's too easy to imagine Silas here with me. He'd stir the water with his fingertips, offer words meant to drive a flush to my cheeks. His eyes would be like melting ice, sending shivers through my body as he ate up every inch of my skin. My thighs rub together softly under the water's surface, desperate to stifle the ache that builds there. I can almost feel his touch—how his fingers would leisurely glide across my face before dipping to the delicate swell of my throat. Before I can even consider relieving the tension building within me, I remember the very thing I wish to be free of.

My violence.

Wide eyes—taken by surprise. Blood. So much blood.

And the shadows.

Anger floods my frayed nerves and threatens to be my undoing. I dig my nails into my thigh, drawing a muffled cry, but not even that pain is good enough. I submerge myself, racing under the water's surface like it will cleanse me of my guilt. My fingers cling to the tub's rim, broken bones roaring as I hold my body under for far longer than my lungs wish. I stay submerged while my rational mind screams in protest and pray that the gods take it all back. This blood. This life.

It cannot be mine. I cannot bear for it to be mine.

My lungs spasm, but I keep my lips sealed—depriving myself of the breath I gravely need. Panic shifts to surrender as I close my bulging eyes and yield, something I promised myself I'd never do. I'm floating, halfway between this world and the eternal agony I crave when my fingers uncurl and I break the surface with a wretched gasp of air. I pull my legs against my chest, choking and sputtering. For a moment, I think I'm free, but then, I see him.

Silas is a plague my mind will never be rid of. A curse I've inflicted upon myself. *I killed him.* And worse than that is the truth I've been denying for days. *I did it because I wanted to.*

I quickly step out of the bath and dry myself with a thickly-woven cloth. The threads scratch at my skin, leaving red marks in their wake. I pay the discomfort no mind; it's fitting, truly. With a huff, I dig through my pack and find what I need. A fitted pair of clean trousers—the fabric black and well worn—and a brown tunic that always reminded me of Kora's eyes. The sleeveless cut of the top shows off my scars, just as I wish it to. I choke back frustrated sobs as my injuries shriek against my every movement.

I have but a single blade in my possession now. Hassan lent it to me this morning, saying it was for my protection. The sentiment makes my lips curl even now. I fear I will never be rid of the hunter's pity.

The knife is a small thing, but sharp nonetheless. I slip it into the sheathe on my belt loop, settling it against my hip. I try not to scowl at the thought of all the expensive blades I've lost to time and men.

As I'm digging through my pack, searching for a cord to tie up my hair, the cool touch of metal stills me. With a shaky hand, I grab the chain and pull it from the bundle of clothes it's fallen between. The sight of silver makes my heart thump dangerously fast.

I had almost forgotten.

I swallow thickly. A tarnished silver ring is looped through the dangling chain, and it all but shatters the cold, dead thing in my chest. I twist it in my fingers, admiring the heavy stain of black that splits through the metal. Like everything shadows slice, it's marked forever.

I let the chain wrap around my knuckles, and my brow furrows. For the first time since I woke up in the safe house, I think of Malachi. He gave this to me a year before I left Artolen; a present for my birthday, though we didn't celebrate such things. He told me it was something to remember him by—a piece of him to keep with me forever.

I thought it silly, for our paths were never supposed to part. My throat tightens with an emotion I don't waste time naming. I slip the chain around my neck and tuck the ring under my tunic without a second thought. I should have gotten rid of the token years ago, but I never could. Somehow, that cold prickle of metal against my skin makes me feel less alone now.

Some part of me—a foolish part—wishes for another Weaver dream, just to get a glimpse. I grumble before pushing the mere thought of that bastard away. Malachi is gone and, for now, so are the dreams. It's for the best—something I should do well to remember.

Numerous attempts to braid my hair leave my broken arm and wrist feeling like I've shattered the bones all over again. Shaky breaths pull into my lungs as I lean over the sink and rest my head against the metal basin. Sweat coats my forehead, and my flesh feels like it's on fire.

You'll see the Mender soon enough, I remind myself. *After that, the pain will be bearable. Maybe even gone completely if I'm lucky and Vish found someone with a modicum of skill.*

I grit my teeth and raise my gaze to the mirror. What I see steals the breath from my lungs just as the bath did. My eyes dart back and forth, trying to understand what my mind refuses to. The markings on the right side of my neck are as they've always been—a single column of black that marks me as Hael's. It's not even what surrounds them that floods me with reckless fear.

Seeing the puncture wounds that were no doubt left by whatever confined me in Letka is no surprise; I had guessed as much last night when I lied down to sleep and felt the uncomfortable pull of scabs against skin. But as my eyes dart across my neck and look past the results of Rohan's barbarity, I all but fall to my knees.

The beginnings of a new column of markings mars the left side of my neck. Dark, inky lines, muddled and thick. Splatters like ink—no bigger than freckles, but darker than night. And among it all, a flow of black like a shadow falling across my skin. The markings are nothing short of orchestrated chaos, mimicking the very nature of their gift.

My stomach rolls. I back away from the sink, shaking my head like, if I try hard enough, it will change what I see. The Shade's marks taunt me, but, no matter how hard I wish them to, they don't go away. I sway unsteadily as the back of my legs hits the tub. My breath is lost to me, as is my mind. I'm sliding into darkness, fading fast as the world I've come to know slips from my grasp.

I should have expected this. It was naive not to. But still, the sight of my new marks is a blade twisted deep into my gut. There is no denying it now—no pretending that the destruction that corrupts my blood is fabled and nothing else. The truth is as clear as the skies. Veles taints my soul, and his mark is now displayed for all to see.

My gaze sharpens as I take one last look at myself. I burst forward in a frenzy, curling my fist back. But before my knuckles can connect with the glass and leave my wrist more battered than it already is, I stop. It's with the breath stilled in my lungs that I take in this new me for the first time.

My amber eyes are violent as I trace every inch of my neck. I turn my head, pulling the left side taut and letting the flickering candlelight paint the marks in a warm glow. The hum inside me grows stronger as I run a careful finger across my skin. My jaw clenches, my whole body tensing. I'm fighting against the very blood I was born with; I know it's foolish.

I force a deep breath and let my fingers trace every inch Veles has claimed. As that constant thrum of power builds under my skin, I snatch my touch away. My eyes burn into the mirror, but the person I see is one I haven't known for years. I see the young girl in me—a girl terrified of her gift and the power it provides. A girl who ran from the world when it sought to destroy her. Weak. Lost. *Abandoned.* My eyes sting with strain as I force myself to see the feeble thing I've become.

I thought I was stronger than this. *But aren't I? Did I not survive the cellar? And the desert? Did I not take down those who wished to barter and use me?*

Silas pops into my head uninvited, but this time, I don't retreat from him like a tortoise. I drag in a slow, hot breath and let my gaze burn into my very soul.

They did not break me.

I think of Silas gasping for air, think of Olen's eyes pooling with fear as my shadows tore into him.

I will not be broken.

I snatch the blade from my hip before I can think better of it. I stifle a scream as my shattered arm raises weakly to grasp a chunk of hair. My eyes darken, amber turning a murky brown as my lids lower and all the hate I feel spills out of my gaze.

Silas is dead.

I begin sawing. The knife cuts clean and quick. Honey-white strands fall into the sink like broken hay. My wrist is bright with pain, and my arm sags boneless and frail as I reach for another chunk.

Rohan is next.

More hair falls. I'm shaking, unable to stop the anguished whimpers that leave my throat. My body is screaming, alight in agony, but I don't stop. When I finally drop the blade into the sink, I slump forward and close my eyes. The inn bustles underneath me, patrons growing rowdier as night falls. It's frantic—loud and sloppy. Instead of shying away from it and letting panic take root, I let it ground me. The yells. The chairs that scoot roughly across the floor before toppling over. I hear the muffled uproar of a brawl before it's quickly subdued. Amidst it all, I feel my own chaos simmering beneath the surface. Anger. Hate. Resentment. It all bubbles near the brim—slithering through my blood and latching a cold, dead hand around my heart. But louder than any of that is the tinge of Veles bewitching my blood.

When I open my eyes, I see her—the version of me that will never allow them to carve my skin or seal my fate. My hair is cut above the chin, severed bluntly and without apology. I stare into the mirror with a gaze that's not a welcome, but a warning.

Let them come for me.

My upper lip twitches as I take one of my scarves and wrap it around my neck, barely draping it over my head. I snatch the knife from the sink and slip it into my belt loop. I've been fighting my nature for too long, dousing the fire in me for fear of burning. But I'm done pretending.

My jaw locks as I tug on my boots and head for the door. The pain twisting from my limbs is nothing compared to the choking fury hardening my heart.

If Veles seeks to claim me, fine. I'll let fate guide me forward, play into the madness the dark god seeks.

I roll my shoulders and take a shuddering breath. The itching under my skin is maddening—a feral desperation that seeks to be set free. A part of me wonders what will become of me if I do just that. Another part couldn't care less about the consequences.

As I cross the room, Silas's words haunt me. His voice echoes in my mind, playing on an incessant loop that pounds louder with each step I take.

Virtue doesn't mean shit if you don't survive.

I grab the door and wrench it open.

He was right.

CHAPTER 7

My eyes sweep the tavern as soon as I hit the bottom step. If it sounded rowdy upstairs, it's unbridled chaos in the flesh.

Pints clink in boisterous cheers while voices boom through the long-stretching room. Dice scatter across tabletops and cards splay out from dirty hands. Two men shove each other, their faces red and furious. A quick fist flies into a cheekbone, and the resulting *thwack* makes my body tense. It's over before I can touch the hilt of my blade. One of the men hits the floor like a downed tree, and I hear the air *whoosh* from his lungs. I'd be worried if not for the garbled mutterings that spill from his bloodied mouth. He'll probably be fine.

The victor grins a drunk, greedy smirk as he shakes his fist out and looks down at his felled opponent. I try to slink around him, but the gods are nothing if not bastards.

The man's gaze slithers across me just as I attempt to pass. "Woah, woah. *Easy there,*" he urges. "Where do you think you're going, sweets?"

As his hand wraps around my broken arm, pain is the furthest thing from my mind. I yank him closer, drawing my weapon without a second thought. His ale-drenched breath hits me hot in the face as I press my knife into the warm flesh underneath his jaw. The asshole has the nerve to grin at me.

"Careful, girl," he purrs. "Best be careful who you hold a blade to. They might just put you on your back where you belong." His gaze grows lustful as he cocks his head at me. "Bet you'd like that. Wouldn't you?"

My blade drags against the unkempt scruff on his throat before I press it roughly into his skin. The force draws a trickle of blood, and the very sight makes mine hum in response. Red runs down the man's neck in a thin river that brings a smile to my face.

"Are you sure you want to play?" I mock. "The last man who shared my bed now rots with Veles." My breath is no more than a tempting whisper against his ear. "Would you like to join him?"

The man's jaw ticks as he weighs his options. He could easily overpower me in the state I'm in. My broken arm is a screeching mess, and my wrist is no better. Every second I hold this blade to his throat is one closer to my body passing out from the pain. But he doesn't need to know that.

I hold my knife steady and pin him with a sharp look. "I require an answer."

"You little fucking bitch," he rasps before loosing a bitter laugh. "I'm going to enjoy putting you in your place."

I press harder, and his throat bobs as another drop of blood slides down his skin.

"My place is right here," I utter. "Making men like you bleed."

My blade bites into his flesh, calling forth more of his godless blood. It slips down his neck, one rolling bead after the other. I watch it stain his tunic, watch his nostrils flare. It seems our little standoff might last forever. Yet, the moment I see the hesitation in his eyes, I know this is over.

Pity. I was hoping a fight might ease this raging ache inside, but the taste of his shame will have to do.

As quickly as I grabbed him, I let the man go. I shove him back toward his friends who stand wide-eyed with weapons at the ready.

I smirk, letting my gaze drift over each and every one. "Another time, gentlemen," I taunt.

As I turn on my heels, I run straight into a firm chest. Before I can re-draw my blade, irritation stills my hand.

"What do you want?" I snap at Hassan.

"You should be more—"

The words still on his tongue as his attention drifts over my shoulder. I follow his gaze to see the table of ale-sloshed men aren't minding their business like they should. One twirls a dagger in his hand while another cracks his knuckles. They all have violence flooding their bloodshot eyes, and the sight pulls an aggravated rumble from my chest.

"Oh, for fuck's sake." I brush Hassan's hand off my shoulder and take a step toward the men. "I'm dying for a reason," I grit out. My voice shakes as I grip the left side of my scarf and yank it down. "*Give me one.*"

The murderous glint in their eyes dies out like a smothered wick as soon as they see what I want them to. One look at my Shade's marks has them thinking better of it. It seems even with their heads swimming deep in a pint, they still value their lives. A few of them actually raise their hands in surrender, apologies slipping from their quivering lips.

The itching under my skin thrums in delight, soaking up the fear I so easily conjured. I hum softly as a twisted smile curls my lips. "That's what I thought."

I quickly fix the fabric back into place before they can steal a glance at what marks the other side of my neck. When I turn around to face Hassan, he's seething. Heavy breath chokes his lungs, and the hazel in his eyes is a searing gold.

"What?" I bark.

He clenches his jaw, seeming to bite back whatever it is he truly wishes to say. "The Mender is waiting," he grumbles. "Unless you'd rather announce to the whole tavern who and what you are first? Maybe get into a fight and injure yourself more?" He shakes his head and scowls at me. "Gods know how much more you've mangled that hand with your foolishness."

My brow pinches. I didn't tell the others that Mirage crushed my wrist. I eye Hassan hesitantly, something thick and heavy rising up my throat. "How did you—"

"The Mender," he huffs. "Now, *witch*. We've been waiting long enough."

My upper lip twitches, eager to hurl a slurry of insults his way, but he's right. My wrist is screaming with pain, and, if I don't sit down soon, he might have to pick me up off the floor.

"Lead the way, *hunter*," I bite.

His eyes flare dangerously, but he doesn't take the bait like I hoped. Instead, he merely mutters under his breath before leading us to the back of the room. It appears my little stunt caught more than a few eyes because as we slip through the tavern, people are quick to part the way. A flicker of pride, mixed with something far darker, swells up in me at the sight.

Good. They should be afraid.

When we finally make it to a secluded nook in the back of the tavern, that smug pride falters. I freeze, breath trapped in my lungs. My boots skid against the floor, and my heart stills. I dare not take another step for fear the sight in front of me is nothing but an illusion. My mouth opens, but I can't speak. All I can do is stare at the man who rests casually at our table as he chats with Savi. Light brown eyes flicker to me absentmindedly. His attention is gone in a breath and back the next. He snaps his gaze to mine and holds it there, eyes instantly growing glassy. I feel heaviness well in my chest, threatening to drop me where I stand. *How*—My mouth pops open, longing to say something. But it's his smooth, honeyed voice that breaks the silence.

"Ren."

He lurches up from the table, charging me before Hassan can even process what's happening. My body tenses upon impact, broken bones screaming in pain. But I don't care. I'd take a thousand years of pain if it meant always finding myself here. Tears spill from my eyes as I clutch Mikel tightly to my chest and unload all of the grief I've felt in his absence.

"How are you—" I rasp. "What are you—"

The words muddy themselves on my tongue, thick with overwhelm and the best kind of ache. I clench my throat, desperate to hold back my sobs, but I cannot. I curl my head into his shoulder and let deep shuddering breaths spill from my lungs.

"I tried to find you," he babbles, voice shaky and tight with emotion. "I've been trying to find you—searching everywhere I could think of."

I feel his own tears wetting my cheek and squeeze him tighter. We stand like that for a moment, doing nothing but clutching each other and finding our breath, until I finally pull back.

A breathy laugh spills free as I wipe away my tears. "*Gods.*" I shake my head. "What are you *doing* here?"

Mikel gives me a beaming smile, eyes still wet and cheeks pulling high on his youthful face. "I was told someone was in dire need of a Mender."

He looks me over, eyes widening oh-so-slightly as his gaze drifts across my body. I try not to tense at the inspection; much has changed since he last saw me. My stomach clenches as he takes his time looking at my scars—at the deeply cut lines that are forever a reminder of Rohan's cruelty. Though I know that alone is enough to send my friend into a fit of worry, there's more to see. My left arm hangs limply at my side. Various cuts and bruises mar my skin. *And my hair...*

Standing under Mikel's discerning gaze, I start to regret how hastily I made the rough cut. I brace myself for endless questions and the scolding I'm due—though he should know by now I'm nothing if not careless. But when Mikel looks at me, all of his concern disappears behind a waggish smile.

"*Veles damn me*, Ren." He chuckles. "You look like shit."

CHAPTER 8

I flinch as Mikel lays my arm across the table.

He lets out a deep sigh, peering at me through thick lashes. "I leave you alone for a few weeks and you come back looking like you've been thrown off a cliff." His smile flashes playfully. "Reckless as ever."

I grit my teeth and try to offer a retort, but it comes out in a hiss. "*Fuck me to the depths*, Mikel," I curse. "Do you have to be so rough?"

"Hm," Riat purrs as he slides into the booth next to me. "I would have guessed you liked it rough, goddess." His eyes sparkle wickedly as he licks his bottom lip and leans in close. "But for you, I can be gentle."

"Oh, piss off," I growl, though I can't help but crack a smile. "Weren't you getting me a drink?"

He slams a pint on the table, smiling like a devil.

As I eye the foamy brown liquid sloshing over the rim, my stomach knots. "No ale," I murmur.

My eyes dart away from it, only to find Mikel watching me carefully. His lips purse in contemplation, but he doesn't utter a word. Instead, he goes back to inspecting my broken arm in a way that feels like individual needles piercing my skin.

Riat groans dramatically before taking a sip of what was supposed to be my drink. "You're lucky I'm in love with you," he teases. "Else I'd find some other pretty thing to give this to."

"By all means," I say, gesturing across the bar with the hand not in Mikel's firm grasp. "I'm sure there's a wife or two around here that could provide the necessary company."

Riat draws a hand to his chest, feigning insult. "You wound me." He laughs before grabbing the pint and pulling himself from the booth. "Rum?" he offers.

I grunt in pain when Mikel straightens my arm. "As much as they'll serve me."

Mikel chuckles, watching the hunter as he saunters away. "Did you two—" My friend smirks. "You know..."

"*Gods*, no." I laugh, then immediately wince as the movement jolts my shattered bones. "Over eager isn't exactly my type," I offer through gritted teeth.

We both turn to watch Riat from across the room. He's standing at the bar, having already found the next subject of his affections. He works quickly, but I'm not surprised. One flash of that mischievous smile is all it takes to flush the face of the young woman beside him. She can't be more than a year or two younger, but she's clearly out of depth. The rosy tinge of her cheeks tells me she's utterly smitten. As I watch Riat chug the ale and sidle up close to the girl, I know my chances of getting a drink anytime soon are less than zero.

Mikel *tsks*. "Yeah, you're right." He shakes his head as his focus returns to my arm. "If I remember anything from our brief stay in Monok last year, you prefer them exceedingly broody and emotionally unavailable." His eyes snap over my shoulder, and his smile grows deviously wide. "Which begs the question..."

I sense his presence before I see him, or maybe it's the way the ornery old goat lets out a deep grumble as he approaches the booth Mikel and I have tucked ourselves in.

My eyes all but roll as I turn to face Hassan. "What?" I sass, to which he offers no reply. "Care to boss me around some more? Am I being too loud? Look too happy? Or is it my mere presence that's the problem?"

He takes in a deep, aggravated breath and stares me down. "Don't push me, *witch*," he utters. "Or I'll be happy to drink this myself."

Without another word, he slides a small glass across the table. I eye it skeptically, ignoring Mikel's stifled chuckle.

"What's this?" I sneer.

"*Gods below.*" Hassan sighs. "You're in pain. Just drink the fucking thing."

My gaze narrows on him, but as much as I want to toss it in his face, I do in fact need a drink.

The ligaments in my wrist writhe in pain as I shakily lift the glass. I keep my face blank under the scrutiny of Hassan's gaze, not letting so much as a grimace show. When the glass meets my lips, I close my eyes and let the rich, sweet taste melt on my tongue. It warms me on the way down, settling my nerves like I knew it would.

When I open my eyes, Mikel is all but snickering, but it's Hassan who has my full attention. His throat bobs uneasily. He stares at my lips, and, for some reason, I can't help but drag my tongue across the bottom one. I taste a lingering drop of rum before the flare in Hassan's eyes has me regretting such boldness.

He clenches his jaw as he slides into the booth to sit next to Mikel. "*Fucking hells*," he mumbles.

"Ready?"

My gaze snaps to my friend. He's smirking like a fiend, barely containing the breathy laughter that wants to spill free. With Hassan right there, I can only glare and nod.

"Resetting your arm is going to hurt like the gods are carving flesh," Mikel continues. "Best we get it over with first."

I nod again, stiffer this time, and down the rest of my rum in one swift gulp. "Do it then."

As Mikel takes a deep breath, worry eats the pit of my stomach. *What will this pain call forth? A glimpse at just how weak I have become? Or will it spark the violence I now possess?*

My eyes dart to Hassan; his focus hasn't wavered.

"The drink is great, thanks," I say snidely. "You can go now."

I stare him down, but he doesn't so much as flinch.

"I'll wait," he utters. "You're not the only one in need of mending."

Though I wish I didn't, I let my gaze dart down to his arm. My handiwork hides halfway under his rolled up sleeve. But it's there.

"Why not get it mended earlier?" I snap. "Did you merely wait so you could remind me what it is I've done?"

Mikel's brow furrows as he glances at the Shade's cut blemishing Hassan's skin. My friend opens his mouth to speak, but ultimately decides against it when I firmly shake my head. Hassan stays silent, though shoots me a deadly look of his own. I match his ire with all that I can muster.

"He wanted me to see to you first," Mikel blurts. "Said you were in a lot of pain and that your injuries were more pressing."

Hassan and I both whip our attention toward Mikel. But while my face is contorted in disbelief, one quick peek at Hassan shows anger tensed across his features.

"Oh, was I not supposed to..." Mikel presses his hand against his mouth to bite back a laugh. He looks from me to Hassan, then back to me again before shaking his head. "*Gods*. You two have it bad, don't you?" Mikel smirks to himself before placing his fingers against my arm once more.

As Mikel's gaze locks on me, I watch his sunny appearance morph into something sober. "Are you ready?"

I know that look; it's one he's given me countless times. But my injuries have never been this bad, at least, not in a while. I give him one firm nod before barring my teeth.

At first, it's a light touch—like a cool breeze across my skin. I watch the veins in Mikel's arm turn as white as clouds. I'm no stranger to Mikel's gift, but despite the familiarity, the sight of his tell draws me in. It's like something slinks beneath his skin, turning his blood milky. The twinge I know but am never prepared for comes next. A biting cold. It seeps deep into me and racks my body with violent shudders. Then, the pain. I whimper and bite down on the inside of my cheek as I feel it all. The bones in my arm forge back together, tearing away from where they've stabbed through muscle and pierced tissue. I screw my eyes shut and pray for it to be over quick.

My body thrashes lightly against the table as I try to control myself. I know there's no fighting this, but my reflexes have a mind of their own. I tug against Mikel's hold and only feel it tighten in return. He can't stop now. It would be worse to leave me half healed and starts this torture over again.

I loose a muffled yell, my lips no longer able to contain the agony I'm facing. My eyes shoot open as a warm hand glides across my cheek. Hassan stares at me, expression wild and unreadable. He leans across the table, holding my face steadily, not letting me look anywhere but him. I cry out as the pain hits its peak. The cold has turned to a raging fire, a blistering sear under my skin. My body shakes and sweat beads my brow. Hassan's fingers press harder against my skin, and I watch as his gaze turns murderous. For a moment, I forget about the pain. Though, it's over seconds later.

I pull in a ragged gasp as Mikel lets go of my arm. The heat subsides and the shuddering stops. I can move my fingers now, but I don't so much as flinch. My eyes hold Hassan's with an intensity that clouds all judgment. Questions burn bright in my mind, but before I can open my mouth to ask them, he snatches his hand back.

Hassan clears his throat, and—despite what happened only moments ago—it seems he can no longer look at me. "Let me know when you're done," he says gruffly, gaze dipping toward Mikel.

He's gone in a breath, and I watch him go with my brow furrowed and mouth agape.

Mikel looses a deep sigh before chuckling. "My dear, reckless friend," he utters. "What in the gods have you gotten yourself into?"

I don't turn to face him. My gaze is fixed on the broad pair of tightly bunched shoulders that now hovers by the bar.

"Nothing good," I rasp.

CHAPTER 9

The rest of my injuries are healed without concern; though some things are too far gone for even a Mender to fix. Mikel tries to keep his eyes off the scars that line my arms, but I know him too well. I catch the moments he thinks I'm not looking. Single, quick glances while he's working on my wrist. A peek from the corner of his eye as he heals the Shade's cut on Hassan's arm. Mikel wants to ask, I know he does. But with the others now tightly packed into this booth with us, he and I both know now is not the time.

I settle against the old, woven cushions as Savi raps her knuckles across the tabletop. She offers me a warm smile before turning toward Mikel. "So" —she looks between the both of us— "I take it you two know each other."

Kai chuckles as he leans over the back of the booth and drapes his arm over Savi. "I don't know Sav," he chuckles. "Doesn't Ren always bursts into tears whenever she meets someone new?" He shoves me playfully, and I brush him off like one might an annoying little brother.

"Hush," I scold him, though my smile betrays me.

I stare across the booth at Mikel and feel myself relax. He's here. He's really here. Just as I open my mouth to ask a million questions, my chance is stolen.

"We need to discuss what comes next."

My eyes flash to Vish. He sits next to Mikel, journal placed on the table in front of him. It's closed, but of course it is. My gaze drops to his arms, where the markings that reveal him for what he truly is are hidden under long, billowy sleeves. His eyes are on mine when I finally raise my gaze. Though I wish it didn't, that calculated stare of his still makes me want to shift in my seat. It feels like doing so will shake his focus somehow. But instead, I force myself to sit still and stare right back at him.

"We've discussed it," I bite. "We need to find whoever knows the location of the Hesha Mol. That's what you told me earlier."

Mikel's jaw drops.

Hassan's eyes go dramatically wide, alight with something like fury and disbelief. He leans forward, flashing me a deadly look before his eyes flicker toward Mikel. I know what he's thinking, so when he actually tries to voice it, my blood boils.

"Are we sure we should be discussing this with—"

"Whatever Vish has to say, he can say it in front of Mikel," I spit, rising in my seat to outmatch Hassan's menacing posture. "There's no one at this godsdamn table I trust more than him." I lean over said table, getting right in the bounty hunter's face. "If he leaves, I leave."

Hassan's jaw ripples with tension as he holds my gaze steadily.

"Ren is right." Vish sighs. "We'll need all the help we can get in order to accomplish what's in front of us."

I flash Hassan a cocky grin as I lower back into my seat. "That okay with you, *boss*?" I taunt.

He crosses his arms over his broad chest, not breaking eye contact for even a moment. I let my shit-eating grin grow the longer Hassan glares. The seething look on his face almost makes me feel better about the fate I've gotten tangled in. We sit there silently, tension seeming to hold the table hostage, until Kai clears his throat.

"Uh, you're the Mender, right? The one who fixed up Riat and Savi?"

I don't let myself ruminate on what injuries I know forced Savi and Riat to see a Mender. Instead, I turn around to catch the sheepish smile reddening Kai's cheeks. My gaze follows his back across the table to where Mikel admires the hunter with curiosity gleaming in his eyes.

"Mikel," my friend offers with a nod.

"Kai."

My focus drifts back and forth between the two, my worry all but forgotten now. I watch Mikel's smile grow—watch his gaze linger on Kai—until the attention forces the hunter to break away.

"So, uh..." Kai fumbles over his words. "What's up Vish? We taking down big bad Rohan once and for a—"

Tariq yanks him sideways, slapping a hand over Kai's mouth to muffle his next words. He waits until Kai has settled before relaxing his grip.

"*All hells*," Kai emphasizes, slithering out of the larger man's hold. "What in the gods was that for?"

"Lower your tone," Tariq implores, pressing a rough hand against Kai's shoulder. "These aren't the type of sands you wage war in."

The table grows deathly quiet as our gazes wander through the tavern. The clamor around us has reached new heights. People huddle in groups playing cards and throwing dice. Men feel up women before taking them back to the brothel next door. A few travelers slink into corners to do deals. No one is aware of us or the words that slip loosely from our lips. But Tariq is right—this is no place to draw even a flicker of attention. Though I wonder if anywhere on the godsforsaken Continent is safe for talk such as this.

"This man" —I press Vish, immediately drawing the table's attention back— "where do we find him?" My molars grind against each other as I realize what I should have sooner. "I'm guessing if it were easy you would have already done it yourself. Am I right?"

I raise an eyebrow, but he lets nothing slip across his face. The table hovers on bated breath.

"You're correct in that it is no simple feat," Vish offers.

An impatient sigh leaves my lips as I lean back against the booth. "Out with it. Where is he?"

Vish's lips purse in contemplation before he finally answers. "Tol Dena."

I can't help the ridiculous laugh that leaves my throat. "*By the gods*—you've got to be shitting me."

He says nothing as I push my scarves back and drag a hand through my hair. The shortened length catches me off guard before I remember the true problem at hand.

"You want us to break a man out of the most feared place on the Continent? A place where we would be thrown into a darkened cell if caught?"

"Yes." Vish lets out a short breath, his annoyance thinly veiled. "Yes, I do."

I scan the table, taking in each and every face around me. Riat leans against the edge of the booth next to Hassan, and that cocky grin of his flashes bright when our eyes meet. *Gods, I wouldn't be surprised if he even heard a word I said.* Tariq and

Savi both hold the same grave expression—one I can't bear to witness for too long. My hope is too threadbare to be stretched even thinner by doubt.

A quick glance back reveals Kai lost in thought, though I easily track his gaze to where Mikel sits across the table. When I finally look at my friend I almost bark out a laugh. Mikel is both appalled and cross with me. His lips are parted in shock, but those light brown eyes are reprimanding. There's no doubt in my mind he'll chew me out for all the trouble I've gotten myself into the moment we're alone.

The budding smile on my face slips when I look to Vish once more. His gaze is as cold and calculating as ever.

"Your man knows where it is? You're sure of it?" I stare into his eyes, tracking every flicker of movement in them.

Vish doesn't even blink. "I'm certain of it."

Veles damn me for eternity.

I drag my tongue across the front of my teeth and grunt out a sigh. "Fine. How many days' ride—"

Hassan's fist slams against the tabletop. "It's a death sentence," he seethes. "You cannot seriously be considering—"

"You don't need to come," I shout back. "I'll be fine on my own."

I make the mistake of meeting his gaze. He looks at me with fury alight in his eyes—like I've drawn a blade on him. It's that same unhinged rage I saw when he held my face earlier. It's wild. Barely controlled. It eats me up with such an intensity that I should want to look away, but for some reason I can't.

"It's already been decided," Hassan grits out. "We all go." He stares at me, eyes flashing as if daring me to challenge him further.

"There's somewhere we must visit first," Vish interjects.

His voice rips me from the vicious hazel gaze I'd somehow fallen prey to. When I finally look away from Hassan, I find I'm able to take a breath.

"And why would we delay—"

"We need protection for the journey ahead," Vish cuts me off. "I have allies in Hira. They'll escort us safely across the desert."

My stomach drops, but I mask it with a bitter laugh. "*Hira?*" I prod. "What a coincidence." I lean forward against the tabletop, pressing my palms against the wood. "Is that why you were so eager to lead me and the bounties there?" I sneer. "Have some friends lying in wait for the great Durit, do you?"

Mikel chokes on his drink, spilling rum down his tunic, but I ignore him. He'll have his answers later. Right now, my blood feels too hot to give them. My focus burns into the small man in front of me—the one who wants me to trust him when he's done nothing but lead me like a blind horse.

I clench my jaw as I get in Vish's face. "What are you playing at?" I demand.

My breath heaves in my lungs as he meets my gaze with an unnerving calm.

"I will confess" —Vish leans back against the booth to put some distance between us— "there is someone in Hira who I thought could help me answer what you might be. But now, there is no doubt in my mind who you are."

"So why go there?" I push. "Why delay our travels any longer? I'm healed. I can take on whatever we encounter along the way. There is no need for protection when—"

"You need a teacher!" Vish seethes. His voice raises quickly, the sharp tone banishing all composure. "Veles's claim on you is volatile. Unruly and unmastered. You cannot keep those around you safe, let alone yourself." He shakes his head and forces a deep breath through his lungs. "He will help you. I know he will."

I open my mouth to ask who he thinks could help me master such chaos, but quickly stop myself. The others are all staring, no doubt muddling over what Vish just implied. I snap my mouth shut and swallow my unease.

My shadows are deadly. There is no denying it. I have no control over my gods-gifted curse, and if I don't get a hold of it soon, it's going to cost me more than it already has.

Hot shame reddens my cheeks as I drop my gaze to the table. "When do we leave?"

CHAPTER 10

I loose a long, deep sigh as I strap my pack to Vish's camel. Caen is bustling, despite the early morning light that barely peeks over the sandstone rooftops. It's a clamor that echoes against the pounding ache in my head, testing my already thin patience.

Voices yell across the earth-packed street, some still drunk and parrying insults, while others prod apprentices along their morning duties. Donkeys bray, and horses stomp. Sacks of grain shush as they're unloaded from the back of carts, and coins clatter as they pass hands. It's all a heaving flow of noise I'll be glad to leave behind.

As mud splashes my boots, I shoot a hot glare over my shoulder. The burly shop keep hardly looks my way, too busy tossing more water across his front steps to rid the stone of clay footprints. When I don't shy away, his sharp eyes pin me with a look that's nothing short of contempt. I'm too tired for a fight and begrudgingly keep my insults to myself as he goes about his morning chores.

"Veles wreck and burn me," I mutter.

I kick the mud off my boots before resting my forearms against the saddle. My camel groans at the intrusion, spitting peevishly. Somehow, it makes everything worse. My head is a living drum, thumping in my skull with every pump of my weary heart. I let out another deep breath and press my head against the worn saddle blanket; the fabric is already growing warm against the rising sun.

It's too early for this shit.

Last night swirls uneasily in my mind, just like the leftover rum in my stomach. Though I wish it was all a blur, it seems the gods would rather antagonize me. I grit my teeth, cringing as it all comes back.

Rum—*so much rum.* At first, it had been to dull the thoughts of what was to come and how I had gotten here. But then Mikel had joined in. *Who was I to deny him the celebration we were both due?* The Continent is a devil, a thing eager to rip away everything you hold dear. It's not often fate leads you back to those you've lost. So, we drank. A lot.

There'd been two empty bottles of rum between us by the time trouble came our way, and Riat and Kai were not to be turned down. Two bottles turned to four as we all played skelt—a card game that prides itself on its losers rather than its winners. By the fifth round, I was fairly certain Riat was cheating, though incapable of remembering how he dealt one hand from the last. So as the cards were shuffled and slapped against the table, we drank more and more.

At some point, Riat had planted a messy kiss on my cheek. I'd no sooner leveled my knife at his throat than we'd all burst into laughter. More drinks. More drunk mischief. It was well past midnight when I finally stumbled up to my room, Riat on my heels like the sly devil he is. I made sure to smile deviously when

I slammed the door in his eager face. For I had made no promises, and he knew better than to assume. I listened to his playful taunts and trailing laughter from the other side of the door as I nuzzled into my bed, still fully clothed with a bottle clutched in my grasp. I had passed out before Riat's voice faded from the hall.

The dream had come for me soon after.

I had felt my boots catch in the sand. Saw shadows swirling around my legs. The canyon—reeking of the gods and the power they claim, spread before me like a giant's tomb. I had been paralyzed with fear, but not because I was trapped in that loop again, waiting for the moment the ground swallowed me whole. No, my fear was new, for I had made it to the doorway this time. But when my boots stirred the untouched sands I had been so desperate to reach all these months, my stomach clenched, and my heart stopped.

I could finally see the markings etched around the door, and what they showed me brought no comfort. It was like my first glimpse inside the Book all those years ago. My breath quivered in anticipation like I was once again thumbing through those weathered pages, straining my eyes against candlelight in a quiet corner of the abandoned tannery my companions and I had called home. But unlike those faraway moments with the Book, my dream left me with no sense of awe and wonder.

In that place where the Weaver sent me, I had run my hands across the carved stone doorway, over the markings I now recognized as my own. Seer and Shade. Knowledge and destruction. My fingers had tingled as soon as I touched the marks, but there had been a pull, too. A strong nudge at the back of my skull. I went without thought. My legs carried me across the stirring sands. Fifty paces—that's what it took me to shuffle across the mouth of the doorway to reach the other column that had been abandoned and left to bake in the unforgiving desert. But these markings were not my own. No. They were something far worse.

I couldn't help myself. My hand had reached out, eager to press against the marks I'd only ever seen in the Book. The Born, one to be created from my very blood. The blood of the brother gods. One touch was all it took for the world to open up around me. It was a great shadow, a violent mass of black and chaos that swallowed me whole and dragged me down into the bowels of the earth. I slipped past black stone as sharp and as smooth as a perfectly honed blade. There was no up. No down. No light. Only a senseless darkness that tunneled into the earth and seemed to have no end. It was then that I saw it. A pair of gray eyes—but it was not the same lifeless gaze that haunts me in my waking hours.

As the torchlight had illuminated his face, I found no gaping mouth. No blood. No violent swirl of shadows. There was only desperation carved into the gaunt angles of his face and a flicker of hope alight in his gaze. It all but brought me to my knees. It was my damnation, and yet something whispered in my ear that it would be my redemption, too. This was not the same man I knew in Letka, but, for some reason, he was mine to save.

I had woken abruptly then, gasping for breath so forcefully I was choking on the air I desperately needed. The hazy white clouding my vision only spurred my panic further. My hands had scrambled across the bedding, searching for my daggers among the rumpled sheets. I found no blades, nor any peace when my eyes finally cleared and the room came into focus. All I could see was that place—the dark labyrinth of my nightmare that had felt so close to the underworld, I'm not sure it wasn't. I had run my nails through my scalp, pulling strands roughly in an effort to find my way back to the waking world. But, soon enough, the waning panic brought on by both my nightmare and my vision was ripped away to reveal the most gods-cursed hangover I've had in years. And now—with the shining sun beating against my back and my head splitting like I took a hoof to the head—I almost yearn for that empty darkness.

"And here I thought I was the only one who couldn't hold my liquor."

I don't bother pulling away from where I'm draped against the saddle. My gaze begrudgingly finds Mikel from the corner of my eye, already resenting his brazen smile and the way he crosses his arms over his chest smugly. His brown hair catches the morning sun, the voluminous curls almost glowing. He looks like a child of Hael—soft golden skin and clear eyes. His markings peek out from the short sleeves of his light-colored tunic, displayed proudly. My gaze lingers on the tightly packed lines that run diagonally across both his biceps and trail down the inside of his forearms. I try not to sink deep into envy, but the pounding in my skull doesn't help.

I huff as I push off the saddle, causing my borrowed camel to groan again. "I can hold my liquor just fine, thanks." My biting tone only draws a bigger smile from him. "I'm not the one who has to touch themselves to get through the morning."

"*Touching yourself*, goddess?" Riat snickers as he slides up next to me. "Sounds like someone should have allowed me into their bed last night."

Mikel raises a brow, opening his mouth to say something I know will only put me in a fouler mood.

"Don't you fucking start," I grumble. I shove Riat off from where he's so casually looped his arm around my shoulders. "Please do it before I snap his neck and leave the world without its most desperate rake," I prod Mikel.

Riat starts on again, baiting me by listing all the ways he could improve my mood. I try to ignore it, until I can't. Something about the not-so-subtle way he talks about the dexterity of his tongue causes my last thread of resolve to snap.

I shove Riat away once again, leveling him with a look that promises more violence. "Silence yourself. *Please*," I grit through my teeth. "Or I'll have no choice but to rid you of that tongue you boast of."

Mikel barely holds back his smirk, shaking his head as he finally steps up to me. "Come here," he urges. "It's too early for bloodshed, even for you."

As soon as he places his fingers on either side of my head, my body tenses. I drop my hands, clenching and unclenching them into fists in preparation for what's to come.

Mikel chuckles under his breath. "Were you always this big of a pain in my ass?"

As I open my mouth to berate him, I'm quickly silenced by an icy cold pressure. It creeps through my head slowly. Deliberately. My eyes squeeze shut, body bracing itself against the intrusive chill. Panic kicks up in my chest. My stomach roils. It feels like Mikel's fingers are slipping into my scalp and snapping the delicate threads of my mind like the strings of a lute. It's over the next second, and I'm finally able to breathe again.

When I open my eyes, Mikel is watching me with his brow raised defiantly. "Feeling better?"

I bite back a smile and roll my eyes. "Yes."

"Yes, *and*?"

I shove him lightly, though my smile only grows. "Yes, Mikel. Thank you, Mikel. What ever would I do without you, Mikel?"

He rests against the stable door, feet crossed casually as he pretends to clean his nails. "You would be dead at the bottom of a dune somewhere, baking in the sun while the lizards pick out your eyes." He looks up at me then, a smirk hidden in the curve of his lips. "Lucky for you, I find the godsforsaken Continent boring without the torture of your company."

Mikel stands there, radiating a warmth that thaws my frigid heart like it has since the first time I saw him all those years ago. It's almost feels like nothing has changed.

I had met Zoah's son, Maurit, at an outpost near Raulik. I was alone, having just left my previous caravan after my place among them soured. And, like many times before, it had been soured by my own hand. *Though, what was I supposed to do? Let their leader lay claim to me like some concubine?* I try not to scowl at the thought. The scar I'd left him—a brutal thing carved across his hip—was sure to remind him to never force his hand again. But there was no staying after that.

So, I had found myself alone in a tavern in Raulik, my pack resting at my feet and a mere fifty yenti to my name. Whether it was his kind eyes or the six pints of ale I'd already had, I'm not sure, but somehow, I agreed to join Maurit's family in the desert. He told me they were in the habit of picking up those with nowhere left to go. Now that I think about it, it must have been the ale that convinced me, for sober-me would have surely met that kind of pity with the point of a blade.

Regardless of what had swayed me, I found myself following Maurit out of the outpost the next morning. He told me their camp was only an hour's journey, and each step of my stolen camel had wound the ball of anxiety within me tighter and tighter. It's foolish to trust strangers on the Continent, but I was desperate. I had been ready for an ambush at any moment, hands twitching for my knives. Only when I'd glimpsed what awaited me at Zoah's camp did my bunched shoulders finally drop from my ears.

Friendly faces.

There was no ambush, no threat. All I faced was an old man and woman surrounded by their grown children and those they'd adopted along the way. I remember the moment Mikel stepped out of that tent like it was yesterday. He had taken one look at me, brow raised in challenge, before beaming a smile as warm as the sun itself. He wore his markings proudly amidst the isolation of the desert—though there was only a small trail of them around his left bicep back then. As he'd made his way over to my camel, I found myself tensing. His hands were tucked casually in his pockets, and—despite the eight blades I'd strapped to myself that morning—I'd felt vulnerable. He'd stopped in front of me and offered a curious glance that made me stiffen even more. He looked me up and down, taking in the dried blood still crusting my broken nose and the red-rim of my bloodshot eyes. He'd tried to hide the smirk on his face as he held his hand out to me, but I saw it nonetheless.

"Mikel," he'd offered simply.

I'd refused to shake his hand, still disarmed by the way he was grinning at me like we were kin. He'd huffed a breathy laugh, bouncing the curls that crowned his head in a golden halo.

"You look like shit," he'd snorted. He'd started walking away, only stopping to flash a grin over his shoulder. *"Meet me by the fire. I want to set that break before it ruins that beautifully violent face of yours."*

That was it—was all it had taken for Mikel to sink his claws into me. We had become fast friends after that. Watching him escape into the Jahaer weeks ago felt like watching a piece of me die. Seeing him in front of me now stirs emotion in my chest, breaking me wide like a dry riverbed that was never supposed to feel turbulent waters again.

I shove him playfully before I can succumb to such dramatics. "Without me, you'd be out of practice." The grin is wide across my face. "Those marks on your arms?" I prod smartly, "*I put them there.*"

"Oh, of course." Mikel laughs. "How could I forget all of the broken bones and bad tempers I've had to mend over the years?"

As I look at him, smile heavy on my face, something quivers in the corner of Mikel's mouth. It's not the smirk I'm used to seeing when he teases me, nor the sly grin that's plastered on his face when persuading me to take another shot. No, it's a wavering concern and gut-wrenching hesitation that dulls those light brown eyes of his. As soon as he opens his mouth, I brace myself for what's coming.

"What the fuck happened, Ren?"

The words tumble out in a heavy breath. My eyes flicker to the right, and I'm all-too happy to find that Riat has wandered off on his own accord.

As I force my gaze back to Mikel, I dig my teeth into the inside of my cheek. "The usual." I shrug, managing to hold eye contact for a moment before it becomes too much. My eyes drop to my boots, and I kick at the dusty earth with a lackluster effort. "When have you known me to keep out of trouble?"

I'm convinced the silence that has found us is harmless until I finally look up at him. *Shit.*

"*The usual?*" Mikel clips. He lets out an aggravated huff, eyes widening as he looks me up and down. Even without my lingering injuries, there's plenty to see. "*For the love of the gods...*" he starts.

His gaze hovers on my scars, pupils wavering like he's seconds away from breaking the tough composure he always tries to keep for me. He knows I hate when he worries, but this time, I've earned every inch of that pinched face he's fighting to keep flat.

"It's fine," I utter against the growing lump in my throat. "I made sure to leave the bastards with scars of their own."

His temple pulses in frustration as he clenches his jaw over and over again. He's trying to let it go, I know he is. But when his eyes flash up to mine hotly, emotion brimming his lash line, I know he needs answers. I don't blame him. If I was the one staring at my best friend's mutilated skin after mere weeks apart, I'd want more than answers. I'd want names.

"They weren't slavers," I start. "But I almost wish they had been."

I tell him everything. The trek across the desert with Olen and Harkin. Denheir. The cellar they kept me in. The ways in which Rohan saw fit to provoke my gift. The entire time, Mikel holds steady. I can see the anger swirling in his eyes, the emotion that's desperate to snap free and promise the revenge I so dearly deserve. But he holds his tongue. He waits. He listens. His brows pinch together when I mention Hassan and Savi finding me—how they patched me up and offered safety. He smirks when I get sidetracked recounting my time among the bounty hunters, almost laughs when I rant about how Hassan is an ornery old goat who thinks he knows best. I ramble on and on, and the entire time, Mikel's focus doesn't waver.

I tell him about the visions, tell him how they were triggered by Silas's touch. I skim over the Berserker quickly, but Mikel clocks the unsteadiness in my voice. He knows me too well to miss such a thing, but he doesn't interrupt. Doesn't press for more. He merely stares at me, holding back all he wishes to say until I've shared every last detail. Only when I pull my lips into a tight line and cross my arms over my chest in resignation does he speak.

"Yeah," he mumbles. "Nothing crazy. *The usual.*"

A smile plays subtly against his lips, but his eyes hold a severity I know not to ignore.

"I'm really glad you're here," I admit, voice softer than I'd like it to be. "That for some reason, the gods allowed our paths to cross again."

He cuts the distance between us quickly, pulling me into a hug before I can think to escape. His face buries into the scarves that cover my face, and I squeeze him tightly in return.

"Don't *ever* do that again," he scolds me, pulling back with fury and pain warping his features. "Don't *ever* tell me to leave you." He clenches his teeth, but I can still hear the shuddering of his breath. "I don't care if your leg's been hacked away and there's a band of Turidens ready to bleed us dry. I'm with you until the gods decide I'm done. Even then, I'll haunt you, if only to ensure someone watches over your reckless ass. I'm not leaving you. Not now—not ever again."

His fingers dig roughly against my arms, all but shaking me. "Do you understand?"

I nod, biting back the tears that wish to spring free. There's been enough of that—for the both of us. Instead, I let a *tsk* slip through my teeth as I brush him off. "Alright, alright. I know I'm your reason for living and everything—I mean, I get it. It must be hard to have a best friend as charming and capable and attractive as—"

Mikel socks me in the arm playfully. "Such a pain in the ass," he laughs under his breath.

I shoot him a cheeky grin that stretches wide. "Your favorite one."

He gathers his horse from the stables as I sort through my pack. I've checked it three times, but it's all I can do to keep busy. There are too many unknowns floating through my now hangover-free mind, and I don't wish to face any of them. When Mikel returns leading a gray mare with a beautifully braided black mane, my heart stutters. My eyes drift back into the stables, where I know Mirage rests with Vish's belonging tacked to her saddle. She wouldn't even let me pet her this morning. As soon as I opened the stall, fresh hay in hand with which to bribe her, she panicked. It was only when I was out of sight that her chuffing breaths stilled. There will be no riding her anytime soon. Something stirs painfully in my chest as I wonder if I ever will again.

Mikel pats his horse, earning a content huff in return. I pry my eyes away, unable to stomach the sight of what I've lost.

"And what of you?" I ask. "How is it you've ended up in this rat's barrel?"

An easy laugh spills from Mikel's throat as he loads up the last of his things. "Looking for you, of course. Figured you'd find your way to the nearest tavern, fiending for a drink and immodest company."

I go to parry a retort, but it gets caught in my throat. Memories of the company I did keep in Mikel's absence flutter through my mind unchecked. Gray eyes eclipsed by blown out pupils, quickly turning black. Rough hands against my skin, holding my hips down. Taunting lips eager to devour me. But the fantasy is short lived and tainted by reality.

It was all a lie.

I let myself remember how the gold clinked in its pouch. How he gasped for air. How the blood flowed from his chest. I clench my teeth hard enough to feel the grooves of my molars, and shut away every last thought of Silas. He's gone. It doesn't matter anymore.

As I come back to the world, Mikel is rambling on—unaware of the darkness I was momentarily lost to.

"...had to make sure they were settled. Kora was being a brat. Told me you'd been teaching her how to use a blade. Said she'd be more useful than I would." Mikel laughs, then shakes his head. "You can imagine how Kiara reacted, hearing you'd been secretly training her little sister."

A small smile slips over my face, temporarily stripping me of my burdens. "So they're safe?"

Psshh. Mikel lets out an overconfident puff of air. "They're probably living like kings now. When I left them, they were headed to Braki. Maurit mentioned something about a boat. Honestly, I think Zoah was ready to get out of the desert," he says, stuffing his hands in his pockets. "I don't think the Jahaer is the kind of place he imagined taking his final breaths in."

Mikel shrugs, trying to look unconcerned, but I spot the solemn glint in his eyes. "If anything, what happened reminded him what madness wracks the Continent. His family is better off in the east. Kora and Kiara, too."

I nod, knowing it's more than true. Zoah was always kind to me, kinder than he should have been to a bitter girl with more trust issues than blades. He deserves peace; they all do. I just hope there's somewhere left on the Continent to find it.

"I headed north," Mikel continues. "Figured if they were slavers, Hira would be the closest market. I spent almost a week there. Lost count of how many I watched be prodded and sold like livestock." He stops for a moment, eyes darkening. "Every day I stood in that market. Every day I looked for your face." His hands clench, and I catch his throat bob before he looks away. "You never came. I wanted to feel grateful that you weren't one of them—that you weren't peddled off to some vile bastard who would rather own another person than pay an apprentice. But I could only think about what fate had found you instead."

Mikel kicks a rock, sending a spray of sand and dirt across the ground. As he puts his hands back in his pockets, I catch tears welling in the corners of his eyes.

"I heard a Mender was needed here in Caen." He lets out a huff of a laugh, not at all amused. "This town might be full of drunkards and thieves, but coin flows here, as it seems to across the whole of the east. I figured if I could work for a few weeks, I'd have enough to last me the journey down the coast. I knew you were out there somewhere." He takes in a ragged breath, clenching his jaw once more. "I wasn't about to forget that."

I pull away, pretending to fuss with my saddle once more. My throat aches, and I don't speak until I know my voice won't betray me.

"You could have, you know..."

His gaze rises to meet mine, emotion pinching his brows.

"...forgotten me." I shrug, though I'm quick to look away again. "I wouldn't have blamed you."

"No. I couldn't," he all but growls. "We're family, dumbass."

He reaches into his bag before throwing something at me. I catch it against my chest, heart pounding with a deep ache.

"Now rub that on your arms," Mikel grumbles. "If you're so set on showing the world just how tough you are with those scars, you need to protect your skin. I won't have you complaining about being as crisp as a boar's head on a pike come sundown." He rolls his eyes, mumbling under his breath as he turns away.

I let out a deep sigh as I open the small tin to do as he says. Eventually, Mikel steals a glance over his shoulder. He offers a pleased hum as he sees me rubbing the paste across my arms, though I make sure to stick my tongue out at him in the process.

Am I reasonable? Yes. But that doesn't mean I can't take a moment to bask in my status as the biggest pain in his ass. Just as an aggravated laugh flies from Mikel's lips, Hassan is upon us.

"We need to go," he orders.

I look behind him to see the others are mounted and ready. They wait at the opposite end of the stables, their animals stomping impatiently around the open barn doors.

I raise my gaze to Hassan and glare like Mikel's gift didn't rid me of my headache. "What's the rush? Afraid someone will see you with a pair of daemons?" I prod. I loose a taunting laugh just to witness the way his eyes flash in anger. "Better move along, hunter. I'd hate to tarnish your reputation."

Mikel chokes back a laugh as a devious smile lights up his face. He begins mouthing something to me over Hassan's shoulder, but before I can read his lips, the bounty hunter steps up to block the view of my friend.

"If you want to find yourself in shackles once more, be my guest," Hassan snarls. He lifts his hand up and slaps a piece of parchment against my chest. "But if you want to live, get your ass on that camel and follow me. Now, *witch.*"

As he stalks off, I let my gaze roam across the paper he left. Mikel wanders over, loosing a low whistle as Hassan furiously stomps toward the others.

"*Veles be damned.*" Mikel bumps his shoulder against mine, leaning in close. "You know, I was certain you'd slip off with that devilish hunter with the scar last night. I thought, why not? Ren has never been one to turn down a good time. But now?" He laughs, and I look up to catch him eyeing Hassan from across the stables. "I'm certain Riat's is not the bed you wish to slip into."

Mikel turns back to me, huffing at my silence. "Oh, come on," he prods. "Surely you can admit that—"

"We need to go."

His voice stills as mine find its strength. I hand Mikel the parchment without another word. He reads silently, and only when I hear his muttered curse do I know he's finished.

"*Gods below*. Ren this is—"

"More coin than what anyone in this place will see in a lifetime."

I feel my heart pounding in my ears as I hoist myself up onto the saddle. Uneasiness is the very life in my veins, the twinge in my chest. My hands shake against the reins even as I clench them into fists. Mikel offers me the parchment, and I force myself to take one last look.

The resemblance is poor, but it will serve its purpose. The full cheeks make me look younger than I am, and the nose is missing the slight bump I earned years ago in a tavern brawl. And my eyes—they got those wrong, too. The fire is missing from the smudged ink drawing. The sketched orbs look flat and lifeless. Numb. Defeated. My heart clenches as I consider if it's not a true depiction after all. It matters little, because the rest of it will surely damn me.

The scars—the scars are my undoing. Raked across my arms like tokens of Rohan's brutality, there is no mistaking them. *And the markings...* My Seer's marks stain the right side of my neck, but the left—the left has been kept blank.

I stare at the bounty, sickness roiling in my stomach as I begin to understand. Rohan does not simply want to be the Born. He *needs* to be the Born. There is nothing he won't do to achieve it, and he'll be sure to be the only bastard who gets the chance.

As I crumple the parchment in my fist and toss it to the barren ground, the sum written in large black ink is all I can think of. *20,000 yenti*. That's what a good blacksmith makes a year in the right city. A chill rolls up my neck as I snap the reins and urge my camel forward.

I was wrong, Rohan won't come for me. That would be too simple, too out of character for the cruel man I came to know so well in such a short time. He won't chase one woman across these vast sands. No, he'll make sure someone else does that for him.

And with this kind of bounty on my head?

I avert my gaze as I pass Hassan, tucking my camel among the middle of the caravan. Rohan has just made me the biggest prize the Continent has even seen. I'm no longer just running from Rohan. No longer simply looking for the Hesha Mol so I can end this talk of prophecies. Anyone who's ever hoped for a better life on the godsdamn Continent is looking for me.

I'm about to be hunted.

CHAPTER 11

The heat is all I can feel—that, and the deep knot wound into my lower back. Every rocking step of the camel shifts my weight, never allowing my muscles a moment's rest.

I'd forgotten how much I hate these saddles. Unlike the leather seat Mirage is fitted with, this one provides little comfort. The wooden frame digs into every bit of me, and the woven cushions resting atop the board are in desperate need of more padding. My ass has fallen asleep more times than I can count, and, judging by the determination set in Hassan's shoulders, we won't be stopping anytime soon.

We've been traveling for three days straight. No stopping—at least not when the sun is high. Only when the day begins to fade does Hassan let us rest; though, there's nothing restful about it. Each night we make camp, and each morning we set off before the first lick of sunlight is even a glimmer on the horizon.

The endless traveling has been good for one thing and one thing only—talking. At first, I kept my distance. Or at least, I tried to. The others—Hassan and Vish excluded—treat me just as they had before Letka. They share stories, pass around canteens, and offer hunks of bread. Even as we journey further north, they treat me like a friend and not the reason for our hurried pace. But I know better, for I can feel the change inside of me. It hums under my skin, an ever-present companion. So, while it was my every intention to keep my distance, only a day passed before I realized it was no use.

Riat is always nearby, teasing me incessantly. Kai is never far either, though it's clear my company is not the one he seeks by sticking so close. Savi and Tariq fill the time by describing what awaits us in Hira—the incredible markets, the people, the way the whole city seems to tower above you. Amidst them all, conversation never wanes. While I initially craved a lick of silence to stew in, I soon realized their chattiness was my opportunity.

I've feigned ignorance over and over again in my hunt for answers, and it didn't take long to find some. No one knew Vish was a daemon, not even Hassan. It wasn't until that day in the gorge—when those two Berserkers came upon us—that the secret had slipped. Tariq told me he'd had his suspicions, but had never wanted to force his friend to reveal the truth. I respect that about Tariq: his acceptance of others, his patience. Gods know he's shown me more than I deserve since I got here. And yet, he always seems to have more to give.

More digging told me that, aside from Vish, no one knows the daemon we're meeting in Hira. Vish trusts this unknown ally, and for the others, that seems to be good enough. I, however, need more than vague assurances. I've tried asking him directly, but he's been tight-mouthed and close-lipped for days. It's gotten worse the closer we've grown to our destination. The only answers Vish offers now are so obscure that I'm left with more questions than I started with. His ally is touched by Veles, and—according to Vish—a powerful daemon. Though he's certain this person can teach me to control my gift, he wouldn't say why. Apparently, there are others in Hira, too—other daemons who will prove valuable for the journey ahead.

The mystery of it all sets my teeth on edge, especially since I'd watched his pupils flicker into dark slits more than once. It was eerie to see something I thought so fabled occur right in front of me. But whatever Vish learned from the gods, he didn't share. Not when I prodded, not when I accused him of keeping secrets just like before. Though his lips were hardly swayed by my hollering, his eyes revealed what he dared not speak. Something about what is to come—what the gods have told him—makes Vish nervous. I could see it in the way his gaze grew flighty, how he snatched it away as if worried I'd find the truth in those green eyes of his. He's unsure of something. Cautious. Though I wanted to press for more, Vish was quick to put distance between us after that. But before he slinked to the front of the caravan, he told me something. Once we find the Hesha Mol, there's a place we can go—a place so deep in the gods-drenched north that it'll prove safe. A hideout of sorts, one that daemons have supposedly been using ever since the Rebellion ravaged the Continent a hundred years ago.

He called it Rikyir.

Now, thoughts swirl in my head—as unsteady as the sway I feel atop my camel. Of all that I learned in the past three days, it's the daemons in Hira that unsettle me most. That unknown factor has me gripping the reins tighter each time I think about it. It's like stepping into a sandstorm, not knowing whether it will bury you whole or leave you unscathed. Ever since I left Artolen, I've kept far from other daemons. It was safer to hide that way, to live as though no gift ran through my veins. It wasn't until I met Mikel that I realized how lonely I had been, how eager I was for the company of another. Someone to confide in. Someone to understand me and the blight the gods put on all those they choose. But companionship is like a deep well in a drought-stricken desert. It can just as easily drown you as save you. I've felt both sides of that coin, and yet I always seem to forget how much the drowning hurts.

"Mikel told me about your friends."

I startle with a lurch. *Gods, I need to be more aware.* I'll likely take a blade to the gut if I keep getting lost in my head like this.

My brow quirks as I look over at Savi. "Huh?"

She laughs, taking in my dazed expression with a smirk. "Still daydreaming?" She raises a brow, her smile deepening. "You weren't fantasizing about stabbing my cousin again, were you?"

I open my mouth to answer quickly—to tell her that Hassan is more likely to die by my shadows than a blade—but stop myself. I don't have the energy to argue over such truths. Besides, I'd rather not remind her of what it is I'm truly capable of—not when her eyes are bright with such kindness.

My lips purse as I look away. "No. Your cousin is safe as long as he keeps his distance."

"Hm."

Savi guides her horse closer, and I stiffen. Her smile threatens to disarm me, and though I know I should bask in the joy radiating off her like the sun—be grateful to still receive it—I feel undeserving to do so.

"Mikel told me about the caravan you used to ride with. They sounded like good people."

My heart warms at the thought of Zoah and the others, but that warmth is quickly smothered by a tightness I can't shake. "They were."

She pats her horse's flank, and Teak huffs happily in return. I grit my teeth as I think of the last time Savi and I rode side by side—how I wasn't fastened to this fucking camel. My hips shift against the wooden seat, but it only pinches more.

"He's talked endlessly of Kora," Savi continues, oblivious to the scowl curling my face. "How eager she was to learn about her gift." She cocks her head and shoots me a grin. "But he said the pair of you got on like thieves in a crowded market. Always up to no good."

My lips pull into a tight line, grimacing to hide what true feelings the sentiment brings to the surface.

Savi leans her forearm against the saddle's pommel, turning to face me fully. "He told me about a time you and the girl snuck a lizard into his bed. Said the thing slithered up his pant leg before he could rid himself of it."

Though I try, I can no longer stop the smile from slipping across my lips. "Did he now?" I muse, casting a sidelong glance at Savi. "And did he tell you how he screamed like a newborn and demanded I search the tent to catch the thing?" A breathy chuckle rumbles in my throat. "He refused to sleep with blankets for a week after that, just to be sure the creature didn't come back."

As Savi laughs, that infectious smile pulls high on her face. We both settle against the heat in the air and the warmth in our chests, but, all too soon, the mood changes. Savi lets out a deep sigh and weaves her fingers through her horse's mane.

"I bet you miss her."

A lump forms in the back of my throat, but I refuse to let it seep into my tone. I swallow roughly, letting the moment tick by, and only peel my lips apart once my breath is steady.

"I do."

Silence hovers between us, and I have no intention of snapping it. I let my eyes glaze over as I stare across the sun-drenched earth, only blinking when my gaze grows dry against the heat. Though I don't want to, I let myself think of Kora. *Gods, she was such a brat.* I smile to myself despite the tight feeling that still lingers in my chest. Always arguing. Always sassing her sister or looking to conspire with me. But more than a troublemaker, she was far too kind for this world.

My heart clenches, but for once, I let myself feel it all as it comes.

I remember how Kora used to hand me a hunk of bread every time I set off for a day's hunt. It would be dripping with khrish flower honey, sticking to my hands and getting all over my saddle as I ate. She would always wake with me on those days, eager to see me off no matter how early I'd risen. Not a moment went by at camp when she wasn't plastered to my side like a shadow. Helping me scour the desert for dead brush to use as kindling. Begging me to teach her how to throw a blade. I once heard her fighting with her sister, arguing whether she should be hanging around me at all. Kiara never liked me, but that never stopped Kora. That kid was too stubborn for her own good.

I shake my head softly at the thought. I wonder what would have become of us all if Olen and his men hadn't come. *Would I be riding side by side with Kora now? Teaching her how to fix a snare in order to catch dinner? Or would the Continent have torn me from her and the others regardless?*

"Do you want a family of your own?"

Savi's voice shatters any peace I found in this fleeting stillness. My jaw ticks as I stare out across the barren landscape ahead of us. There's a bitter feeling swirling in my stomach, but I ignore it best I can.

"Daemons can't have children," I mutter. "Our gods-cursed blood makes it so."

I don't turn to face her, though I can all but feel the words building up on her tongue. My fingers twitch against the reins, preparing for the pity I know will soon come.

"You'd have made a great mother."

I practically snap my neck with how fast I turn toward her. My gaze sears into Savi's, looking for a hint of mocking, but what I find there is genuine. She smiles at me softly, and somehow that's worse. I have to look away.

"I would have made a shit one," I rasp. "Just as mine did."

Conversations grow noisy around us, but I tune them out. It's Savi's voice I wait to hear—to tell me what, I'm not sure. She's quiet for a long time. As I peek at her from the corner of my eye, I expect her attention to have drifted, but catch her frowning instead.

"I can't imagine what that's like," she finally says, "to have a parent cast you out." Her mouth presses into a firm line, pain swimming in her eyes. "But I know one thing." She holds my gaze intently, and I want to shrink beneath it. "You would never abandon someone like that."

My chest floods with emotion, burdening me with a familiar ache I'm desperate to be rid of. As much as I try to speak, I can't. I merely offer her a nod before looking away.

"I'm sorry," she utters.

My throat tightens, and I fix my gaze in front of me. My hands fidget with the reins, fingers flexing.

"No one should have to go through what you have." Savi looses a breathy laugh, though I hear how it weighs her down. "Gods know you're stronger than all of us. But I can't—"

She chokes on the words, and when I finally offer her a glance, my stomach flips. Tears line her eyes, and that carefree smile she always wears is pulled askew by wobbling lips.

"Seeing you in Letka. It just…" She sucks in a breath, trying to settle herself. "It's something I can't forget. *Won't* forget. It makes me angry, like somehow, we let it happen," she admits. "And I know I'm not the only one here who feels that way."

"You're not—"

"You deserved better," she presses on. "From us. You deserved our protection."

She offers me a hesitant smile, pain still wavering in those hazel eyes that are so different from her cousin's. Gentle whereas his are harsh. Vulnerable whereas his are unwavering.

"I regret it deeply," Savi states. "And I can only hope my mistake hasn't cost me your friendship."

My throat grows dry as I stare at her. I try to take her words to heart, to truly believe I deserve her kindness—her apology—but as my gaze sweeps down to the Torch's burn scarred into her arm, I can't. Pain swells in my chest, laced with an anger that's only for me.

"I accept your apology," I announce, voice thick with emotion. "But the gods have already given you a taste of what my friendship can offer. You'd be wise to hope for anything but."

Her brow furrows as she catches my rigid gaze and understands what it is I'm saying. "Ren—"

"Check your cousin's arm for proof if you need it," I utter darkly. "Or the body I left back in Letka."

I snap the reins against my camel, pulling ahead before she can offer another word. My heart is pounding, heavy with an ache that feels unbearable. It feels wrong—like I should carve the thing out with the closest blade. My fingers tingle, all too tempted.

I close my eyes only to find the gray ones I can't seem to escape. My mind flickers to Silas quickly now, like a drunk pondering another pint of ale. It's an urge I can't shake. A compulsion for pain. The journey from Caen has been laced with memories of him. The good. The bad. They all seem to pop up when I don't want them to. I've tried to fight it, but I've learned I can only wait for the bitter recollections to pass and pray they don't carve me hollow.

I killed him, and it hurts. *Gods, does it hurt.*

I shouldn't care. I should have banished him from my mind long ago, but I can't bear to. This suffering feels like penance. *Isn't that the least he's due?* My days are plagued by his gray eyes, though the nights are worse. I thought the Weaver dreams were bad, but my mind has proven it can conjure something far more wicked. It's his dying gaze I see in my sleep, his tempting words that whisper in my ear. Last night was by far the worst that's come—a torturous bliss.

I had been wrapped in his arms, held so tightly I was sure I was to break. My chest had been full of ache, but not the one I've grown so used to. No—it was heavy, but full. Warm. *Relieved.* It tore me apart worse than any violence. Gutted me deeper than any blade. I could barely see when I woke up, too lost to a panic I alone created. It had felt so real.

The memory of it still haunts me now. I dig my teeth into my tongue until I draw blood. Only then does Silas fade away.

Movement pulls my focus, and as my eyes dart to the left, I catch the last thing I wish to see. I resist the urge to scream—just barely. The gods surely find amusement in my suffering.

Hassan is staring again, peering at me from the corner of his eye. I let out a deep groan and curse under my breath, though it does nothing to shake this anger. He's been like this for days. Always watching. Distant, yet somehow nearby. It's taken everything in me not to snap at him, but now, I refuse to temper myself.

"That afraid I'll tear your men to bits?" I huff. My eyes pin him like daggers, only growing sharper when he turns to meet my gaze head-on. "Or are your lingering looks a sign I should have Mikel check your head?"

His jaw ripples as he grinds his teeth together. "Must you be so dramatic?" he mutters.

I let out a *tut*, snapping my tongue against my teeth. Before I know what I'm doing, I've pulled my camel closer to his brown stallion. The horse chuffs unhappily as my boot brushes Hassan's thigh.

"I'm dramatic?" I argue. "I'm not the one staring all hours of the day." His gaze flares hot, and it vexes me more. "Pray tell, what is it? Do you truly fear me that much? Or do you merely wish for me to be constantly reminded of your disdain?"

"I'm not afraid of you, *witch*," he growls. "Someone has to make sure you don't hurt yourself." Those hazel eyes grow dark, searing with something unkind. "Or run off with the enemy again."

"*Oh!*" I seethe. "Because you did *such* a good job of both last time."

His upper lip twitches, and he's barely able to tame the scowl before it slips out. Hassan mumbles something under his breath, and just as I demand he speak up, I get lost along the way. He's glaring like he wants to smite me from the very earth, but underneath that...

My brow furrows as I stare at his face. For a moment, I was sure there was something more there—something I dare not name for risk of sounding foolish. I try to latch back onto his anger, to right myself against this changing tide, but I find myself gazing at the plumpness of his lips. There's a freckle to the right of his cupid's bow. I've never noticed it before. *Or, have I?* The stubble that frames his cheeks and trails along his jaw has grown out since we left Caen. I wonder what it would feel like against my own skin.

I need to look away. *Gods, I should look away.* But my eyes betray me as I continue to hover my gaze over his features for far longer than I've ever allowed myself. Worse still, is how he lets me, as if he, too, is taking advantage of this moment we've fallen into.

"Ten coins."

Mikel's voice pulls me from my trance.

"*Devils below.*" Kai laughs in response. "They've been at each other's throats from the start. Twenty coins says they kill each other before it gets that far."

My eyes snap to the right where Mikel and Kai ride side by side. The black haired bounty hunter has a mischievous grin on his face while Mikel only looks at me smugly.

"Twenty-five," Mikel replies, not at all phased by the violent look I'm giving him. "But she'll be the one to leave after it's done."

Mikel shoots me a wink to which I quickly return with the foulest of gestures. I've heard enough of his teasing over the past few days. If he wants to make inane bets with Kai, let him. It'll be his empty pockets. Whatever he thinks will happen between Hassan and I, he's wrong. I won't be quick to be someone's fool—

won't let myself be too preoccupied with urges to realize the one satisfying them is waiting with a dagger at my back. *Never again.*

I shake my head and turn around to face the person who truly deserves my wrath. Hassan hasn't taken his eyes off me, and that infuriates me more.

"Do you really think I need *you* looking out for me?" I snark, pulling us back to the argument at hand. "I was doing fine before I met you."

Hassan sneers as he prods his horse to keep up with me. "When we met, you were on the brink of death, face down in the sand. You were a lifeless heap, cradled in my arms as I graciously took you back to my camp." He swallows harshly, and his eyes flare like violent suns. "If I'd known that wasn't the last time I'd be carrying you away from death's door, protecting you like a newborn lamb primed for slaughter, I might have left the task for someone else."

I laugh just to spite him. "Such the hero!" I extol. "Was that why you followed me to Letka? To throw it in my face that once again these men had made me weak enough to need saving?"

"You wouldn't need saving if you weren't such a reckless, infuriating woman!" he seethes. "If you'd only trusted me and not that bastard, you wouldn't have been in Letka in the first place!"

"Trust you? With your few words and your hateful stares?" I scoff. "No, trust is a fool's errand. I picked who I thought could help me stay alive."

He sits up in his saddle, getting right in my face. "You picked *wrong*," he growls.

I shove him away and feel my rage burn hot. "Why do you even care?" I demand, tugging the reins as best I can to settle the fussy camel beneath me. "What hold does Vish have over you? What kind of debt forces you to stay by my side like this?"

"There is no debt," he utters under his breath.

"Guilt, then," I quip.

"There is no guilt," Hassan snarls. "Only duty."

"Duty?" I mock. "How fitting for one such as you."

He grits his teeth and prods his horse closer. "I promised Vish I would keep a weapon out of Rohan's hands. I had no idea it was a daemon. No idea it was *you*."

The disdain slipping from his lips makes my heart seize in my chest. Before I can feel the ache it promises, anger chokes from my throat with a scathing bite. "*Oh*, and how you must hate it!" I rasp. "To have your promises and your pretense of virtue tied to me—a daemon you'd have rather left in Letka to rot."

My hands are shaking. I clench them into fists as I realize how careless I've truly been. My gift itches through my veins, eager and laced in hate. I close my eyes and pull in a deep breath. Emotion weighs heavy in my chest, like a stone stifling my lungs with each drag of air I take. Hassan must think I'm breaking, because his next words still every ounce of fury in my blood.

"Even without my promise to Vish, I could never have left you there."

My eyes shoot open. I prepare myself for the bite of whatever he'll say next, but all I find before me is a frightening stillness. His gaze doesn't leave me for even a breath. He swallows thickly, hazel eyes heavy with something far too disquieting. The longer I stare, the more his composure feels forced, like if he dares lose focus, he might be the one to break.

"You didn't see it," he states, voice low and clenched. "Didn't see what he'd done. What he'd reduced you to."

My stomach drops as memories of the dark flash through my mind. The cool press of metal that felt like a hand against my throat, tight and unyielding. The empty drum of silence. Blood slipping down my neck.

Goosebumps erupt across my overheated skin. I search Hassan's face for the hate I know he must feel, desperate to latch onto it once more. I am nothing but a burden to him; he said as much in the canyon. But as I cling to everything he tries to hide, looking for what I know must be there, what I find sets me even more on edge.

"Please," I try to laugh, though my voice breaks uneasily. "Considering I didn't leave Letka with a new batch of scars, I'd say it was hardly that bad."

My gaze holds his with the same severity with which he regards me. I can't help but remember Savi's pain, the guilt she now carries. Panic eats through my stomach, waiting for assurances I'm not certain will come.

"Right?" I prod quietly.

Hassan's eyes lock on my neck, seeming to trace where that collar rested against my skin. "What I saw in that room—" When he closes his eyes to gather himself, the mocking smile slips from my face. "You were an animal in a cage. A weapon to be guarded and hoarded." Hassan's voice is too soft for my liking, much too soft. "Those scars he gave you in Denheir are nothing compared to what he would have done, how far he would have gone to break you." Hassan finally looks back at me, though I wish he hadn't. "Rohan is not a fate I'd wish on anyone."

I crack a sly smile. It's the only thing I can do to keep what I truly feel buried deep. "Not even your worst enemy?" I jest. "Not even a *witch*?"

His gaze is unwavering. Something about the way he's staring at me makes me shift atop my camel. It's as though his gaze has weight, like he's holding me in place, worried what might become of me if he dares blink.

"No," he offers softly. "Never you."

My chest tightens, and I drop my eyes from his. I look to the right, expecting to find Mikel's rapt attention, but he's averted his gaze. So has Kai. They're both silent. I've never known either of them to bite their tongues; that's how I know they heard every word.

I swallow down the sting of emotions I dare not face and quickly snap the reins. My camel picks up its pace with a peevish groan, but still, it doesn't feel fast enough. I want to sprint across the sand, find distance from the unspoken things that cling to my chest. I'm afraid I won't be able to breathe fully until I do.

As my camel slips closer to the front of the caravan, I feel it. Dread chews up my heart, pumping it faster and faster. The haze drifts in, and frustrated tears begin to well in my eyes. I know no peace in this life—the gods make sure of it time and time again.

I remember to tighten my grip on the reins before I go under.

The dark—always, it's the dark that greets me. The air slips across my skin like a wet breath. It's cold, heavy with damp. It prickles across the back of my neck and sends an uneasy fluttering through my stomach. The gaping maw of the cavernous room stops me where I am. My boots are slick against the floor; the jagged, black rock face is coated in a mist of dew. Water flows somewhere, trickling down crevices beyond where my eyes can see.

"Fill up your canteen," a heavy voice mumbles in the dark.

I'm nudged slightly as someone stalks past. Torchlight paints the dark in a flickering glow as I head in the opposite direction—if only to spite him.

"We've been down here for a day, maybe two," the man offers from somewhere behind me. "I won't have you passing out from dehydration. Do as you're told, Serehna."

I want to snap at him, but fear holds my tongue hostage. The crack of bones is a warning rattle. The sound is like a fist around my lungs, stealing my breath like this dank hell I've wandered into. Shadows dance across the room as I whip my torch toward the noise. The voices around me muffle and fade into the background. I know they're speaking to me, but I can't focus, can't think of anything other than what horrors await us.

One long, shimmery leg, as sharp and slick as obsidian, emerges from the dark. My body is stone-still, though the breeze that slips through this nightmarish place keeps my torchlight flaring. Fear coats the back of my neck in sweat. Three more legs appear, the end of each tapered like the sharpest blade. Firelight shudders against the walls as the torch trembles in my grip.

Veles, forgive us our trespass for this is surely our place of eternal rot.

As those bulbous eyes track my every movement, I press my hand to my mouth to choke back a scream. My breath gets trapped in my throat. My terror is barely audible, but even then, I know it's already too late.

I gasp, sucking in hot, dry air as I come back to this day. The white hovers in my eyes for too long, reigniting my panic. I thrash and yell, desperate to see the sun and be rid of that thing creeping through the dark. The camel grunts underneath me, and I feel the warm touch of flesh against my arm. I pull away, tucking myself to the front of my saddle and making myself as small as possible. My breath is a tempest, pulling hot air into my lungs until I can handle no more. I cough and sputter—finally seeing the light trickle in from beneath my lids. The sun greets me violently as I tip my head back and stare at the sky.

I'm in the desert. There is no darkness. No depths of the underworld to torment me.

I feel that touch of warmth on my skin again and flinch away. My gaze snaps to the left, eyes blown wide as I stare at Hassan. His brows are pulled together tightly, and his hand hovers in the air between us like he's considering comforting me once more. I look away only to find more eyes on me.

The whole caravan has halted. Shame eats at me like a worm rotting an apple. I go to nudge my camel forward, but Hassan's voice stops me.

"What did you see?"

As I turn around, it's concern I see on his face—concern that shouldn't be there. I can't look away quick enough. My boots kick against my camel, earning a drawn-out groan. I keep my eyes from Hassan's waiting gaze as I pass.

"Hell," I admit.

My camel slinks through the group, but even as I reach the front of the caravan, I don't stop. I prod onward, into the burning afternoon rays with a chilling certainty pounding in my chest.

Sight is undeniable, no matter what course one seeks to alter. The gods guide with a steady hand—unflinching and unchallenged. Pray not to sway the way they've woven fates, for it is as fruitless as asking the sun not to rise and set.

The words I memorized from the Book gnaw at me with every breath I take. Whatever my future holds—whatever darkened torment awaits me—there is no escaping it.

Though I try to never forget it, I can't help but remember that the gods are nothing if not cruel.

CHAPTER 12

The sight of the city on the horizon—this one just as unfamiliar to me as the last three fate led me to—sets my heart in an unsteady patter. It's the largest one this deep into the Continent's interior and one I have taken great care to avoid. More bodies means more trouble, but it seems I no longer have the luxury of dodging it.

Though we're still hours from reaching the prominent city, Hira's presence looms in the distance like a slumbering giant. Nestled against the most northern point of the gorge that separates the Jahaer from the coast, the city is part of the land itself. Carved straight from the rock face, stone buildings tower to immense heights seen even from this great a distance.

I feel the warm press of leather against my arm and shift my gaze to the flask held out in offering. Mikel's smile is knowing as he pushes it into my hand.

"You look like you need it."

"Hmph," I affirm before snatching it from him.

I make quick work of the cork before downing a few gulps of what I already know is wine. Mikel is never in short supply. I wipe my mouth with the hem of my tunic before tugging my scarves back into place.

"Thanks."

Mikel reclaims the flask to take a sip of his own, though, even as he drinks from it heavily, his eyes never leave me. That unrelenting stare of his feels like a fly buzzing my head. Mikel knows too much, and the way he can so easily see through me grates my nerves more than it should.

I mask the emotions on my face and stare out blankly toward the red rocks we're fast approaching. We're not heading to Hira tonight; Vish thought it unwise to risk detection before seeking out our allies. Though I was inclined to argue—if only for the sake of it—the delay settled the bottomless pit in my stomach that hadn't eased since Caen. *Temporarily*, at least.

There's something about the cities that makes my skin itch. Maybe it's the endless eyes on me. Or perhaps the close quarters— the way cities trap you in their bellies. There's nothing but dead ends and hopeless turns. You're unable to get lost in a sea of sand and simply disappear. But maybe, that's all a lie. Maybe if I'm being honest with myself, it's the aching familiarity that comes with a bustling city. I step inside those gates and see Chani slipping through market stalls, picking pockets. I see the twins, Han and Calen, cheating their way through a game of splint in a back alley. I see a black hood pulled low as shadows slink around darkened corners. It's everything I wish to forget but am forced to remember.

"Do you want to talk about it?"

My gaze snaps to where Mikel is looking at me like he can read my mind. And damn it all, if anyone here could, it would be him. I let out a scoff and turn away.

"Talk about what?" I mumble.

He sighs and guides his horse closer. "I was going to ask about the vision you had earlier—you know the one that clearly scared the gods-cursed life out of you. *But,* we could talk about something else. How about the fact that you're suddenly some mythical daemon? Or the fact that you have an obscene bounty on your head, one that even I considered taking—"

My gaze whips to him in an instant, though Mikel only laughs.

"Kidding," he adds, grinning like a devil as I retract my hand from where I was about to shove him from his horse.

I loose an aggravated breath, but it doesn't help ease the tightness in my chest. Mikel would never turn on me, not like Silas. But still, the sentiment cuts deep.

"If you don't want to discuss any of that, we could talk about how you and that one over there" —Mikel gestures across the desert— "are playing the longest game of foreplay I've seen in all my twenty-seven years of life, simply because you both are too scared to make the first move."

I grit my teeth as my gaze drags toward where Mikel is waving his hand. Hassan flanks the left side of the caravan, deep in discussions with Vish. I don't think he can hear us all the way over here, but it doesn't stop me from shooting a blistering glare Mikel's way.

"You're as blazed as this earth if you think that arrogant, ornery ass and I have any—"

"*Gods above,* Ren," Mikel chides. "Careful or someone might think I hit a nerve..." He shoots me a wink and strokes his chin thoughtfully. "Okay, no talk of that. After all, I'd hate to ruin the fun."

I roll my eyes and *tsk* at his boldness. If it was anyone else, they'd have a dagger to their throat by now. Luckily for Mikel, he wormed his way into my only soft spot long ago. I couldn't root him out if I tried.

We ride in silence for a while, but I know better than to think I've escaped his prodding. The moment I flicker my gaze back to Mikel, I see all that playfulness has fallen away.

"Is it the vision?"

I scoff, waving my hand at him dismissively. "It's not the first time Hael has shown me what threats await. It surely won't be the last."

He mumbles under his breath, like he's cursing the gods *and* my stubbornness. "Come on," he sighs. "Are you going to make me beg? Or are you going to tell me the real reason you're clenching your hands so tightly you're bound to break a finger?

My eyes drop down to my lap where my hands are currently strangling each other. I uncurl my fingers immediately and stare at the angry, red splotches of skin.

"It's the cities," I grumble. "You know I hate them."

Mikel raises a brow, but I'm quick to look away.

"The cities, huh?" he prods. "Nothing else bothering you?"

My fists clench once more, and it's an effort to unfurl them. "I have a bad feeling is all," I mutter. "Coming here feels like a mistake."

Out of the corner of my eye, I see Mikel grimace.

"I'll be honest," he starts, letting out a sigh. "I don't like what we've gotten ourselves into either."

I look him over carefully. It's easy to spot the doubt riddled across his face, and it only makes mine grow stronger.

"We can go," I urge, my voice too low for the others to hear. "Fuck the Hesha Mol. Fuck being the Durit. We can leave tonight and make a break for the northern pass. From there we can head east—to the coast. We'll find a boat. Leave the godsdamn Continent. We've talked about it before. There's no reason why we couldn't—"

"Do you hear yourself?" Mikel seethes through a whisper, eyes wide. "You want to run to the coast and broker passage onto a merchant ship? To where? With what coin?" His fingers press against his temple as if the very idea is causing his head to ache. "Who is to say they won't see past those scarves the moment we step aboard? *Veles rot and bind me*, Ren," Mikel rasps.

He shakes his head as if disappointed. "It's true, I don't like our position here," Mikel admits. "Trusting people I just met, especially ones who have already lied to you, is unwise. They seem to care for you just enough to keep you out of Rohan's hands, but twenty thousand yenti?" He looses a breathy laugh, but I know he's anything but amused. "That kind of coin turns even the most honorable of men into rogues and charlatans."

Mikel forces a deep breath as he stares up at the sky. I watch in silence as he runs his thumb down his markings, only to offer it up to Hael moments later. The sight of his prayers makes my stomach churn, but I don't dare interrupt him. When he's done asking the gods for strength, he turns back toward me.

"None of this bodes well, but until we find the Hesha Mol or that bounty is dropped from your head, these people are the best chance we've got."

"A chance at what?" I argue, whisper straining under my breath. "Surely not anything good. They want me to fetch the godkiller, then hide away in some long-lost rebel camp in the north. The gods-plagued north, Mikel! What future does that promise us?"

"One where you're alive!" he rasps, voice trilling across the desert. We've undoubtedly caught the attention of the others, but Mikel doesn't tear his gaze away from me—doesn't even blink as he glares with his jaw rigidly set. "You might be willing to risk your life, just as you've always done, but I'm not. Not anymore." He looks away just as a stray tear splashes against his cheek. "I've already walked the Continent thinking you were dead," he whispers. "Do not ask me to do it knowing you well and truly are."

I open my mouth, but falter as the words get tangled on my tongue. The pain is evident on Mikel's face, though he's trying his best to keep it from me, even now.

"Fine," I offer.

He raises his gaze, and I gulp down the flurry of emotions waging war in my chest.

"We stay until they give us reason not to," I say. "But the moment fate turns against us, we leave. Agreed?"

Mikel nods, mouth pulled into a taut line. "Agreed."

"Good," I huff. "Now stop being so dramatic." My lips turn up into a smirk as Mikel rolls his eyes. I shove him lightly, drawing a muffled protest from his lips. "I'd hate for your new beau to think you so emotional."

Mikel's eyes widen dramatically. He moves to shove me back, but I'm too quick. He nearly topples off his saddle as I slip out of reach.

"What?" I prod. "Think you're the only one with eyes?"

I let my gaze swoop behind us to where Kai and Riat ride. They're too busy talking about gods-know-what, but that doesn't stop Mikel's cheeks from turning a dark crimson. My friend might have thought me too preoccupied the last few days to pay much notice, but I've seen just how often a certain bounty hunter lingers by his side. I've also seen how the last of that same bounty hunter's rum cake made it into Mikel's hands yesterday as we rode weary and weathered.

"Kai likes his food. *Loves* it even," I taunt. "And for him to share it with you?" A devious smile lights up my face. "Seems he likes you more."

"It's not even like that. He—he was just being nice," Mikel stutters. He's so flustered that he dips his head out of view, pinching the bridge of his nose to hide the blush from me.

I shoot Mikel a wide smile, enjoying how easy it is to rattle him. If he thinks he's the only one capable of being a nosy bastard, he's sorely mistaken. As much as he's teased me about Hassan, I'm all-too ready to give it back. He grumbles and swears at me, but it's not long before his own smile slides into place.

The sun is hot overhead, beating down with such severity that it all but melts the icy burdens in my chest. Somehow, despite the troubles we face, I feel lighter—like a familiar face was all I needed in order to see the good in this world again.

I snatch the flask from Mikel's hand as soon as he offers it. Two deep swigs of wine leave my tongue tingling and my chest warm. When my eyes raise to the front of the caravan, I take another sip for good measure.

Our destination appears before us like a hand of the gods. Vish told us his allies lived south of the city—along the gorge's edge but far from the curious eyes of those in Hira. I was skeptical before, though seeing the house now, I almost think Vish a smart man.

It's tucked in a natural cove, surrounded by towering rock walls and hoodoos. Like the city itself, it's carved into the canyon and juts from its face. If you didn't know a dwelling existed here, it might slip you by.

Just as I'm settling into the idea of trusting Vish's judgment, I'm shaken back to reality by the welcoming we're about to receive. Three men emerge from the house—each a different stature, but all clearly a threat. Even from here I can see the muscles lining their arms and shoulders. The closer we get, the more my fingers twitch in anticipation. I touch the hilt of the knife Hassan gave me simply to remind myself it's there.

Two of the men cease their approach, and my heart patters wildly. My eyes lock onto them, brow raising curiously as something strikes me as familiar. They wait in the shade under a patch of hoodoos, tracking our caravan as we wander closer. But they're quickly forgotten, for the third man now holds my sole focus. He hasn't stopped. He walks toward us with purpose—confidence apparent in every stride. His very presence radiates danger, like he's harboring it in his very soul. Black fabrics cover his torso and face, obscuring everything but his eyes.

Up ahead, Vish slows Mirage. He calls out to the man, but his words are lost on me. I prod my camel forward as an unsettling feeling slinks through my veins. As I take in the cloaked man, my gaze tightens. He stops at the mouth of the canyon, clasping Vish's forearm with his own. Something about the greeting is familiar—something about the way he pulls back to run an assessing eye over Vish sparking memory. The man cocks his head, then crosses his arms in a way that is anything but casual. It's a gesture meant to intimidate—one meant to remind allies that they tread a thin line. I can almost imagine the cocky grin hidden beneath his headscarf.

Tension spreads through me like a sickness, warning me not to get closer. Blood pounds through my ears. My heart stutters, then beats too quickly. I take in the man: his tall frame, the strong slope of his shoulders, the ease with which he carries himself.

The feeling that plagued me earlier—the unease of where this path lead—it all makes sense now. I don't even need to see the man's eyes; I already know.

I'm off my camel before the animal can stop. My boots stomp across the densely packed earth, billowing dust and sand in my wake. I pass Hassan; he tries to hinder me, but his grumbling protests don't slow me down. I'm mere feet from our host when he finally turns to face me. One glance is all it takes for me to succumb to every reckless thought I've ever had.

My knife slides free as I lunge. Though he's not expecting it, he manages to evade my first blow. I'm all too quick with the second. My blade snags his sleeve, ripping the fabric with a rough jerk. The sight of his marked skin only burns my fury hotter. I slash and tear, managing to cut a long gash through his tunic. As my knife comes away without the slick of his blood, I yell with a decade's worth of frustration.

Vish is pleading for me to stop, but I won't deprive myself of this moment. The cloaked figure blocks my next strike with ease before shoving me back. He does it playfully, like this is just a game to him. I can hear the others shouting against the frenzy of my own mind, but I shut it all out. The only thing that matters is the bastard in front of me and the blood I'm due.

I lunge, driving my weight into him. We fall to the ground, and I force my knife down with all my might. It hits the hardened clay with a violent *thud*, striking inches from his face. Those dark eyes lock on me, flaring in wicked amusement. Rage is all I feel as I rip my blade free, but—before I can kill the smug brute—he bucks me off. My body reels back, tumbling into a heap as he slips out of reach. I loose a frustrated yell and stab my knife into the barren earth. I pant and fume, fingers curling against the ground as I plan my next move.

He waits for me to get back into a fighting stance with a casual arrogance that boils my blood. He's drawn no weapon, merely stands with his arms folded across his chest. As my eyes flicker down to the gods-cursed markings that decorate his fingers, I remember he doesn't need a weapon. He is one.

I stalk toward him, hand clenching around the slick hilt of my knife. Hate is the violent twitching in my limbs. It churns through my body—courses through my veins like a blaze of fire. That fury boils over as I shove him hard.

"Do something," I spit. "Fight me!"

He laughs as he steadies himself, and the deep timber of his voice floods me with unbridled rage. I charge him again, knife held so tight in my grip that my knuckles feel like they may shatter. I strike; he parries. It happens over and over again as we dance circles around each other. Just when I think I have him, he kicks the inside of my boot, toppling my stance. My emotions are too loud, too distracting. I'm not thinking clearly, only desperate to draw blood. It's a mistake I know better than to make, but I do it anyway. As I try to steady myself, I'm blind to the opening I've left him. He kicks the back of my knee, buckling my leg with amusement crinkling the corners of his eyes. I curse as my ass hits the ground in a puff of sand and glare up at him through dust-coated lashes. The bastard has the audacity to wink.

Without a second thought, I launch myself at him. My fist slams into his stomach, eliciting a choked puff of air from his lungs. He shoves me away, though with only half his strength.

"You're really want to fight me?" he rasps, pained breath giving way to laughter. "You think that's wise?"

I don't need to see his face to know he's smirking. I can hear it in his voice, can see the flicker of mockery in his eyes. He sidesteps me as I lunge, but he makes a mistake. He thinks I don't actually want to hurt him. He thinks I won't play dirty to draw blood.

Wrong.

I see my opportunity, and I take it. I stagger toward him, breath heaving from my lungs. With my head dropped low, I'm nothing more than weak and beaten in his eyes. I'm mere inches from him when it happens.

I snap up, knife curled tightly in my hand as I aim for the indent of his shoulder's socket. It's going to hurt like a bitch, but that's my goal. Just as a spiteful smile tugs across my face, my wrist is held back. My blade hovers mid strike, obstructed and undelivered. But he's not even touching me; he doesn't need to.

It's not his hand but a wispy tendril of darkness that yanks my arm down and throws me off balance. My blade is still flying through the air, ripped from my grasp, when he barrels into me. A shocked rasp slips from my throat as he claims my center of gravity. I try to fight him off, but it's too late. A flurry of limbs and shadows has engulfed me, working in unison to quiet my resistance. By the time I realize what's happening, he's pressed me up against the rough rock face, and I'm out of breath.

As my gaze flickers up to his, I regret ever getting this close. I should have run away. From the moment I saw him, I should have avoided this outcome at all costs. I was never supposed to let those eyes melt into mine again. But now that they are, I feel myself losing a battle I didn't know I was still fighting. The fire in his gaze stirs something in me—something I hoped was long dead.

I buck against him, trying to shift my hips and sweep his legs out from under him. It's useless. I'm pinned like parchment on a post. I let out a frustrated yell as his shadows trap me further. They wrap around my boots, grounding me to the earth. He looses a deep, rumbling chuckle as I squirm against his hold. Hate is too weak a word for what I feel as I glare at the man in front of me.

"I told you fighting me was unwise," he taunts before finally pulling the scarves away from his face.

Though I already knew who lurked under the mask, my heart still drops to the furthest depths at the sight of him. I reel away, pressing against the canyon wall as he cocks his head at me. His eyes are full of too many things to name, but the worst of them shines bright. *Satisfaction.* As I struggle in his grip, the bastard has the nerve to smile. He overtakes my personal space in mere moments. He leans in close, and my body stills.

"You can't beat me in a fight." His lips graze the fabric covering my face, brushing against my cheek. "I taught you everything you know, Serehna," he coos. "Or have you forgotten?"

He grasps my scarves, tugging them down to reveal me to him. I flail under his shadows' hold, but I know it's pointless. Still, I thrash and curse, straining against the darkness that's always been stronger than me and everyone else.

"I see you still don't know when to admit defeat." He smiles, laughing to himself as I struggle. "Glad to know your training didn't go to waste."

"Fuck you," I snarl.

I thrash like a rabid dog as one of his shadows slinks up my cheek to brush the hair from my face.

"You look good, Serehna." His shadows slip down my neck, teasing the new markings that rest there. "Veles suits you," he purrs.

I squirm against his hold, trying to angle my shoulders in order to slip from his grasp. It's futile. His hands quickly pin me to the rock, boxing me in. He has me right where he wants me.

Somehow, I choke back the urge to scream in his face and find restraint instead.

"Let. Me. Go," I seethe.

"Stop trying to kill me, and maybe I will."

The smirk on his face only stokes my anger. I thrash and claw at him, but his shadows hold me steady.

My eyes burn into his, hoping he understands just how much I want to rip him to shreds. I force a deep, shaky breath from my lungs and beseech the god who laid claim to me so abruptly. I want Veles's fury—*need it*. The man in front of me is no innocent, and, as I glare up at him, I know I won't be pleased until I draw blood.

The thrum under my veins is there like always, but unlike the feral urge I felt that day in Letka, my gift is almost quiet now. Subdued. I try to reach for it, but I don't know where it ends and I begin. *Fuck.* Though my shadows prove as useless as my gift of sight, I have other tricks to use against the man before me—tricks he didn't teach me.

"Let me go, Malachi," I utter with a sigh.

I watch his eyes flare dangerously as his name leaves my lips. It's been over a decade since I've said it, and it tastes like a poisoned berry on my tongue.

He leans in close and grins. "And here I thought you'd forgotten me." His voice is a deep purr as he lowers his face to mine.

For a moment, I falter. The words get caught on my tongue. His gaze ensnares me like a silken web. Swallowing thickly, I drop my gaze to my boots. *Gods, if only.* If only he'd been stripped of my mind years ago, maybe then I could find a full breath now. Forgetting Malachi would be like forgetting the dark hum of night itself. It would be like stripping my soul of its pieces, leaving hollows to grow cold. I exhale harshly, ridding myself of the old emotions his presence rouses. Everything I've been running from—my reason for hiding all these years—is finally right in front of me, and I don't know how I managed to ever stay away.

With a wavering breath, I find the strength to raise my gaze to him. But as I do, I force myself to look past those dark, captivating eyes and the pleased smirk curling his lips. Past the sharp line of his jaw and the way his dimples pop against his cheeks. I look past it all and remember how that same face watched me bleed out in Artolen. How he didn't so much as utter a final word. How he ran.

Eleven years is a long time; this is much overdue.

I stretch up onto the tips of my boots and find a closeness that makes him pause. "I could never forget you, Malachi," I admit with a shake in my voice.

My hands drift across his firm chest, and I feel his heart soar under my fingertips. I tell myself I'm merely playing a game and ignore the way his presence makes my breath grow shallow. When I look up at him through heavy lashes—need dripping from my gaze—I pretend it isn't easy.

"Though after all these years, it seems there's still something you forgot about me," I whisper, breath ghosting his skin.

Like I know it would be, his body is drawn like a moth to a flame. I feel him relax against me—feel his hands loosen their tight grip on my shoulders and slide down to my waist. His shadows forget their purpose, too. They slip away to tease the air around me, and—oh, how easily he falls into old habits.

I pull in a sharp breath, not expecting the touch of shadow that slips across my thigh. My eyes widen, but I blink my surprise away quickly. He doesn't get to win—not after what he's done. I clutch his tunic roughly, and his shadows respond with a similar hunger. They curl like fingers, teasing my hips. As I shift my feet against the earth, embracing the freedom I've unknowingly been given, I can't help but grin.

"What did I forget?" Malachi coos. His hand grips the fleshy curve of my waist, like eleven years was too long to go without me.

I bring my mouth to his neck, teasing my lips against his hot skin. "Your shadows know me," I whisper, breath no more than a feather against his earlobe. "And they like me better than you."

My knee connects with his crotch a moment later.

He's swearing, hunched over in pain as I slip out from the canyon wall. When he finally regains his composure, I've already retrieved my blade.

"When did you learn to play dirty?" He's coughing, though there's a godsdamn smile spread across his face when he turns. "The Serehna I know would call that a cheap shot."

"I'm not the same girl you knew in Artolen," I spit back. My body tenses as he approaches. Like he taught me to all those years ago, I raise my weapon to block my face and ready my stance. "Much has changed."

"Clearly."

He smirks, letting his eyes run up and down my body as he comes to rest in front of me. I try not to shift where I stand, but I feel every inch of my skin heat under his scrutiny.

Gods, it's like I'm a teenager again.

My body chills, snuffed of all tempting thoughts the moment I notice where Malachi is looking. His gaze hovers on my arms—on the scars that now mutilate my skin. I expect revulsion, but instead find fury shadowing his gaze. He stares for too long, jaw working roughly until he seems to come back to himself. When his eyes find mine, it's a familiar smugness that drifts across his face. He slides that playful composure back on like a mask, and I wish I didn't know what that felt like.

Malachi eyes the knife clenched in my grip before loosing a breathy laugh. "Are we still playing this little game of yours?"

he muses, running his tongue across his teeth. "Or can we skip to the part where you're happy to see me?"

I bark out a laugh of disbelief. When he merely cocks a brow, my anger returns hotter than before. "*Happy to see you?*" I fume.

I stomp toward him, and the bastard grins. The sight only seeks to fuel my reckless whims. My blade swishes through the air before I can think better of it. I strike with every ounce of strength I have left, breath raging in my chest as I work tirelessly to draw blood. Though I catch him off guard, Malachi dodges the first blow and the second. But as his eyes meet mine, they flash with something other than arrogance for once.

Doubt.

There's a nasty ache in my chest, one that I wish to carve out myself.

Did he honestly think that, after all this time, I'd welcome him back with open arms?

My lip curls into a scowl. I lunge. Strike. The blade digs into his tunic, once more slashing the fabric across his chest. This time, it comes away red. His hands tighten around my wrists with a brutal quickness, ending this fight before it truly begins. But it's too late; I've already lost all sense of composure.

I writhe and scream in his grasp, tears building under my lashes. Everyone is watching. I can feel the heat of their attention like fire on my skin, but I don't stop. Nothing could make me stop.

I scream and hiss and curse and shake. I've lost myself to the abyss of an agony I tried to keep buried for too long. The only thing I can focus on is the fucking Shade—the one who used to steal food for me until I had the guts to do it myself. My blade is lost to the sand, but my wrath is far from through. My hands slap against Malachi's chest—grasping his tunic, scratching his skin. I shove as hard as I can, but he barely staggers back.

"You left me!" I scream, tears raking down my face now. As they wet my skin, shame burns hot in my chest. "After all the times you said you would be there, you left," I rasp.

Malachi curls his hand around the nape of my neck, holding me steady. "Serehna—"

"Ren," I seethe, ripping free of him. "My name is *Ren.*"

My heart pounds with a force too great to bear. All I can do is stare at him, at the remnants of the boy I thought would never break me—the only person I trusted more than myself. He's bleeding, blood spilling out against his dark tunic, but he doesn't seem to care. His eyes roam my face like he's trying to understand what changed, though he was the one who ruined everything.

I scoff as I drag a hand across my wet cheek, removing any trance of the pain he's caused. Just as I open my mouth to spit the vilest of insults—if only to make him feel as I do—a gentle hand comes to rest on my shoulder.

"Serehna," Vish says carefully.

I flinch against the touch. I'm quick to shove his hand away, not bothering to be gentle about it. "Stop calling me that," I seethe.

My teeth clamp down on the inside of my cheek. I don't let up until I taste blood, but the pain doesn't provide its usual distraction. Even though I know I'd feel better if I did, I can't look away from Malachi. I leave Vish standing to my left, ignoring his unspoken plea. I know we're here for Malachi's help and that I should restrain the resentment I feel for the Shade, but I can't. I want to scream until I'm sick. I want to tear him apart. It's the least he deserves.

I glower at Malachi, wanting my hurt to be his own. But the longer I stare at him—seeing the way he's aged, how the scruff on his face outlines the strength of his jaw, how his eyes are still so brown that they look almost black—I feel myself slipping.

The sight of him before me, after all this time, produces an ache in my chest that should only be possibly if he stuck a blade there himself.

"*Witch.*"

My focus breaks instantly. As my gaze snaps to the right, I find Hassan standing by my side. His eyes are locked on me from under a deeply furrowed brow. His jaw is clenched tightly.

"You're bleeding."

I follow Hassan's gaze down to where Malachi's blood stains my palms. I rub my fingers against the slick of red, smudging it against my skin.

"Not my blood," I utter, almost too softly to hear.

He grunts under his breath before nudging me. "Come on," Hassan prods. "Let's get you cleaned up."

I find myself nodding, retrieving my blade before being guided forward by Hassan. My legs feel like they're dragging behind me, like they want me to stay out here under the blistering sun to suffer this pain. I'm crashing—can feel the strength leaving my bones with every step I take—but I don't allow myself to stop.

All this time, I thought I would kill Malachi if I ever saw him again. So many nights, staring deep into a fire's blaze, I had dreamt of my blade at his throat—of him begging me to spare his life. The sight of his blood on my hands should relieve me of those old burdens. I expected to be free of this pain once and for all; but what I feel now rocks me like I'm still atop my saddle. I feel hollow, like a piece of me has been carved out and stolen. And though I want to feel nothing in its place, I feel everything.

I risk a glance over my shoulder and find Malachi staring. It's only a moment before I realize that violent gaze isn't fixed upon me. No, it's Hassan he glares at with such hate that it sends a shudder up my spine. When Malachi turns that gaze on me, it changes. There is no more heat, no more fury. It's cold detachment that fills his eyes, a muted resentment. He looks at me like I mean nothing, and though it should please me to feel his animosity, it doesn't.

"Let us go inside," Vish offers, shepherding Hassan and I toward the house.

Malachi is quick to join us, though he says nothing. He merely stares at where Hassan supports my lower back with his hand and sneers. When Malachi catches my gaze, I'm quick to look away.

Vish's eyes dart between the pair of us uneasily, and I swear I catch his pupils retract like he's calling on the gods for answers. For once, I don't want to know what truths they offer him.

Vish's lips press into a firm line, though his throat bobs uneasily. "Come." He sighs, heaviness slipping into his tone. "It seems we have much to discuss."

Malachi offers a snide laugh as he heads in the opposite direction—stalking off to where his men still rest in the shade. "Yes," he calls back, voice scathing. "It seems we do."

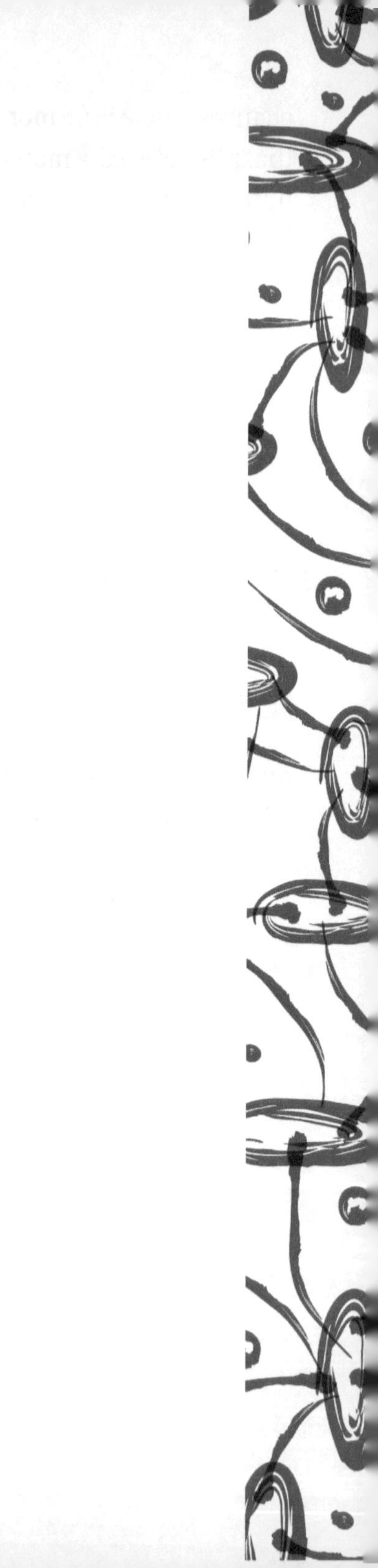

CHAPTER 13

I haven't said a word since I stepped through the threshold. It feels like I've been through battle. My unwelcome reunion with a certain Shade has left me reeling, and I fear I'm tapped out of all fight. I'd wanted to protest when Hassan nudged me toward the house, but I couldn't summon the effort.

Savi and Mikel were quick to follow, their unspoken questions nipping at my heels. As Savi washed my blood-stained hands with a wet cloth, her eyes silently prodded for answers. Mikel wasn't so subtle. His whispered interrogation began the moment the four of us slipped through the door. But I had no words for him— couldn't even manage to look up from the table. My mind was, and is, rattled. I've been hollowed out and left with jaded edges.

It didn't take long for the others to shuffle in, and when they did reality struck hard like a fist to the face. I wasted no time slipping to the furthest corner of the room, eager to melt against the walls. As I rest there now, twitchy like a gutter rat, I want nothing more than to be gone from this place.

Tension eats the room as everyone either sits down at the table or leans up against the walls. No one knows what to say, and I catch their gazes slipping to me as if I can provide the answers. I tuck my arms against my chest and shift deeper into the corner I've all but crawled into, eager to escape their eyes. The house is by no means small, but with this many people packed into the kitchen it's not exactly comfortable. It's suffocating, and the erratic beat of my heart isn't helping. I haven't had a moment to catch my breath since we arrived, and now leftover adrenaline lingers in my body like a coiled snake.

Raised voices float in from outside and demand my attention. The familiar rumble of Malachi's voice makes me clench my teeth, providing an odious reminder as to why we're here. He's arguing with Vish, has been since I settled against this wall. Though I can't understand what they're saying, I know well and good what they're discussing—*who* they're discussing. My suspicion is only confirmed when the door swings wide to reveal Malachi's pinched expression. His eyes immediately scour the room, but when his gaze finds mine, he stills. Two men push past him, but I don't bother to identify them. All I see is Malachi. His frustration. His hesitation. He stares at me like he wants to cross the room to get to me, but won't allow himself to. Something fierce fills his eyes, and I find myself held hostage in that gaze. Seeing him like this brings too many memories back to life, and I'm not sure I can weather their pain.

I curl my arms tighter around my body and pull my gaze from his. The ache in my chest is an anchor weighing me to the floor; I can't escape the repercussions of this homecoming even if I wanted to. The justice I sought for so long is a hairsbreadth away, yet all I feel is outrage that the gods have inflicted such a fate upon me. Though I could soothe this anguish quickly, I can't bring my hand to reach for a weapon. Turmoil twitches through my limbs at our proximity. I can feel him watching me. I should leave, but I have too many questions—harbor too many unspoken words on my tongue to walk away now. This pain would follow me for lifetimes—poison my last dying breath if left unchecked. The only way to staunch this mortal wound is to see it closed. For good, this time.

Once again, I feel the uncanny shiver of eyes on me, but when I finally risk a glance, Malachi has turned away. His voice strains low as he continues to argue with Vish, muttering hostile words that are barely quiet enough to keep secret. I expect Vish to back down from the imposing man towering over him, but the Seeker holds his ground. His mouth moves quickly, uttering things I'm more than desperate to hear. Malachi doesn't look convinced, and I can tell he's not pleased. But when Vish presses a firm hand to Malachi's shoulder and drops his voice even lower, the Shade stills. I can all but feel the tension in the room. More words spill from Vish's lips. Judging by the fire in Malachi's eyes, he doesn't enjoy hearing them. I watch his face contort into a scowl before he shakes his head and leaves Vish standing alone.

"We haven't been properly introduced."

The voice rips my focus from Malachi. As I look across the room, my body instantly tenses.

Fuck. I thought they looked familiar.

"You've got to be kidding me," I grumble.

My hand drops to my side, twitching for a knife. With methodical precision, my eyes rake over the two Berserkers in front of me—the same ones we ran into in the canyon. They're just as intimidating as they were that day, with markings displayed across dense muscle and statures oozing violence. I can't help but straighten my spine as I tighten my gaze on them.

The taller one smirks before speaking again. "Tofá," he offers with a nod.

"I didn't ask."

He laughs softly under his breath before jutting his thumb at the man next to him. "This is Ivar."

"Again, I didn't ask," I retort.

My eyes flicker to Malachi, finding his attention hot on me. I only last a moment under the scrutiny before I have to look away.

"Where's your smart-mouthed friend?" Ivar prods. He lifts a brow, not a lick of amusement on his fire-scarred face. "I had hoped to run into him again to... settle some things."

My nails dig into my palm, leaving half-moon indents. I hold his gaze, but say nothing.

"Hm, how could I forget?" Tofá hums. "Last we saw, you and Rohan's favorite Berserker were quite *cozy*." His smile curves deviously, and his blue eyes flash.

"What Berserker?" Malachi demands to know.

I swallow harshly as my gaze slides to him. A foul feeling slithers in my stomach, bubbling up my throat with a venomous bite. "He's no one," I answer Malachi, forcing the words out roughly. "Just another Veles-cursed who thought my life of little value. No need to tell a story you know all too well."

"Serehna—"

"Tell us, *Serehna*," Tofá taunts, cutting Malachi off. "Where is that leech of yours?"

"Dead," I bite, my voice cold.

Ivar's head tilts curiously. "Dead?" he questions.

"Did I fucking stutter?!" I snap.

The rush of anger I feel threatens to shred the restraint I've carefully leashed myself with. As my gift thrums through my blood a little louder than before, my body lurches in panic.

I squeeze my eyes shut and tuck myself tightly to the wall, curling against the rough stone. My hands clench into fists, digging my nails deep into flesh. I try to shut everything out—try to ignore the uneasy shifting of feet and the murmured voices that heavy my shame. It seems the others have finally found a smidge of worry, as they should have long ago. I ignore the itching in my veins, though it feels harder and harder to each time this happens. With fear clenching my throat, I force myself to focus on nothing but the unsteady breaths shuddering through my lungs.

In and out. In, in, out. In and out. One breath, then another.

Mikel is there before I know it. His presence is a balm to my frayed nerves as he leans against the wall, shielding me. He reaches out and gives my wrist a light squeeze—an anchor in turbulent waters. He utters nothing, but he doesn't need to; his presence says enough. I don't dare open my eyes to see if the others are watching me shatter like something weak and delicate. I know they are.

A *tsk* slips from behind Tofá's teeth, pulling everyone's focus, including mine. "So the prick is dead?" he muses. "Interesting."

"We've lost one enemy and gained countless more," Vish clips, dismissing him with the flick of his hand. "What we need now is to get Ren across the Jahaer before she's seen."

"Crossing the desert quickly will be no easy task," Malachi offers brusquely. "I trust you brought enough supplies to endure the journey?"

Though he directed the question at Vish, Savi is the one who speaks up.

"Our travel here was rushed," she answers. "We're low on a few things but are no strangers to the markets in Hira. It shouldn't take us more than a few hours to procure what we need."

Malachi lets out a heavy sigh. "Fine," he utters. "We leave the day after next. Though..." He levels a scathing look at Vish. "There's still the issue of company to discuss."

He steps forward, letting his ruthless gaze wander across the room. He eyes Savi, then Kai. Riat shoots him a cocky grin, which only makes Malachi scowl. But as his focus drifts to me, he hesitates. Those dark eyes are searing before they shift to take in Mikel's defensive posture. My friend hasn't backed down, nor will he. Mikel glares, all but daring Malachi to step closer.

The Shade raises a curious brow as he spots Mikel's markings. "A Mender will be useful for what's to come," he offers. "But a gang of bounty hunters?" Malachi scoffs, then regards Hassan with nothing but contempt. "That's more trouble than I need."

Vish starts to interject, but Malachi speaks over him.

"We have three of Veles's blood to protect her. Anyone else will only get in my way."

Hassan clenches his fists, but before he can act foolishly, I do it for him.

"I don't need protection," I huff with a bitter laugh. "Least of all from you."

Tofá and Ivar both snicker, voices low and taunting as Malachi turns to face me.

"You're the most wanted person on the Continent," he argues. "Everyone will be looking to collect the prize Rohan put on your head." He stares at me coldly, then lets a smirk slowly drift across his face. "Or have you not yet seen the bounty plastered with that beautiful face of yours?"

I grit my teeth so hard I'm sure I look like a wild animal. "I've seen it," I bite.

"Good," Malachi remarks, amusement shining in his dark eyes. "Then you understand why my protection is more than necessary."

"As is ours," Hassan interrupts. "We've kept her safe thus far. We're not leaving now simply because you will it."

A heavy silence stretches across the room. I see firm nods of agreement from both Savi and Tariq. Kai and Riat are grinning from ear to ear like they can't wait for the trouble that's to come. But something stirs uneasily in my chest as my focus shifts back to Hassan. He's the last person I would expect to offer protection, and yet he glares at Malachi like it's all he hopes for.

"You've kept her safe?" Malachi mocks. He presses his hands against the table, leaning across it to get in the bounty hunter's face. "So what I heard about her being captured and collared in Letka isn't true, then?"

Anger ripples through Hassan, bobbing his throat and tensing every muscle in his neck. "It's true," he grits through his teeth.

His gaze darts to me, and, for the briefest moment, I swear it's guilt that floods those hazel eyes. He steels the emotion from his face quickly before turning back toward Malachi. "We let the Berserker take her to Letka. It was a mistake, one that won't happen again." Hassan lets out a deep breath, though it does nothing to relax him. Every muscle in his body is locked down and brimming with tension as he glares at the Shade. "But we came for her," he states gruffly. "Killed two of Rohan's men and a Torch to free her. And I'll kill a hundred more if I need to."

Both Tofá and Ivar bristle where they stand. Riat clocks the tension, fingers hovering against the hilts of his knives.

"Is that all?" Malachi taunts.

Hassan leans over the table, coming face to face with him. Malachi only smiles.

"I drug her out of that hellhole," Hassan snarls. "I sat at her bedside for days, waiting for the poison to wane. I was there then, and I'm here now."

"You think that means something?" Malachi sneers. "That you killed for her? That you played nursemaid?"

"I—" Hassan starts.

"*I* was the one who saved her all those years ago," Malachi growls. He slaps his hands on the table, veins growing black. "*Me.*"

Vish and Savi tense where they sit as shadows slink around Malachi's wrists. That darkness ripples like a violent tide moments from reaching shore. Hassan holds steady, but as I watch his eyes dart back and forth between the shadows and the one who conjures them, I know it's fear he feels.

"I took care of her," Malachi continues, voice booming through the room. "I made sure she was fed. I taught her to fight. I—"

"You left me for dead!" I snap.

All eyes are on me as I push off the wall and stalk toward the table. I don't stop until I'm inches from him.

"Serehna—"

"Serehna died in that alley, Malachi," I retort. "She died when you decided to leave me behind. When you decided that five years meant nothing to you. That *I* meant nothing to you."

His eyes soften as he stares at me, brows furrowing. "I couldn't—"

"Couldn't what? What excuse could you possibly have for abandoning me like that?"

My breath hitches as his shadows slip down the table legs. The moment those wisps of darkness touch my boots, I go perfectly still. It's a cruel distraction, and one he knows I'll fall for. Anger churns in my veins, but stronger than that is the overwhelming comfort of this touch. It's dizzying. *Familiar*. My hands shake as the shadows slither up my boots, teasing their way across my thighs. It's not until they reach my stomach that panic breaks my trance.

I try to reel away, but Malachi grabs my wrist to keep me there. He holds me steady, eyes piercing as his shadows slip under fabric to touch bare skin. I go to protest, but my mouth grows dry. Emotion builds up in my throat, and, all at once, every ounce of strength I have is lost to me.

He says nothing as his shadows carefully lift the hem of my tunic. I stare at him—glare at him. Venom pools in my gaze, but there's something else there that betrays me. Tears fall slowly and silently as those wisps of darkness that used to brush the hair from my face now brush against my scar.

The jagged line cuts almost all the way across my stomach, marking my skin with a deathly white reminder of that day. I tense as the cool, teasing touch of shadow is replaced by something warm. Malachi's fingers trace the scar softly, and I all but shiver at the feeling. When I look up at him, I find his gaze hardened, focus locked on my skin. His jaw works roughly as devastation contorts his handsome face. Something breaks in me at seeing him like this, but he doesn't deserve my compassion or my pity.

"You did that," I rasp, loud enough for the whole room to hear. "Not the Turidens who came that day. *You*."

I rip myself from his touch, staggering back if only to find distance from the emotions he so easily incited. As he watches me move further and further away, his eyes lose their fire until I'm left looking into empty pools of brown. I know that look, but for some reason I can't help but dig the knife a little deeper.

"If Hassan and the others want to come, then they come," I state. "I need to know someone won't leave when things go bad."

Malachi swallows harshly, and though I want him to break our gaze, he doesn't.

"So be it," he grits out. "Whatever you—"

The front door flies open.

"They didn't have any lamb," a bubbly voice calls into the house. "So you better be okay with por—" A petite woman stops abruptly in the doorway, eyes widening oh-so slightly as she surveys the room. "Oh," she starts, covering her mouth as she lets out a chirpy laugh. "I didn't know we were having guests." She looks us over one by one, not at all fazed by the tensed muscles or weapons displayed throughout the room.

Her eyes shine bright as she smiles. "Hope you all like pork. There's plenty to go around." She sets the wooden crate of groceries on the table, but sucks in a harsh breath when she sees Malachi. "*Oh my gods,*" she frets.

The moment her hands land on his chest, I feel the slumbering thrum in my veins flicker to life like fire catching. I dig my teeth into my tongue as the woman tugs at Malachi's slashed tunic, assessing the cut I dealt him earlier.

"You're hurt," she states.

Malachi grabs her hands and gently pushes them down. "I know." His eyes flicker over her shoulder, finding me instantly. "It's nothing, Quin. I'll patch myself up later."

As Malachi sits down in the chair next to Savi, my eyes rake over the woman. *Quin.* She's delicate and feminine in all the ways I am not. As she leans up against Malachi's chair, he all but dwarfs her. Her curly, auburn hair is cropped to her ears, reveling a stack of gold baubles pierced into the lobes. A peppering of freckles dashes across her high cheekbones, the brown dots complementing her soft, tawny skin. The woman's thin body is adorned in a simple blue dress, but compared to my rumpled tunic, it's almost elegant. She has no weapons. No scars. Just a dazzling smile that she offers without hesitation.

My stomach turns sour.

As I watch her cozy up next to Malachi, my throat clenches. Her presence is a knife I didn't expect to be thrust into my chest. The feeling that overcomes me is foreign, but much too potent. I don't give it a name, I simply seek to leave. But before I can make it to the door, the bitter taste of fate halts my feet.

I stop and stare at Quin's hand. Her slender fingers are draped over Malachi's shoulder, but it's not the casual intimacy of the touch that has me ready to draw a blade—though, it's tempting. My brow pinches roughly as I stare at the pattern on her skin—the small and large clusters of circles that connect in a web of splatters and lines. Her marks span the top of her left hand and run up her forearm in a curving band. The pattern is beautiful, but familiar. I know it well, for the Continent boasts more Weavers than any other Hael-blessed daemon.

I open my mouth, only to close it abruptly when no words come out. All I can do is stare at Quin's markings and jump to conclusions. How I often wondered what a Weaver could want with me. How I wracked my mind for answers that would never come. But the longer I let my eyes roam over the black that marks her as one of Hael's, everything finally makes sense. It's fitting, for only the gods would take pleasure in this mockery of fate.

People around me are speaking. Voices clash against each other, resuming previous arguments. I hear someone say my name, but my focus doesn't waver. Their words slip by me like a hot wind across the Jahaer. I pay it no mind; I know it'll pass, and when it does my burdens will still be here.

My eyes flash up to the soft, innocent expression muddling Quin's face. She looks so happy, so oblivious to the pain she's caused me—the torture she's inflicted. And though I want nothing more than to rip that smile off her face, all I can manage to do is loose a choked whisper.

"It's you."

Her head tilts as she regards me. It's then that she looks at my neck, at both sets of marks that are on display for everyone in this cramped house to see. Her eyes widen before her full lips part in a gentle gasp.

"*Hael, bless us.* You're *her*," she declares. "You're Serehna." She springs from her place next to Malachi in an instant, bounding across the kitchen. "We've been trying to find you for ages. Gods know he wouldn't quit talk—"

She tries to wrap me in a hug, but I panic. Anger and anguish clash inside me like a trapped beast, and I lash out with all its might. My hands are quick to shove her away, harsher than I should have. She bumps against the table as I stagger back.

"Don't fucking touch me," I rasp.

Quin flinches like I slapped her, and gods do I wish I had. I shake my head and put more distance between us. Mikel is at my side at once, steadying a firm hand against my back.

"Who the hells is that?" he whispers harshly.

My hands shake as I clench them into fists. It takes me a minute to find my voice, but when I do, it's booming. "*That* is the Weaver who's been in my head for months," I announce to everyone. My chest feels too heavy, and my breath too shallow. "She's the reason for my nightmares." I turn to face Malachi, pain and rage blurring my vision. "Tell me I'm wrong."

He stares at me with a furrowed brow, but he doesn't deny it.

"Nightmares?" Quin's mouth gapes open like a fish. She stares at me wide-eyed, shock painted across her features. "What do you mean— We didn't.... I never meant to—"

My feet take me across the kitchen before Mikel can think to hold me back. I stomp right up to Quin, towering over her small frame. "Do you know how many times I begged the gods for it to stop?" I spit. "How many nights I woke with a scream trapped in my throat?"

My blood itches with violence, and a shudder runs up my body. I dig my nails into my palms, but even that does nothing to quell what's coming. That sluggish feeling overtakes my blood, heavy and thick, and I instantly drop my gaze to watch my veins turn black. It's a frightening sight, but I don't fear it now.

I close my eyes and tip my head back, letting a slow smirk creep across my face. *Gods, this is going to feel good.*

Malachi's chair topples as he forces himself in between the Weaver and I. "Serehna, let her explain."

He cups the back of my neck firmly. The rough, desperate touch of his fingers on my skin has my gaze snapping open. For a moment, there's only him and me. The sight of those dark brown eyes stills something reckless inside—tempers the violence I was ready to unleash. My blood settles. The room grows distant. The comfort is brief, like coming up for air before slipping underwater once more. I'm back in an instant, pulling in a ragged breath and thrashing out of his hold.

"Explain what?" I rasp. "That you and her have been manipulating me for months?" My boots smack into his as I step closer, eating up the space between us. I glare at him, uncaring that he's almost a head taller and that his shadows could tear me apart. "You sent me into that canyon over and over again. And for what? Me to get a glimpse of you?" I scoff. "You taunted me with your voice. Drew me in only for that darkness to drown me. What excuse could you possibly have for that?"

I smack my hands against his chest, but he doesn't fight back. He lets me hit him until my arms ache.

"Eleven years!" I shout. "Eleven years without so much as a word, and now you send your Weaver into my dreams. *Why?* To lead me here so I can see you playing house? To see how you've only found comfort since the day you left me?"

I shove him away harshly. Though I try to calm my raging heart, it's no use. "Fuck you, Malachi," I rasp against shuddering breaths. "Fuck you for all of it."

"All Quin was trying to do was send you a message," he says steadily. "I needed you to find me."

His eyes are full of pleading, but I know better than to be swayed by that look. Malachi tries to take a step toward me, but my knife is drawn before he can lift his boot. He hesitates. I watch as the muscles in his jaw ripple and flex before he ultimately makes his decision. He stalks closer, undeterred by my promise of violence. His hands raise in surrender, but he's anything but harmless. My knife trembles in my hand as I raise it to his chest.

He stops a mere breath away, letting my blade dig into his already torn tunic. "I needed to get you here," he prods. "After Vish told me what he knew about the Durit, I knew it had to be you."

"So you knew?" My voice breaks. I swallow harshly, trying to find the strength to carry on. "You knew, and yet you thought nightmares were the answer?"

"We had no knowledge they were nightmares," he groans. "*Gods*, Serehna, do you really think—"

"Why did it have to be you?" I rasp, fist choking the hilt of my blade. "After everything you've done, has my suffering not been enough?"

"I don't want your suffering," he snarls back. "I only wished to find you."

"I was not yours to find!" I shout. I grab a fistful of his tunic and yank him toward me. "You should have left me alone."

He leans in close, lips twitching against my ear. "That's where you're wrong, Serehna," he utters. "You will always be mine to find. The gods brought you to me for a reason—then and now. You are my responsibility. Mine to keep safe."

I'm quick to raise my blade to his throat. "I'm not yours," I spit. "Not anymore."

Tofá and Ivar instantly move from their place against the wall, but Malachi holds up a hand to stop them.

"Do you expect me to be flattered?" I sneer. "That after all these years, you still hold some childish claim on me?" My hand shakes, and I tighten my grip on the hilt. "You always were a selfish bastard. I'm just sorry it took me until that day in Artolen to realize you never truly cared."

Without breaking my gaze, Malachi leans into my blade. His eyes flare dangerously as wispy shadows tug at my tunic like greedy hands. "Do it then," he utters, tilting his chin up to bare his throat to me. "If you truly believe that, finish this now and spare me the lecture on how I feel."

He glares at me with a cold detachment. There is no care there. No concern. He's looking at me like I've already plunged this knife into his heart, and I wish that didn't hurt me, too.

The blade wavers in my hand as tears blur my vision. I suck in a deep, shuddering breath before resheathing my weapon as quickly as I pulled it. "Stay away from me, *Shade*," I bark, shoving my way past him. "Or else I might not be so merciful next time."

I'm out the door a moment later, fleeing into the crisp night air.

CHAPTER 14

Breath huffs through my lungs too quickly, threatening to topple me like an overworked horse. My boots scrape against the dried earth and stir up sand as I hurry from the house. I don't know where I'm going, just that I need to go far from here. The desert is an unnervingly silent companion as I quicken my pace. I try not to think about Malachi, but without anything to distract me, he slips into my mind like a thief in the night.

He knew I was the Durit. Knew I was alive.

My chest aches like my last breath has been stolen from me. I stumble forward on unsteady legs, only stopping when my palms slap against the rough red rocks that tower above the house. Labored breaths heave in and out of my lungs as I try to steady myself. The night is a chill across my arms, but the cold does nothing to strip the heat from my face. Hot tears spill carelessly, threading shame tightly through me.

I flip over and let my back slide down the canyon wall until I'm seated firmly on the ground. As I kick my legs out in front of me, I let shaky hands rake through my hair. The short strands feel foreign against my fingertips, ending too abruptly and leaving me with nothing to grasp in all my fury. It's one of a handful of things that feels wrong to me now.

I told Malachi that Serehna died in Artolen, but did a part of me die in Letka, too?

The front door creaks, and I flinch. As murmured voices drift out across the desert, I hold perfectly still—somehow hoping I'll fade into the growing dark. From across the canyon, I watch the others strip our animals of their packs before wandering off in the opposite direction. Only when they disappear around a bend and slip out of sight, do I relax.

I tilt my head up toward the sky, seeking solace in the dark. The moon is at rest tonight, paying tribute to the underworld like it does every month. Stars light the sky, glimmering like torches thrown in a deep well. I stare out into the expansive nothing until I feel that darkness slide over me like a blanket. Moments like this—finding stillness beneath a night's sky—have consoled me since I was a child, but tonight I only feel discomfort.

As my eyes close and the world around me quiets, the heavy thrum in my blood makes itself well-known. It's unsteady, eager to slip free. Every moment I keep it caged, it grows more agitated. It screamed to be free earlier. When I stalked across the kitchen set on destroying Quin, it hummed its encouragement. My gift begged to lash out. Strike. Slice. Wound flesh and forever leave a reminder. And for a moment, I was eager for that violence, too. I wanted to hurt Quin like she'd hurt me. Worse, even. But everything had stilled the moment I'd looked at him.

Maybe it was nothing more than a moment of surprise as our gifts regarded the other—like Veles holding a mirror up to himself. Blood recognizing blood. Though I wish it were true, not even I can be that naive. The violence in my blood was quelled by nothing more than my own weakness. I hesitated. The very man who taught me to be stronger than my enemies was the reason I couldn't be.

I groan as I drop my head into my hands. *Veles damn him.* A soft breeze sifts the sand around my boots and stirs the desert like the thoughts in my mind.

Why must he have such a hold on me after all this time?

My gaze catches on the collar of my tunic and the glint of silver that rests beneath. I thought this ache couldn't get worse, but it seems I was wrong. There's a gnawing sorrow in my gut, a riotous churn I can't shake. I do nothing but stare for a moment, trying to find the courage to face the past and the way it's suddenly tangled in the present. Slowly, I let my fingers pluck the silver chain. The slightest touch feels like a burn, reminding me how deep these old wounds run, but I don't let go. I tug the necklace until Malachi's ring slips free from my tunic. The mere sight of it threatens to tear a sob from my chest. I should rip it off, chuck it far away, and let it sink into the sand. It would be easy to lose it amidst this desert. I would be better off without its memories. But for some reason, I can't. As I tuck it safely beneath my tunic, my heart gives a nasty lurch.

"Foolish girl," I utter, though it's not my own voice I hear, but my mother's.

I squeeze my eyes together tightly, fighting off fresh tears. I try not to think of Malachi sitting inside that house, smug with the fact that—whether I meant to or not—I came when called. The worst part is, I'm too desperate to turn away. How weak I have become, no longer able to make my way across the Continent alone, forced to forge alliances with those whom it would be smarter to run from than with.

Silas flashes through my mind, cutting an ache so deep I fear I might be ripped in half.

Foolish girl, my mind reminds me.

A lone tear slides down my cheek and drips into the sand. All those years I spent running from what happened in Artolen, pretending I didn't miss the home I had found there. More tears fall, and I wipe them away roughly.

But Silas...

The pain in my chest builds as regret digs its claws in deeper. I let myself feel it all. Every twinge. Every blistering ache. I was too eager to replace what Malachi had taken from me. Too desperate to prove I was worthy of what others have denied me time and time again. I had wanted someone to slither through the cracks in my heart and seal them. I thought he wanted to be the one to finally do it.

My throat grows achy, and I swallow back the bitter laugh that threatens to spill free. *Oh, how gullible hope is.*

I think back to those days alone with Silas in the desert, and then to our night in Letka. *Had it really all been an act? A mere rouse to lead the blind hare to the waiting snare?* My fingers dig into my scalp as I force out the ragged breaths that get caught in my lungs. I feel weak, so foolishly weak.

The crunch of boots has me stilling, though I know it's far too late to go unnoticed now. I listen quietly as the steps grow closer, then closer still. Jaw clenched shut, I prepare myself for another argument I'm not ready to have. Not yet. When a pair of boots finally comes to rest in front of me, I can't hold my tongue.

"Fuck off, *Shade*," I grit out as I wipe away my tears. "Whatever you have to say, I don't want to hear it."

A deep sigh sounds from above, followed by a heavy *thump* as someone sits down next to me. My head snaps up, twisting to the left. I don't expect the gentle brown eyes that greet me, nor the way Tariq smiles softly, like he's not at all bothered by my abuse.

"I— uh..." I choke on the apology, stumbling over words I can't figure out how to say.

Tariq merely offers me a steaming mug and settles against the rock face. "It's cold out here, thought you could use some tea."

I swallow the lump in the back of my throat, nodding to him as I take the mug. "Oh. Thanks," I murmur.

The ceramic warms my chilled hands, but I don't take a sip. Instead, I stare out into the night and search for something I know I'll never find. But still, I try. Feigning stillness, I beg the gods to ease this ache in me. I wait and wait, but the knot in my chest only grows tighter. Tears fall without my blessing, and I drink to hide my shame. Tariq doesn't prod. He simply sits with me, occasionally sipping from his own cup. The chill in the air is the type of cold that settles into your bones and fixes to never leave. I should go inside, though I don't; I shudder and draw my knees up to my chest for warmth.

We sit like that for a while—Tariq and I. Not speaking, merely existing. Only our quiet sips and steady breaths taint the still night around us. My eyes flicker to the house too often. I stare at the darkened doorway like I'll find shadows waiting. But nothing and no one stirs from the house, and it deepens the ache in my chest more than I care to admit.

I gulp down a sip of tea, hoping it drowns the swell of emotions lodged in my throat. It only burns my tongue.

Tariq follows my gaze and lets out a deep sigh. "It's never easy," he starts, "when the people we love are the ones who hurt us."

My gaze rips from the house. "I don't love him," I urge. "He looked out for me growing up. Nothing more."

Tariq settles further against the rough canyon wall, getting comfortable. His large hands rest in his lap, holding his now-empty mug with a gentleness I've come to expect from him.

"You know when my aunt was killed, I wanted nothing more than to make the world pay." He stares out at the desert for a long time, as if lost in thought. "There were days when revenge was all I could think about. It consumed my every waking moment, my every breath. I wanted those men to understand what they had done, what they had taken from me."

I look at Tariq and observe the tension ground in his jaw, then the way he swallows roughly. And his eyes—his eyes no longer hold their typical softness. No, his gaze is full of the things that haunt him. I see ripples of anger and pain. Regret and grief. My gaze snaps away as my stomach grows uneasy. I know that look on his face well, for it's the same one the mirror shows me.

"What did you do" —I hide my unease behind another sip— "to ease that burden?"

Tariq sighs. "I met the others." The corners of his mouth turn up as he attempts a smile. "I was in Fála, chasing rumors of those who had killed my aunt. That night, I found myself in a tavern. *The Camel's Back.*" He chuckles. "A wild place, one where just stepping inside means asking for trouble..."

I tug my knees closer and turn toward him. "And I'm guessing that's exactly what you found?" My brow raises. "Trouble?"

He nods. "It's all I had wanted that night. I needed blood on my knuckles. Something to curb the craving for violence I thought I was due to deal." His jaw clenches a little tighter at that, then he sighs almost as if amused. "I was only one ale deep when I saw this kid picking a fight with the wrong people. He was brazen—hurling taunts even as they circled him. Eight against one." Tariq clicks his tongue. "He was mad, but still, the kid wasn't backing down."

One of Savi's stories comes to mind and spreads a smirk across my face. "Let me guess," I offer. "He was a cocky little shit with a penchant for throwing knives?"

Tariq looses a deep rumbling laugh that warms my chest and almost staves off the night's chill. "Yes. Riat couldn't have been older than twenty, but he was just as sure of himself back then. Maybe more than he is now."

Tariq sets his mug down in the sand and crosses his arms over his chest. "*Hael above*, that boy has always been trouble," he admits. He shakes his head before loosing a heavy sigh. "So I'm watching these guys prepare to beat the gods out of Riat. I had no idea what the kid did, but I didn't care. All I saw was an opportunity to get my hands dirty, to unleash some of my rage before it devoured me whole. I wanted blood that night, and I wasn't leaving without it."

Tariq's gaze tightens, getting lost in memories. I can see the emotion swimming in his eyes—heavy and bright. Never have I seen such anguish from him, never did I think he harbored such things. How naive of me to expect to be the only one with burdens to carry.

Shame sours my stomach, and I pull my gaze away before his pain can snare my own.

"The moment I stepped into that circle and stood beside him, something changed," Tariq continues. He takes in a deep breath and lets it out slowly. "Riat froze. The kid turned ghost white, lost every ounce of bravado. Just stared at me."

I lean in closer, my arm bumping against his. "What do you mean he froze?" I balk. "I can't see Riat ever backing down from a fight."

"That's just it," Tariq whispers, shaking his head. "He wanted to fight, but he didn't want me to fight with him. Said he had what was coming to him, that he was going to get the snot kicked out of him and that was okay." Tariq swallows harshly, and I catch his lip wobble. "But he said I didn't deserve to go down with him, that just by stepping into that circle, I had proved I was a better man than him. A selfless man that put others before himself."

Tariq's jaw clicks, and as he sniffles softly, I'm overcome with the urge to comfort him. I should press my fingers against his arm, squeeze his shoulder if only to let him know I'm here. My hand shakes as I raise it, but doubt holds me back. I strangle the mug in my hands instead.

"I stayed by Riat," Tariq continues. "Fought side by side with him and made sure he left the tavern with no more than a scratch. I met Hassan the next morning, learned about their crew—about how they prided themselves on dealing some sort of justice across the godsforsaken Continent. It was then that I realized how far I'd strayed—that by fixating on revenge, I had been sullying the very name I was trying to honor in death."

Tariq pulls in a long, deep breath and finally turns toward me. There's a wet glimmer settled against his lash line, but he doesn't shy away from it. He looks me deep in the eyes and lets an honest smile drift across his face.

"The others helped me realize that violence solves nothing. It's a blight on the soul, a self-inflicted wound that never heals. The only way to shake that darkness off our backs is to forgive. No matter how much you wish to withhold it—no matter how badly it hurts to offer it to those who have harmed you and harm you still—nothing new grows in withering souls without forgiveness."

I open my mouth to speak, but he stops me.

"The forgiveness is not for them, Ren," he urges. He wraps his hand around where mine grasps the mug too tightly. "It's for you."

A flurry of emotions swarms my chest, each one deep and lasting. I blink back tears, feeling foolish for spilling so many of late, but Tariq offers no chiding remarks. He merely squeezes my hand and sits with me.

Time floats by uninterrupted, and the unspoken words between us brim with silent understanding. When Tariq finally lets go, I find the ache in my chest is almost bearable now. I fled the house desperate to still the chaos in my mind, and, somehow, Tariq did just that.

He stands up with a sigh and nudges my shoulder. "Time for bed," he prods. "The others have been setting up our tents around the bend. Riat was itching to share one with you, but I figured you'd prefer to bunk with your Mender friend." He pauses, lips pursing in thought. "Mikel, I think?"

He looks to me for an answer as I pry myself up from the sand. "Mikel and I shared a tent for two years," I say, an easy smile drifting across my face. "It'll be no trouble to do it again."

"Good." Tariq nods before taking the empty mug from my hands. "I'll take these back to the house. I figure it's too soon for that forgiveness we talked about."

I groan, embarrassment flooding my face as I shake my head. "Yes, thank you," I utter. "I'm afraid I would still be looking for blood if I stepped through that door."

I watch Tariq as he sets off, but soon find myself running across the sands to catch up to him. "Tariq. Wait."

The moment he turns around, I slam myself into his barreled chest. My arms latch around his large frame, holding him tight.

"Thank you" —I squeeze him once before letting go— "for your endless kindness."

For a moment, Tariq merely stares at me, struck speechless. But as a quiet smile slips into place, his expression grows almost amused. A blush warms my cheeks, forcing me to look away. If I'm not careful, I fear Mikel won't be the only one who's wiggled their way into my weak spots.

I offer Tariq a final nod, walking back on my heels. "Thanks again for the tea," I mumble, "and if it's any comfort, I think your aunt would be proud of the man you've become."

I turn before I can see the emotions overtake his face; there's been enough of that for one night. Instead, I saunter off toward camp, hopeful that, for once, tonight will offer a dreamless sleep.

CHAPTER 15

I pull the scarves tight to my face, obscuring everything but my eyes. The East Gate looms ahead, and its giant arch of red rocks reaches almost as high as the gorge beyond. Just like the monoliths in Letka, the entrance to this great place is carved in markings. I can't bear to look at them for fear I'll recognize something I'm not yet ready to. The last thing I need is to see the legend of my own blood carved into stone and made real. I shake out my hands, trying to release the tension that's plagued me all morning, but my unease isn't so easily shed.

Last night, Hassan and I had argued about my coming here. He said it was too dangerous—said he and Savi would collect whatever supplies I required, just as they promised to do for the others. But I wasn't satisfied, and I wouldn't take no for an answer. If anything, I escalated things until Hassan was forced to comply. Although, I still wonder how much my victory was given and not truly won. My blade was hardly the threat I'd hoped it to be. The small knife—the very one Hassan had lent me—was easily flicked out of my hands like a twig. It was only when I bluffed—telling Hassan I'd go ask the Shade to accompany me—that he conceded. I'd worn a pleased smirk to bed, but my delight was short-lived.

It was a fitful night's sleep—so full of tossing and turning that Mikel had thrown a cushion to demand my stillness. I was almost grateful for Savi's voice when it slipped into the tent much too early, yanking me from sleep's razored clutches. Though she'd managed to wake me before I dreamt of a certain Berserker, my luck proved fleeting. My morning was quickly ruined by another daemon I'd rather have forgotten, this one very much alive. When Mikel and I finally left our tent to find the others waiting, Malachi's gaze cut to me instantly like he'd been anticipating the very moment I showed my face. He stared silently, offering nothing but unwavering focus. Even as I'd saddled my camel for the short trip, I'd felt his attention like a touch. It slinked and prowled, robbing me of my breath until I remembered one unwavering truth. *I hate him.* I tried to return his ire—had glared over my shoulder to prove I meant everything I said last night—but was swiftly stripped of my courage. One look at those dark eyes proved to be too much too soon, and I'd had to turn away.

The three-hour trek to Hira has given me too much time to think—to stir in thoughts I know are better left untouched. It doesn't help that the Shade is never far away, and that his gaze always seems to find mine when I wish it not to. He hasn't said a word to me, though I don't know what I would want him to say. *Would an apology even help? Or would it merely kick me deeper into this pit of misery I've made a home in?* The thought of it now makes me sneer. He'd have to be begging on his knees for me to ever forgive him.

Though each step of this trip has wound my anxiety tighter, the morning has been relatively uneventful. When we made it to the South Wall—a mass of towering red sandstone that protects the southern edge of Hira—we left our animals and continued on foot. We weren't the only ones. The stable was more than half full by the time we departed—a raucous place I was more than happy to leave behind quickly. I knew it was a bad sign then, and staring at the city walls before me now, I'm only proven right.

It's packed. Time seems to move too slowly and my feet too quickly. Bodies flank our path, brushing past on hurried legs and conversing in eager tones. Savi told me it was Sithtí—one of the many days dedicated to Hael. It's a blessed day. A day promising prosperity and good trade. As I look across the crowds slipping into the city before us, I suddenly wish I hadn't come. Today feels like anything but a blessing.

The back of my neck grows hot and clammy as I stare at the bodies flooding the East Gate. There's too many people. My palms start to sweat. Each breath feels like it's lodged in my throat. My fingers brush against the hilt of my only blade, but it doesn't soothe me. If anything, it serves as a taunt.

As my eyes take in the city's entrance, my heart beats a little faster. The arch is like a portal to another world, a massive thing that casts shadows across the ground that's been trampled by too many boots. The closer I get, the more its markings come into view. It's a mass of flaring lines and roughly chiseled circles. They bleed into each other, weaving a story I don't want to know. Torch's marks give way to Seer's. When I spot the chaotic flurry depicting a Shade, I drop my eyes to the earth. Though I try to ignore it, the blood in my veins hums a little louder now. My shadows beg for release, but, more than that, I fear it's acknowledgment they so desperately crave. I squeeze my fists tight—strangling every instinct that tells me this denial is wrong—and lock my gift away.

It's only when someone slams into my shoulder that I remember where I am. My gaze snaps up, and I instantly reach for my blade. Hira is no place to cower in pity and shame. It will surely break me just as Denheir did if I let it. Nothing good happens in the cities.

When I deem no one around me to be a threat, I slowly release the grip on my knife. Luckily, my skittishness has gone unnoticed. It seems everyone is much too busy bustling about in their own frenzy to care. My boots scrape the hard-packed earth as I slow my pace. It stirs up the sands that have been brought over from the Jahaer by years of wind. Each grain beneath my feet is an odious reminder that—though the desert is only half a day's ride from here—its vastness is far out of reach.

I swallow my fears and trek forward. The East Gate looms overhead now, and red dust trickles from its high crevices. Its presence is as stifling as it is beautiful. The rock has withstood the test of time and the Rebellion's fire. I see varying shades of natural red that couldn't be copied by even the most talented of rug makers. As I gaze up at the arch, observing how the sun shines across it in dazzling glory, I can't help but feel like Hael is looking down on us. The peace I find in that thought is fleeting, however, for the god of knowledge is not as benevolent as people believe.

The moment I step through the gate, the nervous flutter in my gut returns. It's even more overwhelming than it appeared on the horizon yesterday. Hira is a living beast, an imposing thing sculpted by Hael's very hand. Buildings seem to be carved from every towering rock and into every inch of canyon wall. Red rock mixes with sun-bleached stone, blanketing the city in a symphony of contrasting hues. Woven tapestries drape across alleys, shading market stalls from the hot desert sun. And bodies—everywhere there are bodies. Eyes trail over me curiously. Hands accidentally brush me as they pass. I ignore the flicker of panic in my chest and look deeper into the city. The sight has me forgetting the crowd I've found myself trapped among.

Buildings jut out from the most northern point of the great gorge—their impressive structures reminiscent of what the Continent could have boasted if the Rebellion hadn't thrust it into turmoil. There are endless passageways carved into the canyon walls, some spiraling up into great towers to crown this city. As I squint against the sun's glare, I see people passing through those shaded archways, carrying woven baskets and guiding donkeys up winding paths. Hira is beautiful, but beautiful things are often deadly.

My eyes scan for threats as we weave through the crowds. Shops line the streets, as do many faces. Blacksmiths. Butchers. Inn keepers. Travelers. My skin prickles as I catch sight of a crop of fiery, red hair. It catches the sun's light like a warning flare. I stop where I am, frozen to the clay-baked earth when a gentle touch splays across my elbow.

"What is it?" Mikel asks.

I open my mouth, unable to form any words. My blood thrums nervously, increasing the pace of my heart. But as the crowds part, I find that those fiery locks don't belong to the man I fear meeting again, but instead to an anxious teenager. I watch him dodge carts and brush past merchants, brow furrowed in concentration. He navigates the masses with a crate of metal scraps tucked under his arm, determined in his haste. A breath of relief spills from my lungs, and I shake myself free of the threats that still haunt me.

"Nothing," I utter to Mikel. "Let's go."

I can't help but sweep my gaze every which way as I follow the others deep into the city. We pass older women playing maváti under canopies as they're served plum wine. Men lean against alleyways and talk in hushed tones in between puffs of smoke. People pack the streets, bartering for goods and selling their wares. But it's the boisterous thunder of an auction that snares my focus and has my steps faltering.

The stone platform is set high above the crowd. A thing said to once be used for daily calls to prayer now boasts a red-faced man as he yells down to buyers and prods their purchases forward. The breath is yanked from my lungs with calloused hands as I watch a young man shuffle along, body battered and chains heavying his steps. I bear witness to a fate I once thought would be mine and grow sick at the sight. Men yell out bids, placing a finite value on a life that should be priceless. They speak of him not as a man, but as an investment. Muscles lean and good for labor. Broken enough to not cause a fuss. I take it all in, my teeth gritting like a mindless beast. That thrum in my blood grows unruly and charged, like it, too, seeks a terrible reckoning. But it's when that gavel strikes and the young man is declared sold that my control snaps.

I'm barreling through the crowd without a second thought, shouldering people out of my way. My veins are itching—practically burning with the fury I wish to unleash. Memories I'd thought lost to time burst to the forefront like a blast of fire.

A hit to the head in the dead of night.
Waking up to find my hands bound and my mouth gagged.
Days of travel in the wrong direction.

I stop my mind from delving deeper, fearful of what I might find if I prod further. There's only one moment I wish to relive. The memory of his blood coating my hands tunnels my vision and hastens my steps. I'm eager for what comes next, but before I can shove my way to the front of the slaver's auction and kill all those who deal in flesh, I'm yanked back by firm hands.

I have my knife drawn when I spin, though quickly falter when I meet Hassan's gaze. His jaw is clenched tight as he begins to pull me away from the crowd. I thrash, shouting at him to let me go. Hassan doesn't hesitate, simply tugs me closer with an unwavering grip. I want to scream, but his eyes hold a silent fury that stills my tongue.

He looks at the auction behind me, jaw ticking. "Not today," he utters. "But one day. I promise you that."

My brow furrows as I detect the barely restrained rage marring his face, but it's there, and it matches mine. I swallow thickly, reigning in urges I know will only prove to be reckless. He's right. With the city bustling and my face plastered on parchment, today is not the day to settle old grudges.

I don't look back. One mere glance would surely persuade me to soak this market in blood. All I can do is dig my nails into my palm as I rejoin the others and hope that day Hassan speaks of is closer than I believe.

I keep my head down as we follow the crowds through Hira's packed streets. Donkey-led carts cut across our path, their rickety wheels bouncing against the rough earth and billowing dust in my face. I stifle a cough and am instantly hit with the smoky scent of roasting meat. It's only a moment later, when we cut down a side street, that I'm bombarded by the stench of urine. I gag and hold my breath. The alley opens up to reveal more bodies. More noises. More smells. A woman bumps into me as an infant screams in her arms. Ale drifts out from a nearby tavern. Voices chatter. Gold passes hands. It's choreographed chaos—an overwhelming flutter of sights and sounds that has my fingers hovering against the hilt of my knife. Only when we make our way into a clearing deep inside the city do I finally let my tightly bound shoulders drop an inch and find that I can breathe again.

The others begin their chatter, posing arguments and devising plans, but it lands far from my ears. I'm drifting away, far too intrigued by this place we've found ourselves in. My brow furrows as I take in the heart of this great city. It's calm, peaceful even. At its center is a large water fountain, nearly fifty paces wide, with smooth cream-colored sandstone that's worn with age. Thick walls rest hip-high and protect the outer ring—a shallow pool that fills as people crank one of the numerous hand pumps spanning the rim. Women dunk buckets into the welled water before perching them on shoulders and atop heads. A few children laugh as they weave between their mother's legs, only to dash away at the mere threat of a scolding. I catch a glimpse of a golden-haired boy just before he dips his small hand into the tepid waters, splashing those around him. He's quickly thwarted by an elderly woman who snatches his hand and tugs him away kicking and screaming.

The chaos settles back into a rhythmic lull of flowing water and babbling voices soon enough. I take a few steps forward, curiosity getting the best of me. It's been years since I've been in a city like this—a true hub of the Continent. And even more since I've allowed myself a still moment in one.

I let my fingers skim across the water's surface before my focus snags on what lies beyond. No more than an arm's length away rests the fountain's inner ring, though this one is no mere shallow pool. As I lean across the edge, an abyss opens up before me. The stone-carved well plunges deep into the earth, to where the water flows freely. It's the kind of depth I doubt even a stone's throw would calculate. A shiver ripples up my spine as I stare down into its gaping maw for a moment longer before pulling away.

As I turn to face my companions, irritation flares sharply across my face. Six of us have come to the city today, though I would have been happy to lose a few somewhere along the way.

Malachi and Quin have been inseparable since we left the house. Always close by. Always whispering to each other. Even now, the petite woman beams a sunny smile up at him while babbling on about gods know what. Her muted yellow dress, much like the one she wore yesterday, laces across her torso and cinches her tiny waist in tightly. The sleeveless garment reveals the intricate Weaver markings that grace her left hand and trail up her arm.

My lip twitches as I attempt to hold back the scorn I feel. I'm covered in so many swathes of fabric that you barely see a sliver of skin. Though my brown tunic molds to my body, draping just below the waist of my pants, the long sleeves cover every inch of flesh and the scars that now identify me so easily. I've layered not one, but two scarves to conceal my face. To anyone passing by, I'm unknown and unimportant—nothing but a faceless wanderer.

But her...

I grit my teeth as I grant myself another spiteful glance at Quin. She wears her marks without hesitation, showing the world just who and what she is. Bitterness swirls in my stomach like a freshly culled poison. Just when I think my jealousy is only for the simple freedoms she's been given in this life, the gods prove me wrong.

Quin wraps her hand around Malachi's arm, patting the muscle as she presses her ruddy cheek against him. Her words are lost on me, but I don't miss the hopeful glint in her eyes. The sight stirs something more than foul in me—something that would make the gods themselves cringe. I study what I see for too long. The way she smiles up at him. The way he sighs and shakes his head before a smirk graces his face. It's too much to bear with restraint and composure. The wounds of finally seeing him after all these years—and wrapped around someone else no less—are far too fresh. I look away before my pain can fester, but not before I'm caught.

As Malachi's eyes lock onto mine, they lose their playful gleam. Quin continues talking, but Malachi's focus is far from her chittering words. He watches me silently, eating up every flicker of emotion I know my face gives away. That dark gaze sharpens and burns into me with the same heartlessness I witnessed last night.

He doesn't care about me? Fine. He'll see just how little I care about him, too.

I stare at him like I want the gods to smite him from this very earth. And, by all that is true, I do. Maybe if I start praying to Veles, the vengeful one might grant my request.

I tense as Malachi's gaze shifts. It sweeps down my body, gliding over my tunic and down to my hips. My heart beats a little faster, and I curse the treacherous feeling one mere glance brings. His eyes linger far too many places for far too long before slowly rising. When his gaze finds mine again, I can't help but shiver. The cold indifference has left his face, and in its place is a heat that threatens to melt me more than the sun ever could. Suddenly, there's a flush on my cheeks—one I tell myself anger put there no matter how much my body says otherwise. I roll my eyes at Malachi before turning my back on him.

Fuck it all to one of the hells.

I brace my arms against the fountain's rim and watch as small ripples disturb the peaceful surface. As I dip my fingers into the water, those ripples sway, then strengthen. It doesn't soothe me, and it's not nearly enough. I swat my hand against the surface, sending water sloshing over the edge. The sound lulls my temper, but not as much as I hoped. As I watch the turbulence I caused spread, it's helplessness I feel when I only sought control.

My eyes focus and unfocus, taking in everything and nothing at the same time. The daze of it calms me, stills me in a way that lets all else fade. Though the day grows hotter with each breath, I embrace the prickle of heat against my clothes. I close my eyes and imagine it's Hael himself reaching out to me, offering a healing I don't deserve. Each scorch of heat from the god of all-that-is-good chases away the darkness inside, at least for a moment. I pretend the dread is gone, that the lingering fear that has coated my bones for far too long has been plucked away like an errant piece of straw. But when the hairs on the back of my neck stand on edge, I know there's no escaping the fate I've been dealt.

Every part of my body is ripped awake and made alert to the presence at my back. There's a slight tremble in my hands, a charged anticipation. My jaw clenches, but I refuse to open my eyes—not even when that presence settles next to me. If they were going to kill me, they would have done so by now.

As the silence beats on, my agitation rises. "What do you want?" I finally utter.

I recognize the grumpy rumble of his voice the moment it leaves his lips.

"It's time to go. We only have a few hours at the markets before we need to head back."

"Okay." I don't so much as offer a glance his way. "I'll meet you back here before the sun meets its high," I chide. "I'm sure I can manage on my own. I have been in a city before, you know."

Silence eats away the space between us, growing more unsettled the longer Hassan stays by my side.

"We decided it's best if you come with one of us," he says, his voice almost strained. "With the bounty, it's not safe for you to be alone."

I tilt my head and peer up at him from the corner of my eye. "Who decided?" I challenge.

Hassan lets out a sigh and ignores my question entirely. "Savi, Mikel, and I are going to the steel markets, then the spice bazaar." His mouth contorts into a grimace before he glances over his shoulder. "The other two wouldn't tell me where they were going, but he made it clear the invitation extended to you."

I turn around to find Malachi's gaze fixed on me once more. Anger flares in me like torturous flames I can't seem to escape.

"And remind me why I have to go with any of you?" I prod Hassan.

I know I've pushed my luck when he presses himself into my personal space, hip bumping against my waist.

"Because you will not be taken again," Hassan grits out, tone scathing. "I will not be forced to witness what I did in Letka ever again, especially not because of your own bullheadedness."

My lip twitches with a fury I know I should contain—a fury I know is misplaced on him. But I'm in no mood to restrain myself. "Silas didn't take me," I offer snidely. "I chose to leave. And you let me."

His eyes bore into mine as he presses even closer. "Keep reminding me of my mistakes, witch," Hassan grits out. "I will gladly take the cut of your words if it keeps you safely by my side."

Something wicked stirs low in my stomach at the admission. He's so close I can feel the heat radiating off of him. Though I shouldn't, I find myself yearning to let it burn me. I drop my gaze before I can do something so foolish.

"Where did you say you were going again? The steel markets?" I clear my throat and give him a casual shrug. "I do need new blades."

When I finally look up at him, there's a hint of surprise dancing in his hazel eyes. He nods slowly, focus still fixed intently upon me.

"Come on then," he says, gesturing toward the others. "Maybe you'll finally find a dagger that can hold its own against me."

I spin to face him. "Surely you can't be serious?"

As we walk through the city square, I shove him teasingly. "I'll have you remember you almost woke up in the underworld because of me." I raise a brow at him. "Or did you forget that it was only because of your cousin that my blade didn't pierce your heart?"

Hassan crosses his arms over his chest as we reach the others. "Come now, witch," he taunts. "You and I both know that dagger was never going anywhere near my heart." He leans in close, this conversation only for us. "For who would keep that smart mouth of yours in check if not for me?"

My heart stutters as I take in the glint in his eyes—a playfulness that feels as foreign as it does welcoming. I know I should spit a retort back at him, tell him just how badly I wanted to kill him that day, but for some reason I can't. My tongue is tied as I stare at him—at the man who's had my blood boiling since the moment I met him. I search myself for the loathing I once felt so clearly, but the absence of it only unsettles me more.

"We need to get moving."

Malachi's rough voice drags me back to the world and rekindles the hate I was so desperate to feel for another. I glare at the empty space next him, not even bothering to meet his waiting gaze.

"Fine," I quip. "*We* are." I turn to Savi. "How far are the steel markets?"

Her face lights up, but before she can answer me, Malachi steps in between us.

"You don't need to go with them," he states. "You'll surely find better company with us." I don't miss the way his lip twitches as he casts a scathing glance at the man next to me, nor the way Hassan bristles at my side. "Come with Quin and I," Malachi continues. "There's somewhere we're going I think you'll find of interest."

He leans in close, dropping his voice to a whisper that was once so tempting. "There was a time when all we did was dream of this place, of how we would make it our home..." His shadows slink around my wrist, drawing soothing circles. "Just give me this. We have years to make up for, after all."

I snatch myself away from his shadow's touch. "And whose fault is that?" I snap. "Because it surely wasn't me who sacrificed the last decade together."

"*Enough*, Serehna," he sighs. "You can yell at me all you'd like as I give you a tour of the city. Don't let this—"

"I meant what I said last night, Shade," I bite. "*Stay. Away. From. Me.* We might be on the same side now, but I spent many years wishing to spill your blood." As I look Malachi up and down, just as he did to me earlier, I make sure he sees nothing but hate in my eyes. "So much as give me the chance, and I'll be happy to take it."

His jaw ticks as he regards me. Tension purses his lips as if he's holding back what he wishes to say.

I don't give him the chance to utter another word. "Savi," I call gruffly. "Which way?"

She shoots me a hesitant smile, eyes darting between Malachi and I. "Steel markets are due west," she states.

My eyes follow the direction of her outstretched hand. Across the fountain is a maze of alleyways and corridors. I'm walking toward it before anyone can stop me. Though I hear Malachi mumble under his breath, I keep walking. Even when I hear the distance babble of Quin's singsongy voice, I ignore it. She's probably grateful I declined the invitation to join them. More alone time for her and *him*. I sneer as my boots stomp across the square.

Mikel is quick to catch up to me, sliding his arm through mine. "*Damn me to the depths*, Ren," he chuckles. "You never told me the asshole I vowed to hate in your honor was so attractive." He twists around to get what I know is one last look at the traitorous Shade. "*Hael give you strength.* I don't know how you're going to stay away." Mikel looses a shrill whistle before pressing in closer. "If for old time's sake you end up in his bed, I won't fault you," he whispers in my ear.

Gods, he knows too much. I should regret all of those late nights spent by the fire with him and a jug of wine. He knows all of my secrets—even the ones I wished to never share.

"There will be none of that," I retort, shrugging him off. "The Shade is as good as dead to me. Besides, it looks like he already has someone to warm his bed."

I grind my teeth a little too hard as I think about Quin's dainty fingers laced around Malachi's arm.

"Oh, please." Mikel snorts. "That little thing?" He drapes his arm across my shoulder and pulls me in close. "Trust me, she's not who you need to worry about."

I roll my eyes, but the thought nags me. Though I wish to stop it, it's not long before my tongue reveals my interest. "And who should I be worried about then?" I prod.

Mikel sighs as he spins us around to face the way we came. The market street we've wandered down is bustling, full of vendors and people bumping their way through the masses. Though it's a blur of bodies, it only takes me a moment to spot Hassan and Savi. Their tall, muscle-lined figures stand out among the crowds, and the distance others grant them allows the pair to easily maneuver through the busy street. My mouth quirks when I notice the bright smile on Savi's face as she admires the wares in passing stalls. Hassan, however, looks like he's on a job rather than out for a market stroll. I'm surprised he hasn't drawn a weapon with how murderous his gaze looks.

"What did you say you called him when you first met?" Mikel tries to stifle his laugh. "An ornery old goat?"

Again, I regret telling him so much.

I glare at Mikel from the corner of my eye. "What's your point?"

His eyes sparkle dangerously as he tugs me closer, whispering in my ear. "Well that goat looked like he was ready to kill your Shade after you ran off last night."

As I pull back to get a better look at Mikel, he grins like a fiend and waggles his brows.

"I think I heard him mumble something to the older one, the Seeker—"

"Vish," I correct.

"Yeah, yeah, that guy," Mikel says, waving me off with his hand. "Your grumpy old goat said something about having trusted a Veles daemon with you before." Mikel grins, looking all too pleased with himself. "Said he'll be damned if he does it again."

I scoff and push him away from me. "You do realize that *I'm* a Veles daemon now, don't you?"

Mikel shoots me a pointed look and crosses his arms over his chest. "You know damn well he wasn't talking about you." He leans in again, dropping his voice just as Hassan and Savi join us. "All I'm saying is, even if that little sprite wants to keep you away from the Shade's bed, she's not the only one."

Just as I open my mouth to disagree, our privacy is lost. Savi shoots me a warm smile as she comes to stand in front of us, and I swear I see something weighing down her canvas bag. How she's already found time to shop, I don't know, but judging by the delight on her face, I'm sure it'll be the first of many purchases today.

Hassan looms over her shoulder—decked in dark-colored scarves and leveling a gaze that promises violence. His eyes flicker across the crowds as if he expects some merchant to stab me with a blade at a moment's notice. It should annoy me, but my mouth quirks up into a smirk before I can stop myself.

"Steel markets lie just around that bend," Savi states, pointing to a wall of hanging tapestries that sways as shoulders bump past.

My throat grows tight as I realize the calm pause I found by the fountain has long departed. Here in the market streets, people shuffle through the crowds too quickly, offering muttered apologies and insults as they push their way through. I nod toward the chaos, urging Savi to take the lead. As she melts into the crowd, Hassan lingers. His gaze continues to scour the street like threats lurk under every hood. I try to brush it off, rolling my eyes as I tug Mikel forward, but I can't shake the unnerved feeling that creeps up on me.

Does Hassan feel what I've felt all morning? That impending dread on the back of his neck?

I grit my teeth and force my eyes away from the hunter. "Come on." I prod Mikel. "Let's get my blades and be done with this place."

CHAPTER 16

The crowd seems to thicken as we turn down the next alleyway. Bodies press in, shoving their way through the tightly packed passage before ducking into shops and side streets. Savi's head weaves in and out above the barrage, disappearing briefly only to return further ahead than before.

I quicken my steps, but there's only so fast I can press through the swarm. The path before me is choked like a stifled breath. People push past with inconsiderate haste, too careless to even offer a backward glance. A man rushes by with an arm full of crates, stacked too high for anyone's good. I barely have time to stagger sideways before someone bumps into him, sending the whole heap crashing to the ground. Curses rip through the street. Fists are raised without follow-through, and faces turn red amidst threats and belittlements. No sooner does the bedlam begin than is it lost to higher tides.

Hira is a bustling beast, and it has better things to do than ease squabbles. The two men move along, bitter and grumbling.

The street returns to a rush of disorder once more. When I finally turn away, I realize too late that I can no longer spot Savi's scar peeking through the top of the crowds. Fear is a timid prickle in my chest. I'm stretching up onto the toes of my boots, desperate for a glimpse, when chaos greets me like a vengeful friend.

Someone slams into my side, sending me staggering off course. The crowd swallows me, and, suddenly, my sense of direction is as muddied as the ground beneath my boots. My heart rate kicks up, pounding viciously in my chest as I realize I've not only lost Savi, but Mikel, too.

One person bumps into me, then another. The raucous buzz of voices fills my eardrums until it's all just senseless noise. A man shoves past, dragging a hand across my waist before manhandling me out of his way. I lurch, reeling backward before stumbling into another overly warm body. Panic eats me like a starved man. My breath turns shallow and strained. Every unintended touch and lick of hot breath drags me further into the spiraling dark of my mind.

I'm being paraded through the market in Denheir.
I'm twelve years old being circled by men in Artolen.
I'm bleeding out at the feet of a Turiden in that alley.

Sweat slides down my neck. I claw my way through the crowds, desperate to be free of this place. As I shove my way toward the bend up ahead, searching for escape, heat descends on me like a blanket. Where one street ends, another begins. I can smell soot, taste the acidic twang of hot metal on my tongue. Fire flares around me as men sweat over forges and hammer iron into blades. The brutal sound of metal striking metal rings in my ears and makes my teeth grit. I dash forward through a break in the crowds, spying the only solace the gods provide. A small fissure in the wall-lined street provides me a moment's refuge as people trample past.

I tuck myself against the sandstone, burrowing myself deep enough to breathe in its earthy dust. I rip away the scarves covering my face and suck in lungful after lungful of that stale air. Each inhale feels like a gift. My breath is erratic; my heart thumps so loudly it floods my ears. The thrum of my blood is there, too, summoned like a beast ready to hunt. I keep it chained the only way I know how.

My fingernails rake down the rough stone, breaking against the pressure. I taste blood as my teeth chomp into the tender flesh of my cheek. I tense every muscle, ground myself into every sting of pain, until finally, the violent thrum within me ebbs and flows back to its natural state. It's muted, but ever-present— always lurking.

As I come back to myself, I realize I'm not alone. The hairs on the back of my neck stand up. This time, I know who it is. His presence is one I'm beginning to recognize all too well.

I peer over my shoulder, eyes wide and dilated like a trapped animal's. Hassan says nothing; he doesn't even look my way. He's standing with his back to me, as rigid as stone. It takes me a moment to realize what he's doing, and when I do, my throat aches with emotions I'd rather not feel. He's sheltering me here in this nook. *Protecting me.* Mere paces away, there's an endless current of bodies squeezing their way through the street, but they don't touch me. They couldn't get to me if they tried. Hassan's arms are folded tightly across his chest, and his head swivels back and forth as he assesses everyone with a critical eye. He stares down those who get too close and bristles until they get far enough away to no longer warrant his gaze. It happens again and again, his tension never settling.

My brow furrows as I watch him. It's like he can feel my attention because all too soon his gaze snaps to mine. Still, he says nothing. He doesn't berate me for losing the others or chide me for my weakness. He simply looks at me, and I feel too small under his stare. The depth in his eyes—the sheer force of it—makes it seem like he knows every hysterical thought that plagued me moments ago, like he felt every panicked breath I took. I quickly fix my scarves back into place, hiding myself from him the only way I can. It doesn't help to quell how raw I now feel in his presence.

"Savi and your friend are just up the street." He offers it casually, like he didn't just witness me break.

I swallow harshly, trying to find my voice. "Let's go, then."

As soon as I take a step forward, he barrels out into the busy street. I try to steady my breathing, preparing for the worst, but the chaos that overwhelmed me before doesn't even graze me now. Hassan acts as a shield, tucking me to his side without touching me, using his strong arms to part the way when the masses get too close. The instinct to snap at him flares hot in my chest. I didn't ask for his protection. I don't need it. I tell myself this again and again as we move through the crowd undisturbed. But no matter how hot my shame burns, I can't find the right words. I merely follow, allowing myself to be safeguarded like something worth protecting.

For the briefest of moments, I feel a light pressure against my lower back. The touch is startling, quickening my heart with a familiar anxiety. I jolt, but the touch lingers, guiding me to the right with the steady press of fingers.

"Just a little further," Hassan whispers in my ear, breath hot against my scarves.

I swallow my panic down, though my heart keeps its erratic pace. Hassan stays close, prodding me down the street with a patience that almost suits him. For a moment, the city doesn't seem to be barreling down on me. I take a steadying breath, clearing my mind of the last lick of nerves.

Has the street widened? Have the crowds scattered?

When I look around to see that none of the chaos has waned, fear of a different sort fills the pit of my stomach. The city is as frantic as it was moments before, but, somehow, the presence at my side makes it bearable. My gaze wanders up to Hassan, trepidation weaving its way through my chest. This feels foolish, and yet I stay close.

As we reach the others, Hassan pulls away. The loss is sudden—bittersweet for reasons I don't care to admit. Savi shoots us a carefree smile while Mikel's face holds a mischief I know all too well. It's damning, reminding me why certain things are best left ignored. Mikel's eyes roam over Hassan, no doubt observing how close the hunter is still standing to me. I shoot my friend a heated look, silently cursing him to mind his business. He opens his mouth to tease me, but Savi's voice breaks the tension before he can.

"Lorik is an old friend," she offers before stepping up to the threshold before us. "He'll be sure to fit you with whatever you need."

I linger for a breath, but Hassan's impatient grunt has me pressing forward—abandoning all hesitation. My gaze sweeps high as we pass through the stone doorway. Though it looks small from the outside, the interior of the shop is anything but. Cut from one of the many red rock formations that stretch out through the west of the city, entering this place feels like stepping into another world. Rock walls paint the shop in rich, red hues, as vibrant and varied as the city gates. Earthy musk mixes with iron and heat, filling the space with a pungent twang. The ceiling arches far overhead, and sunlight spills in through high-cut windows that cast the room in heavenly light.

As my feet carry me further inside, I'm mesmerized by what I find. A worktable spans the entirety of one wall, its metal surface littered with tools, scraps of metal, and raw cut gemstones. I step around a rack of weapons, their newly polished blades gleaming against the stretching beams of light that slip inside the cavernous room. I can't help but run my fingers along a large dagger whose blade shines almost white. The intricately carved weapon is cold to the touch, and my eyes widen as I catch sight of the design that's wrapped around the hilt and inlaid with black stones. My blood hums contently as I realize the carving is of a vitremi.

Mikel whistles in appreciation as he steps up beside me. "Leave it to you to find the most extravagant blade in this place."

I roll my eyes and shove him away from where he's all but breathing down my neck. "I like my blades pretty," I admit with a smirk. "Makes it even more satisfying when I scar some poor bastard with it."

I give the weapon one last, lingering touch before stepping deeper into the shop.

Twin forges blaze hot in the center of the room. Next to them stands a large, burly man with sweat beading across his shaved head. He sets a smelting pot inside the fiery inferno, and I watch for the briefest of moments as the tips of his metal tongs burn brighter than the sun on its hottest day.

The man discards his tools and tosses aside thick gloves before turning toward us. The smile on Savi's face is nothing compared to his own. His sturdy frame sways like a great tree as he limps across the room.

"Savíana," he bellows before pulling Savi into a bear hug that all but swallows her whole. His callused hands squeeze her tightly, garnering a breathy laugh from Savi as she squeezes him back just as hard.

"It's been too long," she admits.

The man kisses the shaved side of Savi's head before pulling away to hold her at arm's length. He looks her up and down like an overprotective father searching for something as small as a scrapped knee. When he spots the Torch's scar, his forehead wrinkles with concern.

He sighs deeply and gives her a knowing look. "I thought I told you to stay out of trouble."

Savi looses an easy laugh as she pats his shoulder. "It was worth it. Trust me." She looks over her shoulder, sending me a wink before turning back toward the older man. "Lorik, I brought some friends," Savi states, wrapping her arm around his. "And we need the good stuff."

He raises a brow at that. "And what makes you think I'd give you anything but the best this shop has to offer?"

Savi's resulting smile drives a rumbling chuckle from Lorik's throat. "What do you need, kid?"

"First things first," Savi states. "Introductions." She pats Lorik's arm before turning her attention back on us. "This is Mikel" —she gestures across the room—"he's a Mender and a damn good one at that."

Lorik's gaze flickers to Mikel. "A pleasure," he offers, nodding with a reverence that shocks my friend—and me. His eyes then drop to Mikel's waist and the lone dagger that rests there. "Hm," Lorik hums, canting his head to the right.

He saunters over, bringing Savi along with him. The closer he gets, the more I find myself tensing. If not for Savi's beaming smile, my fingers would be twitching for a blade right about now.

Lorik clicks his tongue as he comes to rest in front of Mikel and I. "Mind if I take a look?"

Mikel shrugs. He takes his time unsheathing the dagger, handling his most prized—and only—weapon with the utmost of care. When he places it in Lorik's waiting palm, the blacksmith's eyes shine happily.

"She's a beaut," he mumbles, turning the blade over in his hands. His scarred thumb strokes the tip of the blade, and a content hum sounds from his lips as it pricks him. "Well taken care of, too."

He hands the dagger back with an appreciative nod. "What are you in the market for?" he asks. "I just finished a new falchion that would pair nicely with that. Give you more reach if you're not looking to get close enough for a clean shave."

Mikel laughs, but shakes his head. "This old dagger suits me just fine," he assures. "Besides, I'm not the one who draws a weapon if someone so much as breathes in her direction."

As Mikel's eyes slide to me, I scoff and cross my arms over my chest. "That was one time, and the bastard had just downed a whole pint and a dish of kippered kulpi. I was one more inhale away from passing out due to the stench."

When I look back at Lorik, the man's eyes are locked on me curiously. He stares at my face—at the swathes of fabric that keep it hidden. His eyes are a vibrant shade of amber, deeper in tone than my own with flecks of red. He's Hassan's height, though his large frame makes him seem twice as big. My gaze flickers across him quickly. His hands are covered in various scars and burns, and one of his pinkies is missing. The white sleeveless tunic he wears is stained with soot, soaked in sweat, and stretches taut across his stocky stomach. His hair is shaved to the scalp and his face is peppered with thick stubble like he hasn't shaved in a few days. My eyes slide to his belt, searching every loop and holster fitted to his soot-stained trousers. He wears no weapons. *But why would he when he has the entire room at his disposal?*

As I raise my gaze, I realize he's sizing me up, just as I did him. Though, all he has to take in are my clothes—the wear and use they've gotten over the years. His focus hovers on the leather sheathes Kora helped me sew long ago, all empty except for the small knife Hassan lent me. My fingers tingle for the blade, though I make no move for it. I keep my gaze sharp as Lorik watches me, each of us looking for the slightest tell. As his eyes make their way back to mine, I see a flicker of challenge there.

"A fighter with only one blade and nothing to show the world other than the violence in her eyes."

I flare my gaze dangerously, just to prove his point. He smirks, then chuckles as he turns to Savi. "You've brought the trouble with you it seems."

She shoves him playfully. "Lorik, this is Ren. My *friend.*" Savi glares pointedly, leveling a look at him that I've seen her send Hassan's way a thousand times. "You'd best treat her as such," she teases.

"A friend, ay? She must be a special one for you to bring her here."

Lorik waits for her to say more, but Savi's lips simply pull into a thin line. Her gaze flickers to me, eyes raking over where the columns of my markings are covered. I can all but feel my blood thrumming at the attention.

Savi clears her throat and offers Lorik a casual, but strained smile. "She'll be needing some daggers to replace the ones she lost."

"Lots of them," I say gruffly.

Lorik raises a brow as his gaze snakes back to me. "Is that so?" The burly man steps in close, invading my personal space in a way that has my nerves buzzing. "You know, I don't usually do dealings with anyone who hides behind a mask..." He crosses his arms over his chest and looks down his hooked nose at me. "Keeps me from doing business with those I ought not be."

"I'll vouch for her," Hassan bites, stepping up to Lorik. "It's not like she came blazing in here covered in blood like some of your other customers." Hassan's upper lip twitches as he sneers at the man. "Money is money after all."

Savi lets out a deep sigh and shakes her head. "Lorik, you remember my cousin."

The older man levels a stern gaze at Hassan. "Still without manners, I see." He *tsks*. "You always were an irritable bastard."

A cackling laugh leaps from my throat before I can stop it. Just as my hand slaps my mouth to cover the noise, Lorik raises a brow in my direction.

I cross my arms over my chest and stare right back. "So, are you still pretending to give us a hard time, or can I buy some damn blades?"

A slow grin creeps across Lorik's face before his own laugh jumps across the room. He turns to Savi and gives her chin an affectionate tug. "Never a dull moment with you in my shop, Savíana." He lets out a rumbling chuckle and beckons us back behind the forges. "I've been working on a few things I think you may find interesting. Tell me what threats await you, and I'll be sure to supply you with what you need to meet every sunset unscathed."

As we wander to the back of the cavernous room, the glint of metal catches wayward sunbeams, sparkling like stars. Longswords rest on wooden racks. Daggers lay on tables and sit in leather sheathes. I spot axes, chains, throwing knives, and even glimpse a few shields leaning against the back wall. Though the prospect of replacing my daggers is more than appealing, I find myself hesitating as I scan the rest of the room.

Two large stone statues overlook the space, carved from the very rock this shop was built from. Brightly woven tapestries hang behind the sculpted forms, creating a lush backdrop for what I know is an altar. The moment my eyes meet the stone faces, I avert my gaze to the floor. The thrum of my blood pounds faster, heavier. Mikel and Savi's voices fill the room, bouncing off the stone walls and echoing into the faraway ceiling. But soon, everything but the altar is lost to the haze of my mind.

I step closer, fingers tapping nervously against my leg. My marks itch, though I know it's nothing but anxiety chewing me from the inside out. Still, I keep my gaze locked on the floor as I move, unsure how far I've gone until a stone foot slips into view. I stop and let breath fill my lungs in a slow, methodical inhalation. It does nothing to keep my trepidation at bay. Candles flicker in my peripheral vision, but I don't dare look up—not yet.

I try to find reverence in my heart, but all I can feel is a simmering discontent. The more I stare at the feet of the gods that have caused me so much suffering, the more anger constricts my chest like a snake taunting its prey. Frustrated tears prick my eyes as I finally manage to raise my gaze. If the gods are truly watching me from these effigies, then it will be hate they see.

With a harsh swallow, I stare at Hael. Just like in the Book, his statue depicts him as a tall, powerful man. His beard is short and trimmed, outlining his wide jaw. His robes are cinched at the waist with an ornate rope and flow to the floor with eminent grace. Something tightens in my chest as I stare at his left hand—or really, where his left hand should be. The limb is cleaved at the wrist, severed cleanly. My stomach rolls uneasily as I think about what it would feel like to cut off your own hand.

A shiver racks my body, then turns to a full shudder as my eyes sweep left. *Veles.* Though he rests deep under my feet, far in the underworld where his brother banished him, it's as though I can feel his energy radiating off this stone. His robes have no sleeves, leaving his arms bare, though they're anything but. Markings cover every inch of the statue's skin. The intricately carved marks wrap around his defined biceps and the corded muscle of his forearms.

And his hands...

Gone. Cleaved by his own brother and left no more than stumps. Again, a shiver shoots up my spine.

I quickly lift my gaze from the brutality only to find something worse. His face is chiseled with a wicked beauty. Long hair sweeps down to his shoulders, and—though the red-hued statue cannot show it as such—I know it's as raven black as the gift that runs through my veins. His sharp cheekbones and jaw guide my focus to his mouth, where full lips are spread into a subtle smirk. Hooded eyes gaze down upon me, rousing fire in my chest, yet urging me to shrink under the scrutiny.

My blood hums potently, and, for a moment, I've overcome with the urge to touch the effigy in front of me. It feels like I'm being beckoned closer—like I'm being called home.

I reach out, hand shaking as I will it forward. Closer. Closer still. As I'm inches from the stone, a voice rips through the fog of my mind.

"Ren."

I flinch, eyes blinking rapidly as I come back to the moment. As I stagger away from the statues, I turn around to find all eyes on me.

Mikel raises a brow, worry creased in the corners of his eyes. "I've been calling you for ages," he tells me. "Come see the daggers Lorik pulled for you."

I nod absentmindedly and quickly cross the room. I try to pay attention as Lorik explains his process to me—how he refines all of his metals to ensure the highest quality and strength—but my mind is elsewhere. There's a prickle on the back of my neck, an unshakable urge to glance over my shoulder and gaze upon the gods once more. I dig my nails into my palm to stifle the impulse.

"What do you prefer?" Lorik asks.

I can only blink slowly as I look up at him. "Sorry, what?"

He blows out a deep breath, but I see the hint of a smirk in the corner of his mouth. "Do you need something that will get you out of a tight spot, or something to defend heavy blows?"

My lips purse as I think it over. "Both. Neither." I shrug.

Lorik's thick brows raise high on his face. "*Neither*?" He chuckles. "Then what do you—"

"Something that kills," I offer plainly, though the words cut me with a deep ache I'm eager to ignore. "Man or beast. It doesn't matter."

As I run my fingers across the daggers laid before me, I feel the room's rapt attention and the heaviness it brings. When I finally look back up at Lorik, his jaw is firmly set.

"I've let too many men live and now pay the price of their pursuit," I admit, picking up one of the blades and twirling it in my hand. "For that, there is only one option left for me now."

The dagger is a beautiful thing. Steel honed down to a perfectly sharpened tip. The metal hilt is wrapped in black leather cording, giving it some grip. I toss it in the air and catch it with a steady, practiced hand. The weight is good—not too heavy, but enough to put power behind a thrust.

My lips press into a pleased smirk as I twirl the blade once more before sheathing it in the harness across my chest. "This will do nicely," I mumble, eyes already back on the table.

My fingers dance across the variety of weapons before me. I pick up a large blade with a serrated edge. It's unbalanced in my grip and draws a frown. Setting it down, I grab a different blade, then another. By the end, I've touched every dagger laid before me, and four blades rest in the various sheathes across my body.

An ease settles my shoulders as I count the weapons I now have at my disposal. Two small, double-edged blades that are light enough to throw rest against my hip. In the sheath hidden in my boot, I've tucked a long blade that will pierce a gut as good as any. As my fingers graze over the first dagger I chose—the one that's now holstered at my chest—I breathe deeper than I have in a while.

Though, when I raise my gaze and look to the man who fashioned the weapons I've boldly claimed, my confidence falters. "How much?" I utter.

I shoved all the coin I have into my pockets this morning, but I'm not stupid; I know it in no way covers everything I've so quickly declared mine. Though I still resent the need, I briefly thank the gods my face is covered so no one can see the shameful blush heating my cheeks.

Lorik only raises a brow, a gesture I'm beginning to understand means he's more than entertained. He's said nothing this entire time, preferring to let me examine his wares for myself. Though now, he looks at me with quiet amusement dancing in his eyes.

"You picked four of my best blades." His taps a thick finger against his lips, almost as if he's hiding a grin. "You have good taste."

I realize then I'm fucked. This isn't some outpost blacksmith I can barter with until I'm walking away with coins still clinking in my pocket. Whatever price he gives, there's no way I can pay it.

"400 yenti is the price for any friend of Savíana," he states.

My stomach drops instantly. Just as my fingers drift across the blades resting on my hip, ready to hand them over, Lorik's voice stops me.

"But I'm nothing if not a curious bastard…" He drops his hand, revealing a wide grin. "300 for the lot if you show me what you hide under those scarves."

Hassan opens his mouth to intervene, but I quiet him with the flick of my hand. Lorik clocks the interaction with too much interest, and it's then I know I have him.

"That dagger up front, the white one with the carved snake…" I lean across the table, eyes sparkling dangerously. "I want it," I declare, smiling under my scarves. "Add it to the tab, and we've got a bargain."

Lorik laughs, dragging a hand along the back of his neck. "That blade alone is worth 400 yenti. What makes you so certain sating my curiosity is worth the loss?"

I tilt my head and cross my arms against my chest. "I guess there's only one way to find out."

We stare each other down for so long I see the others getting antsy from the corner of my eye. Lorik expects me to break first; I can tell by the way his mouth is quirked up at the corner. But soon, that cockiness shifts into resignation. I'll stand here all day, and Lorik seems to realize that.

As he lets out a *tsk* and shakes his head, I know these blades are mine. "*Hael guard my heart,*" he laughs. "A bargain it is then."

Just as I reach into my pocket to scrounge up every bit of coin I have left, the tell-tale clink of gold stops me.

My eyes widen as I stare up at Hassan. "What are you—"

"That should cover both her and me," he grumbles. "I need to replace the last sword you made for me, and I need two daggers of your choosing." He levels a serious look at Lorik. "Ones that can pierce fehnári flesh."

Lorik's gaze darkens immediately. His eyes flash from Hassan to me before finding Savi's gaze. He *tuts*. "Trouble indeed."

As Lorik steps away, Savi close on his heels and uttering taunts about him going soft, I wheel around to face Hassan. "You didn't need to—"

"I wanted to," he interrupts.

My throat grows tight. "Why?"

I watch emotions flash through his hazel eyes, divulging glimmers of things I thought I'd never see from him—things I don't dare dwell on for fear of their quick departure.

Is there kindness behind that harsh gaze? Regret?

Surely not.

My brow knits together as I take it all in, trying to figure him out despite knowing better than to.

Hassan's jaw clenches as he rips his gaze from mine. "Think of it as an apology for Letka," he mutters. "Like I told your friend last night, I made a bad call. Letting you leave with the Berserker is a mistake I take full responsibility for."

Words bead on my tongue as my mind fights itself on what to say. Instead, I simply scoff. "The Shade is not my friend," I state.

Hassan's eyes snap to mine, but this time, I'm the one breaking eye contact first. "But thank you," I mumble, "for the blades." I swallow back the lump of emotion as best I can. "It's been difficult without my own... like I've been walking around with weak spots and wounds for all to see. I know it's stupid—"

"It's not." Hassan's voice is firm, but without its usual venom. His throat bobs as he holds my gaze. "I know what it's like to be without the weapons that make you feel whole. To a fighter, it's like losing a limb." He stares at me for a long time before forcing a deep sigh. "But even without your weapons, you're far from weak. Don't let anyone tell you different."

Something warm slips into my chest, spreading until I feel my cheeks grow hot. When Lorik walks back over, I immediately drop my gaze. I dig my nails into the palms of my hands to settle the foolish feeling wreaking havoc on my body. I grit my teeth, and Hassan clears his throat. When I finally look back up, it's to catch Mikel staring. His shit-eating grin is all too obvious and makes my flustered face burn hotter. I glare at him, silently begging him to keep his mouth shut. Mikel looks from me to Hassan multiple times before offering me a knowing wink.

Gods, there will be no avoiding this conversation later.

"This one isn't exactly like your last" —Lorik rests a sword on the table in front of us— "but it should be similar enough that you don't notice any differences when you wield it."

Hassan picks up the sword and raises it high. The sunlight reflects off the polished metal, highlighting a thinly carved line that runs from the hilt to the tip. The hilt itself is wrapped in thick brown cloth, tied off by a small band of hekkriti leather. It's a beautiful thing, and, judging by the gleam in Hassan's eyes as he turns it over in the light, he thinks the same.

He sheathes it with the fluidity of a trained fighter, and I find my focus hovering on the swell of his biceps well after the blade rests at his back. My eyes snap away quickly at the realization, but Mikel still catches me ogling.

Veles, smite me. I roll my eyes and force my traitorous thoughts to settle.

The clink of metal echoes across the room as Lorik sets three daggers on the table. He pushes two toward Hassan. "These will fare well against any beast—though, I trust you know the madness that hunting devils brings?" he cautions.

Hassan appraises the two blades before holstering them in his belt. "Where we're going, it won't be us doing the hunting." He nods to Lorik before heading for the door.

I snatch the final dagger from the table, admiring its white shine and the bejeweled snake before sheathing it against my thigh.

As I turn to follow the others, a sharp *tsk* snaps my attention back. "Now I know no friend of Savíana's would leave without fulfilling their end of the bargain."

I turn to face Lorik once more, but this time, the determined heat in my gaze wavers. This could be a mistake—a grave one. Just because Savi trusts him doesn't mean he's above fracturing an old friendship for 20,000 yenti. *How much steel would that buy him?* I look around the shop, realizing just how carelessly I've gambled with my own life.

Lorik steps around the table, arms folded across his chest. "*Ren*," he prods, brows raising sternly. "Don't deny a man his curiosities."

With a deep breath, I step forward and strip my face of its protections. I note the moment he sees my Seer's marks. His eyes grow sharp. His brow furrows, as if wondering why a Seer would go to such lengths to stay hidden. But it's when his gaze swivels to the other side of my neck—the side that's still new to me—that everything changes.

A strangled curse leaves Lorik's throat as he reels away. His mouth moves quickly, muttering a tangle of words that steals my own breath.

"Blood of the most high. Blood of the darkest depths. Driven by sight and cloaked in shadow. Blood of the brother gods. Blood of the two in one. Hael bless and Veles strengthen. For thou will shake the earth and soak the sands. For the Durit will strip the land bare and leave it reborn."

I'm utterly still—frozen to the spot. My heart pumps too heavily. My blood thrums too easily. Though the prayer ends, I can't stop his words from looping in my mind. It's a blight on my sanity. A curse I can't shake. *How many times did I skim over that very devotion in the Book? How many times was my fate right in front of me, but I was too blind to see it?*

Lorik's eyes are bulging and urgent as he meets my gaze. The look on his face is so overwhelmed, so painfully earnest, that panic bubbles up the back of my throat. I can't breathe. My chest constricts tightly as I stare at the man and the emotions that are splayed across his face. He doesn't see me as a monster, as someone destined for destruction.

He thinks I'm as blessed as the gods who damned me with this fate.

I reel backward, tripping over a pile of scrap metal. I feel an arm reach for me, attempting to steady my frantic steps, but I'm quick to shove whoever it is away. There's an overwhelming rush of blood thundering in my ears, drowning out all rational thought. As I stagger out of the shop and into the bustling street, my hysteria only heightens. My boots skid against sand as bodies push past me. I'm shoved and tossed, forced this way and that amidst the throes of people. My gaze darts left to right, but all I find is inescapable chaos choking me from all sides. The hot sun blares down, heating my face with its vicious heat.

My face.

My fingers scramble for the fabrics that hang loosely from my neck. I tug frantically, desperate to cover my marks. But my fingers are shaking too badly, and the headscarf slips loose from my grip time and time again. Just as alarm slithers up my throat in a choking sob, rough hands find my face. Suddenly the sun is gone, replaced by a stern set of hazel eyes.

Hassan looms over me, holding my focus to him. "Breathe, witch," he urges. "Look at me. You're safe. Just breathe."

His gaze burns hot, silently urging me to heed his words. I try to take in a breath, but it wavers unsteadily in my lungs. My hands shake at my sides and tears blur my vision. Just as I close my eyes in order to escape the unbearable chaos around me, something strokes my cheek. I convince myself it's just the tickle of a breeze, but when my gaze flickers open, I'm proven wrong.

Hassan's thumb drifts across my skin with a gentleness I never expected from him. Though, now that I'm feeling it, it seems foolish to have expected anything less. My brows pull together sharply, but despite the frightened voice in my head telling me this will only bring more pain, I give in. I melt into his touch, letting the tension loosen from my chest. His presence is soothing—better than any balm Mikel could ever make. Each stroke of his thumb settles me more and more until, finally, I can breathe again. But soon his touch ventures further, tracing my face until it reaches the corner of my mouth. My breath hitches, held prisoner to the whims of where that touch may journey next. When his thumb tugs at my bottom lip, all thoughts slip away.

There is no city, no people, no risk of capture. All that exists is the feeling of his skin on mine and the frenzied stirring in my core. My heart patters uncertainly, but just as I part my lips, Hassan's touch disappears. He quickly fixes the scarves against my face, masking my identity once more.

When he's done, he offers me a long look that only serves to disorient me further. "We have one more stop. The spice bazaar. After that, we can go."

I nod, though I can't help but search his gaze for something that will help me make sense of what just happened. He doesn't give me the chance. He steps into the street and slips from view before I can blink. Mikel and Savi appear seconds later, lingering at my side. I don't dare look at them, knowing they not only witnessed what happened in the shop, but what transpired between Hassan and I moments ago. I choke down my shame and straighten my spine before gesturing to where Hassan disappeared to.

"Lead the way," I prod, cringing at how my voice breaks.

Mikel loops his arm in mine, tugging me close. "If you think we're not talking about this later..." he mutters.

I try to laugh it off, though the smile swiftly falls from my face as I stare out into the street. I still feel the ghost of Hassan's touch on my skin. If it weren't for the fabric covering my mouth, I would have already pressed a finger to where he grazed my lips so fleetingly, if only to remind myself it was real.

All my dizzying thoughts are scrubbed away in an instant as an uneasy feeling ripples through me. It raises the hairs on the back of my neck, pebbles a chill across my skin. Though all I can see in front of me is the frantic flow of people, that uncanny tinge of fear remains. It's the feeling of eyes on me, but I find none that are. With a frown, I pull my gaze from the street, heartbeat still unsteady in my chest.

Mikel steps out into the masses, though before we can get too far, Savi tugs at my arm. The sudden touch startles me, but when I turn to look at her, what I see on her face unnerves me even more. Her eyes glisten with unshed tears. My chest lurches for a moment, thinking she's upset at whatever transpired in the shop with Lorik. Though before I can open my mouth to mutter a quick apology, I notice the shaky smile pulled across her lips.

Savi leans in close, dropping her voice to a whisper. "I hope you know you're important to people, Ren. And not just those that see the gods in you." She clenches her jaw against the emotions that threaten to take hold. Before I can pull away, she locks me in a gaze that brims with so much gratitude, it feels misplaced on me. "I'm glad fate led you to us," she admits. "And he to you."

Her words leave me aching, yet dumbfounded. There's so much buried shallow for me to find that it threatens to drop me to my knees. My mind spins like a pair of dice refusing to fall. I don't allow myself to search for the truth in her words—for if I am weighed and found wanting, I don't know if I could bear it.

My gaze drifts down the street, searching for a man who has long since disappeared from sight. There's an aching heat in my chest, a hope I told myself I'd never feel again. I keep quiet as I follow Savi and Mikel onward, letting my body guide me while my mind gets lost along the way. There's something to be said of fate—how it leads you places and then places people in your path. This isn't the first I've felt its heavy pull, but this time, I can only hope it doesn't leave me hollow.

CHAPTER 17

Savi purposefully leads us up streets and through alleyways. Her bright, bubbly demeanor is masked in sheer determination as she snakes through the crowds. She clears the path for Mikel and I, causing more than one person to hurry out of her way. It seems Savi can be as intimidating as her cousin when she wants to be.

Somehow, the frantic buzz of the city feels less abrasive with both my companions so close. Savi is constantly peering over her shoulder, making sure I'm still there, but Mikel allows me no such freedom. He clings to my side the entire time we weave through the city like I'm a child that might be snatched away. Though I want to chide him about treating me as such, I can't help but feel grateful. The crowds grow denser, and my heart rate kicks up in turn. Bodies funnel in from adjoining alleyways, squeezing tightly with a force of heat and sweat. I flinch as one man shoves past with an impatience that has my blood thrumming, but before I can even worry about that violence within, Mikel is hurling an insult over his shoulder. The man returns it with all his fury, but Mikel only flips him an obscene gesture and hurries us along.

My friend sighs, looping his arm through mine and tugging me closer. "I would say it's not usually this bad, but that'd be a lie," he offers, continuing to elbow our way through the masses. "Most of these bastards are just as rude when it's not a holy day."

A small smile pulls at my mouth as I look at Mikel from the corner of my eye. The gods may have dealt me a shit hand, but at least they did right by bringing him back to me.

It's not much further until we reach the spice bazaar. The minute we step foot onto the vendor lined street, the rush of sights and scents overtakes me. But it doesn't bring the same panic that's been riding my shoulders all day. No, far from it. I take a deep inhale and almost relax.

I smell desert roses being crushed into teas. Dried herbs hang from wooden beams and send the comforting scents of mint and rosemary to my nostrils. I spot a man muddling chri berries, crushing the ripe red fruit into a thick paste. Smoke wafts about, purifying the street with the earthy aroma of bofchin.

Against the distractions that pull my focus left and right, I spot a familiar head of dark brown hair up ahead. As Hassan turns at our approach, I feel my heartbeat hasten. Sunlight casts its golden glow across his tan skin. His wavy locks are pulled back into a knot, though a few strands have pulled free to frame his face. There's a small scar below his cheekbone, and I can't help but think of what might have put it there. *Did the other person walk away from the fight with such a small token? Or did they meet a worse fate?*

My chest warms uncomfortably as my eyes rake over Hassan's face once more. His strong jaw. The piercing gaze I've come to know so well, though there's something that hides beneath it now. He's handsome in a way I've never let myself study for fear of what it may reveal. And yet now, one lingering look and it seems I've fallen deep into every line, freckle, and scar.

Hassan's lips purse tightly as he watches me, and I can't help but imagine how they would feel against my own. He raises a brow, and it's then that I realize I'm staring at the man. Blatantly staring.

Gods.

I pretend to look at something else. Luckily, there are plenty of distractions at my disposal. My fingers trail absentmindedly across a bunch of tightly bound herbs, but before I can pull away, a large black thorn catches my skin. I curse, muttering under my breath as I quickly pull my scarves down and press the pricked finger to my lips. The bead of blood hits my tongue with a coppery tang as I suck it clean. I utter one more curse at the herb I now realize is Hvar's pinch. That would have saved me a lot of trouble in Letka. One prick and the thorn's sap would have chased the poison out of me faster than wind across the desert. The sight of it now feels like a taunt from the gods.

As I raise my gaze from the market stall, I realize I'm now the one being watched. Hassan's eyes are fixed intently upon my mouth, so much so that he hasn't even noticed my attention. I watch his jaw clench, and as his gaze flashes up to mine, panic flares through both of us. We look away quickly, each pretending to peruse herbs we definitely don't need.

Mikel chuckles behind me, and I'm able to catch the words *'as flustered as virgins'* before he wanders to the next stall with Savi. The vibrant flush of my cheeks drives me after them, eager to create some distance between the hunter and I.

I pretend to be interested in every little thing in front of me— if only to escape the reason for my pounding heart. Shelves are lined with tinctures, while herbs and oddities spill across tables.

There's more than Mikel could possibly need for his remedies, and a quick glance reveals a giddy smile stretched across his face.

My fingers rake through a bowl of sun-bleached pehmi bones, earning me a soothing *clatter* as they sift together. I've only seen a pehmi a handful of times; the small creatures are sly, only showing themselves when hunting desert hares. It's said their rib bones bring protection to anyone looking to cross the Jahaer, though who can be certain. I roll one of the stark-white bones between my fingers, admiring the smooth feel of it. A scoff leaves my lips before I let the bleached talisman fall back into the bowl. *As if the gods would heed my suffering for such a small creature.*

My eyes catch on a heap of beetle shells as Mikel sorts through the bunch. Each one is a different shade of brown that seems to reflect the sunlight like metal. I have no idea what use they pose, but Mikel pays a woman for a handful of them and some mitan flowers. I cringe at the sight of the black petals as the shop owner slips them into a drawstring pouch. The bloom is a staple in Mikel's remedies and one I should be grateful for. Many use mitan for healing cuts and burns, but its sickly stench—pungent like rotten eggs and wine that's been left in the sun too long—would have you thinking otherwise. Though the smell doesn't reach my nose, I scrunch my face up in disgust all the same.

Mikel shoots me a knowing look as he tucks the purchases into his satchel. "You're such a baby," he chides. "Next time you do something foolish, I'm letting your wounds rot and fester."

I roll my eyes and shove him playfully. "And then who will keep you entertained?" I press. "For surely the Continent would be found lacking without me."

As we reach the next shop, my eyes catch on a basket of dried fruit. I snatch up a handful before chomping on them happily. The sour taste bursts across my tongue, and I audibly moan in delight.

The shop keep levels an annoyed look at me, but I simply jut my thumb toward Mikel. "He's buying," I utter through a mouthful. I make sure to shoot my friend a wink before dashing away.

When he finally catches up to me, Mikel dumps a cloth pouch in my hand. "Don't say I never did anything for you."

My eyes light up as I unwrap it to find more of the sour snack. "Uh! *You*, my friend" —I stuff my face with a handful— "are more benevolent than Hael himself."

Savi loops her arm around my shoulder before stealing some of the green fruit for herself. "*Hael above*," she groans, closing her eyes as she savors the taste. "I forgot how much I loved dried gonki fruit."

I try to swat her hand away as she reaches for more, only to have her tuck me into a headlock.

"*Fuck's sake*," I cackle. My body twists and stretches as I wrestle my way out of her strong grip, all while keeping the fruit at arm's length. "And here I thought I'd only have to hide it from Kai."

She sneaks one more piece before relenting. "I would say that's true, but our bad habits tend to rub off on each other." As she swallows her last bite, she offers me a coy smile. "Who knows what is to become of us now that you're here."

Before I can object—tell her that, like before, my presence is only temporary—she elbows me playfully.

"I give it a month before we're all drawing blades on anyone who dares look at us funny."

A smile breaks out across my lips before I can stifle it. "Good," I huff. "Maybe then people will learn it's not polite to stare."

Savi's lively tone carries on, but I've lost my focus. My boots fumble underneath me as I spot Hassan up ahead. He leans against a wooden post, resting under the canopy that shades a market stall full of tonics and brews. His arms are crossed against his chest, muscles on full display in the sleeveless black tunic he wears. He hasn't noticed us yet, much too focused on his task. His eyes scan over the street with a deadly intensity, and it's only when his gaze flickers to me that it softens.

"You've got a little something" —Mikel's finger drags against my bottom lip and wipes the corner— "there. Got it."

I turn toward him slowly, and though my eyes are full of murderous intent, I'm betrayed by the ridiculous smile on my face. "I swear to the gods—"

"Just a little drool," Mikel muses. "Nothing to be ashamed—"

"—rip your limbs from your body and feed them to the buzzards," I utter through a laugh.

I shove Mikel away, though he's quick to slip back against my side. "Don't worry." He grins. "I've caught him looking at you like that, too."

My eyes widen, but before I can press my friend for answers, Hassan finally joins us.

"Is it all in order, then?" he asks Savi.

She pats the cloth satchel resting at her hip. "Everything we need, and then some."

He nods, but as his focus drifts toward me, he pauses. His eyes slip low, hovering on my lips for a moment that feels too long to be insignificant. A nervous swell rocks my stomach, and I chew on my bottom lip absentmindedly. Though I try not to, I can't help but think of how gentle his touch was earlier.

Hassan's throat bobs uneasily. "You should cover your face," he utters, though his voice wavers. "We need to be careful."

My stomach sinks at the realization, and I'm quick to tug my scarves back into place. "Right, of course," I utter. "Sorry. That was foolish of me."

He hesitates like he wants to say more, but doesn't. With a deep breath, he gestures toward the main street we've wandered from. "We need to head back to the fountain," he grunts. "The others will be expecting us soon."

Without another word he dips into the crowds, leading the way. Savi mumbles something to Mikel, and though I miss what was said, I don't miss the boyish laugh that trills from my friend's throat. Before I can berate them to divulge what I fear I already know is the topic, Savi takes off after her cousin. Mikel merely offers me a shit-eating grin before gesturing for me to follow.

The city is just as chaotic as it was before, and I feel a momentary shudder of panic as we slip onto the central street that runs through this district of the city. Luckily, Mikel stays close behind. He places a reassuring hand on my shoulder, all but guiding me forward. We're almost out of the spice bazaar when I feel it again—that uncanny itch on the back of my neck that tells me I'm not alone, that I'm being watched by unfriendly eyes.

I stop dead in my tracks, causing Mikel to stumble into me. People rush by brusquely, fumbling their way past as I continue to block the street; I pay them no mind. My eyes dart around, hastily searching for the cause of my unease.

Mikel hovers at my side, tucking himself close to me. "What is it?" he whispers. "Do you feel a vision coming on?" His arm snakes around my waist, there to steady me if need be.

My throat grows thick with dread when I finally find what I'm looking for. *Him.*

Shaggy black hair hangs around his face in greasy strands and cloaks the harsh angles of his face. He tilts his head curiously, as if surprised by my recognition. But I would know that face anywhere, for I've seen it before. The black Shade's cut is just as violent as it was in my vision—carved down his face in a twisted line and scarring his left eye with decay. I think about running, about darting down a side street, but it's far too late for that. He stares at me with a devilish smile, one that stretches gleefully up to his cheeks like he's eager for the moment that's found us.

As he steps out of a doorway and into the wide street, my blood thrums in panic. "We have to go," I utter to Mikel.

Mikel goes to voice his concern, but is quickly interrupted by a violent blaze of fire. Screams erupt around me, rising in a frenzy as cutting as the hungry flames that lick at distant market stalls.

People panic and flee, tossing me around like a rag doll among the growing hysteria. Fire blazes across the busy street, and though it's too far to feel the flames, the threat of them is stifling enough. I stagger back into the melee, eyes locked on the Torch as he saunters toward me. He flares another burst of fire across the street, clearing the path best he can. More screams. More waves of heat. But all I can focus on is the determination set in his deadly gaze. Before I can turn on my heels and run like I know I should, a familiar pair of hazel eyes finds me among the panicked flow of bodies.

Hassan shouts over the chaos, but his words are lost on me. Without a second thought, I drag Mikel forward, fighting against the stampede of people. A quick look down the street shows that the Torch is still burning everyone and everything in his path to get to me. And he's getting closer.

When I crash into Hassan and see Savi at his side with her bow drawn, I can barely find my breath. "He's here for me," I rasp as people shove their way past. "We need to leave."

Hassan draws his sword, but I barely have time to admire the fresh gleam of steel before he's puling away from me. "We'll hold him off. Get to the fountain and find the others."

I yank his arm back roughly. "No," I snarl. "You're a fool to think yourself a match for Veles's own flames."

As Hassan's lips curl in defiance, another blast of fire blazes through the bazaar. It slams against the shop next door, splintering wood and blasting shards of now-shattered vials through the air. I barely have time to hide my face before I'm sprayed with fragments of broken glass. When I look back up, the Torch has gained too much ground. But as he steps closer, pushing his way through the mayhem he caused, I realize he's not alone.

Two men flank him, and, though I don't spot any markings, the sheer size of them has my fingers twitching against my daggers.

"Fuck," Hassan spits, seeing the same thing I do. "Go. *Now,*" he orders. "We'll rendezvous outside the city gates—at the stables." As I open my mouth to object, he snatches my face in his hands. "*Godsdamnit,*" he growls. "For once, just listen to me."

Before I know it, he's shoving me toward an empty alleyway. Hesitation slows my steps, but as I look back and take in the desperation in his gaze, I finally do as he asks. I sprint toward the side street with Mikel in tow. Heat chokes the air, as does the thick stench of smoke. Only when I hear a massive crash do I dare look over my shoulder.

The shop we'd been standing in front of moments before is utterly unrecognizable. The canopy is shredded—support beams collapsed and covered in flames. I catch the gleam of Hassan's sword as he circles it above his head just before delivering the first blow. I find my pace faltering even as Mikel shoves me forward. But I can't move; my focus is locked on Hassan as his sword swings toward one of the Torch's men. Steel meets steel. Arrows fly as Savi tries to subdue her own man. I flinch as I see Hassan take a slash to his side. I watch the blade tear his tunic before my view is blocked by a mass of black hair.

"*Fucking hells*," Mikel utters under his breath, tugging me relentlessly. "Now, Ren. We have to go *now*."

The moment the Torch steps into the alleyway, he flashes me a wide smile. It's then that I run.

The city passes by in a blur. My fingers scrape against sandstone as Mikel and I take turns too quickly. Breath heaves in my lungs, tightening my chest. I stare at the back of Mikel's head and the golden halo of bouncing curls as he winds us through narrow passages and across busy streets. I have no idea where we're going; I just hope he does. All the while, a heavy presence rides our backs like a servant of death.

I can hear his heavy footfalls scraping the ground and skidding around corners mere moments after we do. The fire is there, too—licking at our heels. It's an ever-present heat that only creeps closer. The screams are quick to follow, though we don't dare stop to see who the fire touches.

I push Mikel onward, forcing us to outpace our enemy even when my friend's confidence in our direction wavers; it's a split second hesitation that I don't allow. We miss our turn, but I shove us forward anyway, earning a protesting grunt from Mikel. I drive us faster and faster until the threat of fire fades into the background. Mikel takes a quick right turn down an alleyway, and before I can ask how much further, we're thrown into the sunlight. I stumble into the city's center after Mikel, lungs burning and sweat soaking my scarves. It's only when we reach the great stone fountain that I allow my body a moment of relief.

"Which way to the gate?" I ask, breath panting and head hung so low it almost touches the stout stone wall.

"That way," he chokes out, equally as breathless. "Dead east." His hand shakes as he holds it up, pointing across the square. "We follow that street all the way to—"

Chaos explodes around us as a wall of fire cuts through the masses. People scream as they're caught in the inferno's path, and the smell of burnt flesh meets my nose with an ungodly odor. I swallow back a wave of nausea and press my scarves against my face as I look across the square.

He's here. His fingers are stained black like death-touched embers as his gift flows through him. Fire dances in his palm, impatient and eager. Fear churns my blood and makes my heart beat too quickly. But more overwhelming is the knowing clench in my gut, the one that tells me this was a grave mistake.

We should have kept running.

CHAPTER 18

I toss a glance at Mikel. As I note the sweat beading his forehead and the shakiness in his limbs, a pit grows in my stomach. When he swivels his gaze toward me, the panic in his eyes almost drops me to my knees. I feel like I'm about to be back in the Jahaer watching Olen choke the breath from my best friend's lungs. The thought drives a constricting ache in my chest, but stronger than that is the insistence that no harm will come to Mikel on my watch. There's no other choice.

In a quick burst of energy, I shove Mikel away from the fountain—east. He barely has time to react before I'm sprinting in the opposite direction of where I should be going. Mikel's voice bellows after me, cursing and yelling as fear laces his tone. But it's too late. The Torch only has eyes for me.

My pursuer grins maniacally as he runs for me. He doesn't even offer Mikel a parting glance. *Good.* Like the last time we were at death's door, my friend's safety is a comfort, but the consequences of what I've done are too great to ignore. Cockiness will surely get me killed.

One look over my shoulder has a fresh bout of adrenaline rippling through me. The Torch is gaining ground. My legs pump as fast as they can, carrying me west across the square. I weave in and out of those who haven't yet fled, glimpsing the growing terror on their faces as I rush past. Loose rocks have my boots skidding beneath me as I dart down the next street. Breath huffs in my chest and my tunic feels heavy with damp. But still, I don't stop. The streets get narrower, threatening to choke my path. Wide market lanes turn into alleyways littered with broken crates and donkey carts. My heart stutters as I race around a corner only to find nowhere left to go. With wide eyes and blood pounding in my veins, I search for escape. My breath hitches as I spot it. *Yes. There.*

I hoist myself through a circular window cut into the alley, and immediately fall into a private yard. It's only seconds before the wall explodes behind me, sending chunks of stone slamming against my back. My legs give out underneath me as the weight cripples my already weary body. I drag myself from the rubble, stumbling forward with breath seizing my lungs. I risk a glance back and immediately regret it. Flames flare through the gap, only settling to reveal a head of stringy black hair as the Torch steps through. His sinister smile is the last thing I see before I flee.

I hurdle over stone flower boxes and crates; the rush has my boots scrambling to land on solid ground. A woman screams as I dart past, quickly retreating back into her home. I don't hesitate, don't let myself dwell on the ill fate I've brought to so many innocents today. Instead, I stay the course, tearing my way across the red-tiled patio and through the tangle of fruiting trees and blooming plants. My sights are set on the only thing in this godsdamn garden that can save me.

A wooden ladder rests against the far stone wall, rising into the sky like a gateway to heaven. Heavy breath pumps my heart too quickly, and the shattering *crack* of a pot behind me has my legs pushing faster. The ladder is close. So close. But so is he.

Before I even reach the lowest rung, I hurl myself toward salvation. My body swings wildly, careening to the side. I slam into the wall, sending a smarting twinge of pain through my hip. A deep laugh fills the air around me, and my blood runs cold.

I will not die today. I will not be taken.

With a roaring yell, I manage to snatch another handhold to steady myself. Rung after rung, I heave myself higher until there's no higher to go. Rough stone scratches against my pants, snagging the threads as I pull myself up onto the roof. My legs shake underneath me as I come to stand, and, though black splotches my vision, I know I can't stop. The creak of the wooden ladder behind me is a frightening reminder of that.

My boots slap the flat sandstone roof as I sprint across it. Ragged breath constricts my lungs and makes me dizzy. I risk a glance back, but instead of the face of my pursuer, it's a roaring burst of flames that greets me. My body flattens against the roof as I duck for cover. Heat sears the fabric of my tunic, fire mauling the air where I stood moments before. My stomach is in knots as I crawl forward on my stomach, eager to escape the stifling blaze and the death it promises.

"Give it up, girl," a voice calls through the frenzy. "I'll have that reward whether you're intact or writhing in my flames."

As I pull myself up to standing, the muscles in my legs feel wobbly enough to give out. I look out across the city, taking in the maze of rooftops that's spread before me. My gaze flickers down to the wide gap between this house and the next. The only thing it promises is a brutal fall if poorly attempted. My throat grows tight. My heart stutters. It's then I know what I must do.

With my stomach in knots, I slowly turn around, hands raised in surrender. I watch the fire die in the Torch's hands, watch the black fade from his fingertips. He chuckles to himself, gleaming a wicked grin as he takes a step closer.

"Smart choice."

I don't give myself time to second guess what is bound to be a mistake. Turning on my heels, I sprint across the rooftop, not allowing a moment's hesitation. There's no thought as I hurl myself off the roof's edge, only the murmured prayer I send the gods' way.

My gut lurches. My legs pedal against air as if I can defy this free fall. Just when I think I've misjudged the distance and prepare myself for a bone splattering end, my boots hit something solid. I stumble forward, rolling head over heels until I stop with my palms spread across stone. My body twitches with adrenaline, and I don't waste a drop. I'm up on my feet and sprinting across this new rooftop a moment later.

A deranged laugh rips through the air behind me, peppering goosebumps across my skin. I don't dare look back. All I can do is push my legs harder as I hear the telltale smack of boots against stone and the corresponding grunt of exertion. It seems my pursuer is not so easily deterred.

I jump from rooftop to rooftop, paying no heed to the streets that rest far beneath me. Even one hesitant peek at the fracturing fate below would be enough to call forth a misstep, and I cannot afford even one. My boots land with a grating force that seems to shoot up my jaw as I land on yet another roof. I don't turn around to see how close those flames or the one who conjures them are; I just run.

The high sun blazes down on me, its unfriendly heat making my head heavy and my body weak. Breath tears through my lungs, and my muscles ache with exhaustion. For a moment, all that fills my ears is the slap of my boots against stone and the distant clamor of the city. Bells ring, signaling midday. Voice shout and carts trudge down streets. I hear no pursuit, only my own breath as it heaves in and out with a choking rush. Though it's foolish, the silence at my back has me believing luck might be on my side today.

When I see the wide gap and the canopy that spans it ahead, I'm reminded that the gods are anything but merciful. I try to judge the distance, but as I get closer, I know it's a gamble I have to take. Just as I brace myself for the leap—begging the gods to close the gap—a sharp pain rips through my calf. I scream, stumbling toward the ledge with fear filling my heart. I attempt to course-correct, try to kick off and pump my legs in order to make the jump, but it's too late. I'm already over the edge.

My arms flail for purchase, though the air slips through my fingers. There's a rush of wind and a gut-wrenching drop. *This must be the end.* But then I'm jerked to a halt—held aloft by a thin canopy like the gods cradle me in their very hand. I'm eased of all panic for a single breath before the world falls out from under me. I hear the swift rip of fabric, feel its tatters brush my face. And then, nothing. I don't know how far I'm falling, just that I am. All too soon, the ground greets me with a vicious *smack*. It slams into my chest and drives a gagging huff of air from my lungs. My head spins as pain radiates through every inch of me. For a moment, I think I might be dead, but there's too much pain for that.

It's only when I hear the soft thud of boots landing to my right that I remember there are far worse things than the possibility of having broken every rib. I lift my head only to find the Torch leering down at me. His Shade's cut almost glimmers against the midday sun—its eternal decay catching the light like a polished rock. As I try to push myself up, he stomps on my back, forcing me down.

The Torch tilts his head, making the long black strands of his hair sway like smoke. "What a shame," he coos. "To think I'd heard such great things about you—the woman who maimed so many of Rohan's best."

He kicks me firmly in the ribs before rolling me over with his boot. I gasp and feel a surge of nausea race through me at the sudden onslaught of pain. If I had to guess, at least three of my ribs are cracked from the fall. Probably more.

"Get up," the Torch taunts.

As he takes a step away from me, I find the strength to get to my feet. It's with gritted teeth that I fight through the pain. Though, it quickly proves too much. I immediately sway, nearly buckling to the ground when I try to put weight on my left leg. A brief glance over my shoulder has me shuddering. A black dagger is buried in my calf, almost hilt-deep. I fight the urge to tear it free, knowing the blood loss alone will seal my fate. Instead, I bite down on the inside of my cheek and draw the dagger sheathed at my thigh; the one secured to my chest comes next. They're the largest blades I bought from Lorik, and while I didn't think I'd be christening them this soon, I'll be more than happy to with the blood of the man in front of me.

The Torch grins. "And here I thought there was no more fight left in you." He chuckles before withdrawing two identical black daggers from his belt. "I do enjoy a good bloodbath. It'll make your surrender all the more delicious."

I watch him spin each blade in his hands like he has all the time in the world. My eyes flicker over his shoulder to find the bustle of the city so close, yet so far out of reach. A few people pass by the alley, but one look at the dagger-clad maniac in front of me is all it takes for them to scurry away. No one will help me, but it's nothing new; I can hardly blame them. You don't live long on the Continent playing hero.

My eyes track the Torch as he draws closer. He's covered in swathes of dark fabrics, though one lingering look all too quickly reveals him for what he is. His markings are ink-like flares against his pale skin, black tendrils that wrap around both wrists and bleed across the knuckles. Those god-given marks trail up his neck, too—snaking up into his hairline and disappearing under greasy strands. I don't need to see any more skin to know he's covered in the sign of his gift. It's clear in the way he carries himself that his Veles-cursed flames are a mere extension of him, something he confidently wields without hesitation or guilt.

Our boots tread grooves in the sand with each step we take around the other. There's a limp in my gait, and I feel the slow, steady trickle of blood as it pools in my boot. Every breath strains my ribs past what feels comfortable. None of that matters though, only surviving this does.

I clench my jaw tightly, determined to hide the pain from my face. I'm not sure it's worth the effort. It's clear he knows I'm struggling. Every step he takes forward, I take one back. But he doesn't lunge for me, doesn't hurl a dagger or unleash a blast of fire to end this quickly. No, he's toying with me—savoring every wince of pain my face reveals and each staggering step I take in retreat. He's nothing more than a predator playing with his food.

I try to dart to the left—closer to the alley's exit—but he's too quick. A wide grin spreads across his face, flashing sharp teeth at me like a wild beast. He's blocking my only means of escape, and he knows it. I realize then there's no way around him, only through. This alley is wider than most; I can use that to my advantage if only I find an opening.

I grind my jaw roughly as I firm my stance. "A Torch who prefers blades," I remark with a bitter laugh. "Some might call that overcompensation."

He flips the blades in his hands like he's anxious to use them. "Fire is such a swift thing," he muses. His good eye shines dangerously as he smirks. "I much prefer taking my time."

I let the weight of my daggers settle in my hands before twirling the white, snake-carved one into an overhand grip. "Who are you?" I prod.

"I'm a lot of things," he states. His tongue drags across his teeth slowly as he assesses me. "Torch. Devil. *Death.*"

"*Your name*," I utter. "I want to know whose blood I'm to spill."

His smile presses high into pointed cheekbones. "Roel," he offers, like it's the sweetest song.

He takes a slow step forward, then another. There's nothing defensive in his posture as he saunters down the alley toward me. It's the walk of someone who knows how this ends.

"Show me how you play, *Ren*," he coos.

He moves like a burst of chaos, slicing his daggers through the air as his boots stir the dust around us. I barely see his next strike in time to block it with my own. I duck to the right, skirting around his side. Though my body shakes with strain, there's no hesitation as I thrust my blade toward his gut. He sees it coming. With a quick reflex, he rams his arm down into mine and drives my blade off course. I don't have time to prepare before he kicks his boot into my stomach with sickening force. I cough and gag, buckling over as my ribs burn with pain. Bile slips up my throat, but I choke it back. I'm barely able to draw in a breath before he's on me again.

His daggers swish through the air in rapid succession, striking with such force that I feel every block shudder through my forearms. My boots scuff the ground as I parry his advances, twisting and driving my body along in his violent dance. He grins like the devil he claims to be, tongue wagging in his mouth and eyes wide with bloodlust and glee. The sharp clash of steel resounds through the alley, colliding with the heave of our muddled breaths.

My arms ache as I raise them again and again to stave off his blows. Every time I move, blinding pain sears through my ribs and floods my vision with black. Sweat runs down my face, bleeding into my eyes as exertion takes its toll. Just when I think we'll be stuck in this never ending loop of strikes and parries, I see my opening. His right side is slower to react, and it takes only a moment for me to use it to my advantage.

I feign a strike to his shoulder, forcing his left arm up in defense only to aim my other blade for his abdomen. The blow isn't as strong as I'd like, but it slices all the same. As I tear through his tunic, I spy the blood my dagger summons. It's only when his grin widens that I realize I played right into his hand. I'm too close, and somehow, that's just what he wanted.

He barrels into me, lunging low and jamming his blade into my side before I can stagger out of reach. A bellowing curse rips from my throat the instant steel breaks flesh. He releases his hold on me as I stumble away, both blades still gripped tightly in my hands. When I prod my side, my fingers come away with the fresh slick of blood.

It's a dizzying, sickening rush as pain flares from too many places, all at once. With gritted teeth, I lift my chin high and limp forward to face him. And while every step has me staggering on shaky legs, I don't cower or flee. There will be no more running today.

As breath heaves in my lungs and blood pours from my side, Roel stares me down with a smirk curling his lips. "Someone knew what they were doing when they trained you to fight," he admits. The black void of his dead eye almost seems to shine in delight. "But I wonder... how long will that skill hold until it breaks?" He steps closer, daggers twirling in his grasp. "How long until I break you?"

He lunges before I'm ready for it. My ribs scream in protest as I raise my arm to curb his assault. Blow after blow, he drives me further back into the alley. Blow after blow, he steals every last bit of my strength. My mind spins as blood drips into the sand, following me like an omen of what fate has found me. Already, I feel the gods calling me down to the underworld, carving a place for me in the dark.

I won't go.

With a heavy grunt, I slip under one of Roel's strikes before twisting my hips. I send a high kick straight to his gut, driving it with as much force as I can muster. The impact sends a shudder of pain through me, but it's a solid hit. He hacks out a pained breath, and—though his surprise lasts only a second—it's all I need. I strike down with my left hand, driving my blade into the delicate flesh of his shoulder. He yells, and as soon as I feel his body quiver from the blow, I send my other dagger into his abdomen. The blade sinks in deep, sending another tremble through his body. He grunts as I rip both blades from his flesh, unleashing the blood I promised to flow.

His gaze snaps to me. The dark malice twitching in his eye is the only warning I get before the force of his whole body slams into me. We hit the ground with a heavy *thwack*, and I scream as the dagger lodged in my calf sinks deeper. Roel pins his weight on top of me, smile wild and hungry. For a moment, it's not his face I see looming over me, but Olen's. I'm back in the Jahaer, just as helpless as I was before. My mind snaps awake as Roel shifts to press his knee against my windpipe. I choke and gag as panic seizes my lungs. My arms flail—striking and slapping every part of him I can reach. Just as I thrust my dagger toward his face, his own pierces through me with the touch of white-hot fire.

I scream until my voice cracks.

The world stops.

I still underneath him, eyes going glassy and wide. My mouth goes dry and pain flares to life like it's the only true thing. With my body twitching in agony, I manage to look to my left; though, I already know what it is I'll find.

Roel's dagger has gone straight through my arm, pining me to the sun-baked clay. Bile burns hot in the back of my throat. I try to move, but it only jostles the wound and draws a stifled cry from my lips.

As Roel removes his knee from my throat and allows me a full breath, I curse and howl. Tears spill from my eyes, no matter how badly I wish to stifle them.

Tsk. Tsk. Tsk. A rough fingernail scrapes the top of my cheek as Roel wipes a tear away. "None of that, girl," he chides. "We're only just beginning, you and I."

He leans back, resting his weight on my hips, as if seeking a comfortable place to watch my face twist in horror. His fingers prod the hilt of the dagger buried in my flesh, ripping yet another wail from my throat. He merely grins. Sweat beads across my temple as my eyes blur with more tears. The only thing keeping me from surrendering to this fate is the other dagger still held tightly in my grasp. My right arm stirs against the ground, but before I can even think to strike, Roel sparks a fistful of flames. He snatches my weapon and tosses it away before leaning over me. Fire burns hot across his palm, and he brings it so close that I can smell my scarves singeing.

"We've had enough fun for today, don't you think?" Roel taunts.

The flames die in his hand as he cups my cheek. The gesture is anything but tender as he grips my scarves and yanks them away.

For a moment, it's shock that paints his face. Those vile eyes go wide, flickering back and forth between both sides of my neck and the markings the brother gods have left in claim. But Roel's confusion soon turns to glee. He offers me a mocking smile as his warm fingers prod at my markings.

"Oh, what's this?"

I flinch away from his touch, though there's nowhere to go.

He chuckles darkly and leans in close. "When I saw you in the market this morning, I couldn't understand why Rohan had placed such a bounty on the head of a mere Seer..." His sharp, uncut fingernails dig into my neck, drawing a tiny prickle of blood.

"Does he know what you are?" Roel cocks his head to the side, eyes devouring every mark on my skin. "But of course he does." The Torch looses a bitter laugh. "It seems Rohan will finally get what he wants."

My eyes sweep the alley for anything of use, any sliver of escape. There's nothing. All that remains is the devil above me and the steady flow of blood leaving both our bodies.

Roel must see the desperation on my face, because his grin widens to reveal sharp teeth that reek of rot. He slowly drags his fingernails over my marks like he's tallying each one. "The great and powerful Durit," he hums. "The prophesied daemon that's said to be more god than man." He looms over me, letting hot, foul breath slide across my skin. "Such a disappointment to find out Bair's Prophecy is nothing more than a weak woman with no use of her gifts."

"Fuck you," I spit through endless pain and tears.

I try to look away, but he wraps a hand around my jaw, holding my focus to him.

"Even my more ordinary bounties prove more difficult than this. After all, it was mere days ago that I got word of the prize on your head."

His grip slides up my face and pinches my cheeks between his fingers. As his sharp nails dig into my skin, my stomach turns sour. "But then this morning, there you were—traipsing through the market without a care in the world. A little bird fluttering into my web." He lets out a breathy laugh and licks his lips. "What's the matter, Durit?" he presses, voice low and taunting. "Even with sight as great as yours, couldn't see me coming?"

His crazed laughter spills into the alleyway as I thrash underneath him. Pain radiates through my arm as the sunken blade wiggles deeper into my flesh. I let out a desperate cry, but I don't stop. I would rather rip this blade through my arm than be bound and captured ever again.

Roel grins wickedly as he watches me squirm. My other arm comes up and slaps him across the chest, but it's fruitless. He climbs up my body, knees digging into my stomach. I scream at the unforgiving weight pressing against my ribs and glare up at him.

Roel's hand wraps around my throat, tightening without remorse. "Now, how should we get you back to Denheir?" he asks, smile wide and wicked. "How much of your so-called godsblood do I have to spill before you accept the fate you've been dealt today?"

His grip steals my breath, snuffing the last of my adrenaline and peppering my vision with shadows. But as I blink the haze away, I realize it's not my eyes playing tricks on me. The shadows are real.

Like a beast surging from the sea's depths, black tendrils snake around Roel's throat. He releases his grip on me instantly, using both hands to desperately claw at the darkness that chokes him. Before I can fill my lungs with fresh, unobstructed air, Roel's body is tossed away like a boneless heap. I cough and sputter, trying to regain my strength as the man's muffled yells erupt through the alley. A burst of heat barrels into me, though the fire doesn't devour me like it should.

I search for the thrum of my gift, but Veles's fury feels distant amidst all this pain. My head is a pounding drum, and my eyelids flutter heavily. Black peppers my vision, but through the fading dark I look up to see fire flaring across the alley. Shadows crash against flames, slipping around them like air over silk. Roel conjures another surge to stall his attacker, but his gift grows sloppy and frenzied. I see the panic in his gaze, see the shake in his hands. The shadows waver, prowling across the alley like sentries poised for a fight. But the fight doesn't come. The day hangs on bated breath. Words spill into the air, but are lost to the muffled thud in my ears. Roel must know he's outmatched, because with a barreling rush of flames, he jumps through a fresh crack in the alley's wall and flees.

As I watch his black hair slip through the gap, I realize it's finally over. My hand shakes as I lean over and rip the dagger free from my arm. I scream with a devastating force I'm unable to muffle. Bile chokes the back of my throat. As my fingers curl around the black dagger, I watch the blade drip with my own blood. Through the flickering haze of my consciousness, I realize it'll be a good addition to my collection. Before I can sheath my new dagger, shadows descend on me like the depths of night, igniting panic.

Determination has me summoning adrenaline I thought long since depleted. I kick my legs against the hard, sand-dusted ground, frantic to scurry from the encroaching darkness. It's only when Malachi's face appears within it that my frenzy stalls.

All of my strength—my fear, my desperation, everything—crumbles at the sight of him. He crouches down next to me, eyes darting across every inch of my body as he assesses the damage I incurred. I can feel how bad it is, and the look in his eyes doesn't help. A lump forms in the back of my throat as I watch the pain and rage bleed into his gaze, turning his brown irises almost pitch black.

I can't bear to see it anymore. I flip over onto my hands and knees, groaning in pain as I do. My body shakes under the weight and my ribs twinge with a devastating ache that I know will only be quelled by Mikel's skilled hands. *Mikel.* Panic takes root quickly, stealing the breath from my lungs.

"The others," I gasp. "Are they—"

"Fine," Malachi offers harshly. "I ran into them in the city center. The Mender was yelling about a Torch. I came looking for you."

I wince as I pull myself up, but as soon as my weight transfers to my left leg, I collapse. Shadows wrap around my waist before I can hit the ground. My eyes snap up to Malachi, and he looks like he might be sick.

"I'm fine," I grit out.

I brush his shadows off, and even though I know they're hardly swayed by a mere swat, he humors me. The dark wisps drift away, but hover much too close—like he thinks I'll collapse again at any moment. I might.

It's an effort to bend down, but once I manage to, I rip the dagger from my calf. A wailing moan chokes out from my throat before I can smother it. I make quick work on stripping off one of my scarves and tying it tightly around my leg. Malachi watches me the entire time, and I sneak a glance to find his hands clenched into fists.

When I'm done, I retrieve the black daggers that were buried in my flesh only moments ago. Their dark blades drip with a fresh slick of blood, and the sight curls something nasty in my gut. It's the blood of the gods, but Roel was right. It might as well belong to some weak, godless woman.

I sheath both daggers before limping through the alley to collect my own. When the task is finally complete, there's a trail of red following me. I loose a breathy laugh, but one look at Malachi snaps my mouth shut. Shadows flare around him, stirring up the sand with a carefully restrained violence.

"I need to carry you back," he utters through clenched teeth.

A scoff is all he gets from me before I start hobbling down the alley. My vision splotches with black the entire way, but I don't slow. Not once.

He huffs, catching up to me quickly. "*Serehna.*"

I ignore him, and though my calf hurts like a godsdamn ricsin has snapped it off, I quicken my pace.

"*Veles below.*" His shadows flare wildly, brushing against my side. "Were you always this fucking stubborn?" he demands.

Before I know it, he's tugging me toward him. As my body stumbles against his, he quickly unwraps his own headscarf and drapes it across my face. I shoot him a hot glare, but offer him nothing more. I understand I need to hide my marks, especially now that we know what threats lurk, but I refuse to thank him for it.

As I go to step forward, I nearly crumple; it seems whatever leftover adrenaline I had has finally worn off. Malachi lets out a frustrated groan before scooping me up into his arms. He doesn't give me time to protest, merely cradles me like some helpless bride as he stomps down the alley.

"*Ow*," I seethe, swatting his chest. "Put me down, you brute. I can walk!" My hand smacks him repeatedly until the effort makes me dizzy with pain.

He merely tightens his grip and continues on. "Don't be a brat, Serehna," he utters. "I did save your life after all."

"You di—" I bite my tongue when I realize that's exactly what he did. I was well on my way to being bound and carted off to Denheir when he showed up.

My lips curl into a sneer, and I look away from his stupid face before he decides to taunt me further. He doesn't; he says nothing more as we make our way back to the East Gate. The entire walk there, his shadows trail us like the hounds that are said to guard the underworld. No one bothers us—no one even dares to step in our path. I keep my head low as shame burns hot in my chest. That feeling only grows once we arrive at the stables to find the others waiting.

They don't ask questions. They take one look at me cradled in Malachi's arms, bleeding and bruised, and quickly fetch our animals from the stablehand. I catch Quin staring with wide eyes, though I don't have the energy for her. My gaze flitters past Mikel, not brave enough to face the criticism I know I deserve. Instead, I shift my focus to Savi, whose fingers are tightly wrapped around

Hassan's arm. Her cousin is fuming, eyes like golden fires as he stares at Malachi. Hassan goes to take a step toward us, but is swiftly tugged back.

I can't blame Savi. All it takes is a quick glimpse up at Malachi to see the vicious gleam in his eyes, like he's daring the world to try him. The shadows flaring around his boots don't help either.

As Malachi hoists me atop his horse, I protest and flail like an unruly child. My own camel is right there, but too quickly, a wave of dizziness hits me like a stone wall—settling all protests. I slip into unconsciousness for a brief moment before I'm yanked back with a startled breath. Malachi glares down at me, muttering curses from his place behind me. I try not to flinch at the feeling of his chest against my back, but it has my body growing shaky. I blink slowly—wearily—and wonder if I'm truly this helpless against the Shade's touch. My gaze drops to my arm, and the deep hole in my flesh is a helpful reminder. *Not weak for him, just weak.*

As the six of us head back to the house, I feel myself sinking into nothing. My eyelids flutter closed, letting the world fade around me. It's only by the beat of Malachi's heart against my back and the hot blood leaking from my wounds that I know I'm still alive. Murmured voices spill into the air around me, but I haven't the energy to make sense of them. Malachi's horse carries us on steady legs, and the gentle rocking has me slipping into something almost peaceful. The pain is gone now; all that's left is a cold numbness and a heavy ache. As the black peppering my vision grows steadier, the gods make sure to send one last thought my way.

I slipped through Roel's fingers this time, but he'll snag me in his web yet again. He was right; I didn't use my gift to see him coming. Not this time. But Hael hasn't left me truly blind. There's more of the Torch to come—I've seen it—and I'll be ready for him next time.

CHAPTER 19

My eyelids flutter open slowly, strained by the daze of sleep. But before I can fully take in the wood beams that span the stone ceiling above, a searing cold tears through my arm with a vengeful fury. I bellow, jerking upright amidst the heavy weight of blankets. Though I try to thrash and escape the unexpected jolt of pain, a firm hand holds me down.

"I'm almost done," he hisses. "*Gods and devils*, Ren. Stay still."

It's only when my foggy mind clears that I recognize the voice as Mikel's. My heartbeat settles, and I manage to pull in a breath. But as sleep finally leaves my eyes, the sight that greets me is less friendly than I anticipated.

"I was hoping to finish before you woke up, but even unconscious it seems you're a stubborn prick." Mikel shakes his head, mumbling under his breath as he gets back to work.

No sooner does that unnerving cold slip through my skin once more than do I wince and pull away.

"*Fuck's sake,*" Mikel curses, yanking me back toward him. "Do you want me to fix the gaping hole in your arm, or not?"

He's cross with me, clearly. Not even the hint of a smirk rests in the corner of his mouth as he waits for my answer.

I let out a huff before drifting my gaze toward the door, ignoring his attitude best I can. "Get it over with then," I utter through clenched teeth.

I don't watch as Mikel's gift courses through his veins, though I feel the moment it does. It's like being dunked in icy water, like night has fallen and there's nothing left but whipping wind and a sunless chill. But it's still worse than that, because the icy flow sinks deep inside me, through places I didn't know I could feel. I bear down against the feeling and try to ignore the sensation of muscle and sinew forming back together.

In escape of that feeling, I turn my mind to the one who caused it—*Roel.* I think of how that fire of his blazed through streets and left screams in its wake. I think of the tang of his breath as he loomed over me. And as I remember the glint in his good eye and the way he grinned when he drew blood, a shudder rolls through me.

My jaw clenches as the last dregs of freezing ache turn to a burning pressure under my skin. It slips through my arm like fire, though I don't dare squirm or complain. I bear it all silently and without meeting my friend's gaze. Mikel doesn't say anything when he's done, simply drops my limb against the bedding like a dead fish and gets up.

I turn my arm over, inspecting it in the soft candlelight that flickers through the room. "Hm, and it didn't even leave a scar. Thanks."

He turns around slowly. Too slowly. "*Thanks?*"

My brow pinches as I look up to see the fury contorting Mikel's face. "Yeah," I mutter. "Did you already do my leg and ribs? I feel gre—"

"Do you even know how worried we all were?" he shouts. "How fucking sick to my stomach I was not knowing if you were already strapped to the back of a camel, or worse—burned to a crisp?"

I let out a deep sigh and shrug the blankets off. The moment my feet press against the floor I expect the seething bite of pain, but there's nothing but a tingling prickle from being in bed for too long. My lips purse curiously as I flex and stretch my calf. It feels like there was never a blade shoved through the muscle. *Benefits of having a brilliant Mender as your best friend, I guess.*

When I look up at said brilliant Mender, he's scowling. I cross the room quickly, though the closer I get, the more it feels like a mistake.

"Look," I sigh. "I'm sorry, all right? But I did what was best. He was after *me*, not you. I wasn't about to let you get caught in the fray when—"

"*Gods!*" he yells, throwing his hands up in the air. "You know, I thought you'd changed. But clearly you're the same as you've always been."

My brow furrows at that. "What are you even—"

"Stop putting yourself at risk," he admonishes, voice bouncing loudly off the walls. "You don't have to save everyone, Ren. You have nothing to prove!"

I *tsk*, smacking my teeth loudly against my tongue as I roll my eyes at him. "If this is about what happened with Zoah—"

"It's not," he snaps. "It's more than that. Even before those men ransacked our camp, you acted like your life was worth less than everyone else's."

"Oh, *come on*," I start. "That's not—"

"That time we arrived at a well only to find that the rope had snapped and the bucket was floating at the bottom," he gushes. "You scaled down, nearly breaking your leg when you slipped. Then when you managed to climb out, the stones had torn you up. Your hands looked like they'd been through a meat grinder."

I press my fingers into my temple and close my eyes. "What was I supposed to do?" I seethe, my temper getting the best of me. "Let everyone die of thirst? It was five days to the next outpost!"

"And then in Monok" —Mikel pushes into my personal space— "when I cheated those brothers in a game of skelt." He takes a breath. "They were going to beat me bloody until you got them riled—bet the whole tavern you could take them both in a fight." Mikel's eyes burn into me as the words spit from his mouth. "It took me *hours* to heal the bones in your face."

I tilt my head, smirking. "I did win though."

"*Veles strike your tongue!*" Mikel yells in frustration. He raises his hands like he's going to strangle me before clenching them into fists instead. "This isn't funny. You're always doing something reckless, always throwing your life on the line when it comes to others."

"I don't see how that's a bad th—"

"It's like you want to die!" Mikel grips my tunic roughly in his hands and yanks me toward him. "I'm tired of you acting like nobody cares. I care! Do not ask me to bury my best friend because she doesn't see the worth of her own life."

I flinch back like his words have claws and gnashing teeth. And maybe they do, because I'm sure he's drawn blood. For a while, all we do is stare at each other, silence chewing the air between us. I try to form words, try to tell him that he's wrong, but I can't.

Eventually, I pull his hands away from where they're gripping my tunic and hold them in a shaky grip. "I'm sorry," I murmur. "I didn't mean to worry you." I give his hands a light squeeze before pulling away. My bare feet come to a halt in front of the door, feeling too heavy to carry me further.

Emotion is thick on the back of my throat as I spare a glance over my shoulder. "I don't regret it," I admit, voice much too desperate for my liking. "And I'll do it again, and again, and again if that means keeping you safe."

Just as I turn to slip out of the room and escape this moment, the door flies opens. I stagger out of the way, only to be greeted by the last person I wish to see. With a huffing breath, I try to step around him, but he blocks my path.

"Move," I order.

Malachi takes a step closer, forcing me back into the room. "We need to talk."

"*Ha.*" I pretend to laugh. "No. No, we do not."

As I try to step around him again, his shadows trap me.

"Mikel," Malachi utters darkly. "I need a word with her."

A second later, my friend slips out of the room, slamming the door behind him. He doesn't give me so much as a backward glance.

I swear under my breath before turning to glare at Malachi. "*Mikel?*" I prod. "Since when are you two friendly?"

He says nothing, and his shadows flare against my skin.

I cross my arms over my chest and cast a scornful look at the darkness wrapped around my boots. "Get them off me, Shade," I rasp. "*Now.*"

I expect Malachi to hurl a retort my way and loosen his hold, but he doesn't. Instead, he looms closer—leaning down until his face is inches from mine.

"Do you have a death wish, Serehna?"

I scoff and roll my eyes. "*Gods*, what is it with everyone and thinking I—"

"I know you know the cities are dangerous," he seethes. "Just like I know you're well aware of the bounty on your head. You're a target for every power-hungry bastard out there." Malachi's jaw twitches, and his nostrils flare. "So gods tell, why were you alone?" His eyes grow dark as he steps closer. "If I would have known the bounty hunter was going to break his promise so quickly—"

"I wasn't alone," I snap. "I was still with the others when we ran into some trouble. Hassan and Savi tried to hold them off while Mikel and I ran. After that..." Guilt heavies my heart, but I merely avert my eyes and shrug. "We got separated. The Torch came after me. It was no one's fault."

"Separated?" he challenges. "Funny way of saying you ditched the Mender and ran headfirst into danger."

Damn you, Mikel. He must be more pissed than I realized if he's talking to the only person I hate more than the gods themselves.

I pinch the bridge of my nose and utter a grating sigh. "Fine, the fault is mine. I'll make better decisions next time... *if only to spare myself the lecture,*" I grumble. A scowl tugs at my face as I move to leave, but his shadows hold me tight.

"No," he growls, blocking the way. "There won't be a next time." His shadows slink up my legs to wind around my waist. "This would never have happened if you'd come with me today. I would have made sure you were safe."

"Safe? *With you?*" I loose a bitter laugh and lean in close, letting my gaze pierce him. "I'm surprised you didn't leave me in that alley to burn."

Rage floods his eyes, but I ignore the warning and push further. "Don't tell me you thought this was your moment of redemption?" I taunt. "Do you truly think today absolves you for what happened in Artolen?" I scoff. "You're a fool if you do."

He says nothing, though his shadows ripple around me angrily.

"Don't stand there and tell me you would have kept me safe today," I rage on. "You would have surely abandoned me the moment it benefited you."

Still he says nothing, merely glares down at me with untold violence swimming in those dark eyes.

I loose a frustrated grunt as I slap my hands against his chest. "Say something!" I curl my fingers into his tunic, dragging him closer. "Why are you here?" I bark, the thrum in my blood growing as loud as my words. "Why did you save me?"

Malachi's lips twitch into a scowl. "*Why did I save you?*" he parrots. "You cannot seriously be asking me that." His shadows snap and flare around us. "I saved you because I had to, because your recklessness left me with no other choice," he seethes. "I'm here because you need me."

"So that's what you'll have me believe?" I snap back. "That you're merely here to see this journey through? To make sure Rohan doesn't find me or the Hesha Mol?" I shake my head and loose a bitter laugh. "*Please.* You forget I know you, and the boy I grew up with cared not for Bair's madness or what other folly men chased. He only cared for himself."

He says nothing, and it's only by the flare in his eyes that I see I've hit a nerve. I can't help but spark it further.

I lean in close, words soft—yet laced in venom. "You're a selfish bastard, Malachi. You always were. So don't try to play the hero when we both know you'll be the first to leave when this is all over. You would have let that Torch take me back to Denheir if I wasn't the godsdamned Durit," I rasp.

He's on me the next second, hands wrapped around my wrists and shadows slinking up my sides. I try to shake him off, but his hold only tightens. "You truly think that?" Malachi snarls. "That I would have let him take you? That I didn't learn my lesson the first time?" His shadows cling to me possessively as he tugs me closer. "When are you going to open your eyes and see that I'm here. I'm *trying*," he grits out roughly. "I ran through the godsdamn city to find you today, Serehna. Not your so-called friends. Not that bounty hunter. *Me!*"

I thrash in his grip, but there's no escape. "What do you want? Huh? A *thank you*?" I chide. Emotion snakes up my throat and thickens my words. "*Gods above*," I choke out. "*Thank you* for saving me, Malachi. Thank you for not leaving me to die. I guess I should be grateful that this time you didn't abandon me like I meant nothing to you."

Anger flares across his face, but it's tainted by a decade's worth of guilt. "You have no idea what I went through that day," he utters.

"Then tell me!" I try to spit the words at him, but my voice breaks. "Tell me how you left your best friend to die like it was easy." My hands shake, and my chest is so tight it feels like I'm being crushed by stones. As I drop my gaze to where his shadows still cling to me, a tear splashes against my tunic.

When I finally look back at him, more fall. "How could you do that to me?" I ask. "You told me—I thought you..." I can't bear to admit it, and when I feel his shadows loosen, I pull away.

I stagger back, bare feet padding against the stone floor. Only when my legs hit the bed do I stop. I suck in a wavering breath, and with my heart pounding like a scared animal's, I find the strength to look at him again. "How could you toss me aside when I needed you the most?"

His eyes are dark pits of pain, tinged in lingering fury. Shadows swirl around his boots, wild and restless. Amidst the stilted silence that taints the air between us, I let myself truly examine the man I loved for the first time in years.

His hair drapes around his face like wisps of shadow. The midnight strands gleam under the candlelight and brush his ears. A few pieces fall over the right side of his forehead, spilling against his brow like they always have. The urge to brush them away rears up in me with a familiar, unrelenting ache. I clench my fists to stifle the instinct and let my eyes continue to wander.

Dark stubble lines his defined jaw and frames the full lips which color always reminded me of desert roses. When I spot the small scar on his chin—the one I myself dealt when he was teaching me how to wield a sword at fifteen—I quickly lower my gaze.

Foolishly, I let my eyes trail down his body. His marks have grown even more numerous since I saw him last, but I expected nothing less. The chaotic flurry of brush strokes and splotches is densely patterned across his olive skin, like a storm tearing across the Jahaer. Just like when we were teenagers, his fingers and knuckles are covered—a true warning of his gift. The marks race up both arms, bleeding over defined biceps and across the curve of his strong shoulders. There's a large scar winding down his left arm—one I don't recognize—and its raised, white ridge tells me it was deep.

Underneath the loose-fitting tunic he's wearing, I can see where his markings run horizontally across his chest and collarbones. The tight muscles flex and shudder as he breathes hard under my perusal. Above that, two small columns run up the sides of his neck, not unlike my own. The resemblance is enough to force my gaze away.

I stare at the floor, suddenly unsure of where to go from here. My heart feels split in two, and I know being in his presence any longer will only make it worse. I should leave, but before I can, he moves.

My gaze flickers up to him as he takes a slow step forward. I swallow, desperate to rid myself of the ache I feel, but it only deepens. In front of me is not only someone who betrayed me, but the home I lost all those years ago.

"That day in Artolen…"

I flinch at the sound of his voice sweeping low across the room.

Malachi takes a deep breath and steps closer. "It showed me how wrong I'd been."

Just as he raises a hand to brush the tears from my face, I reel back. "About what?" I challenge, voice shaking.

Silence is a roaring lull in my ears, a pained ache in my chest. Malachi's shadows slink up his arm, brushing against the inside of his wrist with a tenderness I know well. My heart drops into my stomach as I watch the darkness comfort him in a way I used to. I can all but feel my fingertips against his skin, calming him all those times the world strained his sanity.

I look up to see Malachi's eyes full of the same ache I know mine harbor.

"When the Turidens came…" His jaw clenches, and he looks away. "It was only a glimpse of what the future looked like for us." He shakes his head. "That wasn't a future I wanted."

It feels like the gods have ripped out my heart and filled my chest with sand. I swallow harshly and look at his boots. "One with me in it, you mean."

His fingers snatch my chin, raising my gaze up to him abruptly. "A future where we were on the wrong end of a blade," he rasps.

"What in the hells is that supposed to mean?" I rave, shoving him away. Though I know my strength is no match for his, he lets me push him back. "If you truly thought Artolen was that dangerous, we could have left. *Together.*"

"It was never Artolen that brought you danger."

My brows pinch, but as I open my mouth to speak, he stops me.

"It was me" —he gestures around the room with impatient hands— "and this filthy world we were born into."

My face contorts in confusion, but every ounce of frustration slips from my face when I feel his shadows. Just like before, they creep up my body until I feel the silky chill of their touch under my tunic. My breath hitches as Malachi lifts the hem with an unsteady hand, revealing the scar we both blame him for. The heat of his fingertips is a blazing fire compared to his shadows as he trails a path along my skin. I melt into it, grief and longing colliding unkindly in my chest. My eyes flutter closed, but the gods are quick to take away the comfort they falsely promised.

"I thought I was strong enough," Malachi utters. "But I wasn't." His fingers dance across my skin like he's savoring every touch. "Maybe I'm still not."

My eyes snap open instantly. "Wha—"

That dark gaze shutters before he comes back to himself. "It was my fault the Turidens came that day." His throat bobs, and his teeth clench. "They were there for me."

Though I yearn for it, I step away from his embrace as my heart patters nervously. My mind spins dangerous webs, and the distraught look on Malachi's face doesn't help to untangle them.

"I was foolish," he grits out. "I thought my gift made me invincible, thought I could spill their blood like they'd spilled so much of ours. I didn't think they'd…"

My brow crumples as I stare at him with a renewed panic pumping through my chest. "What did you do?"

He can't even look at me now. His shadows curl around his boots, almost hiding.

"*Malachi*," I utter, tone grating through his silence. "What did you—"

"I told you I was going to Levahren for a few days," he says. "Told you I was seeing an old friend."

My mouth forms against words I can't manage to utter.

"I went to find them," Malachi admits. "I'd heard rumors of a camp outside Menfi." He grits his teeth, still unable to meet my eyes. "And that's right where I found them."

My gift thrums uneasily. "Mal—"

"I killed three of them before the others woke." He laughs bitterly and forces his gaze up to the ceiling. "I couldn't believe how easy it was, how quickly their blood had pooled into the sand."

I stare at him through wide eyes, heart hammering.

"I got cocky," he seethes. "And it almost cost me my life." He shakes his head and *tsks*. "I should have stayed to kill them all, but they'd dealt their own damage. I knew I needed to find a Mender. But more than that, I knew I needed to get back to Artolen before you came looking for me."

My eyes flicker across his face as I try to put the pieces together.

"I should have been more careful," he admonishes. "Should have spent a few days away and risked your worry rather than lead them home."

Suddenly, everything makes sense, and I feel the world fall out beneath my feet.

"I didn't think—" Unsteady breath saws through his throat. "If I would have known they were following me that day. If I would have realized it sooner..."

"*Chani,*" I whisper. Tears spill silently down my cheeks, but I don't bother to brush them away. My throat feels swollen with grief, though I choke the words out anyway. "You're saying she's dead because you saw fit to taunt our enemies?"

"Serehna—"

"She died because of you!" I yell. "I almost died because of you!"

I stagger back, collapsing onto the mattress as my legs hit the bed. I lower my head into my hands and try to quiet my mind, but the truth is a raging storm inside of me. For a while, I just breathe—breathe and try to understand it all. It doesn't take me long, for things are far too simple now.

When I finally look up at Malachi, my gaze is hatefully dark. "Why did you run?"

"Serehna, please understand—"

"No," I snap. "I need to hear you say it."

His face contorts in resignation. Though I wait for his words, he merely stares at me. He waits like I'll change my mind.

I stand up slowly, eyes blazing like a hundred fires. "*Say. It.*" I bite.

Malachi swallows harshly, but finds it in himself to stand up straight. I watch him mask his face of all emotion, just like I've done every day since Artolen.

"I left because I refused to watch the girl I loved bleed out in the street when it was me who'd brought devils to her door." He takes a step closer, but his words don't lull me like he expects them to.

"You ran because you were a coward," I argue, voice shaking. "You left me to die because you didn't want to face what you'd done."

He grits his teeth so hard his jaw feathers with tension. "You're right," he admits. "I couldn't face it. I couldn't watch you die." His gaze burns into me. "Happy, now?"

A hollow laugh spills from my throat. "*Happy*? For what reason?" I rasp. "That after all these years of wondering, I finally know the truth?"

His brows pinch tightly as he glowers at me.

I shove him only to dig my fingers into his tunic and yank him back. "I'm so glad you've unburdened yourself," I spit. "So grateful I finally know how little you cared for me."

Just as I move to storm past him, he quickly pins my arms to my sides. "What do you want me to say, Serehna?" he seethes, breath spilling over my shoulder as he looms behind me. "That leaving you in Artolen was the worst day of my life? That finding you trapped in that alley today, broken and bleeding, was the second?" The words spit from his lips, as hot and wicked as flames. "Though I assumed you dead up until a few months ago, not a day has gone by in the past eleven years that I haven't been haunted by thoughts of you."

He scoffs and shakes his head at no one but himself. "Do you know how angry I've been since I learned you were alive? How often I wonder what would have been if I'd only stayed?" His fingers curl against my shoulders as he clings to me. "It's devouring me, Serehna. Choking every breath," he rasps in my ear. "As much as you hate me for leaving, I hate myself more."

"Good," I mutter. "Because that hate is well deserved." Tears blur my vision, but I hold them back. "Unlike you, I haven't had the privilege of living the last decade thinking you were dead. I've been well aware that you were out there somewhere, indifferent to how I was left broken and with nothing and no one to trust."

I spin to face him—to show him my hatred—but I can't hide the emotions wetting my eyes. "I don't care what lies you tell yourself when you lay your head down each night. You made your decision that day. There's no changing the past." My lips twitch into a sneer as I stretch on my toes to reach his ear. "And you seem plenty happy with your Weaver for someone supposedly shackled by guilt," I bite through a whisper.

Something curious flashes through Malachi's eyes, but he's quick to hide it behind his arrogance. "Is that what you think, Serehna?" he retorts. "That I'm happy?" He looses a breathy laugh, and runs a hand through his hair. "If proximity is all it takes to make an attachment, I could say the same thing about you and that hunter." His eyes flare dangerously as he leans down to meet my gaze. "Could I not?"

His shadows are a cool, sinful tease against my overly warm skin. My anger fades as I watch his tongue dart out across his lip before his mouth presses against my ear.

"Tell me I'm wrong, Serehna. Tell me this is one, big misunderstanding and I'll gladly say the same."

Breath wavers unsteadily in my lungs. My gift is a constant companion under my skin, and for once, I'm glad for its presence. I want it to strike and wound. I want to make the man before me bleed if only to unleash a decade's worth of pain. But Veles's fury is a quiet thing at present, thrumming as weakly as my own heart. I'm left with only a godless rage, but that, too, feels lifeless.

Exhaustion coats my body like a second skin. So much of Mikel's healing touch has stripped me of all strength. I'm weak and unable to keep the fire lit for long. I have no more yelling in me; I only wish to rest.

In my lull, I've forgotten myself and the man before me. Like they have a mind of their own, Malachi's shadows have curled around my lower back where they now hold me tightly to him. It's a simple comfort, a moment I wish I could suspend time for. If it were a dream I would stay here forever, but this is far from those temporal places only found in sleep. This is something far worse—something I dare not allow myself in the daylight. For it would certainly break me if I did.

I pull away from Malachi slowly and mourn his familiar warmth as it disappears. "I will go with you to Tol Dena," I mutter toward the floor, unable to meet his gaze. "I will search for the Hesha Mol and stop Rohan from becoming the Born."

More tears threaten to spill from my eyes, but I fight them with everything I have left. "But once it's done" —my throat constricts with the force of a heartbreak I thought I was done living— "you will never see me again."

"Serehna—"

"My name is Ren!" I snap.

His shadows flinch, and I glare at him with all the hate I can muster.

"You best get used to the taste of it on your tongue, for it's all I'll be answering to."

His eyes flare with something beastly as he stares back at me. Part of me wants him to argue—to never end this fight—but he simply backs away.

"You slept through the night," he utters. "Now that you're healed, we need to leave." His jaw ticks as he pulls his gaze from mine. "That woman, Savi, packed your bags. Clean yourself up and meet me outside. It's only a matter of time before the Torch gets reinforcements and picks up our trail. We best be deep into the desert before that happens."

I take a moment to survey my surroundings, just now realizing this is not my tent, nor anywhere in the city. It's much too quiet in here, almost calming. The room is dark and cozy, with candles perched atop a wooden desk amidst the clutter of parchment and books. An assortment of charcoal sketches litters the floor, and the mere sight halts my breath. Recognition tugs my chest, and my heart drops into my stomach. I should look away, but I can't, not when I catch sight of my own face among the careful smudges of black. Though I wish I had forgotten after all this time, the memory of marked hands sketching in dark alleyways is still fresh in my mind.

"Whose room is this?" I ask, even though I already know.

For the first time since he burst through the door, the tension seems to melt from Malachi's shoulders. He sighs like the last two days have been as long for him as they've been for me. "I wasn't going to let you sleep in anyone's bed but mine."

His eyes don't leave mine for even a breath, and I scowl as my traitorous body flutters at the attention. "Leave me, then," I urge. "I'll ready myself."

He holds his ground for a few seconds before muttering something I can't hear. I watch him slip out the door, and only when he closes it behind him do I loose a breath and expend all my pent-up frustration.

"*Gods drag me under and mark my blood,*" I curse.

I look for something to kick, then realize the commotion will only have Malachi barging back in here. Instead, I drop to the floor and curl my knees into my chest. As I drop my head into my hands, fresh tears prick my eyes. "*Fucking hells,*" I rasp.

I try to still my mind, but the chaos outside the door is an unwelcome distraction. Pots clang and chairs scoot against the floor. I hear voices mumble, tense and frustrated. It seems everyone is hurrying about—packing up supplies and preparing to leave. I know my time is limited, and yet, I sit a little longer. With my eyes closed, I breathe as steadily as I can. I try not to think of Malachi, or Chani, or that day, but it seems I can't help myself. More tears slip soundlessly down my cheeks until I have no more to offer.

I wipe away the evidence of the weak thing I have become and begin to stand, but stop when I spot what I had so quickly forgotten. My hand reaches slowly—fearful like it may bite. The hesitation is foolish, and I quickly snag the parchment, tugging it out of the stack. When candlelight illuminates the drawing, my throat tightens. I clench my teeth to stave off the tremble I feel, but it's not enough. My eyes race across the page, and the ache in my chest grows the more I study it.

It's a perfect likeness. Though I don't know when he had time to draw it, the sketch reveals me as I am now. Older than I once was, riddled with scars and imperfections like worn pottery. But it's the sight of my markings that has my hand shaking against the parchment. Drawn with meticulous precision, Malachi has captured every flare of Veles's claim in a way I have yet to memorize myself. It's violent and chaotic, but *beautiful.* I suck in a wavering breath as more tears come. The moment is lost to an overwhelming rush of emotions, tossing me from anguish to anger in the blink of an eye. My hand clenches the drawing— suddenly overcome with the urge to crumple it, if only to rid it from this earth. I should, but I can't bring myself to.

It's with a thick swallow and a foolish heart that I carefully fold the paper and tuck it in my pocket for safekeeping. As I get up off the floor, I don't allow myself to think about what it means that he drew it, nor what it says about me that I can't bear to part with it now. Instead, I merely take a deep breath and turn my mind to more important matters.

The door to the washroom is open, and I quickly slip inside to clean the blood from my skin. Once I've rinsed away every last fleck of red, I change into the fresh clothes Mikel must have brought in earlier. I hesitate in front of the mirror, fighting the urge to catch another glimpse of who I have become. *Will I see someone broken by yet another fight with the cruelest the Continent has to offer? Or will I see myself as Malachi does?*

My heart gives a wild thump as I dig through my dirtied clothes without second thought. I snatch the drawing free, only to tuck it into my pocket once more. Some part of me regrets having looked at the thing in the first place, *for how can I forget the past if it's still staining my fingers?*

Fuck. I wipe the smeared charcoal off on my pants and stand up straighter.

As the flurry of voices and the rush of footsteps meets my ears once more, I find myself lingering at the bedroom door. Reminders of Hira buzz through my mind like flies on a fresh carcass, leaving me unsteady and sick.

The bustle of the markets.

The reverent words Lorik uttered.

My gut-wrenching fall and the violence that followed.

But what cuts deeper than those memories is the reminder that some wounds take years to heal, and even after time scars them over, they can be re-opened so easily.

I grit my teeth and open the bedroom door with such force I'm surprised it didn't rip off the hinges. As I wander through the house, I'm hit with an uncanny feeling and a dizzying flicker in my vision. The frenzy around me plays out in a way that feels too familiar, but equally as faraway. I've been here before, though I can't remember when. For a moment, I'm overcome by the bitter tug in my chest—a resentment for the fact that I've never asked Hael for clearer sight. But as I stare out across the room, at the frantic packing and muffled words that pass between tightly pursed lips, I remind myself that it's probably for the best.

There's no changing the past or the future, and even if I could foresee what is to come, the flickers I've been given are clear enough. Whatever the gods have planned—whatever awaits us after this—it's nothing good.

CHAPTER 20

The chaos follows me outside as I step from the house. Saddles are packed with gear. Camels spit peevishly in the sand, while horses chuff and stomp. Everyone moves on quick feet, darting past each other and securing all we need for the journey ahead. They haven't noticed me yet—something I'm grateful for.

I spot Mikel amidst the frenzy, and it's with weighted hesitation that I make my way toward him. He's standing next to his horse, eyes rigidly fixed on the strip of horizon that holds our biggest threat. We'll need to wind around the northern tip of Hira to get into the desert, which means slipping by the city unseen. Something uneasy quivers through me at the thought of heading back there so soon, but I know it must be done.

Mikel's focus snaps to me as I sidle up next to him. There's tension lingering in his shoulders, but he looks away before I can offer anything to clear the air between us. I fidget where I stand, letting the silence eat at me as I bide my time. Though I know what I should say—what I should promise him—I find I'm unable to.

Mikel's gaze stays locked ahead when he finally speaks up. "Vish says the path is clear. The Torch is still deep in the city, nursing his pride and recruiting new men."

I don't ask how Vish knows this for certain when he knew so little of me, so instead I simply loose a deep sigh. "Good," I utter. "I reckon we should be able to make it a few days before I succumb to any more catastrophic wounds." My eyes flash to him playfully, though my stomach is twisted in knots. "Seems you'll have to pull your weight around here some other way."

I wait for the telltale prickle of a smirk or the bite of more icy silence. I hope it's the former, but my body stills in preparation for the latter. When Mikel finally turns toward me, the defiant scowl he offers floods my heart with relief.

"Oh, I think I'll have plenty to manage," he sneers. "For my best friend is a reckless fool." He crosses his arms over his chest and glares. "I don't know whether I should tie you to a post at night or simply toss you into the bounty hunter's tent so he can persuade you to stay out of trouble."

The devious smirk I know and love softens Mikel's face and tells me all is well between us. He steps closer, dropping his voice low even though the others are far too busy to overhear. "On second thought, maybe I'll toss you into the arms of that Shade. He'll keep you put. Gods know you want him, and he you. He practically wrung my neck last night when I told him I'd have to wait until this morning to heal the rest of your wounds."

If I had something in hand, I would throw it at Mikel. Instead, I shoot him a murderous look and tug him by the arm. "Hush," I growl. My eyes dart around, but Malachi is nowhere to be seen. "You know not what you speak of."

Mikel lets out a breathy laugh. "*Please*," he chides. "Save it for someone else. I know you, and it's clear to me and anyone with eyes that something stirs between the two of you."

"*Mikel*," I grit out. "There is nothing between Mal—" I stop myself, choking back the name. It tastes too fresh and bitter on my tongue. Regretfully, I swallow the urge to tell Mikel everything that burdens me. Speaking of it now will only pry the wound wider. I simply avoid his gaze instead. "The Shade knows his place," I mutter. "He's my key to getting to Tol Dena in one piece. His company is a necessary burden."

Mikel raises a brow. "And the hunter?"

I open my mouth to offer a quick retort, but uncertainty muddies my words. The mere thought of Hassan's gentle touches and lingering looks seeks to drown me. With the grit of my teeth, I force my head above the swell.

"An ally," I offer carefully. "Nothing more."

Mikel chuckles, shaking his head as he begins to walk away. "Sure, Ren. Just you, the necessary burden, and the ally."

He hoists himself into the saddle and settles in for the long trek. His horse shoots me a wide-eyed stare as he guides it closer. "I'll be sure to say *I told you so* when I see you leaving one of their tents, utterly and completely satisfied." My friend shoots me a wicked smirk. "Who knows... Maybe you'll fuck both."

I sputter as a vibrant red overtakes my face. "That will never—"

"Oh, speak of the devil," Mikel snickers. "Should we ask him what—"

I slap Mikel's boot and utter threats under my breath as Hassan approaches. The bounty hunter looks from me to Mikel uncertainly, no doubt clocking the shit-eating grin stretched across my friend's face and the panic that's poorly concealed on mine.

Hassan's brow is furrowed with unspoken questions as he stretches out his hand to offer me the reins of my camel. "Your things are already packed. We need to leave now so we can pass Hira's rim before sundown."

I nod stiffly, too flustered to offer any argument. As I take the reins from him, his fingers brush against mine. It startles me more than it should, and once again memories of his warm touch threaten to crack me wide open. My heart beats too fast, faster still as he lingers. Time is lost to me; I can only stare at his strong hands as my mind spins dangerously. When I finally lift my gaze, I see my own unease dancing across his features. It's too raw, too real. With a quivering breath, I pull away.

"Thanks," I utter, heading toward the camel.

I feel multiple pairs of eyes on me as I search the saddle to find that—yes, my things are all there. I quickly dig through my pack to retrieve the daggers Mikel must have tucked away for safe keeping. I could kiss him for such things. After I've sheathed blades in every holster, I count them again, just to be sure. Thanks to that death-bringer of a Torch, I now boast six blades instead of four. As I take a step forward, the stiff pressure in my right boot brings a smile to my face.

Seven blades.

I run my hand along the camel's side, earning a groan that is either appreciative or agitated. I can never tell with camels. With a sigh, I hoist myself up and settle into the saddle. It's the same animal I rode to Hira—an ornery thing I've yet to name. And though I've dreaded returning to the discomfort of my last ride, it seems an extra layer of padding has been added beneath me. As my hips wiggle into the wooden platform, I no longer feel the harsh bite of its edges. I shoot Hassan a curious look, vaguely recalling he purchased some blankets at the market yesterday.

As if sensing my train of thought, he looks away and clears his throat. "Vish wants you in the middle of the caravan at all times. It will lessen the likelihood someone recognizes you and will make it harder for them to attack without retaliation from one of us."

I go to argue that I can handle whatever comes my way, when a cold understanding sinks in. *I can't,* I realize. Yesterday was proof enough. Shame heats my chest, growing with a vicious simmer. Veles's gift is wasted on me. I didn't even think to use it—couldn't even conjure a flicker of shadow when my life depended on it. *And my combat skills?* They're no use against fire.

I sink my teeth into the inside of my cheek and nod. "Fine."

Hassan's gaze tightens on me, as if he, too, expected a fight. He grunts and throws me one more odd look before stalking back to his horse.

When I glance at Mikel, his mischievous smile burns my frustrations hotter. "Utter so much as a word..." I challenge.

He only laughs and guides his horse to where the others are gathering at the mouth of the canyon. I follow, slinking through the group until I've found my place among them.

Mikel settles his horse next to Savi, and the pair quickly fall into conversation. Though the sound of their happy voices should settle me, I'm only left on edge. The day's growing heat already feels smothering. The sun is too bright. The air is too dry. Amidst the typical chaos that accompanies a new journey, my mind spins on its own accord. After all that happened yesterday and all I've learned this morning, I don't know what to think. So, I try not to.

The lively chatter that dances between Savi and Mikel is a harsh contrast to the tensely bound shoulders around me. My gaze flickers about, taking in what is to be—for all intents and purposes—my escort across the Jahaer.

Hassan and Tariq have positioned themselves at the rear; I don't know if I'm relieved or nervous that Hassan will be watching my back the entire journey. To my far left rests Vish and Savi. While Savi is still immersed in conversation with Mikel, discussing herbal remedies for burns, I find Vish's focus locked on his journal. His gaze flickers across the scribbled lines of text, devouring every word before his swift fingers flip the page. I wonder how deep of a sleeper Vish is and where he might hide that journal when he rests his head at night. My fingers twitch, as if eager to prove they can still swipe the most valuable of prizes out from under the most oblivious of noses.

The feeling of being watched rips my gaze from the journal's worn pages. Behind Vish rides one of the Berserkers from the canyon. His deep blue eyes bore into mine as a smile drifts across his face. *Tofá,* I remember—though I care little to. He rests a good distance from the others, flanking the caravan like a watchdog. I repress a sneer and thank the gods I won't have to deal with his company today. I've barely spoken a word to him, but I know enough. He's a part of the group of daemons Vish speaks of sometimes—the ones who are determined to keep the Born from being created.

Or is it Malachi the two Berserkers claim loyalty to?

My brow pinches as I think back to that day in the gorge. The pair was clearly looking for the Durit, and I've replayed enough of Tofá's words to know he suspected me. As I pull my gaze away from said Berserker—who still watches me with morbid fascination and a challenging smirk—I can't help but wonder why Vish kept me from them.

If the plan was to bring me to Hira all along, why didn't Tofá and Ivar join us?

Silas pops into my mind without pause. Like a fresh wound that's scabbed over, I don't let it rest. I know I shouldn't, but the urge to tear and scar is too compelling. Though, instead of the hot rush of blood seeping from his chest or the lifeless stare of those gray eyes, memory takes me back to that day in the canyon. He had seemed so worried for my safety—so possessive. But as my mind replays those moments over and over again, it's like a blindfold being pushed back. Too soon, the true nature of the man I invited into my bed is revealed to me, and I feel sick.

When Tofá and Ivar approached that day, Silas wasn't holding me back for my benefit. No, he was holding me back so no one could snatch away the prize he'd already claimed. Nausea churns deep in my belly, and I dig my fingernails into my palms to distract myself.

I urge my camel forward, finding pace with the others from where I'd begun to fall behind. Just as Hassan said: my place is in the middle. I no longer care that I've been carefully positioned out of harm's way; my mind is swimming far from shore. I barely register Kai and Riat to my right, flanked by a distant Ivar. The pair of young hunters chat noisily, and though a distant awareness tells me they're calling my name, I'm too busy replaying every interaction I had with Silas to notice. Every word. Every gesture. It's all a reminder of what I was so blind to—what I refused to see.

The way he could have easily broken free of his chains and escaped, but never attempted to.

How he always found a way to be close to me—not out of affection, but out of the need to keep his prey in sight.

The things he said to create strife between myself and the others.

All that talk of fate leading him to me in the slot canyon.

I want to scream and destroy everything in my path until the riotous ache in my chest goes away. But as the caravan slowly treks toward Hira, I can only stare ahead with a lifeless gaze.

My mind is a vast storm—one I can't break free of. Every memory feels like the harsh grit of sand against skin as it's sprayed by violent winds. Just when I think I've combed through every false deed and gesture, the reminder of his words cuts deeper. It's like I can hear his voice echoing in my ear, teasing me even now. That deep purr was always laced in temptation and falsehoods, and I let it lead me straight into the hands of my enemies. Worse than his performance, I realize, is the truth he hid plainly.

"Virtue doesn't mean shit if you don't survive."

It was so clear. So painfully, brutally clear. But I couldn't see it. Wouldn't. I had thought he cared, thought he saw us as equals—kindred-spirits trying to survive the godsdamn Continent. Oh, how I had been wrong.

Before I can staunch the pain seeping from me like an open wound, the worst of his truths finds me. On our way to Letka, he had given me clues. He had told me then and there what his intentions were, had spoken them so plainly that reliving it now feels like the air has been sucked from my lungs.

"...there is no kin among daemons. We'll all gladly lie and cheat our way around each other if it means another day alive."

Though my throat is raw and achy, I want nothing more than to bellow and curse the gods for this torture. Instead, I dig my teeth deep into my tongue—for it's my own ignorance that led me here. I beg the gods for it not to be true, for me not to have been so naive. But like it was divinely summoned, Silas's smirk is a taunt in my mind—forever a reminder of how I was so easily bested.

Only when my teeth bite too roughly and blood sprouts on my tongue, do I shake myself from the past. The coppery tang forces me back to the real world, but what I've discovered hangs over me like death's shroud.

All around, conversation passes in muffled tones. There's the occasional laugh or taunt, the latter often muttered between Riat and Kai at Ivar's expense. The Berserker grumbles, shooting hot glares at the pair, seeming less than enthused to be stuck within earshot of them. The caravan lulls and pitches with life like any living thing. Hooves plod against the hard-packed earth. Voices mumble, then still. Canteens slosh, and camels groan. It's all a welcome distraction, a numbing balm for my bleeding heart. I wish it made a difference.

Up ahead, a black head of hair snags my focus, transforming the roaring anguish in my heart to an easy, comfortable hate. Malachi rides next to Quin—his tall, powerful frame towering over her petite one. The rose-colored fabric of her dress is draped across her legs and saddle, making her look like the one in need of an escort across the Continent. As I watch the pair chat in hushed tones, Silas's treachery is momentarily forgotten. The sight is a jarring reminder that not all enemies rest at my back. Though it's been days since my last nightmare, the thought of that gods-drenched canyon is all it takes to stir fresh rage in my chest.

Surely there was an easier way to find me than to torment me while I rest?

My hands grip the reins too tightly. I was foolish to trust Silas, but I would be even more a fool to trust Malachi and his Weaver. My teeth grind as I glare at the back of the Malachi's head. Like sensing the heat of my stare, he glances over his shoulder. When his eyes meet mine, I feel the presence of Veles surge in my veins. The itching. The inescapable pull of violence. I feel the fire in my blood burn ten times hotter. And, by the gods, I will it to burst free. That spark of thrill dies out too quickly though, drifting away as if it sensed how I sought to waste its power on petty heartache. I snarl as the dwindling flow reminds me how weak I truly am.

Malachi hasn't taken his eyes off me, and it's with a flicker of panic that I realize he's slowed his horse. The distance closes between us too quickly, and I before I know it, he's riding next to me.

My body locks down in anticipation, though I mask the unease from my face the best I can. "What do you want, *Shade*?" I ask snidely as my gaze runs over him with quiet contempt. "Do you have more secrets to share? Or did you come to bother me for some other reason?"

"I came to remind you what this is," he snarls. His shadows slither up the reins, though his horse doesn't so much as flinch. "This isn't some leisurely trek across the desert. I don't care what you think of me. I don't care if you ever utter my name again. It means nothing to me."

His throat bobs, betraying his words, but he's quick to recover. There is no taunt in his gaze, no playful smirk. He glares at me with a crude arrogance I saw for years, but was never victim to. It's an effort not to shrink from it now, and as he guides his horse closer, I tense my hands against the reins.

"It's no wonder the Torch tracked you so easily, considering how careless you are," Malachi mocks. "But that ends now."

"I'm not—"

"Cover your face and neck. *Now*, Serehna!" he growls. The fury in his tone makes me flinch. "Need I remind you who and what you are?" His lip twitches as he continues to admonish me. "It's not just your fate you're playing with here. You might be willing to risk your life, but I am not." The look in his eyes makes me feel too small. It's resentment that flares in his gaze, chewing me to pieces and leaving nothing intact. "Cover your marks, *Durit*," he orders. "Or I'll cover them for you."

He kicks his horse's side and returns to the front of the caravan a moment later. I know the others are watching, but I don't dare meet their gazes. Their stares churn my shame and coat the back of my throat thick in emotion. Frustrated tears prick my eyes as I yank scarf after scarf from my pack. My camel saunters forward, following the herd as I obscure myself in drapings of beige and tan fabrics. When I'm done, like always, the only thing left to see is my eyes.

As I glare at the back of Malachi's head once again, I find the hate I feel isn't for him—not entirely. He's right. It was careless to leave the house without concealing my identity. It was foolish to have let my face be seen in the city. There's not a part of my body that doesn't reveal me for who I am. My marks. My scars. They're all beacons for those who wish me harm. I'm a liability to the others if I can't stay hidden.

Every sway of my camel's languid pace tries to lull me into a quiet trance, further fueled by the heat that clings to the morning. But my mind is anything but settled. I've consulted my map; I know just how far the destination lies ahead. Never have I been so far west as Tol Dena, and as my eyes burn into the Shade that leads the way, I'm not sure I can survive the weeks it will take to get there.

Malachi is a dagger pressed to my side. A hutri flea burrowing into my skin. There's only so much more of him I can bear. And if he keeps fanning the flames between us, I might just kill him.

CHAPTER 21

Night has fallen, and with it brings a false sense of safety. We've passed Hira and crested its most northern point. Now, all that lies ahead is the same unforgiving sea of sand I can never seem to escape. The Jahaer Desert.

The steady plodding of hoofbeats against hard-packed earth has been replaced by the soft *swish* of sand. Overhead, the moon provides a soft glow to light the way. Its orange rim paints the desert in lush warmth, but the crisp air that creeps across my skin is anything but comforting.

I curl into myself, bundled in the long tunic I pulled from my pack as soon as night fell. Despite the layers I've draped myself in, the cold is all I can feel. It wracks my body with shivers and seeps deep into my bones. Not even the wine Mikel offered me did anything to stave off the chill.

We've been traveling for hours, but I know many more lie ahead. By the time the sun had sunk below the horizon, Malachi made it clear we weren't stopping. He's eager to reach Raulik before our enemies have the chance to catch up. I'd wanted to argue after pulling out my map and figuring how many days that meant in the saddle, but one look at Malachi's dark, simmering gaze told me it was a fight I wouldn't win.

I've tried to keep my mind far from him, but without fail, I find my focus wandering to the front of the caravan. He leads the way with purpose, never offering so much as a backward glance. We haven't spoken since we left the house, and though I know I should be grateful for the distance he keeps, it only deepens the ache I feel. My thoughts tug me in all directions, all at once. I'm reminded of the reasons I should hate him, then reminded why I cannot. It's only when I sweep my gaze to Malachi's right and spot his Weaver that the bitter twinge in my heart sets me straight.

I grip the reins too tightly and tear my focus away from Quin. I don't need to witness more of the murmured conversations that pass between the pair. I've seen enough over the last few hours. It's always the same anyway. He speaks first, mumbling things that have his jaw clenching and shadows flaring against his wrists. Then Quin's hand is there, bridging the space between them with a reassuring touch. It doesn't matter how often I've witnessed it, it bunches my stomach in knots each and every time. I don't know what they discuss, but Malachi seeks her comfort, and that's all I need to know.

Quin's bubbly laugh is like a stake to the heart. I search for something to distract me, but there's little out here except for the others. Everyone has found their place among the caravan, and quiet conversations drift through the night in hushed tones. A glance over my shoulder shows that Tariq still holds the rear, but Ivar and Tofá have pulled back to join him. As I spot the two Berserkers engaged in deep discussions with him, I can't help but wonder if Tariq feels a sense of ease among them.

What do they talk about? I ask myself. *How godsblood curses some and eludes others? The lives they've lived to bring them here?*

I wonder if he finds comfort in being around those who boast the same gift as his late aunt. As a soft smile plays across Tariq's face, I allow myself to believe that it does.

My gaze drifts back through the caravan, and what I see almost rouses a laugh. Hassan was quick to put distance between himself and the Berserkers, though he always seems to have them in his sights. Judging by the way he grimaces at them now, I'd say the incident in the canyon is still fresh on his mind. As he turns back to continue his conversation with Savi, the tension doesn't melt from his face. Though when his eyes dart to me, that changes.

His hazel gaze locks on mine with a curious depth I can't place. He's looked at me like that ever since Hira, sneaking glances when he thinks I'm not looking. I thought it was anger at first—thought the hate he once held for me was back for good. But what I see now isn't the same harsh glare that used to greet me every time I slipped from my tent. It's more complicated, harder to place. It's hesitation and worry. Heat and wrath. It's a look that unsettles me.

Should I draw a blade? Do I want to?

All I know is that it vexes me. I roll my eyes at Hassan, showing him I'm not pleased with his staring. His jaw clenches before he quickly turns back to Savi. Though I know he hoped it would be quiet enough to be missed, I catch the muttered retort he hurls at his cousin. The night is quiet, and secrets have a way of slipping across sands much too easily. As my name leaves Savi's lips, I still atop my saddle. It's a quick, whispered thing—a comment I barely hear—but I understand the sentiment well enough. My cheeks blush in time with Hassan's, and, once more, I find myself searching for a distraction.

As I look around, eager to forget how Savi teased her cousin for staring at me like Riat does, I catch sight of Mikel. He drifted away some hours ago—tempted by Kai and the taste of a sweet treat Savi got him at the bazaar. Though the candied pears have long since been devoured, it seems Mikel has found a permanent place next to the hunter. Their horses saunter side by side while they chat happily. Only the occasional interruption from Riat is able to break the men's focus from each other.

My chest warms at the sight of Kai's flushed cheeks and the smile that's stretched so wide across Mikel's face I know it must hurt. Though I've sunken into numb silence over the past few hours, I urge my camel closer—if only to hear my friend's rich, infectious laugh better.

"...cornered in this alley. Absolutely no way out except for up. And you know what he does?" Kai asks. His eyes are bright as he looks at Mikel, waiting for the moment the Mender urges his story onward.

"*Hm.* He went up?" Mikel offers with a smirk.

I don't miss the way Mikel holds Kai's gaze with heady rapture, nor the way Kai blushes further at the attention.

It takes the hunter a moment to shake himself out of his stupor and remember what he was even talking about. "He went up!" Kai exclaims. "The bastard starts climbing the walls like some kind of spider. Makes it halfway before he slips." Kai shakes his head, smiling all the while. "So there he is, clinging to a window ledge with one arm, dangling like a madman. What am I supposed to do? Strike a man with his back turned? While he hangs on for his godsdamn life?"

Riat chuckles, popping up beside his friend. "You're supposed to show him what a stupid idea running was." He leans forward in his saddle and gives Mikel a devious smile. "Which is exactly what I did."

Kai groans.

"What did you do?" Mikel asks with a chuckle.

"He climbed up the damn wall after him!" Kai levels an annoyed look at Riat before his toothy smile takes over once more. "I thought I was about to watch you fall to your death. *Veles burn me.*" He laughs before his smile wavers. He winces, then looks at Riat. "Too soon for fire jokes?"

Riat only rolls his eyes and waves his friend off. "Finish the fucking story before I do," he taunts. "You're boring your beloved."

Kai flashes Riat a crude gesture before turning back to Mikel with a scorching blush. "So this idiot here" —he jerks his thumb at Riat— "climbed up after the bounty, sending him into a full-blown panic. He was shaking, swaying from side to side. Started to lose his grip on the godsdamn window. *Fucking hells.* Before I knew it, Riat had climbed high enough to reach him and the poor bastard nearly leapt from the wall by means of escape."

Riat grins.

"And after that?" Mikel prompts Kai. "Did you get him?"

The pride that washes over Kai's face is unmistakable. "He took one look at my swords and turned himself in."

Mikel's eyes flicker to the curved steel strapped to Kai's back. "I've never wielded anything bigger than a dagger." His gaze drifts back to Kai, causing another flush to redden the hunter's face. "Would you teach me?"

I have to purse my lips together to stop the laughter from slipping free. Kai has gone so red it's as though the sun still shines and bakes him where he sits. Even amidst the soft glow of the moon, it's hard to miss how flustered he is.

"Uh, yeah. Of course," he stammers, dropping his gaze as he chokes on the words. "Anytime."

As soon as the breathy laugh inevitably slips from my lips, Mikel's attention snaps to me. I give him a knowing look, and though he scoffs, I spot the happiness hidden beneath his irritation.

"Was wondering when you were going to join us," Mikel says. "You were off in your own little world, moping for ages."

My tongue clicks against my teeth in objection. "I was not *moping.*"

Mikel raises a brow before his gaze darts to the front of the caravan. I don't need to follow his line of sight to know exactly who it is he's looking at.

"No, you're right," he utters. "It's totally normal to be silent for hours, staring ahead with nothing but murder in your eyes." The devious smirk on his face tells me I'm more than caught.

I merely shrug my shoulders. "I'm surprised you even noticed what I was doing." My gaze flickers to Kai, connecting with the man's soft, green eyes before turning back toward my friend. "You seem to be pretty preoccupied yourself."

As the shit-eating grin slinks across my face, Mikel sighs like I was born with the sole purpose of tormenting him.

He should be so lucky.

"We were just swapping stories." He says it casually, but the easy smile on his face gives him away. "Kai was telling me about this bounty they caught in Weshí last year. Reminded me of the time you fought that man in the alley. You know... the one with the pretty eyes."

I tip my head back and let out a deep, rumbling groan. "*Oh gods,*" I mutter. "I forgot about that."

"What happened?" Kai prods. He urges his horse closer as Riat does the same.

Mikel shoots me a mischievous look before he begins. "You see, Ren here hates town. Hates it so much that after she joined our caravan, it took three months to convince her to go on a supply run."

I roll my eyes and shove his shoulder. "You make it sound like I was sitting on my ass the whole time." I lean forward to catch both Riat and Kai's attention. "I went hunting every morning. Brought back my fair share of desert hares. We had food. We weren't starving."

"No," Mikel adds. "But *by the gods*, I could only eat your unseasoned, roasted meat so many times before I wanted to hide your blades and steal your saddle."

"So the goddess can't cook?" Riat comments. "I knew she was too good to be true."

"I can fucking cook!"

Riat chuckles, though his gaze grows feral. "It's okay. I'd much rather cook for you," he coos. "That way I can bring you breakfast while you're still resting in my bed."

"Boss is going to kill you if you don't stop," Kai taunts, elbowing him.

"We'll all be dead before he makes a move," Riat whispers a little too loudly. "Why should I waste my chance with her?"

"*Gods*," I utter, pinching the bridge of my nose.

Mikel snickers.

My eyes flare hotly, though he only winks before turning back toward the two men. "So I bring Ren to town with me," he continues. "It's a few hours journey, and by the time we get there she's as cranky as trapped devils. Had her knives out, ready to slit the closest throat."

Riat sighs. "*Gods*, I love a violent woman."

"Fuck's sake," Kai chuckles, flicking his ear. "Listen to the story."

"Somehow, I managed to drag her to the closest tavern and calm her down." Mikel *tuts*. "Two pints of ale later, and she actually seemed to be enjoying herself."

I smile as I remember that night, however hazy it was.

"Two pints quickly turned to four," Mikel continues. "Granted, I had only known this woman for a few months. I'd never seen her drunk, had no idea how much ale she could handle."

I loose a breathy laugh. "Usually it would have been more, but I'd been so nervous about the whole thing that I'd barely eaten all day. I was drunk to the gods with no worries of where I was or who was watching."

Mikel presses his fingers to his lips, letting memories play through his head. "*Hael above*. It was quite the sight." He laughs. "Before I knew it, she was up on the bar-top, swaying her hips along to the bard's tune, daring any man to take her in a fight."

"So she was always cocksure with a blade?"

My gaze snaps to my left where another rider has joined us.

Hassan looks at me sternly, but soon enough, I see something amused behind the harsh glint in his eyes. "Why am I not surprised?"

Mikel grins like a fiend, eyes flashing between me and Hassan. "Oh, it gets better. The challenge has men lining up at the bar, all eager for a chance at a tilt—one they hope ends in a rumpled bed across the street at the inn.

"Ren is still dancing on top of the bar, and mind you, the barkeep is red in the face trying to get her down. But all of a sudden, a man drops a sack of coin on the counter." Mikel shakes his head as if he still can't believe it. "*Gods and devils*, the sound was so loud, I swear the entire tavern went silent."

I bite my lip, laughing as I think back to it. "Mikel counted it all. 900 yenti. It was triple what Zoah had given us to buy supplies."

"With that kind of coin…" Mikel lets out a shrill whistle. "We would have been feasting in the desert for months."

"So I looked at my opponent—of what there was to look at, that is," I begin, getting into the story now. "He was clad in black, cloaked in swathes of fabric so that only his eyes and hands were visible. I admit, my head was less than clear. I'm not sure I could tell you what he looked like even if his face hadn't been shrouded."

When my gaze flickers to Hassan, a quiet curiosity has replaced the playful heat in his eyes. He opens his mouth to speak, but stops himself. My brow pinches but before I can prod him, Mikel's voice pulls my focus.

"We step out back—into the alley behind the tavern," he states. "There has to be about twenty men surrounding us, all eager to see what happens. I hear them taking bets on Ren. No one thinks she has a chance."

I roll my eyes and scoff. "Ignorant fools. The lot of them."

Mikel grins. "So, I decided, what's the harm? I had my own money. And sparing a few yenti was the least I could do to see the night through."

"You thought she was going to win?" Kai asks.

A rumbling laugh rips free from Mikel's lungs. "*Gods, no.* I was sure she'd pass out drunk before the fight even started. I was betting for her to lose."

"But I didn't," I stress, shooting Mikel a pointed glare. "I won."

Kai's eyes go wide. "How?"

"She cheated."

My focus rips to Hassan. "I did not—"

"Deceit *is* cheating, witch," he rumbles. "Feigning damsel in distress to win a fight?" He stares at me for what feels like years before amusement lights up his eyes. "I should have known it was you after that stunt you pulled on Riat."

"I don't—"

He lifts his tunic, and the sight of his muscled chest underneath makes my mouth go dry. I don't even know what he wants me to look at, too lost in the thick wall of his abdomen, until he taps a small scar on his side.

"Gahven, yes? The outpost where you swindled a man of his coin and left a scar for him to remember you by?"

My jaw drops, gaping like a deep cavern. I can't do anything but stare at the scar—at the small line that mars his side, the exact place I thrust my blade that night.

"*Hells.*" Mikel is barely holding back his glee. "That was *you*?!"

Hassan drops his tunic and lets out a breathy sigh. "You took every coin we'd earned from our bounty that night. I had hell to pay when I got back to camp."

Riat and Kai are staring at Hassan wide-eyed, though the latter is the first to break free of his astonishment.

He runs both hands through his long black hair, absentmindedly pulling pieces from the bun atop his head. "*Ren?*" he raves. "Ren is the woman who bested you in Gahven and took all of our money?!" Kai's laughter cracks through the night air like a banshee. "*Gods.* I wish I could have seen it."

"Hassan was unbearable for months after that," Riat blabs. "Wouldn't stop grumbling about the duplicitous woman in Gahven." He looses a wild cackle, eyes sparkling mischievously when he looks to me. "How did you do it?"

"I—"

"She pretended to be weak" —Hassan cuts me off— "but first, she clutched her blades and began circling me like a devil." He lets out a breathy huff. "She too, was cloaked in fabrics. All I could see was the wild depth of her eyes—eyes the color of poisoned honey. She looked like she wanted to kill me. And then..."

Hassan's gaze drops to mine, and I swear the intensity of it feels like he's seeing me for the very first time. "She lunged for me and immediately collapsed. Fell to the sand and let out a devious, little moan like she'd hurt herself."

Hassan presses his lips together to suppress a smirk. "I ran over to her, of course, to see if she was alright. But when I lifted her, those devil's eyes snapped to mine." He levels a stern look at me before loosing a rare chuckle. "She cut me one moment, and kicked me in the balls the next."

Riat and Kai are booming with laughter, and I have to bite my lip to stop myself from joining in.

"I only had seconds to realize what was happening, and by that time, her blade was already at my throat."

Mikel eyes are blown wide, filled with a deep knowing. I can already hear the word stirring in his mind. *Fate.*

I wave my friend off before he says anything too foolish and turn back to Hassan. "I would say I'm sorry, but all is fair and true in a back-alley brawl." I shoot him a wicked smile, hoping it's returned.

He cocks his head at me, gaze steady and unflinching. I fear the worst, but, soon enough, a smile I didn't know I was craving until now graces that handsome face of his. "You taught me something important that night," he says.

"Oh?" I raise a brow. "And what was that?"

He brings his horse closer. And when he leans in, I fight the urge to do the same. "Never trust a beautiful woman with a blade."

The blush overtakes every inch of my face before I can stop it. I look away quickly, only to be met with Mikel's obvious delight. The zeal with which he grins tells me there are too many wicked words bubbling up on his tongue. I flare my eyes, all but begging him to close his gaping mouth before it gets me into trouble. Mikel, somehow, heeds my plea. I pray the moment has passed, but when I look back at Hassan, I find his gaze hasn't left.

"What did you do with the money?" he asks.

I try to hide my satisfaction, but it's no use. "Bought myself a nice room at the inn—a room with a tub. Spent a couple hundred yenti on new daggers." I grin. "And drank myself silly with rum to celebrate."

Hassan just stares back at me with amusement dancing in his eyes. "I'm glad my loss was well received, but I wonder if maybe a rematch is in order." He hums, and I lose myself in the way his lips spread into a smile I've now been graced with twice. "What do you say, witch?"

"Yes." My breath feels out of reach as I fumble for more words. "I, uh—" I clear my throat and nod, though I feel my cheeks burning hot. "I think a rematch is only fair. How else am I going to rob you of more coin?"

"I'm sure you'd find a way—"

Hassan slips away from me just as the desert does. It comes faster than usual; milky white fogs my eyes and leaves me trapped in between this moment and one far out of reach. When I blink, I'm already there.

"Devil," he utters.

My lips curl into a smirk and, with a flourish, I pull my scarves down so he can see what kind of monster I truly am. The darkness slithers up his torso, climbing him like snakes set on their meal. He thrashes. He yells. The primal panic that overcomes the man before me is a welcome thing. It makes him weak. It makes me smile.

The shadows grow restless, snaking higher still. It's no effort to see it done. Veles knows what I want, and he'll happily oblige.

The man's mouth twitches as darkness brushes against his lips like a tender lover. I feel his fear, taste it in the air. It's a glorious thing. Sweeter than the ripest of berries. I watch him swallow that fear down. It's a balm to my blackened soul, a breath of fresh air against the suffocating abyss of my own pain. I happily embrace it, as does the dark god. This fun could go on for lifetimes, but there are more pressing things to attend to.

I end it swiftly.

Shadows rush down the man's throat. Choking. Mauling. Killing. His eyes bug wide. Sweat pours down his face. Voices flitter against my ears, but their shock is nothing to acknowledge. No one can stop this. I'm enraptured. It's a heady feeling that fills me—pride that weaves its way through my veins like the black sludge of my endless shadows.

As I watch the man die at my feet, I realize there was truth in the words I ignored for so long.

He was right.

Control is only found in the absence of any.

I lurch back into my body, flailing wildly atop the camel. The white fades from my eyes too quickly, only to be replaced by a flare of black. I blink frantically, trying to discern the world amidst the lingering night. Not even the moon can illuminate the flurry of darkness that whips around me like a violent storm. I panic further, my awareness snapping to the thrum in my veins and the beast churning within. Shadows. *My shadows.*

I gasp, pulling in an unsteady breath as horses buck wildly. Through the chaos I glimpse Hassan's face, wide-eyed and riddled with worry. Shadows flood the space between us, locking me in a tunnel of darkness. My camel startles, uncertain and unable to escape the chaos surrounding it. I feel the moment my shadows draw blood, hear the grunt of a voice I don't dare recognize for fear of breaking. I'll have to face it eventually, but maybe the darkness will take me first. Shadows snap and flare, reminiscent of the brutal horror my vision provided. I dig my nails into my arms, trying to subdue the gift that devastates the desert around me. It's only when I feel a swift strike—the ghost of something violent rippling through my body—that my shadows lurch back and fade into nothing as quickly as they came.

As my eyes drift ahead, body still twitching with bone-deep terror, I spot Malachi. His veins are dark rivers, and his gaze holds an inhuman violence. As he guides his horse toward me, I hold my breath. Shadows cloak him in a black maw, and the sight sends chills down my spine. My heart stutters as I remember the feeling of that swift strike. It felt overwhelming, yet distant. Like it happened to me, but didn't split flesh. I don't know how, but I know those were his shadows I felt lashing out to banish my own.

I swallow harshly as he stops mere paces from me.

"What happened?" he grits out.

I balk under the intensity of his gaze, still trying to understand it all. "I—" My eyes dart around, and I inhale sharply when I spot Mikel.

He's working fast, but not fast enough. I spot the cut just as he finishes healing it—though not even he can fade the scar. It's his for life, forever a reminder of this day. As I stare at the violent Shade's cut marring my best friend's cheek, I feel the heat leave my body. Fresh blood drips slowly, sliding down his chin. My mouth gapes open, but there's nothing I can say to fix this. Nothing I can do to take back that which I've done. I try anyway.

"Mikel, I didn't—"

"I'm fine," he says too quickly. He offers me a smile, but it's forced and flimsy.

All I can do is stare at his face and the streak of black that will always stain his flesh. I couldn't find a full breath if I tried.

"Serehna."

I ignore Malachi, my focus rooted to the one person who's always been a light amidst the Continent's dark. I should have known this day would come. When I showed my mother my marks, she'd told me I was damned—destined for wicked things. Foolish girl. Gods-cursed. *Devil.* When she'd slammed that door in my face, I'd believed it, just as I believe it now. Mikel was the one good thing in this life I hadn't touched with dirty, stained hands. I'd made sure of it. But now, his face is proof of the monster I've always been, of the vile blood slinking under my skin.

"I'm sorry," I whisper.

Deep sorrow fills Mikel's eyes. The sight of it is a pain I more than deserve. Just as he opens his mouth, Malachi's voice rips me from the agony of what I've done, only to remind me that my damnation has been for all here to witness.

"What happened?" Malachi urges, harsher now. "What triggered your gift?"

It all comes rushing back, though I wish it not to. The man's sputtering gasps. The shadows that swelled down his throat, stealing all breath. I can't forget the bulging terror I saw in his eyes, but worse than that is a certainty I can't shake.

I killed that man, and I enjoyed it.

Tears flood my eyes, but I don't let them fall. Grief and pity won't save me from what's to come—from who I am to become.

"A vision," I offer softly.

"Of what? What was it?" Malachi prods.

My face pinches as I stare at him, trying with all my might to pretend what I saw didn't mean anything—that it was a trick and nothing more. *For how could I have taken a life so violently, only to be left pleased?* The righteous feeling that had soared through me is now a sickening ache in my gut. It seeks to poison me, to banish me to the deepest of all the hells—right where I belong.

I see the path before me so clearly now, though I've never felt more uncertain. This gift inside me—this curse—is not something I can set free. It needs to be chained, leashed by nothing but my own will. Allowing anything else will only ensure those around me know nothing but violence.

"*Serehna*," Malachi urges. "What did you see?"

"A mistake," I whisper. "Nothing but my own mistake." As my eyes drift to Mikel, taking in the black decay now mutilating his smooth skin, my resolve is only strengthened. "One I'll be sure to staunch before it can spread."

CHAPTER 22

The last four days have been a blur, bleeding together through the heavy blink of my eyes. We've barely stopped moving, only making camp for a few hours to rest our animals before venturing deeper into the desert once more. Raulik came and went, a mere smudge on the horizon we didn't dare visit. Malachi and Vish said it was too dangerous, though I can't help but wonder if I'm the one who's too dangerous.

With each passing day, I feel the shred of control I've been fighting for slip further from my grasp. I worry that soon enough, it will be gone completely. Ever since my vision, I've kept my shadows clenched tight inside me, but, if anything, the outbursts have only gotten worse.

Veles's presence never settles—always thrumming through my blood with wild impatience. It wants out, but I can't let it out. I've already done enough damage, already taken Silas's life and marked familiar flesh forever. My shadows have proved time and time again that they have a mind of their own, and I know worse is yet to come. I thought keeping to the outskirts of the caravan would keep that violence in check, but it was only yesterday that the gods saw fit to prove me wrong.

We were hours from reaching Raulik when travelers crossed our path. I had barely glimpsed the head of blond hair before my panic morphed into something deadly—something I was unable to call back. By the time I realized my mistake, my shadows were already coiled around me like a snake ready to strike. The group of travelers stared wide-eyed with limbs shaking. I saw the fear marring their faces and, though I could not see myself through their eyes, I knew I resembled the monster from my vision all the same. They quickly steered their caravan far out of reach, but not before I saw their leader for who he truly was—or wasn't.

A head of tightly-cropped blond hair gave way to haunted, muddy brown eyes. His pale skin was red from the sun and creased with worry. He stood his ground, throat bobbing as he ensured his companions passed safely before doing so himself. *Not Olen.* That was all I could think about as he eyed me warily. But still, fear clung to my bones, like teeth buried into flesh. That same fear still clings to me now.

My nights are plagued by terrors Malachi and Quin swear they don't send. I nearly attacked the small woman the morning before last, adamant she was tormenting me though I dreamt of a man with piercing, gray eyes she knew nothing about. My shadows had burst from me in violent retaliation before Malachi managed to subdue them with his own. Quin was unharmed, something that stirs both relief and displeasure in me even now. While Malachi was furious about my lack of control, Quin was more accepting. She apologized for my pain, though denied she was the cause. She even offered to weave good dreams for me—a suggestion I vehemently objected. I'm not letting the Weaver anywhere near my head, whether she claims her intentions are pure or not.

Every day, it seems I find more distance from the others. At first, Malachi was adamant I stay in the middle of the caravan, but Vish told him to leave me be. He promised to ask Hael if the path ahead was clear, and to let us know if and when that changed. I didn't expect the quiet man to stick up for me; but, judging by the tense, contemplative looks Vish gives me now, it seems the Seeker is well aware of the chaos broiling within.

Mikel has tried to help, and though I should be grateful, I hate him for it. I wish he'd stay far, far away. He'd be better off, and I'd avoid the constant reminder of what I've done. I can barely look at him without being crippled by the searing ache in my chest. Every glimpse of his Shade's cut feels like being stabbed through; some days I wonder if that might be kinder than that which burdens me.

I've refused to sleep in our tent ever since I unintentionally carved that scar across Mikel's cheek. He fought me on it, but of course he did. He has more faith in me than he should—he always has. But there's only so much he can do when I drag my bedroll away from camp and curl against it each night. The moon has been my only companion, and every time it bears down on me with its eerie glow, I beg the gods to take me from this nightmare.

But though my nights are lonely, my morning are not. Mikel is there as soon as I wake from fitful sleep, tossing me a hunk of bread and gossiping about the latest incidents. Riat and Ivar get into more spats than quarreling lovers, and it seems Hassan has been in a less than pleasant mood of late. Every day, Mikel acts like nothing has happened between us. But something did, and every glimpse of him reminds me as much.

Another day has come, and I find myself once more unable to shake Mikel's presence. The others have allowed me the distance I crave, but not him. He rides much too close, for far too long. The only time I find peace is when he saunters over to the others, happily welcomed back by Kai. That's where he belongs—not with me and the violence I wreck.

Arguing with him is pointless; he's almost as stubborn as me. But, like he can tell when I'm slipping too close to the god of destruction, Mikel knows when to back off. It's a push and pull that has my nerves fried and worry gripping my throat. It would only take a moment for my threadbare control to slip, and I can't let that happen. Not with him. Not again.

I take a deep breath and gaze at the horizon. The blaring sun makes the pounding in my head worse, and, for a moment, I'm overcome with the sickening pressure of it. I squeeze my eyes shut, convincing myself the darkness behind my lids can ease this burden. But when I open them again, the pain remains. I grumble and squint through the glare.

We're mere hours from Tilket, a place we can't risk avoiding. It's the last outpost this far north and the only place to resupply before heading west. I've never been, though I've heard plenty of stories regarding the lost city that borders the gods-drenched north. It's a place sunken into the sands. Buried by time. Ravaged by the Rebellion and left crumbling and aflame by King Achar. Rumors say it's been rebuilt, dug from the rubble and erected in the shadow of its former glory by slave labor. In all my years traveling the Jahaer, I've been careful to keep my distance. Not only is the north said to be uninhabitable—plagued by monsters and wrought with danger—but most who venture there are far from peaceful.

Turidens. Slavers. All those who seek to spill blood and trade in flesh find the northern boundary a stalking ground for the desperate. And that's exactly what the poor souls who wander out of the Jahaer and into those gods-drenched lands are—*desperate*. Those who find themselves roaming the Continent's deadliest sands are more than willing to risk their lives for a chance at something better. It's foolish, but some think the beasts that inhabit the north are not there by chance. The Book speaks of fertile lands set atop cliffs, baked in Hael's light and rich in pleasures. The most zealous think the monsters of the north as no more than guards to a promised land—a place where daemon and godless alike can find refuge.

The very notion rips a scoff from my lips. There is no peaceful place on the godsforsaken Continent, and what lies ahead will be proof enough.

The others won't allow me to go to Tilket—not after what happened in Hira. It seems I'm to be guarded and hidden away like a prized mare. Though I understand it's for my own safety, the sentiment does nothing to settle the resentment I feel. So, while a few of them will venture into Tilket and procure what we need, I will be here stuck amidst the sands, just as I have been for the past week.

Though I hate the cities, I hate being told what to do more.

My camel slows as the rest of the caravan halts up ahead. I shift uncomfortably in my seat, watching yet another conversation pass between Hassan, Vish, and Malachi. They've been talking a lot these past few days, though nothing about the heated discussions or wild gestures I've witnessed bodes well. There's clearly something they can't agree on, and though I should ask, I won't allow myself to get close enough to.

Mikel pops the cork off his canteen and takes a big swig as his horse settles next to me. "Think they'll let us rest more than a few hours this time? My tailbone might crumble into dust if we go on any longer."

I peel my gaze away from where it's burning into the back of Malachi's skull and offer my friend a guarded look. "Maybe Kai can help ease the pain," I muse. My eyes drift toward where he and Riat are busy unloading the packs from their horses. "We both know he would be more than happy to lend a hand. If only you were brave enough to ask."

The taunt is delivered without fire, steeped in humorless challenge. I glance at Mikel from the corner of my eye, hoping he'll leave me for better company. He only purses his lips, and when he sighs I know he's seen right through my poor attempt at driving him away.

"And what of you?" he prods. "Are you going to be brave enough to ask for what you need?"

I turn to face him fully, and it's a mistake. The sight of the Shade's mark marring his cheek makes me yearn for a pain I don't know how to slake. I scratch at my arms, nails scraping over the inflamed bumps that decorate my skin. The sting is a temporary balm for the greater agony I'm due.

Mikel's gaze tightens on my arms, worry darkening his eyes. I immediately cease the scratching. When he looks up at me, there's too much compassion there—compassion I don't deserve.

"You should sleep in the tent tonight," he suggests. "Gods know you need a break. The hutri fleas have been gnawing at you for days on end."

I slip from the saddle without replying, pack flung over my shoulder before my boots can even hit the ground. It's with haste that I strip my camel of the last of its supplies, but just as I round the animal's flank, I run straight into Mikel. His arms are crossed over his chest, and there's a pointed look on his face as he stares me down. He doesn't have to utter so much as a word; if anything, it's his loaded silence that forces a deep sigh from my lungs.

"I have more important things to worry about than bug bites."

Mikel falls into step beside me as we lead our animals toward where the others are tied up. "Such as?" he presses.

I offer him a glare. "Not killing everyone in my sleep."

He tries to make a dramatic face, but I can see the truth in his eyes. He's thought about it, and I wish that didn't hurt as much as it did.

I secure my camel before weaving through what is to be tonight's camp. Everyone is making quick work of laying it; already crumpled piles of canvas are transforming into well-raised tents. I hear a fire crackling to life in the near distance. Voices chitter and pitch, no doubt from Kai and Riat's constantly rumbling mouths.

Mikel and I work in silence to pitch our tent. Though I won't be sleeping in it, I'll be damned if I make him do all the work.

My friend finds my gaze as we hold the canvas taut between us. "You're not going to kill everyone, you know." He sighs. "If you'd just ask him—"

"*No*," I spit, voice snapping through the air.

My temper flares, and I feel my gift quiver in response. It's not just fear that triggers it. It senses my anger now, too. I know that's far from good.

I dig my teeth into my cheek, biting at the tender flesh until my gift settles. Only then do I answer Mikel. "I'm not asking the Shade for help," I retort, breath huffing as I begin to stake the tent into the sand. "I would rather bleed this gift from my very veins than trust him again." My scoff comes out in a reckless huff when I slam the mallet down. "*Gods*, maybe I should. Doing just that would prove easier than enduring this."

Mikel says nothing, though I catch the concern creasing the corners of his eyes as he watches me closely. I ignore him as we finish raising the tent. I don't need his pity. I need his fear. He's far better off letting me deal with this alone. Safer, too. My gift thrums in my veins like it agrees.

I toss piles of cushions and blankets into the tent, making sure Mikel has everything he needs. I light the incense cone, too. Only one of us needs to suffer the wrath of hutri fleas. With only my pack and bedroll, I prepare to banish myself to an empty patch of sand. But when I turn around, Mikel blocks my path.

"Please stay," he prompts, daring to step closer. "You're punishing yourself for no reason. I'm *fine*. It was just a scratch. I know you didn't mean to do it."

I try to step around him, but he merely gets in the way.

"Ren, *please*. You're my best friend," he argues. "I trust you."

I loose a bitter laugh. "Then you're a greater fool than I thought."

I shove my way past him, trudging across the desert. The others are watching—I can feel their eyes on me. But they don't try to stop me. Unfortunately, Mikel isn't as easily discouraged.

He races to catch up to me, and his unrelenting loyalty would warm my heart if not for the risk it poses him. "Let me help you," Mikel begs. "If you just tried what I suggested—"

I reel back toward him, anger burning through me. "Oh, yes. By all means, let's do some fucking breathing exercises," I spit. "I'm sure Veles will surrender once I master meditation!"

Mikel closes his eyes, as if gathering the strength it takes to deal with me. And, honestly? I don't blame him.

"We won't know until we try."

I take a deep inhale, preparing myself, but already I can feel the ache of what I'm about to do. "There is no we," I state.

His brow furrows, and my heart lurches. I carry on nonetheless.

"Do not mistake your pathetic need for my company as something shared. I tolerated you because I was under Zoah's care. And just when I was rid of you—when I'd finally found freedom from your company—you crawled across the desert, trailing me like a kicked dog." I recoil against the putrid taste of my words, but force more out. "I don't want you here by my side. I never did."

He stares at me for a long while, gaze so vicious I don't dare blink. I wait for his hate. I pray for his rage. It takes too long, and fear worms through my heart with every passing second.

Finally, his jaws clenches, and he scoffs. "Do you really think that's going to work on me?" he urges, getting in my face. He shoves me harshly and steps up to me yet again. "Think I'm just going to walk away because you're being cruel?"

He looses a bitter chuckle and shakes his head. "I said it once, and I'll say it again. We're *family*. You're fucking stuck with me. Pretend I'm a burden all you want. I don't care—because deep down I know to all hells and back you care for me like a brother despite the way fear steals your sense." He grips the front of my tunic roughly, and it's then that I see the desperation in his eyes. "Stop throwing yourself to the fire, you reckless bitch. *Let. Me. Help. You.*"

"*No*," I grit out, shaking him off me. Though I'm in grave need of pretending I don't care, tears flood my eyes. "There is no helping me. My future is one touched by such destruction that the gods were too spineless to unleash it themselves. Death is all that awaits those who stand by me. The sooner you realize that, the longer you'll live."

When I try to step around him again, he latches onto my wrist. "Ren—" His face drops in an instant, and I watch as a misty white begins to flutter through his veins. "You—" He chokes on his words. "*You're in pain.*"

I rip my arm away roughly, severing the connection to his gift. "I'm fine."

No sooner than I storm away do I feel his presence at my back. "Your head feels like it's splitting in half," he argues. "*Gods*, Ren. Why haven't you told me?"

I spin to face him, spraying sand around my boots. "Because this pain is *mine*," I snarl. "It reminds me what I am. What this gods-cursed blood can and will do if I lose focus. *This pain* is the only thing keeping me tethered to my sanity. The only thing deafening me to a god's violent song." I step up to Mikel, hitting the toes of his boots with my own. He's barely taller than me, though I stretch to level a callous gaze on him. "Leave my pain to me," I utter. "And leave me the hells alone."

I stalk across the sand before he can even think to follow. My chest aches, though I'm not foolish enough to turn back and apologize. I'm doing this for him. He's better off without me; he always was.

The sun hangs low, a dwindling orb soon to be swallowed by the earth. Darkness will fall within the hour, and with it will bring the agony of another sleepless night. I slump to the ground, chucking my things to the side. I want to scream. I want to disappear. But all I can do is tuck my legs into my chest and stare at the sunset bleeding against the horizon. The sight would be beautiful if not for the tears blurring my vision. I wipe my eyes with the back of my hand and swallow down the pain I feel. It's pathetic—this thing I've become.

My teeth grind together as a reminder of the camp at my back prods my senses. Voices muddle and pitch. Pots clang and dishes clatter. I can even smell the distant waft of cured meat. Dinner will be ready soon, but I can't bear to eat. There's a hole in my stomach, a gaping wound that only necroses the longer I think about what I've done.

Mikel's face is scorched into my memory; I couldn't be free of its torment if I tried. His pleading eyes. The desperation riddled into his face. *His fucking scar.*

I press my hand against my mouth to stifle the aching sob that threatens to tear free. He should have abandoned me like all the others before him—if only to save us both this pain.

CHAPTER 23

Just like every night, I find a place around the fire that's far from the others. The moment I'm spotted, all conversation seems to hush around me, but I pay it no mind. I keep my eyes low as I settle into the sand. I'm the last one to arrive, and both to my relief and dismay, no one dares say anything—not even Riat utters a teasing remark. As conversation resumes once more, I settle into the cracks the silence touches.

With an ache in my chest and a dull thrum in my blood, I stare deep into the fire. The flames dance and spit, and though I try to find the beauty in it, all I can see are Roel's flames licking at my heels. My fingers trace mindless patterns in the sand, though it does nothing to distract me from my thoughts.

Once everyone settles against my presence, the muttering of voices around me swells to a lively buzz. Pots grow hot as they hang above the fire, their contents boiling over and sizzling as dinner cooks. Jokes are told, and laugher rumbles from bellies. I fold my legs up to my chest and continue to stare into the flames—desperate to feel nothing. No searing headache. No thrum in my blood. No guilt. No fear of what's to come. Just the heat on my skin and the growing chill in the air.

Eventually, plates are passed around. I shake my head, muttering my disinterest, but Kai pushes one into my hand regardless. He teases me about something I don't bother hearing, and I take the food from him if only so I can return to my brooding. Once he's moved on, I let the meal I don't deserve and can't bear to eat grow cold in my lap.

As the night grows darker, I feel all manner of eyes on me. Each and every time, I keep my gaze locked on the fire. It doesn't matter who it is; nothing they can say will ease the ache in my chest or subdue the beast slumbering in my veins. If anything, they might tempt it.

Our group is smaller tonight, though that fails to ease the discomfort I feel. Any company is too much of late. Tariq, Hassan, and the two Berserkers left hours ago, setting off for Tilket. They'll be back in the morning with everything we need to continue west—water, food, supplies. I'm grateful for the replenished provisions, but our need for them makes me jittery. Plans have changed, though only slightly. No longer will we be skirting the northern boundary on our way west. Instead, we'll be slipping over it completely, stumbling into the gods-drenched north like reckless fools. I don't know why they've chosen to lengthen our journey, only that we'll be out here for weeks now. Traipsing across the unknown north. Hiking up the godsdamn Kohe Mountains. The path ahead only gets more treacherous from here on out. There's no telling what we'll find in the north's cursed sands, or the dangers we'll encounter when we reach the Continent's western coast. I can only hope I'm prepared for it.

I'm pulled from my thoughts and into the conversations around me as voices holler and roar in amusement. The others swap stories—sharing anecdotes of travels and divulging treacherous tales. Kai's cackling laugh rips across the desert, followed by Mikel's dulcet tone. I try to pretend the sound of my friend's carefree voice doesn't make my chest burn, but it does.

I drag the wooden fork around my plate, poking and prodding pieces of meat I know I should eat. I'll need every bit of strength for what's to come, but I can't bring myself to take so much as a bite. My appetite has been missing for days, and already hunger has become a comfortable companion. The twinge of it almost distracts me from the pounding ache in my head. *Almost.*

I close my eyes and grit my teeth against a pain that hasn't eased in days. My mind is like a string stretched too far, always ready to snap. A wave of lightheadedness passes through me, and I squeeze my eyes shut a little tighter. If I can't see the black spots that have been constantly peppering my vision, it can't be that bad. That's the lie I tell myself anyway. I know I should accept the help Mikel would so freely give, but I cannot. There is no other choice than this. Veles is waiting at the gate of this pain, eager to step across its threshold the moment it eases. I can't surrender to my gift. I must fight it.

It's gotten late, though no one has left their place around the fire. Rum sloshes from cups and voices carry loudly across the desert. It's lively—joyous, even. I wonder if they're celebrating the fact that we've made it this far north without incident, or simply letting loose before that danger inevitably finds us. Either way, I'm grateful for the buzz of excitement that's kept me safely in the shadows. Alone and unbothered. Just as it should be.

I take a sip from my cup and let its contents fill the emptiness inside of me. Rum is just about all I can stomach lately. Another swig passes my lips, then another. The pain begins to ebb slowly, so I drink more. That searing ache is still there, but dulled to my senses now. My eyes flutter closed. The rum warms my chest and loosens the tension from my shoulders. For a moment, I think I've found peace from all that plagues me, but that peace is shattered the moment I hear Quin's voice.

It takes me a second to understand what Savi asked her, but when I do, my jaw clenches tight. She wants to know how Quin found her way to Hira—how she found herself here with us. The Weaver's mere presence makes me bitter, and though I shouldn't care—shouldn't want to know her story—I can't help my curiosity. With my gaze still hot on the fire, I lend an ear to the conversation.

"I was offering my gift in Madras, a small city near the coast," Quin chirps happily, unaware of how her voice heats my blood. "Women would come to me, desperate for their children to sleep. So many young minds plagued by the darkest of nightmares. So much pain." She purses her lips in a frown. "I made a living there for a while. Stayed years, though I never expected to. It was a safe life for a Weaver—safer than anything else I thought I might find." She sighs, but all I hear is contentment. "Rewarding, too. I was helping people, and though I knew word was spreading about my gift, I didn't fear anyone would come for me."

My gaze lifts from the fire just in time to see her elbow Malachi playfully.

"Little did I know, some scary Shade would turn up at my door, ordering that I help him slip into someone's head." She looses a bright laugh, but it quickly wavers. Her eyes briefly flicker in my direction, as if suddenly remembering I'm here. Quin clears her throat and continues.

"At first, I thought he was crazy," she admits. "I had never given credence to Bair's Prophecies, but when I saw Vish and the mark of his gift, I believed." Quin all but shakes her head in disbelief. "I'd barely known Malachi a week before we started our efforts to reach the Durit." She squeezes his arm gently before sheepishly turning to address me from across the fire. "He was eager to find you, Serehna."

Malachi tenses next to her, and though my gaze is locked on Quin, I know he's staring. We haven't talked in days, and I don't plan on breaking that streak anytime soon. It's easy to forget Malachi when his Weaver is looking at me like she is. Quin's smile is soft, scrunching the freckles across her cheeks. She grins like she's done me a favor, like by dragging me into hell night after night, she's helped me find destiny.

I clench my hands into fists and pull my gaze back to the fire. I will the violent ache in my chest to steady, digging my nails into skin to stifle the rage that's trying to claw its way free. It would only take a moment of weakness to unleash my gift and give in to the dark god's bloodthirsty call. It would be too easy, and the Weaver's head would be the first one I'd take.

Quin's cheerful voice fills the night air once more, and the violence within gets harder to tame.

"A few weeks later, Malachi brought me to stay at the house," she tells. "I wasn't sure how much progress we were making with the dreams, so he wanted me there to ensure the connection to my gift was strong." Quin gently presses her fingers against Malachi's arm. "There are other benefits to keeping me close, too."

The look she gives Malachi sends a shudder of rage through me, and my blood hums eagerly.

"Ivar and Tofá were quick to follow, and pretty soon we started to become something of a dysfunctional family." Quin's laugh is airy and comes too freely. "I never expected to be on an adventure quite like this," she adds. "I'm grateful Malachi needed me to tag along."

I scoff without care, my voice ripping across the fire. The rum only serves to fuel my indignation. Gazes snap to me instantly, and I can all but feel the quiet dread that's settled over the group. The night waits on bated breath, as do the others. But when my eyes lift from the fire, there's only one person I see.

"I'm *so* happy you're enjoying yourself," I mock Quin. My gift thrums like a caged creature that's found their chains stretched too far. I don't try to rein it in. "*So* glad Malachi has taken you on this little adventure."

Quin's face falls, and maybe if I still had a heart that was whole, I'd stop. But it's been skewered and scarred too many times for me to care.

"*Serehna*," Malachi warns.

His command only stokes the anger I've kept buried deep for too many days now. My jaw twitches, gaze sharpening on Quin. As I lean toward the fire, its flames cast a wicked glow across my skin. I wish they burned.

"Tell me, Quin," I seethe. "What fun have you and your Shade been up to?"

I feel my blood run thick like sludge, feel my heart beat too heavily. My vision tunnels on the small woman in front of me and the terror filling her eyes. A good person would stop, but her fear only eggs me on.

"Do tell me how he took care of you. How he made you feel safe. How he made you feel like you finally had somewhere to belong." My breath is a heaving beast in my chest, spitting words like the fire before me. "How did you two pass the time all those months I was screaming in the dark, I wonder? Were you getting cozy? Dreaming of the future? Sharing meals around the godsdamn kitchen table?!"

My shadows snap out like a whip, rushing across the fire. Quin gasps, reeling back before the darkness can strike her dead. Malachi lurches up from the sand, his own shadows pooling at his feet like smoke. I ignore him and the threat he poses. It means nothing to me now. The violence within me is too incensed to be so easily distracted. There is only the Weaver. My chest heaves with heavy, erratic breath, and even as my shadows slink back to me, I don't take my eyes off Quin.

Her fear is palpable, and though it tastes bittersweet, I swallow it down hungrily. I'm a feral thing, a monster created by the dark god himself. I should be ashamed. I should be sealing myself off from my gift and welcoming back the pain of its confinement. But instead I let my shadows flare around me, swirling atop the sand while I sit rigid. Though my rage may be temporarily sated, I'm far from done here.

I lean forward, eyes blazing. "Tell me," I utter through gritted teeth. "Did you have fun dreaming up such a place for me to visit night after night? Find amusement in how I would never quite make it far enough?" I take a deep, settling breath, but it does little to abate the heat in my chest. "Does that gods-touched place even exist? Or was it merely another way to torment me?"

Quin's brow is a fuddled mess that conflicts with the fear flooding her eyes. Her lip quivers, then purses. It's as if she's trying to make sense of all I just said and did and is coming up more troubled each and every time.

But it's Malachi who fills her silence. "Snuff your shadows, Serehna," he demands gruffly. "I won't risk anyone here because of your temper."

My eyes snap toward him, and I feel my gift thrum a little louder in my veins. "You mean you won't risk *her*."

His gaze darkens, mouth twitching. He says nothing more, and silence hovers between us like dry lightning. Volatile. Smothering. Desperate like a choked breath.

Quin shifts uneasily, breaking my focus from the Shade. "What place?" she asks softly.

"Don't play the fool," I argue. "The place you sent me to for months on end. That gods-cursed canyon with the doorway carved in markings." My gaze pins her to the spot. For a moment, I consider all the fine blades at my disposal and how they might loosen her tongue. "Why?"

"I don't understand," Quin starts. "We never—"

"What was the point of it?" I interrupt, teeth grinding against each other as I try to keep my violence in check. "You wished for me to find you in Hira, did you not? Why trouble me with the hells of that place? Did you merely wish for me to suffer?"

Quin tries to rise from the sand, but the snap of my shadows against the ground has her stilling where she sits.

"*Serehna*," Malachi growls, taking a step closer. "Leash your shadows before I do it for you."

I stand up to match his looming presence, and though I wish to strike him down, the sight on my left has me faltering. Mikel stares at me with worry riddled in his brows. His eyes are filled with concern, and though I wish it wasn't, I know it's for me. I swallow harshly when I spot the black scar staining his cheek.

The guilt comes quickly, followed by a shame that burns my chest too hot. My nails bite into my palms, and only after the prick of pain steals every thought do my shadows fade into nothing. As I slam the door on my gift, the searing ache in my head returns much too soon.

Quin looses a deep breath—one that's heavy with the distress she clearly feels. "A canyon? A doorway?" She shakes her head, eyes darting to Malachi.

I follow her gaze, hoping to find the truth in plain sight, but the look Malachi gives her is unreadable.

"I don't know of such a place," Quin utters uncertainly. "I only sent Malachi into your dreams. Linked your minds in sleep so he could deliver a message. We never— I don't know how…" She shakes her head again before pressing a dainty hand to her lips. "None of this makes sense."

Malachi glares across the fire to where Vish sits quietly. "*Explain.*"

There's an uneasy hesitation gracing Vish's face, one I've rarely seen. He gives Malachi a long look before his eyes flicker with the evidence of his gift. The black of his pupils constricts, swallowed by the green of his irises in the span of a singular breath. When he comes back to us, the fearful look on his face drops my heart into my stomach.

His gaze shifts between me and Malachi before he finally speaks. "It seems Hael sent Ren somewhere else," he utters. "Somewhere fate will take her to see it done."

Silence hovers around us, heavy with things no one dares speak of, especially me. *Hael sent me there? Is Vish saying that all this time, my Weaver dreams have been tainted by visions?* My heart beats unsteadily as nausea churns in my gut.

Malachi's voice breaks through my teeming panic, ripping me back with the shout of his words. "Where was she sent?" he demands to know. "What did she foresee?"

Vish swallows uneasily, but his eyes don't flicker or blink. He doesn't call for Hael's knowledge. Doesn't hurry to flip through the journal resting in his lap. Instead, he stares at me silently, and

I swear it's regret I see shadowing his gaze. He opens his mouth, then closes it abruptly.

He gives me one last, lingering look before turning to face Malachi. "North. That is all the gods wish for you to know," he states. "The path is clouded, for it is her alone who will take it."

My hands shake with a fear I cannot place as I think back to the Weaver dreams. That place had felt so real, because it clearly was. The canyon. That cavernous doorway. The sand that dragged me to all hells.

What fate will lead me to such a place?

As I go to speak, I bite back the shake in my tone. "And what is it that I need to see done?"

Again, Vish hesitates, and the sight takes the last lick of warmth from my skin. His unwavering focus pins me in place, but there's no strength there. No, it's a deep-seated anguish that taints his gaze.

"I'm sorry, Serehna—for the burdens this life has placed on you."

"Tell me what must I do," I rasp.

He looks to Malachi once more, but when Vish turns back to me, his swallow is thick and heavy with things unspoken. "Something I fear you're not yet ready for."

I don't need to ask. Somehow, I already know. My mind slips to the vision—to the violence I wielded without care or concern. I can all but hear the man's gargled screams as the shadows took his life. It's too easy to imagine how that gleeful pride flooded my chest; it warmed me better than any sun. The glimpse Hael offered of the future has been plaguing me for days—a nightmare I can't shake. But worse than what the vision showed is what my waking moments have proved. This control I keep on my gift is slipping.

And when I finally lose the grip on its leash?

My throat aches with that unbearable truth. There is no denying it now, no pretending the gods have anything in store for me other than dealing death. The prophecy was right. I will bathe the Continent in blood.

I stagger backward against the sand, feeling the world bearing down on me with too much certainty. Mikel calls to me from across the fire, but the concern seizing his voice only makes this worse. I'm dashing across camp the next moment, heading to where my bedroll waits for me—cold and empty. My boots carry me quickly, though my legs sway as panic leaves them shaky. I pass Mikel's tent, then the other's. Before I know it, camp is a faraway flicker of firelight at my back, and I'm shrouded in darkness. When I finally see my sad excuse for a bed, I let the lump in my throat slip free. My lips part in a muffled sob as I collapse on top of the thinly woven pad, letting the weight of all the things I carry crush me.

I want nothing more than to scream, though I dare not do anything but let quiet sobs shake my chest. I close my eyes, eager to escape the night, but what I find in that dark nothing is too frightful to face. A swell of shadows. A stranger gasping for breath, just as Silas had. It's all too real, and I cannot bear any more reminders of the monster I have and will become.

As my lids flutter open, heavy with exhaustion, the moon greets me through wet lashes. Its orange hue shines out from behind dense clouds, as if hiding from the gods. Whereas the sight usually reminds me of my father—of how he always used to search the skies for the moon, telling tales of the omens each shape brings—it offers no comfort tonight.

I close my eyes again and breathe. I breathe and breathe, though no amount of it soothes the fitful beat of my heart. Panic bubbles quick in my chest, choking my breath and leaving me gasping. I think of Silas then, of how his last moments were spent breathless and weak such as this. Maybe my penance is to live the rest of my days experiencing just the same.

All at once, it hits me. The pain of everything I've ever felt and everything that is to come consumes me in a rush. Fat tears spill from my eyes, sliding down my cheeks in rapid succession. I don't want them—don't want to feel their slick on my skin or the quiver they drive through my lungs—but they come nonetheless.

My palms hit the sand as I sink forward to press my forehead to the ground in desperate reverence. "Gods, *please*," I utter. My voice breaks, and the tears flow harder. "Take me," I rasp. "Take me, and rid me of this suffering."

My chest twinges in pain, tight against the swell of ragged breaths. I dig my hands into the sand, fingers curling roughly amidst the grit. My hair has fallen in front of my face, and a few strands stick to my tear-soaked cheeks like they're dipped in honey. I want nothing more than to sink deep into the earth and never return, but the gods have other plans.

The sudden *shush* of sand snaps me awake. My panic soars, pumping adrenaline too quickly and clenching my heart. As I spin around on my hands and knees, my shadows lurch before I can. A flurry of black lashes out against the creeping night, but its fury is short-lived. No sooner does my gift whip from me like a blade than does it clash with another. I feel the impact of it like a hand to my throat—squeezing firmly until my gift melts into nothing. Only then can I pull in a deep breath.

"Your shadows are unstable."

When I finally look up, I find Malachi's dark gaze baring down on me. It's as though all the warmth has drained from those brown irises. I wish the sight meant nothing to me.

He folds his arms across his broad chest as disdain drips from his bottom lip. "Worse than that, you can't even hold them against a simple attack."

I quickly pull myself to my feet. "You think I don't know that?" I snarl. My gift hums through my veins, but unlike seconds ago when panic set it free, it simmers beneath the surface. "Is there a reason you followed me out here?" I snap. "Or did you merely wish to lecture me?"

He regards me for a moment, but soon all that arrogance slips from his face. "Were you crying?"

My heart sinks into the raw depths of my stomach. With an unsteady hand, I wipe away the evidence of my tears. "Fuck off, Malachi," I mutter. "Go back to your Weaver. I'm sure she's anxiously awaiting you in the tent I know you both share."

Something wavers in his gaze, though I don't wait around long enough to see if it's pity or guilt. I turn on my heels and walk deeper into the desert. It's stupid to wander farther than I already have from camp, but the storm of emotions brewing in my chest overrides all rational thought.

Malachi's hand slips over my shoulder, pulling me back to him. "Serehna, stop."

I whip around, gaze feral as fresh tears line my eyes. "Stop, *what*?" I argue. "*You're* the one following me. You're the one who spent months calling out to me. And for what? So I can retrieve some mythical dagger? Because I'm the Durit?" I loose a snarky laugh and shove his hand off me. "Don't give me some false story about wanting to do the right thing. You never gave a donkey's shit about being the good guy before. So don't lie to me now and pretend you are one."

His jaw clenches as he glares down at me. "You're right. I'm not the good guy."

He steps closer, and the warmth of his body overwhelms me. My breath wavers, though I don't move. I tell myself I'm merely standing my ground, but the heat flushing my skin reveals me for the liar I am.

Malachi's eyes are like black pits of tar, sucking me deeper into his gaze. His focus drops to my lips, and I let my mind think unforgivable things as he lingers there for too long. By the time his gaze drifts back to my eyes, I'm unmoored by thoughts of him.

He leans in close, and my breath hitches. "I'm a ruthless, selfish bastard," Malachi utters against my cheek. "You've told me as much."

I feel his shadows slip against my tunic and tease the soft curve of my waist. My mind screams at me to pull away, warning me that this is a mistake. I know it is, and yet, I stay. Compared to the numb existence I've been living the past few days, this moment is the sweetest of poisons. A drop will kill me, but gods if I don't want a taste.

"Do you know what it's like to have that which you desire most ripped from your hands?" Malachi asks, voice laced with something heavy and aching.

Shadows slink across my skin, tightening their grip on me.

"It feels like dying," Malachi admits.

His breath is hot on my cheek, and my eyes flutter against the overwhelming need coursing through me. Just as I lean into the temptation of it all, he pulls away.

"I'll be damned if I feel that again," he mutters.

My eyes snap open. Malachi has put considerable distance between us, and though I don't want it to, it hurts. Rejection is a vicious beast—scraping against my ribs, desperately seeking to shred my heart.

How easily I fall into bad habits, swayed by the mere illusion of affection.

My anger flares like an inferno, but it's quickly dampened by the throbbing mess in my head. Pain is an anchor for my thoughts, reminding me some battles are best ignored. I'm too tired to fight anymore tonight. Too tired to care about someone who long stopped caring about me. I shake my head free of all its foolishness and head deeper into the desert.

"Your friend is worried about you," Malachi calls after me.

My boots still against the sand as his words root me to the spot. A lump forms in my throat, and as much as I try to swallow it down, it refuses to budge. I hear Malachi's footsteps pushing through the sand and stiffen when he settles behind me. Still, I don't turn to face him. I can't.

"Let me walk this path with you," he implores. "Let me help you, Serehna."

"Why?" I scoff, spinning around to face him. "Has the weight of your guilt grown too heavy over the years?"

"Yes."

I can only stare at him blankly as a new kind of ache burrows into my chest. We do nothing but stand across from each other for a while. Staring. Waiting for the other to yield first. Sand blows softly against our boots, stirred by the night's chilly breeze. There's a helplessness hidden in Malachi's eyes, a desperation I hadn't noticed before. It should be a relief—to witness the turmoil there—but it only pains me. With tears creeping across my waterline and a pounding heart, I push past him and head back toward my bedroll.

He looses a groan and quickly follows. "*Veles spare me.* Tell me when this is to end, Serehna," he demands. "Tell me what I must do to show you we want the same things!"

When I get to my mat, I don't sit down. I can't—not with him prowling after me like a hunter stalking his prey. I turn around to face him, knuckles bone-white as I clench my hands too tightly.

"And what is that, huh?" I sneer. "What exactly it is that you truly want?"

He stops mere paces from me, his anger quickly melting into hesitation. I stare at him, at the man I swear I know, but it's clear to me that my familiarity is a lie. Though there was a time when I knew him better than I knew myself, much has changed. I can no longer pretend he's the same boy from Artolen, which is why my heart beats loudly in my ears as I wait for his reply.

"I want you to trust that I have our best intentions in mind," he offers. "No matter what happens. No matter what you hear."

I debate considering such a thing when he swallows thickly and his eyes shift down. It happens so fast, I almost miss it. But I don't. I might not know who Malachi has become over the past decade, but I know his tells. *He's nervous.* I try to scoff, but it comes out weak. Unease flares in my chest as I contemplate what secrets Malachi might be keeping from me.

"You want me to trust you? After everything you've done?" A humorless laugh spills free from my chest. "Why should I?"

"Because everyone here cares too much about the fate of the Continent," he argues. "They want to use you to make sure nothing changes. They're idiots. Change is how we survive."

His gaze grows heavy, and as he takes a step forward, I rush to take one back. He all but snarls at the distance. "I'm the only one you can trust, Serehna."

I flinch against the strength of his conviction, though my heart grows cold at his words. My throat bobs uneasily as I take another step back. "You're not the first person to say that to me," I utter. My hands tremble at my sides, though I desperately try to quell their shake. "The one before you reminded me just how foolish trust is. I won't be so easily swayed by honeyed words and the kinship of tainted blood this time."

Malachi merely stares at me, but when that stare begins to search my face for answers, I'm quick to look away.

"You're talking about him, aren't you?" He takes a step closer, and my chest grows tight. "The Berserker."

I don't dare look up, can only try to remember how to breathe as gray eyes flood my mind and I'm reminded of the man who begged for a mercy I didn't offer.

"Vish told me what happened," Malachi admits. I hear the force of his inhale as he comes to rest mere inches from me. "Told me his name, too." He *tuts*. "Silas," Malachi grits out.

My gaze snaps to his. The sound of that name tears at me like talons grazing wounds that were halfway healed. What Malachi sees on my face must vex him, because his gaze tightens on me as he leans in close.

"Who was he to you?" he demands to know.

My eyes drop to the sand before Malachi can see tears begin to flood them. I've already proved I'm weak. He doesn't need another reminder.

"A lesson," I utter almost soundlessly.

Shadows immediately tug at my chin, forcing me to face this moment. "I need more than that," Malachi grits out.

My throat aches as I choke on the words. "He was the same as you were to me—a glaring reminder of something I too often forget."

Malachi cocks his head, lips twitching in annoyance. "And what would that be, Serehna?"

A moment of strength has me yanking my face from his shadow's grasp. I glare up at him, reminding myself that there is nothing between us but a past we cannot even begin to mend.

"Attachments are as foolish as the Continent is cruel. One should hardly mistake them for something lasting." I scoff, and it sounds with a bitter ring. "Pretty words and reckless touches only disguise one's true nature. Affection is a thing forever entangled in lies. Always given in the hope of something gained and never that of love."

My jaw ripples with tension as I try to bite back the emotions that threaten to drown me. "You taught me that," I admit. "As did he."

With a knot in the back of my throat, I snatch my things from the sand. My heart beats wildly in my chest as I stomp across the desert in search of a new place to rest my head tonight. I don't know how far I walk, only that when I finally drop my bedroll and risk a glance back, Malachi is nowhere to be seen and camp is a faraway smudge of tents.

Everything I've learned tonight swirls dangerously in my head, but I don't give the torturous thoughts time to flay me bloody. As I curl up against my bedroll—the wind stirring goosebumps and fleas nipping at my skin—I sink into the heady thrum of pain and let it consume me. Darkness follows, hovering over my skin like a blanket. When my body finally succumbs to sleep, I pray that the gods finally wake me from this nightmare. Or maybe, if I'm lucky, they'll dispatch me to the pit of a hell lesser than this one.

CHAPTER 24

I'm pressing the blade to skin before I can even open my eyes. As I blink the sleep away, hand flexing around the hilt of my dagger, it's a wry smile I see carved amidst the waning dark.

"You still sleep with a blade?" Malachi asks as he leans over my bedroll, unconcerned with the way my dagger is pressed to his throat. "Seems I taught you well."

It's the purring rumble of his voice that has my mind ripping from the tangled webs of sleep. I shove Malachi away with a quick hand and scramble upright.

"What in the gods are you doing?" I rasp, trying to remember how to breathe. "Were you watching me sleep?"

An easy grin spreads across his face as he eases up to his full height. Towering over me like this, he looks like the devil I know him to be. "For a moment," he admits. "Lately, I find you most delightful when you're silent. It seems to be the only time you're not hurling insults and accusations my way."

I roll my eyes and tug my threadbare blanket closer from where it slipped. "And I find you most delightful when you're out of my sight," I seethe. "Now leave. I want to sleep."

"Is that so?" He purses his lips, but I see the amusement he's trying to hide. "You could have fooled me. I would have thought you liked the look of me with how often I turn to find your eyes."

My face heats, but I quickly recover by shooting him the nastiest look I can muster. "You know what they say," I sass. "Keep your enemies close."

"Enemies, huh?"

Malachi leans over my bedroll, dark hair falling in front of his eyes. He's much too close, and as his hot breath fans across my neck, I tell myself the shudder running up my spine is from the morning's chill.

"If you need a reason to keep me close, Serehna," he purrs. "I can think of plenty."

I watch as his mouth curls into a subtle smirk, watch the way those dark eyes bore into mine with too much heat. He's fucking with me, and I wish it wasn't working. Last night I went to sleep with a cold heart, but this morning it seems Malachi is determined to thaw the dead thing. Gone is the demanding brute he's been for the past week, and in its place is something worse. Something I'm not prepared for.

My throat bobs uneasily. How I wish he'd grown ugly and disfigured after all these years.

I pull my gaze from his before I can be swept under unsteady waters more than I already have. "Is there a reason you're bothering me?" I huff. "Or did you simply wish to deprive me of sleep?"

Malachi's lips quirk into something devilishly pleased. "I'd find a much better way to deprive you of sleep if that was my aim." He offers it casually, like his words aren't laced in the best kind of threat.

I can't even put words together. I simply stare at him with too many thoughts—none of which I can share. My face is flushed red, and my heart beats so loud I'm worried he can hear it. He merely cocks his head at me, eating up every bit of my stunned expression.

Gods, it's too early for this.

One look at the horizon shows the sun is a barely-there haze among the gray. When I look back at Malachi, his shit-eating grin is still locked in place. Oh, he's enjoying this far too much.

I stand up quickly, fumbling against the blanket that's trying its best to trap me. My blade is still gripped tightly in my hand as I glare at him. "I trust you can find your way back to camp. Surely you have someone else to bother at this hour. A delicate, little Weaver, perhaps?"

"Quin is sleeping," he says. "Would you truly prefer I head back to my tent and wake her?"

I all but stiffen. Anger flares through me, though I do my best to keep it off my face. "I don't care what you do," I sneer. "Stay in bed with her all day if that's what you desire."

Malachi raises a brow, and gods how I want to slap the amusement off his face. My gaze burns into him, unflinching. My fingers twitch around the hilt of my dagger, and just as I consider using it to motivate him to leave, he sighs.

"I came to wake you for training," he offers, growing a little more solemn. "Like I said last night, your shadows are erratic." I go to argue, but he stops me. "You need someone to show you how to harness your godsblood. You're too stubborn for your own good, and you need a teacher."

I scoff, though my lungs squeeze at the thought of learning how to tame this violence within. "A teacher? *You*?" I sheathe the blade and cross my arms over my chest. "What are you going to teach me other than how to be an unbearable show off?"

As if to prove my point, Malachi's shadows spill out from his boots, slithering across the sand like dark serpents. They slip closer, but before I can shoo them off like a street dog hounding me for scraps, they ebb back to him like a tide. He says nothing, but his lips quiver into a smirk.

I roll my eyes. "And what's in this for me?" I prod. "Why should I let you teach me?"

It's a stupid question; I know it the moment it leaves my lips. I should be grateful he's offering his help, should be desperate to learn how to control my shadows—and a part of me is. But a larger part of me resents every bit of this.

Malachi stalks closer, and when his eyes darken, I know I've fucked up. I tense as he comes to rest inches from me.

"*What's in it for you?*" he parrots, not an ounce of kindness in his tone. "How about owning that power in your veins for once in your life?" He presses closer, and I feel his shadows weave their way through my legs. "How about being able to defend yourself so I don't find you bloodied and broken in an alley again?" he growls.

My jaw clenches as I fight the words that wish to spill from my lips. He clocks the scorn on my face, I know he does, for the next thing he says guts me.

"What's in it for you is learning how to not kill us with that temper of yours."

I flinch, chest aching at the truth of his words. *Damn him.* My eyes shutter closed, and it's there I see the scar on Mikel's face. I see the terror in Quin's eyes. I see the blood seeping from

Silas's chest. Everything in me hurts, and it's with little option left that I utter my agreement.

"Okay," I say quietly. When I look up at Malachi, his gaze has softened slightly. Though, it does nothing to make this any easier. "Teach me, then," I prod. "Teach me how to harness this curse. How to tame it."

"Tame it?" He sighs, running a hand through his hair. "There is no taming it. Veles is nothing like Hael. Your gift has a mind of its own. It doesn't take well to being controlled, nor dismissed."

"Then what—"

Malachi steps closer, and I suck in a breath at the proximity. His shadows slink up my legs and tug my belt loops, holding me against the daemon who calls them.

"There's only chaos," Malachi utters. "Frenzy. *Submission.* You must bend to the beast within."

I try to scoff, but it comes out weak and uncertain. "How the hells am I supposed to learn how to control my gift if there is no control?"

He shoots me a smirk and begins to take backward steps away from me. "Come find out."

I give him an incredulous look, but ultimately give in.

What other choice do I have?

I'm out of my depth here. No control? *Submission?*

I tug my boots on quickly, stumbling after Malachi as he treks across the sand. His tall frame covers the distance swiftly, and I have to jog to catch up to him. When I do, he turns around to face me with an all-too-pleased look on his face. That grin tells me everything I need to know; he's going to enjoy this much more than I am.

I fight the urge to roll my eyes and instead roll my shoulders. My muscles are clenched tightly against the chill, and it takes a few swings of my arms to feel the warmth return to them. I crack my neck, breaking the tension from sleeping so poorly for so many nights. But when I look up, I see that Malachi is staring at me, almost unblinking. I offer him a scowl, but he keeps at his blatant ogling. I'm dressed in what I slept in. I couldn't be bothered to change for this little sparring session, though now I realize I probably should have. A loose pair of pants hangs off my wide hips and I'm wearing a sleeveless tunic I cut with a blade long ago. The frayed hem rests atop my ribs, exposing my navel, where Malachi's focus is now locked. But as his brows knit together, I realize it's not the curve of my waist or the soft plush of my stomach he's staring at. It's the seven-inch scar he can't seem to look away from—the one his arrogance caused all those years ago.

I shift uncomfortably and clear my throat. "Okay. So what am I learning first? Striking? Blocking?"

Malachi's focus snaps back as he looses a playful scoff. "You think you're ready to learn combat skills?" He raises a brow. "Honestly, Serehna. You know I'm a better teacher than that."

I grumble, and he smiles. And gods is it a handsome one.

"Do you remember the first thing I taught you?"

"I don't know," I sass. "Was it how to be exceedingly irritating and annoy your opponent to death?" I cross my arms over my chest and level a bored look at him. "Because you're clearly an expert at that."

It's his turn to roll his eyes. "And you a quick study."

I go to offer a retort, but my mouth twitches into a grin. *He's got me there.*

"Fine," I concede, letting out a deep sigh.

I purse my lips as my mind takes me back more than a decade. Malachi had wasted no time teaching me what it would take to survive in Artolen. Though there were other children in our pitiful pack of orphans and outcasts, he refused to let anyone else train me. It had been months before he taught me hand to hand combat, and a year before he even let me touch a blade.

The space between my brows wrinkles as I search my memories. When I find what I'm looking for, I groan loudly. "You've got to be kidding me," I whine. "We can't start with that. It's insulting you think my skills that deficient."

Malachi looks me up and down, his smile growing devious. It's drenched in far too much arrogance, and it suits him.

"I'm not a child," I argue. "I can fight. Just teach me."

He says nothing, only stares at me with mischief flickering in his eyes.

"Where do you expect me to hide out here?" I babble, hands gesturing wildly around me. "There's nothing but sand."

"That's not the game we're playing," he comments.

As he steps closer, my whole body starts to buzz. It's panic, anticipation, adrenaline, and something else I refuse to name, but know too well.

Fuck.

I wish he were ugly.

Gods, it would be so much better if he were ugly.

"Malachi," I press, voice wavering in its strength. "What is it you're teaching me today?"

"What's the one thing you always hated?" he prods with a devilish smile. "Even though it got you out of trouble more than once."

I dig my teeth against the inside of my cheek when he comes to stand in front of me. He's too close. His presence is intoxicating—the kind of vice I shouldn't imbibe. Malachi cocks his head to the side and raises a brow. The gesture should grate my nerves and urge me to find a dagger, but I'm having trouble remembering how to breathe. I know what's coming, and so does he.

"Run, Serehna," he coos.

CHAPTER 25

My boots stumble against the sand as I take off. I barely hear the deep rumble of Malachi's laugh or the way he begins to countdown from ten. The blood pumps raucously through my ears and muffles all sound. Adrenaline makes me light-headed and hyper-focused.

My gaze is fixed intently on the desert in front of me, miles and miles of undisturbed sand. Muted darkness. Emptiness. Nothing to save me. Nowhere to hide. My lungs burn with every rapid breath I heave in and pant out. My legs flex and drive, propelling me across the sand without a second thought. I'm panicked, yet giddy and eager. But I don't stop. That's not the game.

I sprint across the desert, hurling myself up the small dunes that cover this land and down their shifting faces. Every foot strike is treacherous, threatening to throw me off balance and surrender me to the threat at my back. But even when my boots slide and my legs shudder to course-correct, I don't relent. My body is flushed with blood and surging with energy. I'm high off the chase and the victory I can all but taste. For a moment, I think I've outrun him, but then I feel it.

It's nothing but a tickle at first, a teasing brush against the back of my neck. The mere touch drives panic through my chest, yet makes my mouth curve into a wild grin. My arms pump harder—*faster*—urging me forward with everything I have. The next brush of shadows has me yelling in frustration. I slap my hand toward the tendril that slinks along my hip, but the motion breaks my focus. My boot slips across a sand dune, sending my whole body staggering sideways. I'm still stumbling forward, legs desperate with momentum, when another shadow prods me. But this one is more than a light tease.

It wraps around my waist, coiling tight. I don't have time to prepare for the moment my body is yanked. Like I've hit some invisible wall, I come to a violent stop, limbs thrashing around me. Though, I don't fall. I'm rooted to the spot—held too tightly. I know it's just a game, but, right now, it feels far from one. Panic begins to eclipse my sanity. It's his unholy strength—Veles's inescapable power—that summons brutal thoughts.

Silas throwing me to the sand.

Pinning me down.

Shattering my arm.

I was no match for the dark god's strength then, and I feel weak against this facet of Veles's power now. My mouth grows dry, but I refuse to lose this time. I thrash with everything I have in me.

The shadow holds me in place as my hands scrape against it. My blood thrums, spiked with desperation. I know better, but even as my fingers slip through the darkness surrounding me, I don't stop trying to claw my way free. The itching in my veins turns hot as I struggle.

It *burns.*

It wants out.

How do I let it out?

I'm hyperventilating now. Deep down, I know Malachi won't hurt me, but my mind is back in Denheir. I'm chained to the chair. I'm being kicked by Rohan's boot. Then, it's Letka. Asha's fire sizzling against my cheek. Silas abandoning me, offering me up like a cheap whore.

Veles, help me.

My gift is angry. Feral. I can almost feel it snapping through my veins, so violent I fear it'll break skin. A tiny flare of darkness whips out from my wrist, only to be quickly engulfed by a much larger shadow I know isn't mine. For a moment, the feeling of being swallowed—consumed by eternal nothingness—rakes chills across my skin. My body loses all heat. I'm gone—lost to this world. I'm floating in the abyss of damnation until a sharp breath snaps me back, and my body feels whole once more. Though that oblivion is gone, my panic remains.

I yell and struggle in his shadow's grip. Gasping breaths choke my lungs. My hands tug violently at the darkness that keeps me. I'm a doll with no stuffing as it flails in the wind. Hysteria spins my mind and tosses me back into dark waters. I see the alley in Letka—see the shadows slicing flesh and spilling blood. See Silas's gray eyes fading into nothing. But the torture of past memories are ripped away as I suffer future ones. It's the stranger I see next—the one whose name I don't know but whose life I will take regardless. Nausea clenches my gut. I try to blink it all away, but that violence is inescapable. My nails scratch down my arms, desperate to free myself from this torment. It doesn't work, and I'm left desperate.

I search for the thrum in my blood, and though it's there, it's trapped—banging against the vein. Out of reach like a deeply buried well inside me. I feel the shuddering, unnatural force of it, eager to break through a door of my own creation. It's slamming against the wood, splintering corners but kept sheltered. My hands shake. My own breath strangles me better than any foe.

I open my mouth to scream—to beg the gods to take me away—when all of a sudden, a firm pressure calms my raging heart. It's strong. Unswayed. *Familiar*. My gaze flicks down to find one of Malachi's shadows pressed to the center of my chest. Everything slows, then stills. The touch is much too comforting; it always has been. That cool wisp of darkness settles my panic better than any tonic. Awareness washes over me like fresh air. I remember where I am—remember what we're doing here. I remember who I'm with.

I'm safe.

With panting breath and rigid muscles, I relent and ease against the shadow's hold. As Malachi steps in front of me, he grins. He's arrogant, satisfied, and completely unaware of just how violently my panic poisoned me. I tell myself it's a good thing. *For why would I want him to know the depths of my guilt? The things that terrorize me in the dark?* They're nothing but weaknesses to use against me, and he already has enough at his disposal.

"Good to know that old trick still works on you." His eyes drop down to the shadow that's caressing the steady beat of my heart. "You always loved my shadows. It seems some things never change."

The way he's looking at me makes my hand twitch for a blade. It would feel too good to spill his blood right now. I can't help but wonder what else might feel good right now, and that thought makes me angrier than anything.

"Why do I feel like once again, you're trying to prove a point?" I seethe.

I wave his shadows away, and he appeases me. That darkness slinks back to him, but not before caressing my cheek.

I reel away, face flushed and words stumbling across my tongue. "Would you stop doing that?" I snap, my heart beating too quickly. I huff and cross my arms over my chest. "What was the purpose of all that?" I chide, gesturing back to the sands I just sprinted across. "I can outrun my opponents just fine. I don't need a lesson in that."

He gives me a pointed look, amusement dancing in those brown eyes of his.

"Don't fucking start," I retort. "Most of my opponents aren't Shades. Do you truly expect me to outrun intangible darkness?"

Malachi sighs deeply like it pains him—like *I* pain him. "And what about Torches?" he counters. "If I hadn't found you in that alley—"

"I was doing fine in Hira," I argue. "If the bastard hadn't lodged his dagger in my leg, I would never have fallen off that roof. I would have made the jump."

Malachi's eyes go violently wide, and his face drops all glimmers of that playful smugness. "You. Fell. From. A. Roof?" Though his tone is flat, it's anything but calm.

"It was fine," I mumble, waving him off. "You didn't even notice."

Malachi closes his eyes and takes a deep breath. "*Veles, unburden me and carve it from my very chest,*" he utters begrudgingly. When he looks back at me, his irritation remains. "When I caught you just now, what did you feel?"

I roll my eyes. "You're seriously asking about my feelings?"

He runs a hand through his hair, brushing the strands from his forehead. It's only a matter of seconds before they've fallen back into place. "I'm not asking about emotions," he rumbles. "What did your gift feel like?"

I glare at him, feeling once again like a child failing to grasp something my mother is teaching me. Though I know I'm being a brat, I smirk anyway. "Like it wanted to kick your ass, but decided you weren't worth the effort."

His shadows flare in the span of a single heartbeat. No sooner do I see them in front of me do they grip my jaw. He approaches me slowly, stopping only once we're face to face. I try to thrash in his shadow's hold, but it only tightens—forcing my gaze on him.

Malachi raises a brow, not bothering to hide his satisfaction. "Try again. And this time, an honest answer."

I loose a deep sigh, if only to remind him what a burden he is. "It felt like it was going to burst free, like it was desperate to get out."

My brow furrows as I stare off into the desert and really think about it. I sink into myself and allow every flicker and hum in my blood to speak for itself. It was wild. Hungry for violence. *Trapped.*

My throat grows heavy, and I force a thick swallow. "It felt like it wanted to help me but couldn't. Like it was stuck inside somehow," I offer. "I didn't understand it—everything happened so fast. But it felt... *angry.* Like it was feeding off my panic and desperate to make sure what happened before didn't happen again."

Malachi's gaze tightens at my words, but he doesn't press. He merely stares at me like I'll spill everything that's befallen me since Artolen split our fates to different paths. He'll be waiting until the gods fall before I tell him anything.

The restrictive hold on my jaw fades along with his shadows, and I stretch my mouth to rid myself of the feeling.

"What about when I swallowed your shadow?" he prompts.

"It felt like…" I drop my eyes to the sand as chills rack my body. "It felt like being devoured by an animal. Like one moment, I was afraid, and then… nothing. Oblivion." I chew my bottom lip. "It was almost like, for a second, I died. Like I'd been sent down to the underworld." I swallow harshly, utterly unnerved by the admission, but when I look back up at Malachi, he looks pleased.

"That's because part of you did die." He must see the panic flashing across my face because he quickly continues. "Your shadows are a part of you, but they're also outside of you. They are limitless, but impermanent. Incorporeal, but destructible."

I know confusion has seeped across my face when Malachi looses a breathy laugh. "Only shadows can destroy other shadows. Brute strength accomplishes nothing. Fire can only sway them off course. But when I swallowed your shadow with my own, I broke its form and made it nothing. You felt that because it's a part of you. But because it's also outside of you, the attack didn't draw blood."

I open my mouth, but swiftly close it to form a pout. My brows knit roughly as I stare at Malachi. "You're saying I can feel my shadows because they actually *feel things*? That there's some tangible connection between them and me?"

Malachi rolls his eyes like it's the most obvious thing ever. And maybe it is. Maybe I realized it all along and simply didn't want to believe that the feeling of something trapped under my skin was real.

"Yes. It's the same with all Veles daemons," Malachi continues. "His power flows through our blood, linking us to him. You will never escape his influence—always feel the constant urge to use his gift. But you must master it, else it master you. That's why some Veles-cursed never outgrow their violence. We not only have to control our impulses, but those of a god."

"But I thought it wasn't about control?" I protest. "You said Veles desires submission."

Malachi utters a deep sigh. "He does, but there's more to it than that. You must give up control when it comes to your gift, but not when it comes to yourself." He levels a stern gaze on me. "What did you feel last night when you attacked Quin?"

"I didn't—" The look on his face has me holding my tongue. I loose a heavy breath and press my lips together firmly. "I was angry."

His brow lifts in amusement, but he offers nothing, waiting for me to say more.

I grumble under my breath before relenting. "I was pissed off, okay? I wanted to hurt her like she'd hurt me." My arms cross over my stomach protectively, though it does nothing to shield me from Malachi's unrelenting gaze. "Is that what you wanted to hear?" I sneer.

"Hardly," he mutters. He stares at me for another moment before I notice he's gritting his teeth. "Your emotions make your shadows unruly, Serehna. You need to learn to master them. Veles requires that you submit to your gift, but you must not let it be driven by the chaos of your mind. That very thing has driven more than one Veles daemon into unthinkable violence and endless madness."

Something churns uneasily in my stomach. All I can think of is that vision—of the cruelty it promised. That's where fate will lead me. *But which path? Submission? Or restraint?*

My silence makes Malachi impatient.

"The truth is, it's not going to be easy," he admits. "Veles is nothing like Hael. He thrives on all of it—rage, fear, desire. He'll use your emotions for his benefit. But if you can master yourself, you'll stay in control."

"But what if I can't do it?" I ask too quickly. "What if I'm cursed to be driven by that madness and violence?"

"Look at me, Serehna," he orders, his stern voice pulling my gaze up from the sand. "Do you think I'm ruled by my gift? That I don't have the control you're desperate to claim?" Malachi softens his tone. "It's possible, but only if you give in to the power that flows through your blood. It's the only way."

I swallow uneasily. "And what happens if I do? Give in, that is."

His shadows slither down his arms before I can blink. And before I can take a full breath, they've bridged the space between us. Darkness swirls around me, slinking up my body until it's teasing my throat. A sane person would fear being ensnared by a Shade's touch, but I can't deny the thrill that races through me.

"Your gift will act as an extension of you," Malachi all but purrs. "All the enemies you wish to end, any obstacle you must face, everything you desire..."

I feel the feather-light touch of a shadow against my cheek before it brushes back my hair. That darkness snakes through the strands, raking against my scalp like gentle fingers. My gaze stays locked on Malachi the entire time, though my eyes briefly flutter closed. I surrender to a moment's bliss before I remember myself. My heart beats with thunderous hesitation, and I swallow thickly.

When I look back at Malachi, his gaze has grown dark and heavy. "Your shadows can help you obtain it all," he utters.

We stand there in the silence of the desert, inches apart as his shadows slide across my skin. I feel my cheeks heat despite the brisk morning air, feel longing ache in my core. In those few moments, he looks exactly as I remembered him. Deep, intense eyes that are almost black. A gaze that never seems to end when fixated on me. It's like he can see through me—read each thought and every whim. There's an unrelenting mischief etched into his face, too. Even now, I can see it heat his gaze. He looks at me with such devotion that I nearly believe him.

But then I remember where we are and what's lead us here. I remember that he's selfish and unpredictable. And most importantly, I remember that he's shared a tent with Quin every single night since we started this journey.

My heart clenches unkindly as I pull my gaze from his. I take a few steps back, and, to my surprise, he lets me. His shadows retreat, and I wish the distance didn't feel like part of my soul was being ripped away.

I cross my arms over my chest, burdened by the morning's chill once more. "What's the next lesson?" I ask.

I'm met with silence, and when I finally look up, I see Malachi's expression has hardened. Though I want to root around and find the cause of his callousness, I know it will only leave me hollow and aching.

"Feeling your gift," he mutters, not taking his eyes off me for even a second. "Chasing you was merely a way to trigger it. Now that you know what it feels like, it should be easier to latch onto that awareness."

I nod and take a shallow breath. "Okay. I can try." I shift on my feet, if only to put more distance between us. With one last lingering look at Malachi, I take a deep breath and close my eyes.

It's there are soon as I reach for it—that thrumming in my veins. My blood feels heavy, but I can feel the power it promises. I try to grasp for it. *But what am I even grasping for?*

A soft breeze sifts the sand around me, but I pay it no mind. Instead, I clench my eyes shut and focus on my gift. It's slippery. Wild. Each time I attempt to snatch it, it stings with a violent bite. It feels impossible. My head aches from the strain.

How am I to do this? How can control feel so forced when Malachi says it will come freely?

I hunt the flickers of my gift, seeking to trap it inside me. My stomach lurches as I feel my blood hum a little louder in my veins. There's a pressure, an expanding force that seeks to pop my head like an overripe berry. A soft whimper leaves my throat. I tighten my hands into fists, baring down against the unbearable feeling.

My eyes shoot wide open as Malachi's fingers unfurl my clenched hands. "Relax," he whispers behind me, his front now pressed to my back.

The feeling of his breath on the shell of my ear sends a shudder down my spine. I swallow thickly and nod before closing my eyes once more. My hands relax as I draw in a slow breath. I try to focus on the feeling of my gift without strangling it, try to harness a modicum of stillness amidst the frenzy. Like it wasn't expecting me back so soon, my blood thrums with curiosity. I prod it gently, and it prods me back. My chest rises and falls steadily until everything but my gift melts away. I don't force it, don't leash it with tight chains as fear wishes me to. I merely breathe, and wait, and ask for its presence.

It starts off small, little flares of power that slink through my veins and set my heart aflutter. But soon, the dark god answers my call. That thrumming is all-consuming now. I feel it quivering through every inch of me. Raw. Potent. Keen. Veles is here, hovering on the bridge of this connection between us. My hands twitch and my heart beats with wild excitement.

Gods below. Mikel was right.

When I feel a familiar, sludge-like pressure in my veins, panic flares. My breath shudders; my chest grows tight. But instead of ripping my eyes open like I want to, I tether myself to the unsettling itch that swims through me. It's like honey slinking under my skin. Like molten lava creeping steadily as it cools. The moment I feel the tell-tale glide of shadows across my skin, I tense. I know it's not one of Malachi's; I can sense its origin. My throat bobs as I quell panic and welcome my gift with forced patience. I squeeze my eyes closed a little tighter, pull my breaths in a little deeper. The wisp of darkness is still. Then, it flees. Nothing happens for a while. I almost feel disheartened, but my gift returns all too quick.

That cool touch grazes my wrist, twirling against my skin like smoke. I don't dare open my eyes, not yet. Instead, I take in another deep breath and ask for more. The godsblood in me hums eagerly. It wants freedom and promises power in return. The question is: *am I ready to give it?*

I feel a slight pressure, a tugging in my veins. It wants out— badly; I know that more than anything now. My hands shake but I keep them relaxed, latching onto every twitch and swell in my blood. My heart leaps in my chest when I feel a shadow graze my arm. I open my eyes; I can't resist.

It's there before me, a slinking bunch of darkness. They're small, but they're there. *They're mine.* My blood thrums at the acknowledgment, almost purring in satisfaction. It wants me to claim it, I realize; it's desperate for it. Shadows hover against my skin, teasing flesh and swirling through the cool morning air. I'm drunk off the feeling—overwhelmed by the power flowing quietly through my veins. I turn my hand over, willing my shadows to skate across my palm. They flutter and fade, and it's then I feel something pressing against my mind, fighting me. I swallow harshly, willing my shadows to come back with a little more force now. But that's not what it wants; I can feel it protest. The moment I compel Veles's gift to do my bidding, I lose my tentative grip on it.

It surges inside of me, pounding against the vein. Panic floods my chest and a burst of shadow snaps from my wrist like a snake. The unfettered violence is too familiar and has me grasping for control. It's the memory of shadows slicing through Silas that has my nails digging into my palms, cutting so deep they draw tiny pricks of blood. My gift revolts, crackling under my skin as I trap it behind stone walls. It happens quickly and brings a pain I'm now well acquainted with. An agonizing twinge tears through my mind, blackening my vision and stripping me of all strength. I gasp and stagger backward, only to fall against a firm chest.

When I spin around, my hearts stutters. Malachi looms over me. I expect a lecture—for him to tell me my obsession with control is hindering my progress—but all I find is awe. He's speechless, beaming down at me with such pride that I can't help but laugh. The moment the cheerful noise slips from my lips, I slap a hand against my mouth. It feels foreign on my tongue, but I can't deny the warmth flooding my chest. That warmth only grows hotter as Malachi continues to stare.

The look in his eyes is no longer proud—no, it's flooded with something much more potent. The world ceases to spin as he reaches out to me. He doesn't rush, merely takes his time as he grasps my wrist and raises it to his lips. He gazes at the spot where my shadows just were and smiles to himself.

"Incredible," he utters.

His mouth is hot on my skin. He plants a gentle kiss to the inside of my wrist before his eyes dart to mine. The look on Malachi's face soothes an ache that's a decade in the making, and yet it terrifies me. The feeling churning through me is foolish and unwise. It will ruin me. It has before. I should pull away and end it now, but I can't deny myself this.

Shadows wrap around my waist, tugging me closer. He's still holding my wrist, and it's with heat blazing in his eyes that he plants another slow, agonizing kiss. I shiver, body flooding with a craving I thought I'd kicked. I press against him, desperate for every bit of his warmth.

As soon as Malachi loosens his grip on my wrist, I'm quick to weave my fingers through his hair. When I pull on the strands, he growls.

"*Serehna*," he warns.

The rumble of his voice sends a shudder through me, but I only press closer. "*Malachi*," I taunt.

His hand snatches my waist, dragging me against his body roughly. Shadows skate across my thighs, squeezing my ass and pressing me into him. I bite back a moan as I feel his hard length against my stomach. His mouth drops to my neck, his breath fire on my skin.

"Tell me to stop," he rasps. His fingers slink under my jaw, holding my gaze to him. "Tell me to stop right now or I swear to the gods—"

His lips suck at my neck, and I can't help the gasp that slips from my throat.

"*Gods*," I moan. "Don't stop."

Malachi grazes his teeth against my skin as he rumbles a groan into my neck. "All these fucking years," he utters. "I thought you were lost to me."

He sucks the tender spot beneath my ear, pulling another panting breath from me. I tilt my head back to demand more, and he all too quickly obliges. His mouth traces a hungry path down my neck, making my toes curl in my boots.

"And to think, after all this time, you were merely out of reach." Malachi rasps against my skin. "Fuck the gods for all of their games."

My throat grows thick with emotion as I scratch my nails again his scalp. "I'm here now, Mali," I breathe. "I'm right here."

He pulls back instantly, pupils blown wide. I would feel the sting of rejection if not for the feral delight flooding his gaze. Without a word, Malachi hoists me up against him. My legs circle his waist as he drops us to the sand, and I let out a muffled shriek as I fall into his lap. He grins like a fiend, and for the first time since Hira, there's no tension on his face, only a look that promises me too much.

"Say it again," he utters against my neck as he starts kissing me once more. "Call me that again."

I'm silent for a moment too long, and his gaze snaps up to mine. His eyes are wide. Desperate. I bite my lip against the words that threaten to slip free at the sight of him so raw. My fingers run through his hair softly, lingering in the dark strands. As I stare into his eyes, I realize this was inevitable. Our paths had split before this fate found us, but it seems the gods are willing to give us a second chance. *Why should I fight it?*

My heart clenches in my chest, but for once, it's not with stifling ache. I take my time tracing my fingers across Malachi's face, committing him to memory once more. Every scar. Each and every way his features have shifted from that of a boy to a man in my absence. Strong jaw. Stubble-lined skin. He closes his eyes as my fingers brush against his lips. His body shudders at the touch, and molten heat spreads through me.

"I missed you, Mali," I whisper. When he looks at me again, tears line my eyes—though, they're far from the sad, pitiful things I've been shedding of late. I swallow thickly and offer him a hopeful, aching smile. "So, so much," I admit.

He grabs my face in both hands, staring deep into my eyes. The heat in his gaze makes me squirm in his lap, stoking the fire between us.

"Tell me you want this, Sersi," Malachi demands, the old nickname slipping off his lips like a vehement prayer. "Tell me you want me."

"I—"

The confession dies on my tongue as my eyes flood with a haze of white. I don't even have time to blink. Malachi is gone in an instant, and in his place is a hell I cannot seem to escape.

The pain is all I can feel, that and the slick of blood.

It's everywhere. Soaking my tunic. Dripping from my fingers. But the pain, the pain rises above it all.

It's a searing heat razing my strength. A scorching fire that seeks to chew through my veins. My blood feels like it's boiling, and there is nothing I can do but endure.

My scream is lost to the night.

Both gods are warring inside of me. Clashing. Fighting for dominance as their blessing drips from my flesh and leaves me wanting. Shadows surround me like a windstorm—a wild flurry of darkness that has no master. Though chaos rages, my darker gift is a mere flicker in my veins, a thrum that grows weaker every second. I try to reach for it, but it's too busy abandoning me to beckon my call.

This is not what I asked for. This is not the path I chose.

As I feel the grip on my waist tighten and flex—as I hear the owner of that touch yelling in all his fury—I wonder if this isn't exactly what the gods had promised after all.

My knees crash against the damp ground. The pain is back, and with it comes a cold chill spreading across my skin. My hands drop to my stomach, fingertips stained in the godsblood that pours from me. My head lulls, consumed by an agony I cannot face. I know the gods are coming for me at last, but before I can wander into the dark to never return, I'm yanked back by a desperate touch. My gift reacts before I can, fueled by anguish and an anger I cannot leash.

The shadows strike; I feel every inch of skin that they carve. The muffled yell comes next, its familiar tone yet another blade driven into my gut this day.

Black spots speckle my vision as I glance over my shoulder, but I see enough. Too much. Malachi's face is drenched in blood. It seeps down his cheek, flowing like a river his frantic hands cannot seem to dam. His mouth is agape, cursing so loudly it rivals the clamor around us. His voice rises above the chaos, driving my own pain higher. When those dark eyes flicker to mine, I know things will never be the same.

I try to stand, but disorientation has me collapsing once more. My fingers dig into loose dirt, strangling wild grasses as I scream. The world is a roar of shadows and violence. My blood is shuddering under my skin. I feel myself slipping, feel my strength leave with every painful pulse of my stomach. My fingers blindly slap at my skin, trying to stop the life from pouring out of me, but my hands feel as distant as my mind.

I'm floating, drifting toward that place I've craved for weeks. But it wasn't supposed to be like this.

The gifts I neglected for so long are now taut threads threatening to snap. I can all but feel the gods' fingers yanking at them, unkind in the way they pluck and pinch. They wish to take, because I have allowed everything to be taken. Though worse than the agonizing sensation clenching my chest is a truth I cannot escape no matter how fast my consciousness fades.

This has all been for nothing.

My head lulls once more, chin dropping to my chest with a violent jolt. The world fades only to be snapped back with a bellowing roar. I know I'm the cause, though I cannot find it in me to feel guilt.

He did this to himself by seeking me out.

My eyes close like the lid of a tomb, but all too soon, rough fingers rip me awake. When my lids flutter open, it's a black-eyed gaze that meets mine—one so wrathful I wonder if I've already found my way to meet the dark god. Disorientation paints his face in a blur and the blackened night works to conceal him in shadow. My heart aches with knowing, though I'm lost to what that knowing reveals.

The one I thought lost is yelling. His fury pitches across this battlefield as he speaks to someone beyond what I can see. Shadows curl around my wrists, easing me the only way they can with the last shred of strength they have to offer.

That violent gaze returns to me before I'm ready to confront it. He grips my face without tenderness, only anger and desperation. He's yelling at me now, words spitting with a violence that should scare me. As he yanks me toward him, everything goes black.

CHAPTER 26

I gasp as Hael thrusts me into the world. Fear stutters my heart. I know I'm back—that I'm safe—but all I can think about is what's coming for me. I thrash and yell, desperate to escape this fate, but hands hold me hostage.

Terror races up my spine, stirring a panic I know now more than ever is unwise. But it's untamable. My mind is stuck in that vision—spinning in the memory of the pain and chaos I witnessed just moments ago.

It felt like I was dying. I *know* I was dying. But worse than that was the agony that I was to leave this world worse than how I found it. I don't know how, I just know.

I can't catch my breath. I gasp and flail, but there's a tight grip around me that doesn't relent.

"Serehna, stop," Malachi utters breathlessly. "It was just a vision. You're here with me."

The white fades from my eyes in a leisurely flow that has me cursing Hael. It's too slow. I need to see. *Gods, help me see.*

The desert comes back to me in pieces, and as I blink furiously, I see shadows whipping against the sand. I feel it in my blood—that thrumming frenzy, that stifled fury. My gift is all but begging to be free. Chomping at the bit. Waiting for me to give up control. I force breath after breath into my lungs, but the terror doesn't ease. The panicked gulps of air I take only drive my heart rate higher and make my skin clammy. And, amidst it all, my gift rages on.

Shadows lurch over mine like a great, black tide; Malachi's gift swallows my own in a crashing wave. I gasp against the assault—violently consumed by that nothingness before I'm yanked back into the daylight.

My panic rises, but when I feel the hot press of lips against my neck, my body stills. It takes me a moment to understand what's going on, but the realization brings nothing but anger. Malachi kisses me desperately, sucking at my neck like he can soothe this frenzy—like his touch can change things. But there is no changing this, no easing out the knife the future has buried deep. No removing the target on my back, or the violence under my skin.

I scramble out of Malachi's arms, sprawling across the sand as I suck in desperate breaths. My forehead presses into the earth, and I beg the gods to take this fate from me. But I can't escape it; I can't even find a breath. My mind is spinning, lost to a future I still don't understand as blood throbs loudly in my ears.

All too soon, a warm hand grazes the small of my back. I lurch away, but not before Veles's violence lashes free. The shadow strikes before Malachi can stop it. It slices his chest, cutting through his tunic and drawing a fresh trickle of blood. My face pales as I watch the edges of his flesh turn black beneath the slashed fabric. The cut is shallow and small, but it's there. Though I thought I broke long ago, it seems there were still pieces of me to shatter.

I act before I can think of a better solution. I drag my dagger across my palm, breaking flesh and spilling blood. It stings—*gods, does it sting*—but it's not enough. I curl my fingers into my hand, summoning every ounce of a pain I more than deserve. As the blood spills across my palm and drips into the sand, my shadows finally fade into nothing.

Malachi is there moments later, kneeling before me as he snatches my hand with a rough, unyielding grip. "What in the gods did you do that for?" he rages.

He wastes no time ripping off his torn tunic, though when he tries to use it to staunch my wound, I reel away.

"*Serehna,*" he urges. "You're hurt."

My eyes are blazing fires as I take in what I've done. Malachi's chest is bare, and though I was clawing at him with lust only minutes ago, the sight of his marked, muscled body does nothing for me now. All I see is the Shade's cut marring his skin and the blood that seeps from it. Yet again, I've scarred familiar flesh, and the longer I stare, the more I hate myself for it.

Malachi scoffs as he finally notices where my attention lies. "For fuck's sake. It's barely a scratch. Do you truly think your Mender friend incapable of healing such a small thing?"

I don't answer. I can only stare at another token of my violence made permanent. But as I look at his new scar, I'm quickly reminded of another he'll one day come to have. The vision races through my mind in violent flickers. The blood seeping down his face. The rumbling pain as a yell ripped from his throat. The look he gave me after I'd carved his flesh. Even for a life as cruel as this one, it's too much to take in.

Malachi does nothing but watch me for a moment, confusion muddying his gaze. He ignores the bleeding wound on his chest and instead searches my eyes for answers. The scrutiny is overwhelming. One look at his handsome face only seeks to remind me that one day, no matter how hard I fight fate, I'll scar him just as I have Mikel.

My hands begin to shake, and even as hot blood continues to drip from my palm, all I can feel is a cold chill rushing up my spine. "I'm sorry," I utter, breath barely more than a whisper. "I never meant to—" My cut flesh burns against the desert's breeze, and I flinch as a prick of pain dashes through the wound.

Malachi's eyes dart to my palm, and his gaze turns murderous. "Is that why you did this to yourself?" he snarls. "You feel guilty?" He reaches for me again, but I scramble away.

"I—" My tongue feels too heavy. I try to find the words, but I don't even know where to begin.

Malachi pulls himself up from the sand, brushing off his pants. I can't stop staring at his chest—at the damage I have once more inflicted on another.

"This was bound to happen. You're not going to master your gift in one day." He lets out an exasperated sigh. "You think I didn't expect a little bloodshed when I decided to train you? No Veles daemon grasps any sort of competency without mistakes. It's expected. It's *normal*."

He moves toward me, but I'm quick to step back.

"Things will get better once you give in," he urges. "Your gift won't feel so volatile once you learn to master your emotions."

I let out an unbelievable laugh. "Are you serious?" I balk. "How could you possibly ask me to give in to this violence after what just happened?"

Malachi grumbles and stalks over to me before I can flee. He snatches my wrist, but unlike before, his touch isn't laced in desire. It's with frustration that he pushes his ruined tunic against my hand and forces it to mop up my blood.

"None of this is easy," he states. "Do you think I suddenly woke up with marks and was able to conjure shadows at whim? It took *years* of practice. *Years* of failing to harness my potential. The fact that you were able to summon anything at all is not something to dismiss simply because you're scared. You have more power than you realize, Serehna."

"I don't care about power!" I shout, ripping my hand free of his grasp. "I care about the threat I've become. The danger I put everyone in. If I submit to Veles, who is to say I won't do more damage next time? Who is to say I won't accidentally take Mikel's eye instead of scaring his cheek? Or— Or..." It's Malachi's face that comes to mind, the future version of it that will always bear my mistakes. "I can't— I won't let..." Panic rushes up, squeezing my throat. "This gift is a curse. One I am better off without. I cannot give in to it. I will not give in to—"

I don't realize I'm crying until Malachi pulls me into his chest. His arms wrap around me, and his shadows press against my back.

"You must," he utters, squeezing me tight as my tears wet his skin and mix with the slick of his blood. "Mikel told me you're in pain. It will only get worse. The more you resist Veles, the more reckless he'll grow. You need to give in. Let him have the control you're so desperately clinging to."

"I can't," I rasp against his chest. "If you'd seen what I've done, what the gods would have me do..." My breath shudders as I bite back the sobs that wish to spill free. "I only bring *suffering*, Mali. Suffering and death. I am the monster the prophecy claims me to be."

He shushes me softly and runs his fingers through my hair. "You are far from a monster, Sersi. Don't worry about what the future brings. I will be there to make sure none of it happens."

As he presses a chaste kiss against the side of my head, fear of a different sort seizes my chest. I shove him away quickly.

"*Don't*," I snap. "Don't make promises you can't keep."

"Serehna—"

"There was a time you promised the same thing. And you *left*," I croak, emotions swelling my throat. "You left and forced me to survive this life without you."

He says nothing, only stares at me with a look that pains us both.

I swallow thickly, steadying my tone. "What do you want from me, truly?"

Malachi's face pinches into something guarded, though his eyes are much too desperate. "I've already told you. I want you to trust me."

"But for what purpose?" I plead. "Why is my trust so important?"

His jaw ticks, and he takes his time finding the words. Each passing second of silence makes something nervous shift through my gut.

Malachi sighs. "Because the Continent is heading into chaos, and the only way we keep ourselves free from its shackles is together. You and me. United against our enemies."

I let out an exasperated groan. "What is that even supposed to mean? *Our enemies*? You mean Rohan?" My head aches with how desperately I'm holding my gift at bay. It had a taste of freedom, and now it wants more. "I thought the plan was to destroy the Hesha Mol? Rohan won't be a problem after he learns he can't be the Born. Our enemies won't exist then."

Malachi's expression falters before he shifts to regard me with pity. "We will always have enemies," he chides. "Anyone who glances at our markings with hate in their eyes. All who seek to use daemons for their own benefit. Every Turiden who wishes to send godsblood back into the earth. It's us or them, Serehna. And it's not going to be us, not again. Not ever again."

I open my mouth to argue, but something stops me. It's a knowing apprehension, a dreadful ache twisting through my gut. I don't need to ask the gods to sense that something lingers between the words Malachi fervently speaks. Though I know I won't like what I find, I seek the answers anyway.

My brow furrows as I dare to step closer like a stablehand approaching an unbroken stallion. "I don't understand," I prod. "You're acting like you want to take on the entire Continent."

Malachi crosses his arms over his chest and tilts his head at me. "And what if I do? This hellscape could do with another Rebellion."

I laugh unceremoniously, right in his face. "You've gone mad. There's no other explanation." My hands gesture wildly between us. "Another rebellion? Against who, Malachi?" I press. "There is no king!"

He leans in close, giving me a good look at the zealous fury scorching his gaze. "Not yet there isn't."

My heart stutters as I mull over his words. I open my mouth to speak, but can't find the strength. Surely, he can't be serious.

He sighs, rolling his eyes with an arrogance I'm finding less charming with each passing second. "The Rebellion had it right," he lectures me. "The Continent belongs to us, not them. Our blood runs through its veins. It's us who should rule over it."

I stare at him, mouth agape. But as he glares back at me with that superior look on his face, I can't stay quiet. "Milias Nayer wanted daemons to be equal to those the gods haven't touched," I state. "It was never about ruling over them. It was about peace!"

Malachi sneers. "There will never be peace as long as they covet and villainize our blood."

"So, what?" I snap. "You want to conquer the Continent? Have daemons reign?" I loose an unfriendly laugh and squeeze my fingers against the bridge of my nose. "You're mad if that's your aim in this. Madder still if you think I'll help you. You want another Rebellion? How could you possibly think that wise?"

Silence greets me, heavy and unwavering. When I look up, there's no humor on Malachi's face. He's staring at me like I've disappointed him—like he's angry with me. I want to laugh, if only to ease this tension squeezing my chest, but I can't muster so much as a scoff. I wait for Malachi to say something, but it seems he, too, is at a loss.

"Please think this through," I request. "The Rebellion took the lives of *thousands.* Left the Continent in heaps of rubble and scarred it beyond repair. Still, the chaos of that time stains our lives. No safety. No promise of a future. Only anarchy and greed to embolden us all."

He says nothing. I wait in the drowning depths of this quiet, hoping for something to ease me. The desert breeze stirs the sand against our boots. Behind Malachi, the sun has risen above the horizon, but the start of a new day brings no hope.

My head aches and my palm throbs, though I don't relent. I step closer, fingers splaying across his shoulders. "Nothing good will come from ideas such as this," I declare. "Surely you don't wish to lead the Continent into war? *Daemons against godless?* It'll be a bloodbath."

"If that's what it takes, then so be it."

I pull in a wavering breath. "You can't mean that," I prod. "We've been fighting to exist our entire lives. A Rebellion will only bring more of that. For us and everyone else."

"That's the whole point, Serehna," he argues. "We've done nothing but survive, and for what purpose? What gain? I don't need to know what happened after Artolen to know this life has not been kind to you. I can see it in your eyes, in the way your hands twitch for a blade when you get restless. Surviving this world has left you with scars, and I won't stand for any more to be carved. I'll burn it all down if I have to."

I scoff, though my heart patters frantically. "You think you can change any of it? Prevent more hardship?" I snark. "This life has been for me what it is for all people. There's suffering in survival, Malachi. It's inevitable. It's pain, and violence, and misfortune. But I will continue to let the gods ravage me with this fate, because at least it means I'm still alive. Every scar is proof I've lived to see sunset after another day's hell."

"You're *wrong*," he urges, hands wrapping around my waist. He shakes me gently, grips me tightly. "There's power in our blood, and though others have hunted us for it, it will cull the worst of them. We can remake this world, decide our own fate. There will be no more pain. No more watching those we love die for the burden of their blood." Malachi rubs soothing circles against my skin, eyes softening as he regards me. "Everything will change when I force the Continent to bend a knee. I promise."

I slowly remove his hands from my waist, letting them drop between us as I seek distance from his touch. My chest is tight, and I pull in a forceful breath before uttering my fears. "You speak as if you've already decided your role in all this," I state. "Like you wish to be the one to lead us out of one darkness and into another."

"No one else will do it. Why not me?" he offers. "I have Veles's blessing. His strength. His fury. As do you. With you by my side, there will be no stopping what's to come. *Open your eyes.* The world is ours for the taking, Serehna. It's time we did just that."

"Do you hear yourself?" I rave. "You're telling me that you wish to rule? That you seek to be king?"

Again, it's silence that greets me. As I watch Malachi's lips purse into a firm line, it seems the answers I need will never come. But the longer I stare at him, I find I'm wrong. Though he says nothing, the truth rests in plain sight. It's hidden in the restraint pinching his face. There's determination set in his deep, brown eyes. Then, it's disdain I see. It's flighty and fleeting, but I catch it regardless. *How could I not?* Time may have separated us, but it did nothing to erase the memory of him. How he manipulated merchants so we could steal their cargo. How he intimidated black market traders until they offered us a better price. How he lied to countless others. At his core—good intentions, rotten pit, and all—I know Malachi. And though I shouldn't be surprised by this hurt devouring my heart, it guts me nonetheless.

"That's it, isn't it?" I utter. "You hope to become king... But what of me?"

He admits nothing, and it's louder than anything he could manage to say. His throat bobs, his eyes dart to the sand, and my stomach drops. Grief contorts my face as the truth lays herself bare for me. All along, it was obvious. *Wasn't it?* I just didn't want to see.

"Why are you here, Malachi?"

He stands up straighter and levels me with a stoical gaze. "Because the gods have finally woven fate in our favor."

I laugh, but the sound is filled with too much ache and not enough anger. "*Fate,*" I rasp. "Is that what you wish to call it? The real reason you're here? Why you're so invested in this violence I can barely contain?" My expression is hardened, my world gutted. "Call it fate, Malachi. I don't care. But it's not me you want. It's merely my gift that's drawn you back."

"Sersi, *stop*," Malachi grumbles, running a hand through his hair. "Don't let this ruin what we—"

"Admit it," I choke out. "Suddenly I have a shred of power, and what? I'm worthy of your attention? Of your hands all over me?"

"*Enough*," Malachi orders. "You know that's not—"

"You never had the guts to make a move on me when we were younger. Never did anything other than stick by my side and scare off anyone who showed interest. But now there's something to gain by trapping me with your affections, isn't there?"

"*I'm* trapping *you*?" he protests. "You're acting like I didn't spend months grasping for you in my dreams, like I didn't agonize over every fleeting glimpse I got of your face. The gods might have sent you to a different hell, plucked you from Quin's weavings by reason of fate, but I was living my own nightmare each night I was denied your touch or a mere whisper from your lips. I knew you were somewhere out there, alive, and yet I couldn't reach you."

I'm frozen to the spot, though my fists shake violently at my sides. My mind is a hazy cloud of pain I fear will soon flatten me. I consider letting my shadows loose to ease the burden and sate this agony with Malachi's blood, but I can't. Not yet. He still hasn't admitted this. And though it will destroy me, I deserve to hear it from his own lips.

"Tell me the truth," I insist. "You're using me."

Malachi sighs in frustration. As he takes a step closer, I can see the falsehoods forming on his tongue. I don't give him the chance to utter any more.

"Why else would you have come back after all this time?" I argue. "You wouldn't stir up the past unless it was for some benefit. My gift. The prophecy." My words spew like fire, fueled by the fury I wish to feel for him but can only muster for myself. "What other reason would you have to suddenly want me?"

"I have *always* wanted you, Serehna," Malachi snaps. "Just because I seek more from you than your affections doesn't mean my feelings are absent. My ambition changes nothing when it comes to you. Two things can be true at once."

"Finally. You admit there's more to this than a decade of longing and regret." The world grows heavy on my shoulders, weighing me down like the gods themselves desire me on my knees in supplication. "You're not here for me. Not truly. You're here for the Durit." My chest aches like I've been struck and beaten. "How pleased you must have been to realize they're one and the same."

"Serehna, *listen to me*," he urges, placing heavy hands on my shoulders. "It's you and me. *Together*. Don't let your mind poison what could be. Trust that I will see us through what comes next. I would never forsake you."

His eyes are turbulent, dark storms, yet I hold his gaze with none of the same fervor. "You did once before," I utter. "Why not again?"

He flinches, but I feel no regret for uttering the truth. Everything slips from me in an instant. Every ounce of rage. Every drop of pain. Numb is all I feel, a distant tug pulling me into the abyss I've craved for days. I stare at him quietly and as he does the same—unable to assuage my fears—I realize I should have expected nothing less.

"You're just like him," I offer weightlessly.

Malachi's careful mask slips as his face contorts. "Who?" he prods, quickly pressing into my personal space. "*Silas?*" His jaw twitches as he regards me with utter contempt. "I am nothing like him, Serehna. That bastard was spineless. He thought he could—"

Malachi stops himself, eyes flickering with something I can't place before he straightens. In an instant, the hate that overcame his features so quickly shifts to something of amusement. "Silas was willing to fuck over anyone if it got him what he wanted. You did us all a favor by killing him."

His claim does nothing to ease me. I've latched onto his words with desperate claws, unwilling to let go. "You speak as if you knew him," I whisper. My skin breaks out in chills, and dread fills my stomach like a horde of dead beetles. "But you didn't know him. You couldn't have."

A scowl slithers across Malachi's face as his shadows flare against his boots, slapping the worn leather with violent *thwacks*. "Didn't Vish tell you?" he coos. "Silas and I were friends."

"You're lying," I murmur. But I know he's not.

"Am I?" Malachi taunts. "Is that why you look so frightened?"

I can't catch my breath. My mind spins, rehashing things I wished to never revisit. I think of the journey to Letka. Silas hadn't stopped humming that damned tune—the same one Malachi had always sung to me. Everything makes sense, yet nothing does.

"You're the one who gave him that scar on his chest, aren't you?" I press.

Malachi's gaze tightens on me. "You saw that?" His upper lip curls into something unfriendly, and his shadows tug at my waist like greedy hands. Malachi scoffs under his breath. "I guess Tofá was right after all."

"Tofá doesn't know shit," I seethe, trying to swat away shadows that won't budge.

"*Oh?*" Malachi mocks. "So Silas didn't lure you into his bed like one of the little whores he fancied? That's the bet my men made among themselves. Care to tell me if it's true?"

I slap him before I can stop myself. I should regret it, but I don't—not with the smug look etched across Malachi's face. I move to back away, but his shadows are quick to hold me.

"You did, didn't you? *Fuck him,* I mean." He's silent for a while, though I don't miss the way he's gritting his teeth. "Do you want to know how I knew him? How foolish it is to compare the two of us?"

Malachi doesn't wait for my response. He simply wraps his shadows around my jaw and forces me to look at him. I thrash and scrape my nails down his arms, but he doesn't relent. There's a simmering rage in his gaze that tells me there's no escaping what's to come.

"I was in Lehro. Had been working for a slimy son-of-a-bitch who liked the idea of a Veles-cursed collecting his debts." Malachi *tsks*, lips curling distastefully. "It was a worthless way to make a living, and I was eager to line my pockets with something more substantial... And then I met your beloved Berserker." The resentment darkening his gaze bites like it has teeth. "Silas told me of a man who paid handsomely. I'm sure you can guess who that was."

My mouth grows as dry as the desert around us. I don't think I could say anything even if I wanted to.

"Rohan viewed my gift as the ultimate weapon. Together, Silas and I were the most valuable things he had." Malachi looses a laugh, but I hear the anger harbored within it. "It wasn't until a year later that I saw Rohan for who he was—a prejudiced bastard who enslaved anyone he could exploit." Shadows stray from my jaw to brush against my cheek, though I loathe the touch. "Many men are forced to do Rohan's bidding simply because they're afraid of what would happen if they didn't. The moment that bastard knows your weakness, your life isn't your own."

I loose a taunting scoff. "Is that to be your excuse?" I prod Malachi. "Rohan discovered your weakness and exploited it?"

"No," he states tersely. "I had no weakness. Not then. I thought mine long dead." He leans in close, breath hot and angry on my skin. "For I'd watched someone shove a blade through her."

I feel sick. This is all too much, but I can't afford to be left in the dark any longer. I hold Malachi's gaze, swallowing uneasily. "So you worked for Rohan?"

"Yes," he grunts. "I worked for him—helped him gain control over Denheir and the surrounding cities whether by blackmail or force. It didn't matter to Rohan, and it didn't matter to me. I had power. I had control. There was no one who could stand against me—no one who dared. Silas was the first devil Rohan sent to your door, but me? I was the second. I was the one he sent when things went south. The things I did..."

His jaw ticks, but he doesn't look away. He levels that vicious gaze on me, letting me imagine all of the horrible things he did on behalf of an even more horrible man.

"It wasn't until he ordered me to look for the Durit that I realized Rohan was amassing power that could easily be mine." Malachi sucks his teeth and glares. "I told Silas as much—told him we were fools to fall in line like weak men. I thought we wanted the same things, but he was too desperate to take fate into his own hands."

Malachi's eyes pass over my shoulder, growing lost in thought for a moment. His shadows fell from my skin long ago, and though I could easily walk away now, I don't want to. I'm hooked on his every word, addicted like a dying man off the first hit of merchen root.

I swallow harshly. "What happened?" I ask.

His mouth pulls into a grimace when he looks back at me. "He told Rohan of my plans to unseat him," Malachi states. "Even let the bastard convince him to lead a scouting party to track me down and purge the threat." He huffs, growing smug for a moment. "They never stood a chance. It was only by my mercy that Silas left with his life that day, for surely I could have sent his blood back into the earth like all the others. But I wouldn't. If I spilled godsblood as carelessly as our enemies, there would be no point to all of this, would there?"

My brow quirks as I regard him differently, like a tapestry whose weave was so elaborate I missed the pattern the first time. "That day in Hira..." The back of my throat grows dry. "You didn't kill Roel."

Malachi gives me an odd look.

"The Torch," I utter. "You could have easily killed him, but you didn't." Silence permeates the air like a rotting carcass. "You let him get away."

The wince that flickers across Malachi's face is so quick, I almost miss it. "The Torch wasn't there to hurt you—only capture," he says softly. "And I didn't let him take you. Nor would I have."

I nod, though I feel anything but at ease. "And what of Silas?" I ask. "Do you know why he turned his back on you? What led him to betray your trust?"

The tension snaps back across Malachi's face in an instant. "Why?" He scoffs. "Wondering if there's an excuse for what he did to you?"

I flinch, desperately trying to keep the hurt off my face before he can see it. If he does, Malachi doesn't let it deter him. He leans in close, eyes dark and searing.

"Silas was a treacherous bastard at his core," he utters, anger seeping through his tone. "I should have known better than to trust him, but he had a way with his words, did he not?"

The look Malachi gives me is cruel and taunting. I step away, already having heard enough, but he doesn't let me escape so easily. He wraps his hand around my wrist, yanking me back.

"You want to know? You truly do?" Malachi goads me. "He loved that godless brother of his too much, and he let that love destroy him. I told Silas to keep Sasha in line, but he was too preoccupied with it all. Gold. Drink. *Pleasure.* Everything Rohan so temptingly dangles in front of his men in order to keep them sated and simple-minded." Something bitter washes over Malachi's face before he shakes it away. "Silas was too weak to do what needed to be done, and because of that he lost the one person he was desperate to protect." Shadows snap against the sand as Malachi's anger grows. "If he had only listened to me. If he had only done what—" Malachi grits his teeth and shakes his head. "I should have seen his betrayal coming from a mile away." He looses a spiteful laugh. "As I'm sure you should have, too."

I don't say anything for a while. As I mull over Malachi's words—his story—I feel a tight knot forming in the pit of my stomach. It's an understanding I thought I wanted, but hate the taste of. A knowledge that brings as much clarity as it does pain. I swallow thickly before taking a deep, steadying breath.

"Virtue doesn't mean shit if you don't survive," I utter, my voice as weak and uncertain as I feel. "But he wasn't just trying to survive for his own sake, was he?"

Malachi's face contorts in displeasure, lips pulling down roughly. "Don't tell me you pity him after what he did to you?" he berates me. "He let Rohan take you without any plan to get you back." Malachi's shadows whip through the air, cracking violently around us. "You might think me a selfish bastard, but there are worse things to be in this world," he utters darkly. "Make no mistake, I am not Silas. He and I are nothing alike."

I wait for his shadows to calm, staring at him quietly until the sand stills. His face is a conflicting mask of emotions, but I can't find it in myself to be swayed by any of his ire or desperation. It's a numb emptiness that washes over me. A bone-deep ache. The rising sun is the only warmth that graces my skin—the only thing that lets me feel anything at all, really.

As I slowly step away from Malachi, the space between us feels like a growing chasm. Endlessly deep and uncrossable. My teeth grind into each other as I stare at him and see a stranger—the same one who left me to die all those years ago.

"You're right. You two couldn't be more different." I give Malachi one last look, trying to memorize this moment so I don't find myself so foolish in the next. "I think Silas betrayed me because he had no other choice. But I fear one day, you'll betray me simply because it suits you."

I turn my back on him and leave. He doesn't stop me, and, somehow, that hurts most of all. As I stalk toward my bedroll, tears brimming in my eyes and agony hardening my heart, I realize just how blind I've been.

CHAPTER 27

Sand stirs beneath my fingers, swishing despite the fact that not even a breeze drifts across this land. The black tendrils that flutter atop the ground elicit yet another smile from me. That's twice they've come when called, twice they've twirled above the earth like tiny sandstorms simply because I will it.

After four days and nights of sitting on the outskirts of camp, of stilling my breath and coaxing forth my gift like a hesitant predator, I'm getting somewhere. Of course, my ability to wield these shadows is far from where it should be. I've yet to grasp that theoretical control—or give it up for that matter—but it's a start.

All in time, I tell myself.

I loose a sigh as the truth outweighs tonight's fleeting success. I don't have time. The closer we get to the Kohe Mountains—still just dark blurs on the western horizon—the closer the inevitable grows. Tol Dena. The Hesha Mol. Whatever is to come after that. Each obstacle feels like a weight on my shoulders, eager to crumple me against the path I've somehow found myself on.

My fate is coming, though I wish it weren't. I have much to learn before the future finds me. Too much. And some days, I wonder if I'm merely making things worse by awakening my gift.

I haven't had any visions since that morning with Malachi, but that doesn't mean I haven't been deep inside the memories of those that came before. Reminders of pain, violent hums of power, and gut-wrenching guilt is all that greets me when I close my eyes. I'm haunted by what the gods have planned, and my sleepless nights are worse than any nightmare a Weaver could send.

I grit my teeth and swipe my hand through the shadows, banishing them back into nothing. The thrum in my blood is loud—hungry for more. But just like every time I've loosened the leash on my gift in the past few days, I'm quick to tighten it once I'm done. There's a familiar pressure as I do, like hot coals burning against my skull. It hits me like a punch to the gut. I feel queasy, and it's with a harsh swallow that I stifle my budding nausea.

The pain has gotten worse, though I haven't told Mikel. He thinks every lesson I take up with my shadows lessens the burden, but that couldn't be further from the truth. The searing ache has given way to blinding pain. It's all-consuming, and I have no one to blame but myself. I know what will make the pain go away, but I refuse to give in to what the dark god desires. Control is not something I can offer, not when I know what my submission will cost.

Suffering. Destruction. *Death.*

Again, my mind spins as I recall my last two visions—the chaos my blood wrought and the pain it left in its wake. I will scar Malachi, and I will kill that stranger. It will happen regardless of what I do; I'm not foolish enough to think I can change the fate the gods have woven for me. But still, I'm not ready to accept the last shard of this cutting truth, so I keep my gift locked behind walls of my own creation.

My fingers clench roughly in the sand, but as much as I wish to choke every grain, they merely slip through my grip. A soft *shush* alerts me to footsteps. Though instinct has my hand reaching for a blade and my nerves buzzing for a fight, I don't turn. Whoever it is, I can't find it in myself to care.

Silence climbs my back like a devil as the footsteps slow, then cease. I resist the urge to peer over my shoulder, only dig my fingers deeper into the sand and let more grains slip through like a fate I'll never catch. My jaw locks as anticipation churns through me. If it was Mikel, he would have said something by now. And if it was *him*... It's a foolish thought, one I quickly shake away. Malachi and I aren't speaking. We've hardly looked at each other in days. I know it can't be him, so when my visitor finally plops down beside me, I find the courage to face them.

Savi shoots me a warm smile before knocking her shoulder against mine. "Just me. Riat was eager to come bother you, but that boy is easily distracted."

It's brief relief I feel as I look at her, mixed with a shameful twinge of disappointment. I tell myself I don't want Malachi to be the one in front of me—that I haven't been waiting days for him to beg my forgiveness. But I can only lie to myself for so long.

I press my lips into a firm line to keep my expression clear of all that I feel.

"You're out here late," Savi prods. "Meditating, again?"

I stifle a scoff. *Meditating, indeed.* It's all I've done for days now. Even when I'm not sitting cross-legged in the sand, eyes closed, and breath steady in my chest, the godsblood in my veins is all I can think about. It's ever-present, reminding me just what's at stake. So, I've been relentless. Waking up hours before the others, stewing in silence while my shadows buzz under my skin like flies. Staying up with only the moon for my companion as Veles's gift snaps out in fleeting wisps, simply to demand more. And finally, like tonight, sneaking away from the fire before the others can notice, only to beseech my shadows to come when I call. Though I've tried to keep my lessons to myself, it's proved difficult with a group like ours. Nosy, the lot of them.

The first night, Riat snuck up only to have me draw a dagger and lay him flat on his ass. He was delightfully amused at that. Me? Not so much. I'd yelled at him to leave me be—scolded him like a rowdy child who'd broken a priceless vase. But even after my outburst, solace wasn't found so easily. The next morning, Hassan came grumbling over to toss me a hunk of spiced bread he'd procured in Tilket. He'd mumbled something about keeping my strength up before slinking off into the gray morning light. And Mikel...

After hours of argument, he convinced me to return to our tent a few nights ago. There was no keeping secrets from him after that. I had told him everything—well, *almost* everything. I detailed the fight I had with Malachi, fuming about the foolish crusade he seeks to embark upon. Only after I explained the pain-staking progress I'd made with my shadows did my tongue cease wagging. I spoke nothing of my visions—nothing of the havoc the gods have proved I alone will cause.

Mikel knew I was holding back. I could see it in his eyes. He's always had a sense for these things—for sussing out my secrets— but he's allowing me to keep them for now. But while it seemed Mikel was eager to have us both forget what burdens I carry, he wasn't above proving a point. To say he was smug when I told him that stilling my mind *was* indeed the way to tame these shadows is putting it lightly. Though he didn't say the words, the glint in his eyes was the loudest *I told you so* he's ever sent my way. And I've received more than my fair share over the years.

A smirk slips across my face now that all I can think about is Mikel. My friend has barely left my side for days, poking me with taunts and teasings in an attempt to cheer my ever-sullen mood. He even suggested we slip peshen into Malachi's drink to disrupt whatever goes on in his tent at night. It was a ridiculous, wild scheme that had shaken me from dark thoughts quickly and without hesitation. Even now, I can barely hold back my laughter as I think of how Mikel wanted to make the Shade impotent—temporarily, at least. Though I'd rejected the notion, I'd appreciated the sentiment and the way it'd cracked a smile on my face, one that seems to be rare as of late.

When I look back at Savi, she's watching me with a patient knowing. It's often that I slip into my thoughts these days, all too quickly lost to moments that have long since passed and a future I have no chance of changing.

I sigh and offer her a calm smile. "Meditating, *again*," I affirm. "Don't tell Mikel, but he taught me another way to breathe earlier, and it's proving effective."

Savi shoots me a conspiratorial smile. "Your secret is safe with me."

I nod again, but before I can turn back to the empty desert before me, her appearance catches my eye. I raise a brow as my gaze slowly drifts over Savi. She's dressed for bed, wearing a loose pair of pants and a baggy tunic that dwarfs her muscular frame. Curled in her hand is a thin piece of hefri. The sturdy, flat-shaped root is found in the Continent's east and often used by nomads to clean their teeth when far from any outpost. It looks like she was minutes away from sleep but stumbled out here instead.

"You're up late, too," I prod. "Any reason?"

She gives me a sheepish, though bright, smile. "I was just about to turn in when I peeked out of the tent and saw you. Thought I'd come see how you were doing."

I hum thoughtfully and pull my gaze from hers. "Fine. No need to worry about me." I try to smile, but it quickly fades from my lips.

I don't turn to meet Savi's gaze, but I know it's there—locked on me steadily with a concern I don't want to face. So, I don't. Instead, my eyes search the endless dark for a distraction, but there are none to find. The night is still, nothing stealing the quiet but the steady beat of my heart and the soft breaths that spill from Savi and my own lungs. Yet, the silence feels charged. Impatient. I can all but hear the thoughts churning in Savi's mind, the things she wishes to say but hasn't. It's been like this for days—with her, and the others. I've kept to myself, and if it weren't for Mikel's constant prodding, I know I wouldn't speak at all. There's too much on my mind, too many burdens nipping at my resolve like razor-toothed fish. There's nothing to say that will make any of this better, so why try?

Unfortunately, Savi does. The minute I hear her open her mouth to speak, I prepare for everything I'm not ready for. Questions. Pity. Anything she'll offer will be too much right now. I don't want it. I only wish to seep into the earth and disappear. But I'm granted no such favors.

"Are you really?" Savi prods. "Fine?" Her voice is quiet yet steady, like she's worried she might spook me.

I try to swallow the lump in my throat, but it doesn't budge. My jaw clenches, flexing under tension as I refuse to let emotions take hold. I know I won't be able to utter a word without my voice giving me away, so I nod my head instead.

Savi sighs and pulls her knees up to her chest, getting comfortable. "You're stronger than all of us, Ren. Gods know how you do it."

I chew on my bottom lip, but say nothing. Though I know she didn't mean them to, her words circle my mind like a hungry beast looking for weak spots.

Strength. Is that what they think this is?

My blood thrums under my skin, reminding me of the raw power that could raze the Continent if I let it. It's a temporary distraction and does nothing to quell this unease inside me.

Is it strength that keeps me moving toward a fate I wish to escape? Or is it something else, something much more shameful?

I grit my teeth, attempting to stave off the flurry of ache that blooms every time I think of what has come to pass of late.

Was it strength that kept me moving from caravan to caravan all the years since Artolen? Never settling and always waiting for the knife to appear at my back? Strength that kept me alive in Denheir? That had me barreling out of that house with blood on my hands?

My stomach knots with a twist, holding me hostage to all I've done and who it is I've become.

Was it strength that killed Silas?

A shudder runs up my spine, laced with a pathetic truth the others would pity me for if they knew.

No. It wasn't strength that got me this far in life. It's been fear.

"I've been talking to Vish," Savi states, ripping me from the pain of my thoughts. "About Rikyir."

My body stills, and I look at her from the corner of my eye. Vish has scarcely mentioned that place since we set off on this gods-cursed journey, and I've been eager to forget its so-called existence. I loathe to think of that place deep in the gods-drenched north, untouched by greed or hate. A place where daemons and godless can exist in peace. Untroubled. Happy. The very idea of it sets a vile clench in my gut. Such a place doesn't exist, and if it did, I surely wouldn't be welcomed there.

I don't say anything, and, eventually, Savi fills the silence.

"I know that look," she teases, catching my heavy gaze. "Hassan gave me the same one when I brought this up yesterday."

I try to bite back my scowl, but it doesn't work.

Savi sighs. "You both think it's merely a trick or a lie, but I have faith the gods haven't abandoned us fully."

The bitter laugh slips from my lips before I can stop it. "Oh, the gods are still here," I state. "They make sure I feel their presence in every breath I take. Reminding me just what they're capable of."

I spear my gaze on Savi, but the compassion pinching her brows douses my fury like water on a candle's wick.

"I just mean" —she lets out another sigh and gestures across these desolate sands— "there has to be someplace out there where life doesn't feel like constantly fighting for air. Someplace where a morning's peace is felt all throughout the day until night brings even greater contentment." She leans back, supported by her forearms. "Don't you wish for something more than this?"

I practically flinch. A retort bubbles up my throat, coated in rage and a resentment one could only feel after being denied something so many times. But before I can spew my disdain— berate her for assuming I don't want a peace I will never find— what I see on Savi's face settles me. I swallow harshly before dropping my gaze to the sand.

"What is it you wish for?" I offer, voice threatening to crack under strain. "What do you hope to find in Rikyir that you haven't found yet?"

Savi pulls in a deep breath, and when she lets it out with a heaviness I didn't know she harbored, I can't help but look at her.

A fragile smile rests on her lips, wavering slightly as she begins to speak. "A life where we could all forget the blood spilled from our flesh or by our hands. A day where I could wake up and see happiness on my cousin's face instead of the crushing weight of his self-inflicted duty. A moment where I'm smiling because this life merits it, not because it's needed to make it through."

She holds my gaze steadily, not at all bothered that I can see the glimmering tears in her eyes. "I want all of that, but more than for myself, I want it for the others. Each has things they wish to forget, devils they hope to escape. No one here wants to hunt men to make a living. Or to pass a slaver's auction and have no option but to look the other way. If such a life exists in Rikyir, I want it for us all—no matter how fleeting it might be."

My heart aches, clinging to a future Savi painted so clearly.

How would it be to wake up in the morning and not worry about what the day might bring? To wander through a place without wondering which hungry-eyed traveler might pull a blade on me?

I clench my jaw, biting back emotions I know won't benefit me. Such a life doesn't exist, and if it did, the gods surely wouldn't grant me that peace.

"I hope you find it," I offer. My lips wobble into as much of a smile as I can manage. "If anyone deserves it, it's you."

Concern pits the space between Savi's brows. "And what about you?" She sits up and turns to face me fully. "Do you not think you deserve such a thing, too? After everything you've been through?"

I scoff, though it comes out weaker than I hoped. "If you've seen what the gods have in store for me, Savi" —I loose a deep sigh, and it shudders passed my lips — "you wouldn't think I deserve much of anything."

Her hand snatches mine, squeezing tightly. "*Don't*," she chides. "Don't weigh your worth by the burdens this life has placed on you. You could be miles deep in the underworld and still be more deserving than those who boldly claim Hael's love. You are worthy of happiness, Ren. More than you'll ever let yourself believe, I fear."

I press my lips into a flat line as I slowly tug my hand away from hers. The loss is an ache, but a necessary one. I can't let her words sink in, for if they root into the marrow, I just might believe them.

"You should get some sleep," I utter stiffly. "I heard we're leaving at first light."

Though I've all but dismissed her, Savi doesn't stir from her place in the sand. I know I shouldn't, but I look to her regardless. She's staring at me with too much anguish in her eyes, with something I want to call pity—something I wish I could resent. But the look on her face is much too caring to be such a thing.

"You are so much like him," she states. "It would be funny if not for the lack you both see in yourselves."

My brow pinches as I chew her words, searching for answers. She gives them to me before I even have to ask.

"There's a story my father told me as a child. *Fiohr's Lament.* Have you heard it?"

I shake my head softly.

"Hm," she offers. "If you're anything like my cousin, you'll call it folly. But just give me a moment."

She shifts, getting comfortable once more. Around us, the night seems to wait on bated breath. And though I would never admit it, I'm just as eager for her words.

"The story speaks of a man. *Fiohr*," Savi begins. "A trader who wandered this world in search of riches. He traveled all his days, going from city to city to sell his wares. The more coin he earned, the more he thought he was following the path the gods had carved for him. So he chased gold—chased the high that the *clink* of coin brought—and saw to nothing else. But one day, he met a woman. Risha. A carpet maker with little to her name expect for a crumbling shop and the sun-faded fibers within it. Red hair that shone like a brilliant flame. Eyes golden like that of the coin Fiohr fiended for. He was smitten, tangled up in the threads of her fate like a bird in too-strong winds. But following the true path the gods had laid for him wasn't so simple. The gold weighing down his pockets wasn't enough. His mind betrayed him, spinning tales of lack where there were none. Fiohr told himself he needed more coin—needed to show the woman who had caught his eye just how deserving he was of her affections. So he left the city, left Risha with an ache in his heart, and chased the same fate he'd decided long ago was his. Days passed, then turned into months. No matter how far he strayed, no matter how much gold touched his hands, he felt like the gods had snared his foot. He knew what it was—who fate was trying to lead him back to—but he resisted. He told himself if he just acquired more coin, if he just became a man of great wealth, he could journey back to Risha and make her his.

"The months turned into a year. Fiohr's pockets grew so heavy that he saddled two camels to carry his riches. It was then that the gods sent their first lesson. Thieves came in the night and stripped him of every lick of gold. When the sun rose, the only thing that remained of Fiohr's was a bedroll he'd acquired through his travels—something Risha's own hands had made. But Fiohr denied the gods and the message they'd so clearly sent. He set off, even more determined than before—traveling the lands to acquire that which he sought more than food or rest. Another year passed, followed by two more. It was then that Fiohr's wealth spanned the backs of three camels. Pride filled his chest, as did a newfound relief. It was time. He was finally ready to meet the fate the gods had so clearly chosen for him. So he returned to the city that called out to him so viciously, to the carpet maker that never left his thoughts no matter how much time stood between them. Though, when he arrived, all he found was an empty shop filled with dusty, sun-bleached fibers and cobwebs in every corner."

Savi takes a deep breath, lips pulling into a tight line. "The gods had taken Risha, leaving Fiohr with an ache in his heart— one that rivaled the hearty weight of his pockets. He left the city, eager to forget the fate that had slipped through his fingers, the love that would never be his in this life or the next. With nothing else to fill the gaping pit in his chest, Fiohr chased coin like it would pump the blood through his dying heart. Decades passed. He attained riches unlike all others, became a man whispered about in passing, leered at like a king. But nothing eased the numb ache in him. Nothing quenched his hunger or relieved his lungs of strain. He was a husk, no more alive than the gold that clanked with every step. His fate was to walk this life hollow—for the gods don't take kindly to being ignored. When Fiohr finally died, too many years later, it's said he wailed all the way down to the deepest of the three hells. Finding nothing in its endless abyss but the *clink* of coin and the fleeting visage of red hair as it slipped from view time and time again."

I loose a heavy breath, forcing a scoff as a merciless pressure clenches my chest. "Quite the story," I mutter. "Though I appreciate the warning, I think you'll find my empty pockets to be nothing of concern."

Savi's voice breaks the air around us as a disbelieving laugh slips from her lips. "How maddening that both you and Hassan missed the point of that story."

She tugs on my shoulder, forcing me to look at her. "Fiohr resisted the fate the gods had so clearly woven for him because he found himself unworthy of what they offered," Savi states. "Even when the gods tried to steer him back on the right path, he resisted their pull and damned himself and his lover in the process. If only Fiohr had seem himself worthy of Risha, had only given in to what the gods had already divined, this life wouldn't have been the first of what hells he faced."

I stare deep in Savi's eyes, trying to hear what she's telling me without truly feeling it. All this talk of fate has my stomach spoiling what little dinner I ate earlier.

"What are you saying?" I rasp. My face sours as a bitter taste slinks up my throat. "That I need to give in to my fate or else I'll be damned? I *am* damned, Savi. Nothing can change that. And if you're worried I'll bring that fate to anyone here, don't be."

I tear out of her gentle hold as I pull myself up from the sand. "I won't be joining you wherever your path leads. Back to the Jahaer. In search of Rikyir. It doesn't matter. Our paths split—as they always should have. I know what fate the gods have woven for me, and I'm not running. I have endured every searing moment—every torturous ache—without turning away. I will see it to the end. I will let it destroy me because I have no other choice but to. So do not lecture me on fate. It has been my affliction for much too long, and it is far from done with me yet."

Savi stares at me with grief lined in the corners of her eyes. For a moment, she says nothing. I feel the weight of the silence between us like it's pushing through my ribs and digging into the muscle of my heart. It's a familiar pain, but an unwelcome one. I don't deserve her sympathy.

With a heavy swallow, Savi addresses me once more. "Have you ever considered that this destruction is not your fate?" she utters. "That maybe it's merely the suffering of resisting it for so long? For not seeing the worth you already carry?"

My stomach answers with a revolting flip. The breath in my lungs stutters, but I quickly wipe the shock off my face. With a hardened jaw, I shake my head at her. "Suffering *is* my fate," I reply. "I don't need a parable to tell me as much."

Without another look, I stalk back toward camp. My heart is a thundering storm in my chest, a riotous pang that I don't know how to relieve. With each step, Savi's story returns to my mind like a taunt, coaxing me to see things in a new light. But I can't. It would only make it worse to hope for something that will inevitably be ripped away.

As I pass by a certain Shade's tent on the way to my own, I pretend the thump of my heart is not that fabled tug Savi spoke of—tell myself it's not fate guiding me home. It's nothing more than another one of the gods' wicked games, and it'd be best if I remembered that.

CHAPTER 28

The fire crackles and pops, filling the silence around me. I take a bite of the stew, chewing slowly—deliberately. The richness immediately hits my tongue, but on the end of that decadent, buttery flavor is a slow burning heat. My eyes all but roll back as it dances over my taste buds.

"*Gods.*" I smack my tongue around my mouth softly, trying to savor every bit of the lingering spice. "Is there gahva in this?" I take another bite as my eyes dart between the pair who made the dish.

Savi's face gleams in delight, while Tariq merely offers a rumbling chuckle. "There is." He turns toward the others and gestures to me with the flick of his fingers. "Pay up," he announces. "She's the only one who got it right. None of you were even close."

Grumbles sound around the fire as gold passes hands. It clinks and travels until there's a nice pile resting in my lap.

I hold one up in front of the firelight and grin. "Easiest coin I've ever made."

I toss a piece into the air, laughing as I catch it. The breathy tone is soft and breezy, and, for a moment, I wonder where it came from. It's too relaxed and carefree to belong to me.

When was the last time I felt something other than overwhelming dread and lingering panic?

Days. Close to a week since such a feeling left me. A quick look across the fire reminds me why. I don't hold Malachi's gaze for more than a half-breath. The small smile drops from my face, and as I stuff the winnings into my pocket, I feel melancholy take up its rightful place in my chest once more.

"Where did you even get gahva?" Tofá asks. He leans back against the sand, bowl cradled in his lap. "I heard it only grows on trees amidst the southern edge of the Kohe."

Savi smiles. "It does. But I was lucky enough to find some in Hira."

Hassan sighs deeply as he looks over at his cousin. "And how much did that set us back?"

She *tsks*, gesturing him away with her hand. "I didn't use our supply funds. I have plenty of coin saved up, you know," she reasons.

Hassan remains unconvinced, and just as he starts to object, Savi shoots him a stern look. "We all deserved something nice. Now eat your damn dinner. Didn't you just say this was the best meal you've had in months?"

Hassan looks annoyed, but I see the flicker of amusement quirking his mouth. "It's edible," he offers.

Savi huffs, and this time, the smirk on Hassan's face makes a full appearance.

"Anyone want—" Kai starts.

Mikel cuts him off by snatching the bowl from his hands. He's able to ladle two full helpings into the wooden vessel before Kai has a chance to close his gaping mouth.

As Mikel hands the bowl back, he shoots the hunter a knowing look. "Seconds?" he prods.

Kai blinks slowly, like his mind is fighting to catch up. As he looks from the refilled bowl of stew, back to the Mender, I swear it's love I see in his eyes. With a blush staining his cheeks, Kai mumbles his thanks before digging into the food.

Mikel's smile is soft, and as he turns to me, I can only raise a brow. I expect an eye-roll or a gesture that tells me to shut up and mind my business, but, to my surprise, my friend appears almost bashful. He looks away quickly, covering his mouth with a hand to no doubt conceal the smile creeping into place.

Conversation continues around me, but I'm too focused on my best friend to care. I watch Kai and Mikel as they talk. They're sitting close, folded legs brushing against each other. Smiles line their faces, though there's a shyness emanating from both of them that I've never seen with anyone else. As Kai offers a spoonful of his food to Mikel, my heart leaps so fiercely I think it may jump out of my chest. I purse my lips together, staving off flutters of an emotion I'm not used to. Never have I seen Mikel this happy—this giddy and untroubled. He's not nagging me about my recklessness or fretting about the amount of supplies we have. He's just here, in the moment. *Living.*

My throat clamps down on the swell of joy I feel. As much as I don't want to, I have to turn away. It's not only the emotions that threaten to consume me, but the fear of what comes after such happiness. If life on the Continent has taught me anything, it's that moments like these? They don't last long.

As I face the others, I can't seem to escape the contentment blooming through camp like a desert rose. Drinks flow and conversation grows to a lively buzz. To my left, Savi chats with Quin. They talk of cooking and family recipes, of ingredients they would die for, and what they could whip up together for tomorrow night's meal. Their voices raise and pitch, excitement bubbling out freely and without concern for the volume. I sit quietly, but as conversation shifts to their families, my stomach lurches. With graceful tact, Savi admits it's only her and Hassan now. My chest aches at the reminder of her past—of the destruction dealt by Rohan's heavy hand—but I stay silent.

I listen to Savi offer vague answers with a subtle strength that doesn't reveal the heartache I know she must feel. A pain like hers doesn't simply go away—not even with time. Thankfully, Quin is observant enough to steer the conversation toward her own family. Apparently, she has a younger brother who lives in Hanta. He's godless, she states, though she shares that he's never treated her as anything other than a sister. When Quin admits her brother is too stubborn for his own good, Savi is quick to groan in understanding. She begins to rant about Hassan, and though she drops her voice low as to not be heard, it carries loudly across the sand.

As Savi tells of a time when her cousin refused to stop for directions and spent two days wandering the coast, utterly lost, I can't keep back the laugh that puffs from my lungs. Savi shoots me a knowing glance, but just as she opens her mouth, we're interrupted.

The man's shadow looms over Savi, and she sighs. "Yes, Riat?"

He tries to look casual as he twirls a blade in his hand, but it's obvious he wants something. I can see it in the way his eyes wander back and forth, never really landing on the woman in front of him.

"My hair's getting a little long... Don't you think?"

Savi laughs, shaking her head. "Is this your way of asking me to cut it again, without actually asking?"

A mischievous grin stretches across Riat's face. "So kind of you to offer, Savs," he coos.

Just as he tries to sit down in her lap, she shoos him away. "Nuh-uh," she objects. "Last time, you not only fell asleep mid-cut and caused me to nick you, but you left me covered in hair. And" —she points her finger at him, voice raising as she does — "you promised you'd clean the dishes for a week straight." Her brow arches. "You never did."

Riat opens his mouth, but thinks better of it.

Savi groans, though there's a lighthearted nature to her chiding. "You're like a street dog." She *tsks*. "You beg and then run off when needed."

He smirks. "But a devilishly handsome street dog. Right?"

Next to Savi, Quin looses a bouncy laugh. The sound calls the dog in Riat like a whistle. As he turns his attention to her, I watch as rakish charm spreads across his face.

"What about you?" he purrs. "Care to help a man look his best?"

Quin looks to Savi who simply gives her a dramatic shake of her head. The young woman laughs before turning back to Riat. "Only if you do the dishes for Savi tonight."

Riat grins like a fiend.

"And tomorrow," Quin prods.

"Deal." Riat sits down in front of the Weaver before she can rethink her decision. He shoots me a playful glance as Quin pushes his head to the side to get a better look at what she's gotten herself into. "Don't worry, goddess," Riat tells me. "I only have eyes for you."

Quin shoots me a hesitant look, fingers stilled in Riat's hair. "You two are together?"

Riat's grin is too wide, but I speak before he has the chance to. "No," I state. "Riat has never been in my bed. Nor will he get the chance to."

He has the audacity to gasp and pout like this is news to him. His devious smile is back by the time he looks over his shoulder at Quin. "Guess that means I'm all yours."

Quin looks to me, for what I'm not sure. Though I want to offer a snide comment—ask her how she could have the energy to warm two beds—I decide I don't want to know.

"You two have never...?" She hesitates, drawing my focus back to her. "Why? Are you with..." I don't follow wherever her eyes drift to. "Is there someone else?"

I grit my teeth hard enough to tear flesh like a predator mauling fresh prey. Sadly it's my own blood that fills my mouth as I catch my tongue. There's a worried expression muddling Quin's delicate face that only serves to drive my irritation higher. It's as if she's waiting for me to utter something that will ruin everything for her. Like one name slipping off my tongue will rouse the guilt we both know she deserves to feel. I can only scoff.

"If you want to bed Riat, do as you please. But know he'll be gone before the sun rises."

Riat stares at me with his mouth gaped open like I've betrayed him. The dramatic sight is the only thing keeping me from drawing a blade just to spook the gentle woman across from me.

"Don't let his charm convince you otherwise," I tease, utterly ignoring Quin now. "Once a rake, always a rake."

Riat tries to argue, but I'm already pulling myself out of the conversation. It's only when the Weaver's bouncy voice breaks through the fray that I'm viciously snapped back into it.

"I fear I'm not suited for something so brief…" Quin chews on her lip, her nose crinkling almost sheepishly. "Besides, he's not exactly my type." Her eyes drift across the fire, and my stomach tightens into knots.

"I'm everyone's type," Riat grumbles, though his words barely meet my ears.

I grit my teeth and try to keep the tension off my face, but it's there as loud as the night around me. The jealousy I feel twitches my lip and burns my gaze hot. I look across the fire, past where Tariq and Vish sit, to find Malachi. He's deep in a rowdy conversation with Tofá and Ivar, oblivious to my eyes on him. The three men lounge against the sand, passing a bottle of rum between them. Judging by the way they laugh and gesture wildly, I'd bet the bottle is close to empty. Just as Malachi offers me a fleeting glance, my gaze drops to the fire.

I know it's stupid, but I can't stop the way my chest seizes at the mere sight of him. Ever since our fight, he's kept his distance and I've kept mine. Passing glances are all we've allowed ourselves. And for good reason. If I look at him for too long, uncertainty takes root like poison. I know what he's here for—what use he has for me—but that doesn't stop my mind from spinning excuses for a man who deserves none.

But would it be so bad? To fight my way through the world with him by my side?

I take a deep, shuddering breath and look up from the fire. Quin is watching me, and she doesn't try to hide it. Her brow is knit curiously, hazel-green eyes riddled with questions. She parts her lips like whatever she wants to say is on the tip of her tongue. The sneer on my face works as intended, because Quin closes her mouth and looks away.

"How am I to cut your hair?" she asks Riat.

My anger flares just hearing the airy timbre of her voice. So calm. So unburdened. I quickly raise my cup and take a long swig of rum to stifle the petty fight I wish to start.

"Just shave the sides down to the skin, is all," Riat says. "Maybe a little off the top if you think you can manage."

As Riat winks at her, I find myself unable to watch any longer. I tune them out, trying not to think too hard about why the Weaver is here and whose tent she sleeps in every night. My fingers grip the neck of the bottle too tightly as I lift it to my lips. *Cup be damned.* It will only slow me down to refill it. Two long gulps of rum slide down my throat, then another. The sweet warmth provides a necessary distraction, but it's not enough. It hasn't been enough all night.

I swirl the bottle around in my grip. It feels too light, and the gentle sloshing inside the glass provides the reason. I tip the bottle all the way back, draining the last of its contents in a desperate swallow. As the rumble of Malachi's voice reaches me from across the fire, oblivion calls my name with purpose.

Immediately, my eyes scour the sand for salvation. *Ah.* With a quick, though unsteady, hand, I snatch a full bottle from where it rests at Mikel's feet. I don't look up to see if he and Kai have cuddled closer—I'm sure my friend will entrust me with such details tomorrow. Instead, I wrap my hand around the only thing that will bring me any comfort tonight.

The cork falls away with a muffled *pop*, and I waste no time. I drink, and drink, and drink until my breath is ragged and my chest is full of heat. The fire roars as Tariq piles on another piece of wood. Riat flirts shamelessly with Quin, though she only offers soft giggles in reply. I watch as she gently angles his cheek up toward the night sky so she can reach the side of his head. Her dainty hand grips the hilt of his throwing knife with a careful steadiness as she scrapes the blade across Riat's scalp.

I take another sip of rum. One more after that. Savi turns to me and smiles, oblivious to the storm raging inside. She starts asking me about my blades—the ones I purchased from her friend in Hira. I mutter a reply in between sips of rum, though I don't recall the words that leave my lips. She tells me how she and Lorik came to know each other, how she stumbled upon his shop during the first year she and Hassan had taken up bounty hunting as their trade. According to Savi, Lorik has always been cold to Hassan—though she thinks the old blacksmith secretly views her cousin as the stubborn son he never had.

When the bottle isn't sealed to my lips, I utter meaningless replies so she knows I'm still listening—or trying to, at least. Savi goes on and on, and though I know she sees how my eyes drift across the fire, she doesn't ask why. Savi tells me stories, and each one helps guide me into numb oblivion. Time passes, and the rum flows. Half of the fresh bottle now rests in my gut, but there's more to be had. Another pull of the spicy spirit warms me like the sun on a kind day. But as my eyes shift across the fire once more, expecting to see the side of Malachi's face as he sits among friends, it's those dark eyes of his that I find. Time seems to freeze, then blur before me. The Shade's stare is molten fire—like he seeks to damn me where I sit with the bottle gripped loosely in my hand. Maybe it's just my imagination, because when my eyes flutter closed, then back open in a lethargic blink, his gaze is far from mine.

My head spins, and I shake it to find my way back to this moment. Savi's laugh is a rope tossed down a well—salvation out of rum's hazy depths. I cling to it like it will help while drowning myself deeper. Each drag I take from the bottle muffles her voice until it's all a raucous buzz. I nod and hum thoughtfully, though I'm utterly lost to what tales she weaves with that bright smile of hers.

I blink sluggishly as I raise the bottle high. Savi's talking about my new dagger—the white blade with the etched snake. I strain my ears to listen, try to focus on what she's saying, but my mind wanders with a dizzying pressure. I can't stop thinking of Malachi. Of the future. Of the rum that promises a reprieve from it all. Another swallow burns its way down my throat. Savi tells me there's something unusual about the way Lorik gets the steel that color. Something about how he smells it. No—*smelts* it. With white obsidian and pulverized frihn roots. My brow furrows, trying to understand it all, but her words only add to the muffled roar that thumps in my ears.

My skin is flushed, yet the trailing breeze that runs through camp rakes chills across my flesh. I pull the blanket I'd been sitting on over my shoulders and hunker down into it. Savi looks at me quizzically, cocking her head as if waiting for me to say something.

Were we having a conversation?

I can only shrug and take another sip of rum. She offers me a small, hesitant smile before patting my shoulder and turning back toward the others.

My heart beats loudly in my chest, pounding like a drum. There's a light tingle across my cheeks, like bugs scurrying over the skin. As I raise my gaze to the darkened sky, I feel my head bob on my shoulders.

Shit.

My breathy laugh spills out into the crisp night air without concern. I smile, though I don't know why. The grin curves wider as I lift the bottle. One gulp. Two. Rum spills over my bottom lip, and my tongue darts out languidly to catch every drop.

I close my eyes as the desert spins around me. It's dizzying, whirling with a sickening pace. *Gods.* I swallow thickly and wait for it to pass. When it does, I pull a shuddering breath in through my nose. I open my eyes to welcome back the night, but just as I raise the bottle to take another sip, what I see across the fire stills my hand.

Hazel eyes burn into me with ire. Hassan sits beside Tariq, but his focus is far from his friend. He's staring at me, eyes blazing as hot as the flames between us.

I grimace, not at all liking that look on his face. "*Ornery old goat.*" I slur the words and flip him an obscene gesture.

He doesn't so much as flinch. My gaze tightens on him, though my vision quickly sways. Everything around Hassan spins and dances, but the man is as still as stone. Just as I raise the bottle to my lips once more, the image of him shutters and lurches. He moves too fast for my hazy mind to track, like a ghost among shadows. Before I can even finish taking my sip, he's there ripping the bottle from my hands. A moment later, Hassan hauls me up by the scruff of my tunic like a scrawny kitten clamped in a devil's maw.

I sputter and flail wildly as my body and mind try to get on the same page. "What are you—"

He sets me on my feet just before the harsh press on his hand on my lower back drives me forward. "It's time you went to bed."

A petulant whine leaks from my lips, but as I turn around to face him, my legs get tangled underneath me. My body follows, slumping like a too-heavy sack and slamming me against Hassan's chest.

"I don't want to go to bed," I grumble. My fingers tangle in the fabric of his tunic. I don't know whether I do it to stay upright or because the warmth of his body is much too enticing. Either way, I find myself leaning into him. "I was having a perfectly good time befor—"

Hassan growls as he wraps a hand around my upper arm and guides me toward the tents. "You've done nothing but bury yourself in drink for the past hour," he utters roughly. "You're not having a good time."

"Who are you to say that?" I ramble, teetering in his grasp. "You wouldn't know a good time if she sat on your face."

His lips curl into a snarl as a flicker of something dark passes through those hazel eyes. "Careful, *witch*. I'm in no mood for your taunts."

He practically drags me across the sand as my boots stumble behind me. Only when he peels back my tent flap and pushes the both of us inside does he relent. I teeter unsteadily before pitching down against the mass of cushions piled around my bedroll.

My face scrunches up as I look at him. "*Ornery*," I state. "Ornery old goat who wants me to suffer."

His jaw clenches so violently that the muscles in his neck tense.

"You just can't stand to see me happy, can you?" I argue, voice pitching high. "What did I ever do to you?"

"*Exist*," he mutters. His words are only for himself, but I hear them nonetheless.

The admission is like a slap to the face. It sobers me, as much as it can. My chest aches as I stare at Hassan—at the pain and anguish strained across his features. But it only lasts a second before the recklessness that comes from two bottles of rum returns with a fury.

I push myself up from the ground, crawling forward until I mange to get on two legs. "What is wrong with you?" I rasp. "Why do you hate me so?"

He laughs. It's a vicious thing, full of resentment and vexation. He takes two steps toward me—that's all it takes to bring us face to face. "Hate you?" he chides. "*Gods*, I thought you were smarter than that."

My face contorts into a sneer. I'm shoving him before I even know what I'm doing. "You're an ass," I yell. "I won't be dragged to bed like a child because you're in a foul mood. Get out of my way." I try to storm past him, but my body stumbles sideways.

"No," he growls. He grabs my hands and pins them to his broad chest. "I won't let you go back out there so you can drink yourself sick. All for what? That daemon?" He scoffs. "Though I don't know all that's happened between you, I know enough to say he doesn't deserve it."

"Deserve what?" I snap. "My anger? My hate?"

"*Your attention*," Hassan rasps. He forces a deep breath and releases the grip on my hands. "*Hael above*. All you do is stare at him with that haunted look in your eyes. I thought it was pain for whatever it is he's done, for however he betrayed you. But when I got back from Tilket..."

Hassan steps back and runs a hand through his hair. The wavy, brown strands slip through his fingers before settling against his neck. "I realized it wasn't resentment you were harboring. It was something far worse."

"What is it, then?" I snap. "Since you pretend to know me so well. What is it you think you see?"

"Hope." His eyes hold an anguish I've never seen, or maybe I just haven't been paying attention. Hassan's jaw ripples with tension. "You looked at the Berserker the same way. He didn't deserve you, and neither does the Shade."

My breath hitches, stilling like the world around us. I search his face for answers, but my mind spins from too much drink to find anything useful. He stares at me, utterly silent, but there's something brewing underneath that rigid demeanor he keeps. It's always been there, though I haven't had the nerve to poke and prod. But with my body buzzing with heat and curiosity, I can't stop myself from finally finding out what it is.

"You didn't like Silas," I state. The rum is a devious companion, dousing my thoughts in liquid fire. My body moves on its own accord—treacherous and delighted. I take a step toward Hassan, then another. I keep going until he's mere inches from me.

"I didn't trust him," Hassan says gruffly. "And for good reason it seems."

My heart aches in my chest, but I ignore it. It's easy with the way the world spins in a haze of drink. "And Malachi?"

Hassan almost flinches at the name. His eyes flash darkly. Angrily. As he takes a step closer, his thighs press against me. "I think it's pretty clear what I think of him," he grits out.

My tongue darts out across my lip as I stare up at him. "You're jealous."

He sneers, but he doesn't deny it. As he stands there, rigid and furious, I let my eyes wander over him in ways I've never allowed myself—at least not when he's been watching. The stubble on his face has grown out since I first met him, framing his strong cheekbones and jaw in a thick, short beard. Somehow, I stifle the urge to trace my fingers along it. My eyes drop between us, to the way his pants cinch his tapered waist and fit snugly around muscular thighs. It's then that I notice his hands are quivering at his sides. They're curled into fists, like he's fighting off the urge to reach out and touch me.

Gods, I hope that's exactly what he does.

As my eyes flash back up to him, I realize I've been fighting this for too long. Maybe he has, too. My heart patters nervously as my hands slither up his chest, feeling every inch of hard-packed muscle underneath his tunic. This is foolish. Reckless. But the feral look flooding Hassan's eyes only stokes my boldness. Desire pools deep in my core, parting my lips and arching my body into his. I should be mortified—ashamed of the things I'm imagining. Wanting. *Needing.* But my body is coated in a flushed warmth; the rum has taken away all hesitations and blinded me to future regrets. All that remains is a hunger that needs to be satiated.

My nails dig into the loose collar of Hassan's tunic. "Tell me, *hunter*," I taunt. "Did you drag me into my tent only for me to go to bed alone?" I look up at him through my lashes, eyes blown wide. "Or for once are you going to join me in having some fun?"

A deep growl rumbles from his chest as he looms over me. "You don't want me. You're just looking to distract yourself from him."

A laugh slips from my throat. "Is that what you think?" I raise up onto the toes of my boots to get in his face, swaying slightly. A soft sigh escapes me as I lean into his neck, teasing my lips against the shell of his ear. "Oh, Hassan," I chide. "I thought you were smarter than that."

"*Witch*," he seethes. His hands are rough and desperate as they find the soft curve of my waist. He pulls me tightly against him, leaving no space between us. "You're tempting fate."

He stares at me with a brutal focus, like he can see through to my very soul. I don't think about what dark, pitiful thing he might find there, too fueled by drink to feel any shame. Instead, I wrap my hands around the back of his neck and press up against him.

"Then tempt it," I coo.

My nails scrape against his tan skin, dragging another rumble from his chest. But when my eyes find his, the fire in his gaze wavers, then dies out.

"You're drunk," he utters. He gently tugs my hands down and steps away.

The loss of him feels worse than the cut of any blade. I try not to care, but I'm immediately met with the overwhelming weight of his rejection. It feels like sand packed on top of my chest, burying me in a humiliation I thought so unreachable. I can't bear to look at him, can't bear to raise my gaze from where it's fixed on the ground. Out of the corner of my eye, I see him shift forward.

"Don't," I rasp. My gaze shoots toward him, as sharp and broken as shards of glass.

"Witch—"

"Get out."

He rolls his eyes and forces a heavy breath from his lungs. "*Gods below*, would you—"

"Get. Out!" I yell. I've drawn a blade before I realize it. My hand shakes unsteadily; whether it's the drink or adrenaline that unnerves me now, I'm not sure. My fingers grip the dagger's hilt too tightly, turning my knuckles white.

Hassan takes one look at my fighting stance and scoffs. "*Typical*," he mutters under his breath.

"Come again?" I spit.

He looks at me through heavy lids, his gaze unrelenting. He takes a step closer, not at all fazed by the dagger in my grasp. "How quick you are to draw a weapon when things don't go your way," he scolds. My lips curl into a scowl, but he doesn't give me a chance to argue. "I wonder, will we ever have a conversation without the threat of your blade?" He clenches his jaw. "Or will it be others that always muddy this space between us?"

I swallow uneasily as disgrace eats my heart with unrelenting teeth. I drop my gaze from his and stumble as I attempt to find distance between us. My legs are unsteady from drink, but it's my heart that feels lost to me.

Hassan sighs roughly. "Nothing good can come from this," he utters to himself. "Savi was wrong."

My gaze snaps up, but the severity marring his face has faded into a look of utter exhaustion. I stand there silently, mind reeling. The warm buzz of rum has morphed into an empty sorrow now. It seems the night has finally caught up to me. My stomach roils, and my head throbs with a vicious pressure. I blink over and over, taking in the man across from me slowly and with fresh eyes. His tunic is rumpled, slightly untucked from where my greedy hands tugged and pulled. His mouth is tense, strained into a firm line. My eyes widen as I remember every salacious thought that swept through my mind like a sandstorm just moments ago. I can almost feel the heat of his touch lingering on my waist. I had wanted more—so much more. My stomach lurches as I realize, even after he turned me down, I still do. I grit my teeth, feeling a fool evermore.

I drop the blade in my grasp. It clatters to the sand with a muffled *thud*, and my chest aches with burdens I thought I'd forgotten. My hands wring together, squeezing bone and twisting ligament. When I finally meet Hassan's gaze, he shakes his head and mutters something under his breath too quiet for me to hear. I open my mouth to demand he leave, to no longer bear witness to my humiliation, but his focus has slipped elsewhere.

I watch Hassan fumble to untie the small flask from his belt. He says nothing as he crosses the tent, merely presents the flask like a silent peace offering. I raise a brow in question.

He sighs, exasperated, and shoves the flask into my hands. "Drink," he orders. His firm gaze holds my uncertain one, and his jaw ticks with impatience. "It's water. You need it."

Only when I pop the cork free and take a swig does the tension release from his shoulders. I close my eyes as the moisture hits my tongue and slides down the back of my throat. I drink desperately, knowing it's the only way to chase the devils from my mind and Hassan from this tent. I drain the entire flask and pass it back without meeting his waiting gaze. He stays silent as I wipe my mouth with my sleeve. But still, he hovers—offering nothing but the oppressive weight of his presence.

When I finally look up at him, I feel the scorching burn of that thing he accused me of.

Hope.

It's too much. I turn my back on him, kicking off my boots as I go. The remnants of rum pump through me with a dizzying indifference, and, though I know he's still here, I begin stripping off my clothes. Only once I'm down to my underthings do I drop onto my bedroll with a drunken *plop*. I worm my way under the layers of blankets, loosing groaned huffs as I struggle to get comfortable. When I finally roll over and look at Hassan, he's as motionless as the dead. His hands are curled into fists again, and his brow is furrowed deeply. Though his eyes are wide in shock, I don't miss the feral heat in them. He stares at me for a moment longer before he seems to shake himself from his thoughts. He curses low, then leaves.

I smirk, content that, even if he doesn't want me, I can still get under his skin. "Goodnight," I call after him, my tone sickly sweet.

With him finally gone, the tent fills with unnerving silence. I close my eyes and try to sink into my bedroll, but my body is restless. There's a pounding ache in my skull, and the world spins behind my eyelids. I toss and turn, but it does nothing to relieve me of how drunk I am. The rum sits heavy in my gut and sends quivers of nausea up my throat as soon as I think I've found comfort. I groan and press my face into the pillow, waiting for the feeling to pass. I hear the distant babel of voices, the faraway crackle of the campfire. Though I wish it would lull me to sleep, it only reminds me of things I'd rather forget.

I begin to sift through my unsteady mind, though it quickly proves unwise. When the harsh rasp of Hassan's voice comes back to me, my stomach turns even more sour than before.

All you do is stare at him with that haunted look in your eyes.

I roll over and stare up at the tent's pitched roof. *He's wrong.* I hold no hope for Malachi and me. The past is too wide of a chasm to overcome. I tell myself this again and again, tossing and turning all the while. No matter how much I try to deny it—try to make excuses, or write Hassan's words off as careless bickering—I taste the lies on my tongue. I'm desperate for sleep, but the anger inside of me doesn't allow it. It's potent. Wild. I wish I could blame it on my gift, but the thrum of my shadows is quiet. I roll over once more before I decide I've had enough.

Fuck.

I kick the blankets off roughly before tugging on pants and slipping a loose tunic over my bound breasts. My legs wobble beneath me as I yank my boots on. I have to steady myself against the tent pole until the drunken moment passes. As soon as it does, I step out into the crisp night.

The air rips into my lungs like cold water, clearing my mind of drink's lingering fog. I roll my neck to the side, cracking away any stiffness. I take three steps from my tent before voices have my boots stilling against the sand.

Two shadows slink through the night, dancing across canvas walls as they journey forward. The moment I recognize Quin's familiar, bubbly tone, my heart turns to rock in my chest. But before I can turn back and escape this small torture the gods have provided me, I see them.

Quin bounds happily across the desert, her long dress twirling with each step. But it's him I can't tear my eyes from. Malachi walks behind her like a wraith stalking the dark. He always had a certain presence about him, even as a lanky teen. The moment Malachi would step onto Artolen's streets, every head would turn his way. He was the darkness no one wanted to cross, and I was the girl in his shadows.

I take silent steps back into the opening of my tent and will the night to hide me. I know I should escape and save myself from what I'm about to see, but something foul keeps me tethered to the spot. After everything that's happened tonight, I need to feel this ache—this reminder that there is no hope.

The moment Quin and Malachi reach their tent, my heart flutters uneasily. Words pass between the pair, and I know it's a blessing I can't hear them. Malachi holds the tent flap open wide for Quin as she slips inside with a soft smile. I don't miss the way she pats his arm tenderly on the way. My nails dig into my palms, leaving deep indents in the skin. I think I've seen enough.

Just as I take a backward step into my tent, Malachi's head whips toward me. My stomach drops as his gaze locks with mine. In the fleeting moment when my heart cracks and I'm left hollow, I realize Hassan was right.

"Serehna—"

I rush into my tent with a twisted gut and something too heavy for my chest. I pace around, if only to keep myself from dropping to my knees and screaming.

Why?

Why does it still hurt?

My legs tremble as I slump to the floor. The room spins, and I close my eyes against the nauseous churn of it all. I press my hands to my mouth, desperate to keep every drop of rum down. After what feels like hours of breathing in and out of my nose as steadily as I can, I turn toward the front of the tent. I let myself picture Malachi ushering Quin to bed just as I've seen him do so many nights before.

How easily he's replaced me.

I shouldn't have expected anything else.

My head drops, and I press my face into the gritty sand that peeks between mounds of cushions and blankets. The dusty scent of earth chokes me with every breath like I'm fresh in the grave. Though I know I'm painfully alive, I can't help but dream of how that nothingness would be less burdensome than this.

Finally, I find the strength to tug my boots off. I chuck them across the tent, pleased with the way they *thud* against my pack. I do the same with my clothes, though they lack the solid consequence of destruction as I fling them into various corners.

I tuck myself under the blankets once more, but this time, my body is no longer buzzing with drink and shame. As my eyes close and consciousness fades, all I'm left with is the cold reality that I am alone—just as the gods wish me to be.

It's foolish to hope for anything more.

CHAPTER 29

"What do you call a bastard with a bad temper?" Riat asks.

Sighs spill from those around me, but Savi's voice is the only one that ventures forth. "I don't know, Riat," she gripes. "What do you call them?"

"A daemon," he answers.

Savi groans in annoyance, and I spot both Berserkers shooting Riat foul looks. Just as Kai tries to suppress his amusement, Mikel catches the snicker leaving his throat and raises a brow.

Kai immediately grows red in the face, stumbling over his words. "I wasn't—" he flounders. "It wasn't funny. I was just—"

Mikel's stern look quickly slips away as he clasps Kai's arm and lets out a breathy laugh. I swear the hunter's shoulders slump to the sand in relief. "Easy now," Mikel chides. "It *was* funny."

Riat is undeterred, continuing on with his ramblings like he has for the past hour. "What do you call a beautiful woman?" That playful gaze shoots to me, and I can only roll my eyes.

We're far west of where we slept last night, and yet Riat's incessant chatter makes it seem like we never left camp. My head pounds in my skull, a violent throbbing that's made of my own doing. Mikel offered to ease my pains this morning, and though I was eager to forget all that rum soured, some lessons are better left remembered in agony. Judging by the sullen looks on some of the other's faces, it seems I wasn't the only one to imbibe a little too hard last night and come out of it with regret.

"A goddess," Riat finishes, his tone laced in seduction.

Hassan grumbles, the first noise I've heard slip free from him in hours. He rides far to the left, flanking the caravan like a distant guardian. The tension in his shoulders is nothing compared to the way his jaw is clenched tight. I'd think he was as hungover as me if not for the hard detachment set in his eyes. There's a sharpness there—a vicious clarity that tells me it's not the twinge of leftover rum that plagues him. I've caught his gaze darting away from mine too many times to think anything but the truth.

He's avoiding me.

"And what do you call a daemon with a goddess waiting in his bed?" Riat prods.

The question hovers in the air unanswered. More sighs follow, including my own, though my vexation is stirred by far more aggravating things than Riat.

Finally, Quin turns around from where she rides up ahead. "Lucky." She grins, eyes bright like she had the most refreshing sleep.

Just seeing her makes my headache worse.

Riat *tsks*, though that cheeky smile never leaves his face. "*A liar*," he corrects.

A few snickers spill out among the caravan. Tariq shakes his head before pressing his fingers into his temple. The way he groans into his hands tells me just how much fun Riat and Kai forced him to have after I went to bed.

Tofá offers Riat a bitter laugh, though it's Ivar who snarls in response. "Must you talk so much?"

I can tell by the way he grits his teeth that his head is splitting as badly as mine is right now. Riat opens his mouth to utter what I know will be a cocky retort, but Ivar has already had enough. He urges his horse forward, curses spilling from his lips.

Tofá is quick to follow, though he lingers as he passes. He levels a steady gaze at Riat and hums curiously. "Do you know what they call a godless man who gets on a daemon's bad side?"

Riat grins, waiting for the punchline.

"*Dead*," Tofá utters coldly. He looks Riat up and down, a dark smile growing on his face, before pulling ahead to join Ivar.

"So sensitive," Riat calls to the Berserkers as they reach the front of the caravan. He looses a breathy laugh and turns toward the rest of us. "*Gods below*, you think they'd be able to take a joke."

Savi is barely holding back her frustrations when Tariq looses a deep, rumbling sigh. "You know," he starts, "it would be wise to make friends of them. They're our allies after all."

Psh. Riat waves him off. "And who says I'm not? The tall one thinks I'm hilarious. It's the short one who has a stick up his ass." Riat's voice is obnoxiously loud, and his taunt doesn't go unnoticed.

Ivar turns back to glare at him, but Riat only grins in response. He waves his hand slowly and deviously like the rascal he is.

"*Gods smite the earth and leave it better than before*," Savi murmurs. "Riat, behave yourself. *Please*."

Playful argument sparks from Riat, but I don't have it in me to listen any longer. I force a deep breath and let my eyes scan the horizon ahead. Another day has come and gone. The sun now hovers in its late afternoon cradle, blanketing these desolate sands in sweltering, orange heat. Though I wish for nothing more than to blur my gaze on the monotonous view that's held my attention for days, the scene before me has shifted into one that's not so easily overlooked. No longer are we heading due north, deeper into the gods-drenched lands we slipped into so soundlessly. We've turned west—toward the mountains and the bleak task they promise. The Kohe looms in a distant blur on the horizon, its darkened peaks beacons of an ill-advised fate. It's our guiding point; its presence is better than any map. But with each step that brings the mountain range closer, I'm reminded just why I'm here and what it is I am to do.

It's something I've avoided thinking about—that place that waits for me far to the west. A place that binds those who make too many enemies or commit wrongs too great. A place whose name strikes fear into the most cold-hearted of men. *Tol Dena.* My body shivers against the day's heat. I had hoped to never visit that place of nightmares, but like the cities at my back and the gods-drenched north under my feet, it seems I never had a choice.

Though it will take many more days to reach that far-away place, every step forward fills my stomach with the most riotous of dread. Our proximity to the gods-drenched north made me uneasy before, but now that we've crossed its threshold and trek its treacherous sands, my body churns with anxiety. It's not just the threat of the beasts and monsters that stalk this land, it's the suffocating presence that's quickly found me here.

This place feels alive, like it's tainted with the gods' own power. I know better than to question it's anything but. My darker gift hums in anticipation, rippling more wildly through my blood the longer we stay in this place. Its raw excitement taints my body like a festering wound. Something is coming—stirring. I can practically taste it in the air.

My mind is a restless thing, clinging to false hopes that harsh truths quickly swallow with endless, black maws. Too often today, I've drifted to thoughts of Weaver dreams and the canyon that plagued me for months. The eldritch force blanketing that place was palpable even in sleep, and now that the same feeling is pressing down on me from all angles, panic has found a warm cavity in my chest to call home. I asked Mikel if he feels it, too—that overwhelming pull, that compromising fear. He doesn't, and that unsettles me most of all.

My camel groans and fusses underneath me, though I don't know if it's my own unease or this place that sets it on edge. I offer the animal a firm pat, but it provides no comfort—for it or for me.

Movement up ahead halts the caravan. As I watch Malachi and Quin's horses stomp restlessly, I quickly avert my eyes, needing no further reminders of last night.

"*Gods below*," Riat mutters next to me. "Is that really what I think it is?"

Just as I open my mouth to ask what's wrong, the quick flash of scales provides an answer. Though the act feels foreign, I allow a smile to drift across my face as I watch legs scurry through sand. The creatures dash across the desert, moving so fast I dare not blink, else I miss them.

As one crests a dune and locks its beady, black eyes on us, Kai curses under his breath. "They won't, you know…"

I turn my head just in time to see Kai gulp uneasily.

His wide-eyed gaze meets mine. "They won't eat us, right?"

I laugh, and Mikel quickly coughs into his hand to cover up his own.

"Hekkriti lizards prefer smaller game like pehmi," I assure Kai. "Though, someone once told me they'll take down a merov antelope if given the chance. They are carnivores after all..." I flash my brows at him. "We're *probably* safe."

He blanches. "Probably?"

I stifle another laugh as Kai turns to watch the lizards dart past. They're much too invested in whatever they're tracking to give us any trouble—though I don't tell him that. The shock gaping his mouth is much too amusing. I smirk to myself before following his gaze.

Each creature is longer than a man lying down, and with two rows of curved, stumpy teeth, I don't blame Kai for being wary. I've never heard of hekkriti lizards attacking caravans. Though, as rare as it may be, I am grateful for not only our numbers, but the tall animal on which I ride.

I watch the lizards' long, red tongues flicker out to smell the air. The pack hisses, then darts northeast. I'm mesmerized as thick, squatty legs carry them across the sands with staggering speed. The honey-colored scales that flank their bodies shine in the sunlight and provide a natural armor I'm more than familiar with. As the last of them slips from view, I let out a content sigh and turn back to face the path ahead.

"One day, I'm gonna ride one."

My brow arches as I look to my left. Riat's eyes flash with a cocky mischief I don't think I'll ever grow tired of. "Really?" I laugh. "And how do you plan on doing that?"

He shrugs from atop his horse. "Rope one. Hop on. Ride it straight to the closest tavern." He flashes me his brightest smile, and the scar that cuts through his lip tugs fiendishly. "Simple," he coos.

Next to me, Mikel shakes his head and laughs. Kai is still staring off into the empty desert as if the lizards might change their mind about what they're hunting.

"Straight to the tavern?" I ask, another laugh nipping at my words. "Do be sure I'm there to witness it" —my gaze tightens on him playfully— "I know how you love to embellish a story."

"*Ren.*" He smacks a hand to his chest and gives me a wounded pout. "How can you imply such a thing? Me? *Lie?*" The sad act lasts only a moment before a mischievous grin flickers across his face. "You must know I would never perform such a feat without you there. Whoever would I seek to impress, if not you?"

"*Just once,*" Mikel whispers as Riat and Kai pull ahead and fall into conversation. "Bed him just the once, if only for my amusement."

I roll my eyes, but can't stop another smile from drifting across my face. "The moment I bed him, no one will get any sleep around here."

Mikel's smirk is wicked. As he opens his mouth to offer what I know is a sordid comment, I rush to stop him.

"No," I stammer. "*No.* That is not what I meant, and you know it." I press my fingers to my forehead and loose a low chuckle. "He would be unbearable if I were to give him the attention he so craves. We would know no peace."

Mikel laughs, then purses his lips in contemplation. "Now that I think about it, it's a bad idea," he offers. He shoots me a sideways glance, though his focus quickly shifts elsewhere. "If Riat beds you, I'm sure a certain someone would call for his blood..."

I don't follow his gaze to where it now rests over my shoulder. I know whose hazel eyes Mikel seeks to find. My throat grows dry, and when I try to swallow, the words get stuck. I shouldn't have told him about last night, but I couldn't help myself.

"It would hardly concern him," I offer quickly. "He's already proved he has no interest."

Though it aches from too many hours in the saddle, my spine goes board-straight as I roll my shoulders back. I try to keep my face flat—like this topic we've barely encroached holds no bearing—but I know the act is wasted on my friend. Mikel's eyes hover on me with too much focus, like he can see the falsehoods seeping from my pores.

I clear my throat and force my gaze ahead. "Besides, I should be grateful. He stopped things before we did something we'd only come to regret. Nothing good can come from it. Anything between the hunter and I will only chafe the aversion we already have for one another. I don't know what came over me last night. Gods know rum makes me foolish."

The silence prods my vocal cords, begging me to fill it further. I force myself to look at Mikel, already knowing I'll find his gaze on me. But when I face him, the tick in his brow makes me bite my tongue. The empty words I wish to offer will only give my friend more to berate me for. And after all these years together, I know better than to keep spewing horseshit he can clearly smell.

Mikel holds the silence for a little longer, if only to let me stew in it. After what feels like days, he mutters something under his breath before finally addressing me. "You're an idiot. You both are, though I thought one of you would've been brave enough to fix the issue by now."

I go to argue, but Mikel shoots me a deathly look that tells me he's not in the mood.

"Keep lying to yourself," he urges. "Keep telling yourself he thinks ill of you, and you the same. But we both know that's a lie.

And sooner or later, you won't be able to stand the taste of it on your tongue. I can only hope by then, fate hasn't passed you by."

I scoff bitterly and look away. "You've been talking to Savi it seems…"

Mikel looses a deep, weary sigh. "Everything you've ever wanted is right in front of you. Why can't you let yourself reach for it?"

I blink, stare ahead blankly, and try to find an answer. Though, the question leaves me with more of my own.

Is this everything I've ever wanted?

My eyes drift up ahead to where Savi and Tariq converse with bright smiles on their faces. And then to the right, where Riat and Kai now bicker like brothers over something before laughter rumbles from their bellies. But it's when I look over my shoulder—at the man that's no more than a brewing storm of tension—that an inescapable knowing curdles my gut. This could be a new life for me if I allow it. But what would I give up in the process? For surely I wound find consequences in search of such happiness.

Would the gods grant me mercy?

Or would they be quick to remind me of all the reasons I can never have what it is I truly desire?

All of these agonizing thoughts slip from my mind the moment commotion breaks out ahead. I expect to see more hekkriti lizards, but when I look to the front of the caravan, my stomach drops into the deepest pit the underworld can offer.

Vish is barreling toward me, panic bleeding through his sharp, green gaze. He nudges Mirage's side, making haste if only to close the distance between us sooner. The hot sun shines across his olive complexion, beading sweat over his forehead and into the tension lining the corners of his eyes. Malachi is close behind, though I dare not meet the Shade's gaze for fear of what I might find. When the pair finally stops in front of me, my chest fills with a dread I can't place. Though, Vish is quick to give a name to it.

"Cover your marks," he urges. He looks at my arms, and his hands shake as he gestures toward them. "Your scars, too."

Mirage stomps underneath him, making my camel groan in return. Over his shoulder, I see the Berserkers covering their markings. Another sweep of my gaze shows Quin draping herself in swathes of fabric, shielding her own from view. My breath shallows at the sight.

When I turn back to Vish, his panic is now my own. "Who is it?"

His throat bobs. "Trouble," he utters. He looks behind him—out to the barren stretch of sand that leads west. "They'll be here soon."

My brow furrows, but all confusion drops from my face the moment I look across the desert—really look at it. The empty landscape isn't as empty as I once thought. The mass of shadows that bleeds across the horizon is faint, but undeniable. *Riders.*

My heart kicks up in my chest. "Who?" I repeat.

Vish grimaces, but as he opens his mouth to answer, Malachi pushes his horse in between us.

"Do as he says," Malachi orders. They're the first real words between us in a week, and they're far from kind. "*Now, Serehna.*" He clenches his teeth, and his jaw ripples with tension as he stares me down. "Cover up before I'm forced to do something that'll make you hate me even more."

I want to protest, but the violent flicker in Malachi's eyes keeps me silent. My hands dig through my pack, feverishly tugging out scarves and the extra daggers I'd been too lazy to brandish this morning. Ever since we left Hira, my unease has dwindled until all that remains is overconfidence. No one else has come for us, and this far north, I didn't expect them to.

It seems I was wrong.

CHAPTER 30

By the time I've bundled myself in layers and layers of fabric, Vish has spread the warning of what's to come. *Travelers*, though we don't know what kind.

Just like that first day we left Hira, our caravan is tightly packed. There is no avoiding this. According to Vish, it would only look worse if we changed course to flee. No, we have to face them head on—whoever they are. Vish still won't say, but judging by the anger flaring across Malachi's face—contorting his lips into a violent sneer—I'd say they aren't going to be friendly.

Hassan has glued himself to my side. His horse chuffs hotly next to my camel, as if sensing the growing agitation tainting the air. Everyone is quiet, but this day is anything but calm. As our animals trek forward across the sand, anticipation weighs heavily on each of our shoulders. I grit my teeth as the first rider comes into view. But when I spot the rest, my chest grows tight.

Men. All of them are men.

My eyes scan their caravan quickly, but what I see only deepens the nervous pit in my stomach. There's twenty of them, each as intimidating as the last. They sit proudly atop horses—braced strongly like they know all too well what is to come. I try to dismiss the unease I feel, but their built frames are evident even underneath their dark tunics. These men are lined with muscle, the type carved from combat and strife. Steel braces their forearms like armor, and leather cordage is wrapped tightly around their knuckles. They approach us with an arrogance that has me clenching my jaw. And their gazes... sharp and unforgiving. It's the look someone gives you before they slit your throat. The disdain of someone who would leave before the blood even cooled. Everything about them is brutal—like warriors carved by the gods themselves. As they halt a mere twenty paces from our caravan, my fingers twitch in anticipation.

"Grand passing." The greeting slips out from thin lips, and its lush composure sends chills across my skin.

I stare at the man in front of the group as he offers us a wide smile. It curls against his gums, his teeth bared like a starved predator set before a fresh kill. His gaze wanders across each and every one of us—cutting in its assessment.

"I must confess, your appearance upon these sands is a surprise," he states. "We didn't expect to find travelers this far north."

When his eyes finally find mine, I feel the day grow a little colder. There's a darkness lingering behind his gaze, a cruelty that rivals even that which I saw in Rohan. I shift nervously atop my camel and let my hand splay across the hilt of the dagger strapped to my thigh. He clocks the gesture, lifting a brow.

His commanding voice sweeps across the desert once more as he guides his horse closer. "What brings you to these forsaken lands?" he asks us all. The man comes to rest in front of Vish and Malachi, before dipping his head in contemplation. "Surely you must know the dangers that persist here..."

Though I didn't think it could, his grin grows wider. His horse brays and stomps before nipping at Malachi's stallion. I watch the muscles in Malachi's back tense and strain against everything he's trying to contain. I wait for him to say something—to snap a smart-ass retort back at the man—but Malachi's mouth stays clenched shut. As I watch his chest rise and fall with rapid breath, anxiety wraps around my heart like bloated, waterlogged roots.

"You'll find we can handle whatever the gods send our way," Tofá offers brusquely, hands flexing at his sides.

The man looks over at him, mouth curling in amusement. "Is that so?"

Tense silence floats in the empty spaces between us until Vish clears his throat. "We heard of unbroken lands to the west, at the base of the mountains"—he gestures toward the Kohe with a slight shake in his hand— "ones that are free to claim as long as you can tame the earth and its beasts."

"There is indeed plenty of the west yet to claim." The man before us purses his lips, face contorting in playful challenge as he regards Vish. "But this far north? Seems rather unsafe for a band such as yours," he notes. He guides his horse along the edge of our caravan slowly, like he's got all the time to spare. "After all..." He grins, eyes wandering hungrily over Quin. "You do have women among you."

I find myself holding my breath as he drifts closer to the petite woman. Quin tenses, leaning back in her saddle as if desperate to put more space between them. The fear filling her eyes is potent, claiming all of her usual brightness. Tofá and Ivar are fuming silently next to her, gazes burning. Though they're a force to be reckoned with—even with their gifts unknown to these strangers—our guest is hardly intimidated. He ignores the two men as his focus stays locked on Quin.

His eyes run up and down her body, lingering much too long on the swell of her breasts. My jaw aches from how hard I'm gritting my teeth. Though I shouldn't care, my blood burns hot at the sight of Quin's unease. Suddenly, I can't find it in myself to harbor any distaste for the Weaver. I shift in the saddle, but this time, it's with a violent type of restlessness. It takes every ounce of my self-restraint to stay put, takes every shred of my resolve to keep my blade from flying through the air. It would feel too good to cut this repulsive bastard down from his horse, and I don't need to look around me to know that sentiment is shared. Fury radiates off each of our backs, blinding us to the real threat. By the time the man passes Quin, offering nothing more than a muttered laugh, it's already too late.

We're surrounded. His men have spread out with an efficiency that makes my stomach churn. Though he uttered no words—gave them no command—they've moved across these sands with deadly precision to cover our flanks. My heart flutters uneasily as I take in the silent riders once more. They stare at us with blood-lust in their eyes, each resting atop a beastly horse that chuffs hot breath like hellfire. The men's muscles are locked tightly, stiff with tension, yet poised with a practiced patience. As their leader makes his way down our ranks, his men say nothing—do nothing. The air is heavy with expectation, and though none of us cross that invisible boundary between us and them, our hands fidget and clench quietly around sheathed weapons. The only noise that spans the desert is the stomping of horses and the groan of camels as, one by one, we subtly maneuver to face these unknown adversaries.

To my right, Mikel is breathing heavy. His hand is tucked inside his tunic, no doubt griping the dagger he keeps there. Behind him, Riat and Kai are practically snarling at the men who have become a threat in as little as a breath.

Words pass between Malachi and Vish gruffly. They're arguing; it's clear in the furious spray of the Shade's words and the way Vish seems desperate to contain them. Whatever Vish offers in reply doesn't sit well. Malachi is fuming, and it's only moments before he's nudging his horse forward, matching pace with the leader as the man wanders closer.

If the stranger notices Malachi stalking him like a shadow, he doesn't care. He merely smirks as he guides his horse along our ranks, making sure to appraise each and every one of us as he passes. My eyes track him the entire way. Every detail, every aspect of his being is filtered through my tight gaze as if it will help me prepare for what's to come. *And what that is?* I don't know. But I feel its tension like a bow string stretched much too far.

My breath is tight in my chest as my eyes roam across him. His scarves have been pulled away, revealing blond hair that's plaited in two tight braids—formed neatly and with strict care. They stretch taut against the sides of his head until they reach his nape where the long strands flow down his back. My lip curls into a barely concealed scowl as I study his face. It's cocky. Pleased. His eyes are the palest of blue, and his gaze drips with a superiority only a king could rival.

I watch him regard Tariq for a moment, though his focus quickly shifts. He licks his lips at Savi, and once again I feel anger rise within me. I debate withdrawing a blade, but I'm quickly shown there's no need. Something akin to a growl slips from Savi's throat as the man tries to maneuver his horse closer. A smirk dances across his face before he offers her a chuckle and moves along. It isn't until he comes to rest in front of Hassan and I that I realize how close he's actually gotten. But before those ghostly blue eyes can lock with mine, Malachi draws all focus.

He pushes his way past Mikel and guides his horse next to me, forgoing all sense of personal space as he crowds my camel. No words leave his lips. He doesn't so much as spare me a glance. With a look in his eyes that would scare most, Malachi glares at the man before us. His body is practically vibrating with rage, tense in a way that tells me he's barely holding himself together. I'm surprised he hasn't loosed his shadows. My curiosity only grows when I look down to find Malachi's hands not only covered in leather gloves, but choking the reins in his grip. Something nervous slithers through me at the sight, but when I raise my gaze, all thought is quickly stripped from my mind.

The stranger is staring at me. Being locked within the chilly blue of his eyes is akin to tasting death. His focus is taunting. Cold, yet scathing. Eager. *Amused*, even. My stomach clenches as his gaze grows heavy and takes in every inch of my form. The attention feels final, like a threat my next breath may not come. I force myself to stay still—to not betray the apprehension I feel creeping across my skin—but unease buzzes through my veins. He takes his time as if he can feel the tension building in the air and seeks to provoke it further. My fingers twitch. But, as much as I want to, I don't dare pull a blade. I'm not foolish enough to damn us without knowing the consequences.

"How curious..." The man's focus lingers on my thighs before his eyes flash back up to mine. "I've never seen a woman such as you."

To my left, Hassan's horse stomps roughly into the earth, betraying its rider. Though, I don't dare shift my attention away from the threat before me. The Continent taught me long ago to never take your eyes off an opponent—not for even a breath.

The man smirks at my silence, head canting to the side with curiosity. Though he can only make out my eyes amidst the mass of fabrics concealing my body, I feel too exposed under his persistent gaze. He leans back in his saddle, regarding me further. As his eyes scour my body for a second time, I feel the need to scrub myself raw with a densely bristled brush.

"...fitted with enough weapons for three men and dressed in leathers any mercenary would be envious of," he utters. "And your face..." He clicks his tongue. "The other women don't cover theirs, though yours is hidden from my sight."

Next to me, both Malachi and Hassan tense. If the man notices, he doesn't show it. His gaze is locked on me, rife with a curiosity that clings to me like dried blood. It feels like I'll never be rid of it in this life, or the next. He smiles like a devil, and I have to dig my nails into skin to suppress the shudder that wishes to rip free.

"Now, why is that?" he quips.

Just as I open my mouth to speak, I see it. It is a blaring scream ringing through my ears. A punch to the stomach. I look at the red markings that decorate the man's hands and feel my limbs begin to shake. My tongue seems to swell, incapable of forming words. I want to yank on the reins and run—rid myself of this day and the fate it brought—but I cannot. I close my eyes as panic takes root, begging the gods to relieve me. They don't.

Behind dark lids, I see the alley. But not the one from Letka. *No*, I see the one that broke me long before that. My breath is a heavy burden in my chest—restless and stifled. No matter how many ragged breaths I take, it's never enough.

"She was in an accident as a child," Hassan offers gruffly. "She prefers people not stare at the scars."

"I see..." the man utters, amusement palpable in his tone. "And has the disfigurement left her mute? Or can the woman speak for herself?"

My eyes snap open only to find his predatory gaze on me. And though his harsh, pale eyes demand answers, I can only look at his hands. The red ink is a vibrant brand on his alabaster skin. Every harsh stroke is like a claw mark ripping flesh. I count twelve lines in total, and feel nausea bubble up my throat.

Voices muffle through the air, and horses stomp nervously. But it's all lost on me. All I can feel is a terror that clenches my chest like I'm seventeen again. It's like I'm back in that alley, staring at those marked hands as they snatch my friend by the hair and slit her throat.

"She does not speak," Hassan states roughly.

The man hums in response, clearly not fooled. I feel his eyes on me, but I don't dare look up. My hands won't stop shaking, no matter how hard I grip the reins. Tears well in my eyes, but they're not for me. I made a vow long ago—whispered one over a dead body. As I stared into the emotionless depths of her eyes, I promised Chani if I ever saw a Turiden again, I would strike them dead without hesitation. My blood thrums happily at the reminder, churning with a potency that promises retribution. I could do it. Veles would help me. The dark god would gladly let me spill the blood of those who have spilled so much of his children's. I need only ask.

But even as I try to grasp the power that rests tumultuously beneath the surface, I can't shake the fear that strangles my throat with unyielding hands. It's childlike. Devastating. It seeks to drown me, if only to force me back to the surface for another go.

I look up to meet the Turiden's eyes and can almost feel myself bleeding out. I feel the thrust of a blade through my skin, feel it fumble around my insides if only to cut deeper. It's like the death I evaded long ago is breathing down my neck, eager to claim what was once denied.

The man before me now must see those ghosts bleeding through my gaze, because his interest peaks, and he grins. I steel my gaze away, but I know it's already too late. He chuckles darkly under his breath, then moves.

I still atop my saddle, aware of the way he dismounts his horse with ease. His boots hit the sand with a *thud*, though his manner is anything but rushed. He's relaxed as he steps forward and presses closer. He's taller than I thought, rivaling even Tofá's outrageous height. I'm eager to ignore the looming threat of his presence, but a disgusting hacking sound snatches my focus. He spits into the sand, a glistening wet offering that rids this moment of all friendly pretense. Tavern brawls have been started for less.

"Rumor has it there's something fleeing across the Continent." He paces in front of us casually, like he's discussing the prices at market. "Something that has every bounty hunter racing off to find it first..."

As he turns his back on us, I sneak a glance at Malachi. He's been too quiet, and one look at the harsh set of his jaw tells me everything I need to know. He's aware of who we deal with, and my anger is nothing compared to his own. The browns of his eyes are pits of darkness—seeking to consume the Turiden where he stands. Malachi's breath is fast and shallow, chuffing like a wild beast that's been collared too long. It's then that I remember I'm not the only one with scores to settle. Not the only one who watched someone die by red-marked hands.

I reach out to grasp Malachi's arm, squeezing it tightly in my grip. His gaze snaps to mine instantly, though the fury doesn't leave his eyes. He stares at me like I'm hurting him, like the fear and panic in my eyes is carving him hollow. I swallow uneasily, not knowing what to say—not knowing what will turn the tides of this day and steer it away from bloodshed. But maybe that's what the gods desire, and I know there's no changing their minds.

I open my mouth, but Malachi's rumbled whisper stops me. "Tell me not to do it."

My gaze tightens on him strangely. I tilt my head, but when the implication of his words grows clear, it hits me like a stone flung against my chest. "Mal—"

"Vish told me it'll only make things worse, but I want to," he utters through gritted teeth. "*Gods*, do I want to."

Dread pools low in my stomach, gnawing with a promise that this day will not end well. "You can't," I rasp. My grip on his arm tightens as I pull him closer. "The others—"

"Fuck the others," Malachi all but growls.

His voice breaks out of a whisper, and I tense. A mere glimpse reveals we have the Turiden's rapt attention. His curiosity is brimming over, and the wicked flash in his eyes tells me he's eagerly awaiting whatever comes next.

I swallow thickly and turn back to Malachi. "*Don't*," I breathe. My fingers dig into the sleeve of his tunic. "There's too many—"

"It seems as if the woman does speak," the Turiden states.

My eyes widen, but Malachi is the only one who holds my focus. I silently beg him to fight the violence I know courses through his veins. I urge him to see reason, but the look on his face tells me he's far beyond that.

"Whatever has you two so flustered?" the Turiden prods with a taunting purr. "A lover's tiff, perhaps?"

My eyes flash to him, and he grins.

"My men don't take well to whispered conversations," he states. "Makes them think enemies lie in wait."

Whinnies break out across the desert. The horses surrounding us are antsy, as are their riders. As my eyes sweep through the horde, my stomach sours. Some of the men stare at us blankly, giving nothing away, while others sneer violently. Though I know there's more at my back, my gaze focuses on the handful of Turidens in front of me. They're built as ruggedly as their leader, a trait I now understand comes from their calling. It takes a lot of strength to kill a man, and judging by the red hash marks tattooed on every single one of their hands, they know that better than most.

My heart thrums uneasily, though it's not my gift that makes my pulse thump. I drag my eyes up and down each of the men, assessing what weapons they carry and where they keep them holstered. My focus snags on one man who bears a vicious Shade's cut on his face. The blackened flesh runs down the side of his jaw, ruining the smooth brown of his complexion. He grins at my attention, fingers tapping against the long spear that's fastened to his saddle. The sharp, iron tip gleams against the high sun as if in warning.

"Have you heard of the Durit?"

I look back to the man holding our fate in his hands.

The Turiden's leader smirks as he stares at me. The moment hovers in heavy silence, only to be shattered by the shrill whistle that leaves his lips. Every weapon around me is drawn instantly, including my own. But as an apple is tossed into the man's waiting palm and his men stay in place, I know the mistake we've all quickly made.

The Turiden offers us a wide, devious grin. "Nervous, are we?" he muses.

I don't dare holster my blade, even as I watch Savi and Hassan exchange uneasy glances before lowering their own. Malachi is all but twitching next to me.

"We've heard the fabled talk of him, yes," Vish announces. "Though we're not so desperate as to chase myths."

I don't miss the way Vish plainly declared the Durit a man, nor the way the Turiden lets out a breathy laugh before breaking the apple's shiny flesh with his teeth. Juice drips down his chin and into his short, blond beard as he chews.

"No. No, I'm sure you're not," he teases. He wanders away from us, back toward his horse. The apple bounces in his hand as he tosses it up before snatching it in his grip once more. "I'm sure you good people would be keen to slip into the west, never to cross paths with the filth that taints these sands."

His eyes gleam wickedly as he takes another bite and licks the remnants of the apple from his lips. "I can only pray that one day, our kingdom will be restored to its former glory and the blood of every gods-cursed blight will spill down the pits of all three hells, never to return."

At the front of the caravan, Ivar's looses what can only be described as a tortured growl. I watch as he grits his teeth, then drops his head. His chest expands roughly as he fights to get his breathing under control. All the while, my heart beats erratically, knowing that it's only a matter of time before Ivar's gaze fills with black.

The Turiden watches on with an amused grin, taking one more bite of his apple before chucking it to the sand. He looks to his men, and something silent passes between them before the leader turns back to us. With every step he takes, I feel my throat constrict in panic. *He knows.* The blatant hatred that shines in his eyes mixes unkindly with the smile on his face. I can't help but look at his hands one last time, though it feels like torture to witness the lives of my kin tallied across his flesh.

"It's a little hot to be wearing gloves. Isn't it, boy?"

My gaze snaps to Malachi and the black leather gloves that cover his hands. The durable, thick material is much too hot amidst the desert's brutal sun. Sweat beads on the back of my neck as I think of the markings that stretch across Malachi's knuckles—the ones that reveal him to be the very thing these men hunt.

Malachi's lips twitch into a sneer, and though he says nothing, the fire in his eyes speaks for itself. His breath grows heavy, and I know just how close he is to calling the darkness he claims.

"*Mali*," I plead.

His eyes flash to me. I begin to shake my head—to warn him off this path I know he wants to take—but before I can, his hand snatches mine. He rubs his thumb across the back of my hand, teasing my skin with the glove's supple leather. I can practically feel the heat radiating off him—feel the burn of the barely contained rage that Malachi is holding back by the sheer grit of his teeth.

"Just know, every drop is for you," he rasps. "For *us*."

My eyes widen, and my blood thrums in anticipation.

"How many of you?"

The Turiden's voice rips my attention off Malachi, forcing a shuddering breath into my lungs. As he stares at us, I swear his eyes grow a shade darker. Silence follows, and my body twitches against its weight.

"Tell me how many of you rot with tainted blood, and I'll consider sparing the rest," the man offers.

Hassan tenses atop his saddle, tugging the reins and prompting his horse to stomp against the earth. "The rest of us are happy to take your life while standing beside them," he snarls.

The Turiden's gaze flares before eyeing our band once more. Though they outnumber us, there's no saying how many of his men he'll need to sacrifice to leave here triumphant. The sound of Savi's bow stretching in her capable hands makes the man's ear twitch like a dog. He takes in the lot of us, weapons ready and faces drawn tight, and grins.

"So be it," he muses.

He yanks a dagger from his behind his back before I can pull in a full breath. This time, weapons on both sides are drawn without hesitation—held high without remorse. Behind me, I hear Riat muttering curses, taunting the men around him. As my eyes dart from threat to threat, I can't help but focus on the man who started it all. The jagged blade clutched in the leader's hand gleams in the sun, stained with a murky, faded red. My scar throbs, and I clench my hand around the hilt of my weapon to stave off the trembling I can't deny.

The Turiden grits his teeth as he regards each of us. His gaze moves slowly—strategically. When he looks back at me, his grin is so wide that his lips peel back into the gums.

"It will be an honor to kill a blight such as you," he states wryly. "The Durit belongs in the ground with the rest of the useless dead of your kind."

Malachi's fingers latch onto my arm, nearly tugging me off my saddle with how hard he clutches me. His breath is a hot rasp, huffing wildly as the day around me grows even hotter. His forehead pulses with contempt and barely-concealed rage.

"Leave us be," Vish beseeches, "and all of your men will see tomorrow's sunrise."

"*No*," Malachi growls. "They all die here."

I tense as Malachi's shadows slither down the sleeves of his tunic. It's a bold move, but one that doesn't go unnoticed. I watch as two of the Turidens mumble under their breath, eyes widening. Shades are almost as rare as Seers among the Continent, and though a Berserker's ability to snap bones and a Torch's talent for fire is nothing to be scoffed at, there's something about death carving flesh that makes any man wary.

Their leader chuckles, a wicked smile drawing across his face. "The abomination that rides among you is right," he tells Vish before addressing the rest of us. "No one leaves here until cursed blood soaks the earth."

The Turiden's eyes blaze with heat, but as he registers Malachi's possessive hold on me, a predatory glint fills his gaze.

He cocks his head at Malachi and smirks. "I think I'll start with the woman."

"And I'll start with you."

Shadows explode around me like night has swallowed the day. Everyone lurches, hoisting weapons and dodging Malachi's violent whips of darkness as they flare across the desert. Animals panic, a frenzy tensed reins can barely leash. Men scream, and all too quickly blood is drawn by snapping black. The spray coats the sand, flecking each grain with the troubles of this day. I kick my camel's side, desperate to fight my way through the darkness to join the fight. The others have chosen to stand with those of us marked by the gods, and I won't leave them to battle alone. A rider lurches from the chaos, his horse rearing up against a whip of shadow. I hurl a dagger at the Turiden quickly, and it embeds in the center of his throat with a sick proficiency. A good person would feel guilty, but the sight only seeks to fill the gaping whole in my chest that's existed long before this day.

This is no time for mercy, and these men deserve none of mine. I've already reached for another blade by the time his body drops from the horse. The melee rages around me, as wild as fire that seeks new kindling. I try to catch my breath—try to will my shadows to join the fray—but before I can harness that fleeting whip of power, I'm ripped off my saddle.

The earth greets me with a vicious hand. The breath flattens from my lungs, screaming out in a wheezed gasp that is quickly filled with the dusty grit of sand. Shouts echo through my ears, followed by the violent clang of metal. My eyes strain against the blinding daylight and the black that muddies my vision. It takes me too long to clear my head, and by the time I do, I feel hands on me.

I'm being dragged across the sand by rough fingers that claw at my tunic. The fabric bunches at my throat, choking the rasping breaths I'm desperate to take. My legs kick and flail as I slap against the unseen enemy that snared me so quickly. Dagger clasped tightly in my grip, I lurch back and strike. My aim is blind and frantic. Over and over again, the blade greets only air, until finally, metal bites skin.

I hear a howl of pain and strike again. Harder. Faster. My arm burns against the strain as I flail and stab. Someone's horse stomps dangerously close to my face, sending up violent sprays of sand, but I don't waver. Don't relent. As my weapon draws more blood and provokes another roar from my captor, the choking grip on my tunic loosens. No longer being tugged across the sand, I flip onto my stomach and search for my target.

A man glares at me from mere paces away, forearms weeping blood. His green eyes are locked on me with an ire I've seen from many men, but it's the Shade's cut along his jaw that catches my focus. As he cocks his head—sending his mop of brown hair falling across his forehead—I see that his ear was long ago severed by shadow, too. I can only hope to add to his poor luck.

The scarred man grins, eyes flaring with manic violence as he grabs his spear from where it'd fallen amidst the chaos. He raises the shaft above his head, angling that vicious steel point down toward me.

Everything around me blurs and quiets. It's a knowing that takes over—a certainty that this moment will be my last unless I use that which the gods gave me.

Deep breath in, though I don't let it out. Not yet. The thrum of my blood is an unsteady companion inside me. Eager. *Vengeful.* I can feel every swell and flicker of Veles's power tearing through my veins, growing hotter as it slinks underneath my skin and seeks to claim every inch of me. It wants out, and all at once, I let it.

Just as the Turiden takes a step closer, looming over me with that brutal weapon held aloft, I call on the shadows. The hum in my blood answers in turn, sending darkness forth. The shadows twitch and writhe, finding their weight against the world. When my eyes raise to the Turiden, the flicker of doubt I see on his face curls a smile on mine.

This is for Chani.

Darkness whips through the air, barreling toward the man who dared come for me. He raises his hands to shield his face, but can't escape the riotous bite of my gift. I feel the will of Veles's power as it cuts into flesh—feel the ease with which it tears open his torso. My arms pepper with goosebumps at the sensation, and breath shudders in my lungs.

The Turiden drips with blood, and I watch with sick contentment as decaying black sizzles along the rim of each and every wound I dealt. His green eyes widen slightly, as if the gods just revealed the death fate chose for him. He takes a staggering step back, and the fear that fills his gaze inspires me—burns the violence in my veins hotter. Just as the shadows billow around me, preparing to lurch in what I know will be a killing blow, I meet resistance.

It's a fist pounding against a door that won't open. A stone wall that's too high to climb. My gift revolts in my veins, and I watch as the shadows waver before me. I try to call them back—try to beckon them into the light—but pain is all I find. I'm instantly struck with a piercing ache, one that blinds me in a haze of shrieking agony and a truth I'd rather forget.

The shadows are not mine to rule, for I refuse to give them what they ask for. *Submission.* I all but choke on the suffering it costs me. The gods surely think me a fool.

I gasp against the pain, dragging myself up onto my knees, only to collapse back into the earth. My hands fumble through the sand, searching for the dagger I dropped in folly. I thought I had no more use for such things—thought I was a weapon forged by gods. I snarl against my own stupidity. By the time my fingers latch onto the rough, leather-wrapped hilt, it's much too late.

Like always, it arrives an unwelcome guest. That encroaching cold. That stillness that slips up my body without care or concern for the dangers around me. Panic has my shadows snapping free with a burst before fading into the air like they never existed. Dread floods my chest. Though I wish there was, there's nothing I can do to stop this.

My gaze raises just in time to see the Turiden retreat. He hasn't seen it yet, but the white has already begun to spill into my eyes. Through its fog, I watch as my adversary's fingers shake around his weapon, barely holding the spear in his grasp as he stumbles and slips from view. I try to drag myself forward, try to will my shadows after his bloody trail, but he's too far, and I'm much too weak.

Out of the corner of my eye, I see Malachi's shadows tearing through Turidens like parchment. I want to feel relieved—want to feel proud—but can only crumble beneath the weight of my own failure.

Before I can beg the gods for mercy, Hael calls me under.

The sun burns high above as blood seeps down my face. I wipe it away with the back of my hand and take a step forward. My jaw throbs from how hard I'm grinding my teeth.

"More?" He laughs.

The sound of that voice still sends an ache through my chest each time I hear it. I can't bear to look at him right now, so—though it's poor practice for a fight—I don't.

My eyes stay locked on the sand, fixed to where his leather boots step sideways. I mirror each movement, being sure to keep the distance between us until it's time.

"It's been two hours. Yield." he prods. "I thought by now, we'd have found ourselves soaking in a tub."

He lunges, but I clock the moment the toe of his boot lifts from the sand. Shadows explode from me, twisting into a violent hurl of black. I don't need to look up to know where it's aimed. I can feel it in the air, in my mind, in my blood. The spear of shadow rips apart just before it greets his flesh, exploding like a web. He wasn't expecting that. He's bested me all morning by dodging my blows or dealing his own before I've had the chance. But now, I'm tired of playing.

He laughs wildly, undeterred by the darkness overtaking him. I look up as my gift squeezes him in its viper hold. A flicker of panic eats through me at the sight, but I hold strong. Though he's in no pain, I don't know if I'll ever be able to stomach watching my shadows smother him like this. Memories are shackles I should have shed long ago, but some are harder to break.

He thrashes against the inky black, his eyes deeps pits of tar. White teeth gleam against the daylight as he laughs and jeers. He doesn't give up, but he knows he's been beat.

I saunter closer, boots gliding across the sand. Though something in my chest burns with every glance, Hael keeps me blind to the man before me. A shiver runs up my spine. Each step allows me time to reign in my unease. When I finally reach him, his gift has faded, forcing me to face the playful glimmer in his eyes.

"You've been holding back, haven't you?" He cocks his head and shoots me an easy grin. "Your shadows are strong again. You're ready."

I hate the way that smile strums the severed strings of my heart. I scoff and look out across the desert before me. It's still, and though I know no one is coming for me, I search the horizon all the same.

"I need more time," I utter. With the flick of my fingers, my shadows fall away.

Just as I turn to leave the training grounds, his hand finds my waist. I still, losing myself to moments I never thought I'd get back. He presses his lips to my neck, and I stifle a shudder as he kisses the tender spot where my shoulder slopes.

"You've been avoiding me," he mumbles against my skin.

I shrug him off before I can succumb to more of his touch. "I'm going away for a few days," I utter.

His brow furrows in a way I'm eager to forget. I can't face him, and it's because of my own weakness that I turn my back.

"I'll be needing someone to spar with when I return," I press. "I trust you can keep yourself alive until then?"

He lets out a breathy laugh. I feel him press closer, but don't dare turn to face him. His fingertips drift across my skin, tracing where markings now bleed recklessly over scars.

"Careful," he coos. "If anyone hears you talking like that, they might think you care for your precious traitor."

CHAPTER 31

I gasp as the moment comes back to me.

All around, sand flies in vicious sprays. My head throbs with a splitting pain, and it takes me a moment to realize where I am. The panicked groan of camels and the squelch of blood against slicing skin thrusts me into the now like I've been dumped into tempestuous waters. I come up for air in this reality shuddering and shaking. The clang of metal reverberates in my ears as I crawl forward on all fours, limbs shaky underneath me. I flinch as a body drops to my left, but the sight of a dead Turiden does nothing to still my racing heart.

The haze of my mind feels like I never came out of that vision, though the chaos around me proves I'm far from that future thread. Savi yells across the desert, and my gaze snaps to her just as she looses an arrow into a rider's chest. Another battle cry leaves her lips as she quickly nocks a new arrow and launches it into her opponent's eye. He stills instantly, and the spurt of blood that pops from his ruined socket churns nausea in my already unsteady stomach.

I stand on shaky legs, and—with the white now faded from my eyes—take in the havoc of this day. Horses rear up in panic as riders on both sides are yanked off their saddles. Blades clash and grunts of exertion join the loud thump of blood in my ears. I catch sight of a violent quiver of shadow just before it slices through a Turiden's throat. My own gift twitches in anticipation, though it doesn't slip from my veins. Just as I tighten the grip on my blade and ready myself to rejoin the fray, I'm slammed into the ground.

Dust clouds my vision as my back connects with the earth, forcing out a pained shout. Everything aches. My eyes flutter open, but the sight I find only serves to stir my panic. A Turiden crawls over me, pining me with his weight. I can't pull in a full breath as his knees dig in to choke it from my lungs. Dagger lost to the sand, my hands slap wildly, nails breaking skin like claws.

The Turiden—a man whose features are much too bland to be remembered as the last I'll witness—hits me across the face, silencing the fight in me. It happens again, and again, and again until the impact fades, and I'm left pulling in weak, gasping breaths. Agony alights my face. The building pressure of swollen tissue and shattered bone assaults me with a pain so fierce that everything fades to black for a moment that lasts too long. I blink, and through spotting vision, I spot the red-tipped blade aimed for my heart.

My gift quivers within me, laced with unbridled rage and screaming in self-preservation. I can feel it snapping at its leash, begging me to free it. Its promise of violence is so close, but much too far away. With my vision fading and pain accompanying every breath, I wouldn't know how to unleash my shadows even if I tried.

As the man towers above me—a devil blocking out the sinking sun—I wish it was another's face guiding me to the afterlife. I pull in a quivering breath, head throbbing from the blows I've been dealt, and prepare for a fate I knew I could never escape. Death is inevitable, and though I thought the gods would grant me more sunsets than this, I don't mourn the loss. I just hope the others survive.

I shudder and flinch as it happens. The blade falls against my tunic, and blood flows over me like a river. I gasp, blinking through the murky red haze until I'm staring at the face of death itself. Though, it's not my own he came for.

Hassan stands over me, breath huffing wildly in his chest. His eyes are blazes of golden fire, violent and unforgiving. My skins chills at the raw power washing over him, but as my gaze drops to the severed head gripped tightly in his hand, I roll over and vomit.

My body shakes with dry heaves until I feel a firm grip tug my arm. Hassan hoists me up quickly, dropping his sword so he can plant both hands on my shoulders. He scans every inch of me—eyes darting around in a panicked rush. Only when he finds no life-threatening wounds carved into my flesh does he let out a heavy sigh and release me.

My gaze drops to the sword resting in the sand—its blade coated in shiny, fresh blood. As my eyes wander along a dripping trail of red, I find the source. The Turiden who was seconds away from claiming my life now lies face down in the sand, slumped like the empty carcass he is. As I spot the head Hassan quickly discarded—stare into those distant, glassy eyes that can do nothing but stare back—another wave of nausea rolls through me.

I sway and gag, only to have Hassan pull my gaze toward him with a gentleness that conflicts with the slick of blood coating his fingertips. He holds my jaw firmly as those deep, hazel eyes scour my face. His brow furrows, and as his thumb glides across my cheek, blood spreads amidst the loving embrace. I flinch as he grazes a tender spot—a place I know will grow black and blue with time. When I look back up at Hassan, something feral burns in his gaze.

"I should have taken my time," he grits out, both hands now tracing my swollen face in pained reverence. His jaw clenches as I wince against the soft touches. "His death was too quick."

The space between my brows knits as I witness the agony eclipsing Hassan usually guarded expression. There is no stifled fury amidst his eyes. No hesitation in his glance. He looks at me like he's been flayed wide—like there is nothing left to hide. My breath catches in my throat, and as I stare back at the man I swore I loathed, I consider if I'm done hiding, too.

Hassan is quickly shoved away as Malachi barges in between us. The Shade stares at me with the same intensity Hassan just displayed, only his is not so gentle.

His hand grasps my chin, yanking my focus to him. "Are you hurt?"

I wince and try to pull away, but his hold only tightens.

"*Fucking hells,*" he curses, tilting my face so the fading light can catch where I know the Turiden's blows are now forming into violent, red splotches.

I don't need to see; I know it's bad. I can feel it with every aching breath I take. He growls, dropping his hands from my face as he scours my body for bleeding wounds, just as Hassan did. As his fingers dig into my waist and pull me closer, I'm shaken out of pain's daze.

"I'm fine," I grunt, shoving him off me. "Let me breathe for gods' sake."

Malachi's mouth twitches in annoyance, though he doesn't move to close the distance I've quickly put between us. "What happened?" he prods. "I looked over and you were gone. One moment you were there, and the next... I thought they— I thought you..." He swallows thickly, eyes dark and wild as they burn into me, almost pleading in their intensity. "This should never have happened."

Just as Hassan's was, Malachi's gaze is too much for me to take. I'm not ready to face what lies beneath those endlessly deep eyes of his, not yet. Not truly.

"No. It shouldn't have," I utter. "I told you not to do it, and you didn't listen."

He gives me an incredulous look, and a bitter laugh drips from his lips. "And what did you want me to do? Let them slaughter us?"

"I wanted you to temper Veles's violence," I argue, finally finding my voice. "I wanted you to control your emotions just as you've lectured me to for weeks!"

He's in my face seconds later, shadows billowing around me like a storm I can't escape. "That *violence* kept you alive today," he snarls. "Do you truly think they would have let us go? That they would have looked the other way when they clearly knew what we were?" Malachi's fingers dig into my waist, holding me tight. "It's just as I've already told you, Serehna. This world is cruel, as are its people. They want nothing more than to condemn our blood to the earth, and I'll be damned if I let them spill any more of yours."

"You put the others at risk," I snap, shoving him away. "Not everyone has shadows that answer to their beck and call, Malachi. Not everyone is untouchable!"

He stills instantly, gaze tightening as he regards me for a moment. The minute his face alights in understanding, I feel much too small.

"You still haven't done it."

I try to scoff, but I can't summon the energy. It dies in my throat with a pitiful sound, leaving me raw under Malachi's scrutiny. It's disappointment that suddenly floods his gaze—that, and pure rage.

"Stop fighting your fate," he seethes. "I will not have you die because you're too stubborn to give in to the gods!"

"I'm not—"

"No," he growls. His shadows slap against the sand, growing restless. "Don't try to convince me otherwise. You're rejecting the gift Veles has given you, just as you've done with Hael. The gods have blessed you with untold power, Serehna. When will you see that it's our salvation?!"

"*Salvation?*" I balk. "This power is a *curse*. One this world is better off without. The gods have promised me nothing but darkness in the days to come. Forgive me if I will not freely step into its abyss."

Malachi's fists clench at his sides, and his shadows snake around his shoulders like writhing serpents. "I will walk through it with you—just as I've promised," he seethes. "Why won't you trust me? *Give in*, Serehna. Stop fighting this!"

"Leave her be," Hassan orders, his deep voice shattering the moment as he steps between Malachi and I. "We need to move before anyone else finds us."

His words rip me back to what it is that's truly happened here. I look to the blood still staining his hands, then to the sword clenched in his grip—now dried with gore—and my stomach churns. But before sickness can claim me, panic rings true.

Mikel. The others.

I stalk across the sand, boots stomping the earth as a nervous pit floods my stomach. The chaos greets me quickly, unforgiving with its humid stench and bitter twang.

Death. So much death.

I slap a hand over my mouth, but even that isn't enough to keep the smell at bay. My breath is a prisoner in my chest as I rush to identify the corpses that litter the desert—crumpled and bloody.

Gods, please. Don't take anyone from me this day.

I take quick steps across the sand, boots bumping into things I dare not glance at for too long. One look is all I offer the hardened, lifeless faces beneath me, just enough to search the carnage for familiar ones. After stumbling through the mess of gore, the gods finally reveal the truth to me.

My people aren't among the dead.

The realization allows me to draw in a full breath.

My heart lurches as Mikel suddenly appears before me, blood sprayed across his face and coating his tunic. I race over to him, tripping over limp limbs as I go. As soon as my hands wrap around his torso, I bury my face into his neck. Deep, quaking breaths heave in and out of my lungs, and I barely fight back the tears that threaten to flow.

Mikel looses a deep sigh in my ear as he holds me tight. "Never a dull moment with you, is there?"

He must be waiting for a snarky reply because when it doesn't come, he pulls away to hold me at arm's length. One look is all it takes for that easy smile to drop from his lips. "*Gods*, Ren. Your face..."

His hands are on me seconds later. He doesn't give me a moment to protest before his veins flood with white and a biting chill sears through me. I grit through the pain, knowing it'll be over soon enough. Just as I bite back a whimper, healing's vicious touch fades, and Mikel drops his hands from me. His eyes dart across my face diligently, and when he looses a heavy breath, I know he's rid me of the evidence of yet another's violence.

As the others make their way over, I can't help but scour the desert. It's a vast field of death. A tribute to the dark god himself. My gift thrums in my veins, reminding me that I could easily be capable of such violence—that one day, I'll deal it with my own hands. I shut my eyes tightly, staving off memories of visions I wish I could forget.

"You know... I thought they would be harder to kill."

Savi's voice pulls me from dark thoughts, and as I open my eyes, I glimpse her ripping arrows free from where they're buried into the backs of lifeless Turidens. She quickly resheathes the good ones in her quiver, tossing away those that are splintered and stubbed.

"Speak for yourself," Kai argues. He settles by her side, air heaving through his lungs in ragged breaths. "Those bastards fought hard."

Both of his long, curved swords are gripped loosely in his hands and glisten with red. Blood is flecked across his pale cheeks like freckles. Through the tears in his black tunic, I spot two deep gashes in his left arm.

Mikel dashes across the sand, coming to his aid in seconds. "*Hells below*, you're a mess," he mumbles. He gazes up at Kai, concern mixing with compassion across his face. "You're worse off than Ren, which—given her proclivity for danger—is saying something."

I try to smirk at the taunt, but the scene before me quickly sullies any joy I might feel. It's... familiar. Blood cuts through the sand in a river, connecting bodies like a map to the underworld. Riderless horses pace restlessly, while some have already wandered far from this chaos. It cuts me like a hot blade through an open wound, drives my teeth into my tongue with the need to cloud my mind. Something prickles the back of my neck—some inner knowing that this day played before my eyes long ago, and the gods wish for me to remember it now. I shiver as that uncanny feeling slithers up my spine and takes root somewhere unshakable.

How many visions like this have I lost to time? How many have I kept buried in dark corners if only to pretend they never existed?

I swallow thickly, pushing back the hot rush of sickness that seeks to rear up from the depths of me.

"Well, that was something."

When I turn, my heart stutters at the sight of Tariq. His beige tunic is soaked with so much blood that the fabric clings to his thickly muscled chest. It's only after realizing none of the blood is his that I remember how to breathe again.

As my gaze flickers across the desert, I'm relived to see the others are more or less unscathed. To my right, Ivar and Tofá hover around Quin like guard dogs, eyes still flooded with black despite the fact that no threats remain. The petite woman shakes nervously between them, and though fear widens her gaze, a quick glimpse reveals she's untouched by today's brutality. A closer look at the Berserkers gives me an inclination as to why. Both Ivar and Tofá's hands are covered in blood, so much so that—from this distance—it looks like they're wearing gloves. It coats them like a second skin, trailing all the way up under the sleeves of their tunics.

Vish stands behind them, his focus far to the west. The sight of his eyes constricting—the spectacle of his gift flooding his gaze—makes my heart beat unsteadily. I won't ask him what he sees, for I doubt he'd tell me. But even if he did, I'm not sure I want to know.

Though I can feel Malachi lingering nearby, I don't look at him. Instead, I look across the sands to find Hassan and Riat approaching. While Hassan still looks like death himself, grip tight around his sword, Riat is grinning like a child during a Hecfrí celebration.

He steps his way in between the bodies littering the ground until he's sidled up next to me. "Looks like we found ourselves in a bit of trouble." He lifts a brow and gives me a goofy smile. "Good thing I took care of it."

Savi barks a laugh. "I forget... who was it that saved your ass before a Turiden could slice your knees off?" Riat *tsks* dismissively as Savi crosses her arms over her chest and grins. "Oh yes," she finishes. "That was me."

"I was hardly in danger," Riat debates. He loops an arm around my waist and pulls me into his side. "But it was a deadly fight, to be sure. One I would be more than happy to recount later... in my tent, perhaps?"

I loose a breathy laugh before wrapping my fingers around his jaw. "Never going to happen," I utter, shaking his face before giving his cheek a playful pat. "Save it for some poor maiden at the next outpost."

"Oh, but I've been saving it up for you, goddess," Riat coos, hand drifting much too close to my ass. "One night laced in untold bliss." His fingers curl tightly around me, and he waggles his brows. "Gods know you'll be screaming my name for all to hear."

I loosen my hold on him, if only to shove him away. It sends him stumbling back, and he almost trips over the crumpled body at his feet before he manages to right himself.

"Next time that hand slips too low, I'll carve it away like Veles's own stumps," I warn.

His eyes widen at the threat before he sees it for the empty thing it is. "Oh, *come on*, goddess," he groans. "One chance. That's all I ask for."

I offer a heavy sigh, though a smile peeks out from my tightly-pulled lips. "Not in this life or the next, Riat."

"What will it take? Help me out here," he prods. "I mean, I could understand that white-haired daemon. *Fuck.* Even I got a little hot watching the way he looked at you. But don't tell me you still have your sights set on these grumpy bastards?" He gestures wildly, and though I wish it wasn't so obvious, it's impossible to miss who he's referring to.

My cheeks burn, and I glance up at the sky, desperate to look anywhere but where curiosity baits me to. Though, it seems I just can't help myself. I steal a quick glance at both Hassan and Malachi and redden further when I find both of their gazes locked on me.

"Seriously?" Riat groans, catching my blush. "I'll be deep in a grave before either of them make a move."

I can't bear to meet anyone's gaze, but luckily, Savi comes to the rescue. She clears her throat—and the tension—with a cough that couldn't be more obvious, but is appreciated nonetheless.

"So..." she utters. "What are we going to do about" —her hands gesture loosely to the heaps of dead bodies— "*them.*"

Tariq lets out a deep sigh. "It all but proves we were here. It would be safest if we buried—"

"Let them rot."

My gaze snaps to Malachi, finding a look I could only describe as murderous.

"They're food for the buzzards," he declares, voice as sharp as any blade. "Nothing more."

"Damn." Riat chuckles. "That's cold as all hells." His eyes flash to Hassan playfully. "What about you, boss? Any wishes for the devils who almost got their hands on our goddess?"

Hassan grumbles, and the look he sends Riat is answer enough. Something thumps against my boot, and I slap Riat's chest to get him to bugger off. He only grins at me deviously— batting his eyes for good measure.

"They were moody bastards. That's for sure," Kai pipes up.

A quick glance shows that Mikel has already healed his wounds. I can't help but smile at that.

"Do they really hate daemons so much that they would have slaughtered us all?" Kai continues.

"Turidens see daemons as the downfall of the Continent," Tariq starts. "They were the kingdom's holy soldiers back in the dark times of King Achar. After the Rebellion, they viewed cleansing this land of daemon blood as their greatest duty." His gaze tightens as he looks out to where our enemies came upon us so suddenly. "They'll raze a whole outpost just to kill one of the gods' own children. I've seen them do it."

"They would have done worse if they'd gotten their hands on her," Malachi interjects sharply. "A massacre is kind in comparison."

Another thump has me turning toward Riat with agitation crinkling my brow. He merely offers me a smile. "They would never have gotten her," he declares. "Not with me so duty-bound and love-stricken as to protect our precious Dur—"

It happens too fast. A lurch of sand. A blood chilling *thud* followed by a *squelch*. I see the red bubble up from his lips before I hear the gurgle of his breath. It's strained and misplaced on that bright face of his. Riat's hands slap carelessly at the spear jutting through his chest. Before I can even process what's happened, Tariq reels down to stab the Turiden who dealt the strike.

Riat teeters like a withered tree, and I barely have enough time to catch him as he drops to his knees. His face buries against my shoulder, heavy and limp. I can feel the blood seeping out of his gaping mouth, wetting my tunic. His breath is shallow and strained, laced with a sickening, wet rasp that echoes in my ears. I doubt I'll ever forget the sound.

I stare wide-eyed, searching for proof that this isn't real, but the look on Riat's face fills my chest with a devastating certainty. My gaze snaps behind him to the half-dead Turiden just as Tariq delivers the final blow. But there's no justice in his death, not even as I glimpse the six red hash marks inked across his hand. His execution won't change anything, but I spot something that does.

The Shade's scar cut across his jaw glistens in the sun, reflecting the rot that found its way there long before this day. Those wild, green eyes of his are now lifeless, and that brown mop of hair sticks to his stone-still face in clumps of sweat. The breath in my lungs grows stale in my throat, unable to slip past my lips. As my eyes drift over the freshly decaying cuts marring his torso—the ones that weren't strong enough to deliver death—a truth I never wished to carry buries itself deep in my chest. I can't bear to name it now, though even without the words, I know its taste and feel its blame.

My mind snaps awake as the body in my arms begins to shake. As I pull back, Riat stares up at me, eyes full of something I can't place, mouth wobbling against unsaid words.

"No," I rasp, breath finally pouring from my lungs. "*No*. This isn't— this wasn't... I never saw—" Panic chokes me. "Mikel!" I shout. "Mikel, help him!"

I blink away tears to find my friend already at my side. He guides Riat back gently, though I find myself clinging to the hunter with desperate hands. As Mikel pulls him away, the sight I find rips a vicious sob from my throat.

The spear is buried deep in the center of Riat's chest—the steel point so far through flesh that I can see the weapon's wooden shaft. Savi drops to her knees next to me just as Mikel lays his hands on Riat. A pained, shuddering gasp leaves the young hunter's mouth, and I can't stand to watch. But when my gaze raises to Savi, I wish it hadn't. Her hazel eyes burn with hot tears, driving the ache deeper into my chest like the spear struck me first. There's a quiver in her bottom lip that she tries to stifle by biting, but it's no use. I watch her cling to Riat's arm, silent sobs shaking her whole body. It's too much. Too horrible. I sink into numbness, clinging to the desperate notion that this can't be real.

When I finally look back at Mikel, anger and desperation mix violently in my chest. "What are you doing?" I rage. My eyes dart back and forth between Riat and where Mikel's hands are hovering in the air, no longer touching skin. "Do something!" I order. I lash out at my friend, tugging his hands down. "Heal him. Fucking *do something!*"

Mikel grits his teeth and looks up at me with a shadowed gaze. He shakes his head once, only once. "It's done. There's nothing I can do."

My eyes widen, but it's the wailing sob that tears from Savi's throat that drives me forward. I snatch Mikel by the collar of his tunic and haul him over Riat's body. "You're a fucking Mender," I urge. "*Fix him!*"

He laces his hands over mine and squeezes tightly. The look he gives me holds none of the frustration I deserve, only a deep pity.

When he finally speaks, I feel the day grow cold. "It pierced his heart," Mikel whispers. "The gods have already taken him."

More wails bellow through the air as Savi buries her face against Riat's tunic. She cradles him, rocking them both back and forth as grief consumes her. Hassan sinks down behind his cousin, laying a heavy hand on her shoulder as she cries and clings to the body that grows colder with each passing second. Suddenly, it all hits me.

I reel back, scrambling away from the devastation I alone caused. When I get to my feet, I feel the gentle press of a hand on my back but quickly flinch away. I shove Tariq off, breath quaking in my chest. My boots trip over bodies as I stagger back on shaky legs, but I don't stop moving. With every backward step I take, my focus stays locked ahead. I can't seem to drag my gaze away from Riat's limp body, nor the devastated woman that clings to him. But it's the sight of a lone figure standing amidst it all that halts me where I stand.

Kai rests in place, as still as a statue. He hasn't so much as taken a step closer, but the shock is written clearly across his face. He seems hollow—like all of the life has leeched from his skin. His eyes hold a faraway look, as if trapped in his own mind—like what he's watching is only a dream. A nightmare.

Gods, please let this be a nightmare.

It's only when Vish approaches Kai—pulls the young hunter's face against his shoulder—that I watch the world crumble. The scream that tears from Kai's throat feels like the sky itself has cracked wide open. It's a gasping wail—a desperate howl that sounds like all of my worst memories joined together. Kai slumps against Vish, and it takes all of the older man's strength to hold Kai's trembling body upright. Vish strokes his hair like a father consoling a petrified child, but when Vish's gaze shoots across the sand to find mine, I see his pain, too.

It's the last knife to my chest—the final answer to the questions I've asked for so long. I'd wondered why death seemed to follow me, why the gods had cursed me to bear such pain in this lifetime. As I stare into Vish's eyes, that once critical gaze now riddled with anguish, I realize this life was never about my suffering.

My knees sink to the sand as I'm stripped of my last ounce of strength. Riat's blood coats my hands, sticky between my fingers. I bury my fists into the desert's grit just to be rid of the sight, eager to strip myself of the touch of it. Tears line my eyes, but I refuse to let more fall. They're a sign of weakness—one I can no longer afford, one I don't deserve. Instead, I lower my face to the sand and scream. I wring every last breath from my lungs until all that's left is a violent ache in my throat and a well-deserved burn.

When I raise my gaze, the view is the same as before, though the distant wails of grief no longer stir my own. They only act as evidence of what I have allowed to happen, and now what I must atone for.

I pull myself up from the sand, staggering with the heavy weight of exhaustion. As my gaze burns across the desert—at the tragedy the gods have woven here today—I feel rage bubble up in my chest.

I was wrong all these years.

So wrong.

It's not my suffering the gods have woven into the very tapestry of my fate.

It's everyone else's.

CHAPTER 32

The pyre burns bright against the night's brooding darkness. Soot and smoke drift across the sand on a cold, trailing breeze that stings my eyes. I want to look away—if only to escape the burning fumes for a breath—but can't bring myself to.

All is silent around me, leaving the desert with nothing but the crackle of flames to keep it alive. The time for bellowing wails and babbling tears has long since passed. Grief will not bring Riat back, and those around me seem to know it, too. Any tears shed now are silent. *Accepting.* They slid down faces in slow rivers, refusing to be brushed away. And yes, while grief will not bring Riat back, the agony of his death lingers—worse than the stench of burning flesh and charring bone that clings to the air like plague.

My gaze stays fixed on the fire and the smoldering body it consumes. Even as, one by one, each member of Hassan's crew steps up to offer their goodbyes, my focus never wavers. It starts with Savi. She's still covered in blood, and the dried gore almost shines against the flush of firelight. For a moment, she does nothing but face the pyre and stare into its abyss—gaze into the lapping flames that dismember her friend bit by bit. But eventually, her hand moves. It's achingly slow, as if she's merely sleepwalking; I know she wishes it were so. Her fingers are curled around a bottle, and as she gently tips it forward, the flow of rum sizzles against the fire.

No one hurries her along or steps closer to hear the words she utters. It isn't until a while later—after she's walked back to find her place among the others—that the next person approaches.

The hour that follows is full of nothing but the hot lick of flames and the endless sifting of sand against boots. I watch them all pay their respects. Vish. Hassan. Even Malachi and the daemons that followed him on this gods-cursed journey take the time to send Riat off. It isn't until Kai steps up to the flames that my growing numbness wavers, and grief tears through my heart with fresh claws.

The young man before me is a shell of himself. A walking corpse. His swords are missing from his back, and there's no sign of the carefree smile he's worn every day since I met him. In its place is a cold emptiness, carried forth on heavy, staggering footfalls. I'm holding my breath, clenching down on every part of myself as Kai reaches the pyre. I pray for strength—for the devouring maw of grief I know so well to release its hold on him. I would gladly bear it all in his place.

Flames flare against the night—chewing at wood and bone, spitting a hiss as if in warning. Kai doesn't back down, not even as soot falls into his hair like snow. Shoulders slumped, eyes distant and glassy, he sticks out his hand. He stretches as if to touch the pyre; or maybe it's the body within he's so desperate to reach.

I watch the first kiss of flame as it licks at his skin and flinch as if it's my own flesh held to the fire. Yet, Kai holds steady. He stands there, entranced as tongues of heat curl against his fingertips and begin to burn. I'm so mesmerized by the way he takes the pain—how he fights every instinct to pull away—that I miss the figure racing across the sand.

Hassan reaches Kai quickly. Wrapping a firm arm around his chest, he begins to tug the young hunter out of the flame's reach. Though as soon as he tries to guide him back toward the others, Kai snaps out of grief's trance with a shudder of violence. He thrashes and flails, fingers digging against Hassan's arm in a desperate attempt to slip free. The larger man holds him in place, though Kai's adamance to return to the pyre is evident in the kick of his legs and the wild yells he shouts into the night. Hassan doesn't so much as flinch. He merely braces himself, taking the assault as if it's due. But I see the way his lips move, watch how he offers a flurry of words to calm his friend.

Though I don't know what passes between the two—am grateful not to hear whatever heart-aching comfort spills from Hassan's lips—it works. In an instant, Kai goes rigid. Though, it's only seconds later that his head lulls back and true agony finds us all.

The mournful wail that cracks Kai's voice and brings him to his knees carries across the desert like death's own cry. I fight the urge to plug my ears as he yells Riat's name over and over, beseeching the gods to bring his friend back. I know they won't, for this suffering is of their own creation. As Riat's name echoes through the night, I pray the sound won't brand itself in my ears like the other horrors this life has seen fit to gift me.

Kai yells and thrashes, trying to break Hassan's hold once more. He begs Hassan to let him go—insists he needs to pull Riat from the flames. The sound of Kai's agony muffles the frenzied heartbeat that thumps through my ears. It drowns out all other noise, leaves me raw and exposed. Kai screams his denial, telling us this is only a trick of the gods. It can't be real.

Gods, I wish it weren't real.

Hassan has to wrestle Kai to the ground to keep him from dragging himself into the pyre. All the while, Kai wails and pleas. He makes one last attempt to shake Hassan off before his anger gives way to something he can't ignore. *The truth.*

Kai buries his face against Hassan's stomach and sobs like a child. Heavy tears pour down his face and breath heaves in and out of his lungs with such severity that I can hear it across the sands. My hands shake as I watch Hassan comfort Kai, unsure how he can still find the strength to do so. But it's the sight of silent tears streaming down Hassan's own face as he cradles his broken fighter that well and truly wrecks me. It churns the guilt in my stomach so violently I think I may be sick. I take a few steps back—desperate to slink into the night and forget this suffering—when a firm tug stops me.

My gaze drifts down to find a tendril of shadow latched around my leg. I swallow the lump of emotions I'd rather not face and search for the one who called forth this darkness. Malachi stares at me from across the pyre, gaze heavy and unrelenting. His lips part as he offers me one silent word. A command. *Stay.*

Tears prick my eyes without consent, and the soft brush of shadows across my cheek only makes them flow harder. My heart is an open wound, one I fear will always bleed and never heal.

I rip my gaze away from Malachi and watch as Hassan guides Kai toward Savi. She quickly pulls him into a crushing embrace like a mother protecting her child from nightmarish horrors. She whispers in his ear, and I watch as fresh tears flow down Kai's face.

They wet his cheeks, slipping into his dark hair. The silky strands have long since unraveled from his bun and now hang limply over his shoulders. His brows are crumpled and beaded with sweat. His eyes are distant, sorrowful pools that shimmer and sway against the firelight. I barely recognize the man I see before me—the man grief has turned him into.

As Kai grips onto Savi like she can liberate him from his pain, I feel yet another tug from the darkness. Malachi's shadows twirl around my wrist, tugging me forward with a gentle touch I don't deserve. I shake my head vigorously—eager to return to numbness and flee the tragedy today has brought—but Malachi is as stubborn as I am. Another shadow slithers around my waist, slipping to my lower back before nudging me toward the pyre. As I stumble forward, multiple pairs of eyes flicker to me. Each and every gaze is like a knife held to my throat. I have no choice now.

My heart pounds as my body leads me places I'd rather not go. One step, then another. My feet stumble. My chest aches. I've reached the pyre much too soon, and as I pray for a vision to take me from this moment, my petition goes unanswered.

I dare not breathe, but I must. The smell assaults me with a brutal truth I couldn't deny even if I hoped to. Riat's body rests amidst the flames, skin giving way to bone. His soul left this world long ago, but I feel the weight of his life as I stare into the fire. I try to think of the good times—of all the jokes he made, of all the shared laughs and mischievous grins. Each and every memory is stripped from my mind as soon as I call it forward, leaving me to latch onto things I'd rather not touch. All I can see is the hot gurgle of blood pouring from his chest. The confusion blown out in his eyes. The tip of the spear that pierced his heart. It's the dying gasp I hear next, the one that slipped from his lips so quietly I almost missed it.

Nausea torments me, and I barely keep it at bay. I force strained breaths in through my mouth, though easing the smell leads me to other horrors. I can taste the char of soot on my tongue. Acidic. *Foul.* The fire taunts me. *Sizzles* and *pops* haunt my ears, echoing deep inside my mind. The sight of flesh peeling from Riat's skull threatens to buckle my knees, and it does. As I waver and sway, a firm pressure on the back of my legs keeps me upright. I don't turn to see the shadows. For if I turned from the pyre now, I know I would never return, and Riat deserves better than my cowardice.

It hits me then—everything I hoped not to feel. Grief. Regret. *Guilt.* My hand clutches my chest, but the pressure does nothing to ease these burdens. Like my mind wishes to torment me more, I ask myself questions that will never be answered.

What if I had offered myself in exchange for everyone's safety?

What if I had looked down and seen that it wasn't Riat who prodded my boot?

What if I had killed that Turiden when I had the chance?

Though none of these answers will drag Riat back from the underworld, I berate myself with them endlessly. It is my punishment—my senseless penance. I stare ahead, letting the pyre's heat dry out my eyes to the point of pain. The fire is the only constant, a reminder that there is no changing the gods' plans.

I raise a shaky hand and—with a fluid motion that allows no hesitation—drag one of my daggers across my palm. I watch the blood bead and trickle over my skin before offering it to the flames. A violent *sizzle* fills the night air, until finally, stillness returns. I stand there, motionless, for what feels like ages. The fire is warm against my skin, casting away all chill. It seems almost foreign—the calm settling into the air—but, then I remember its cause. Though the threats of this day have passed, the days that follow will only bring more. I'm certain of it, for the gods love their misery.

I back away from the pyre slowly, not daring to take my eyes off the body of the young man who rests within its inferno. Every *pop* of heat and curl of smoke is like a venomous whisper in my ear, and it repeats the same thing over and over.

He's dead because of you.

For a moment, all I can do is stare into the fire and wish it would consume me, too. But that would be too easy, and I deserve far worse.

When I retreat from the pyre, Tariq takes my place. I watch him toss something into the flames—some small piece of carved wood that looks like a pehmi. The sight of the cunning, yippy little creature shatters my heart more violently than it already has, reminding me just who we've lost. Tariq mutters soft-spoken words, peering into the fire like Riat is there listening. I can only hope he's far from this place, basking in a paradise I don't even know if I believe in.

As I watch tears slide down Tariq's face in slow streams, that incessant voice in my head grows louder. Stronger.

He's dead because of you.

I swallow thickly and squeeze my eyes shut, but the voice doesn't fade.

He's dead because of you. Who of them will be next?

A shuddering breath tears into my lungs as I reel back. My legs don't stop, seeking to take me further and further away from these horrors. This truth. Eyes follow me as I stumble against the sand, but no one stops me. It's only when Hassan's gaze meets mine that I start running. Those hazel eyes, broken and angry, are all I can think of as I sprint across the sand.

Every step haunts me. Though we're an hour from where we left the Turidens face down in the sand, the desert seems to swell like a sea of blood. I know it's only a trick of the fading firelight, but my heart lurches all the same. It beats too quickly as I stumble into camp. I can still glimpse the pyre burning bright against the night, though it's far enough away that I can no longer taste death on my tongue. If only memories of such a thing would leave me be.

With every forward step I take, grief accumulates in my chest—growing heavy like piling grains of sand. It weighs me down. Steals my breath. I wonder if this pain will simply stop my heart from beating. It feels like it could, though I know it's a foolish thought. That would be too kind.

Moonlight illuminates my path as I step around tents in search of my own. Night has fallen heavily over the desert, and it won't be long before the others leave their watchful place before the pyre. There will be no dinner tonight. Riat's body will find no nourishment on its journey to the underworld, so neither will ours. Much too soon, everyone will be slinking off to their tents for what I know will be a fitful night's rest, and I need to be long gone by then.

Finally slipping into my tent, I pull in a deep breath. It wavers, shuddering in my chest like a scared creature. I'm forced to grip a handful of canvas to steady myself, and even then my knees give out. Slumped against a pile of blankets, I squeeze my eyes shut and push away the doubt that gnaws at my resolve. I've had plenty of time to think this through—have done nothing but contemplate my future in the hours since Riat's last breath. My decision has been made. This is what must be done. Not for my sake, but for everyone else's.

I move quickly. With rushed hands, I dig through my pack and quickly find what I'm looking for. I strip myself of every bloodied piece of cloth that clings to my body and chuck it into a heap; I would burn it all if I had the time. My leathers stay on, too precious to part ways with even though blood coats the scales. I tug on a fresh tunic, then fumble for my blades. I sheathe every one I have before draping my body in layers of fabric. When I wrap the last scarf over my head, tucking the tail around my neck, not even a sliver of skin is showing—nothing but my eyes.

My boots bump into cushions and trip over mounds of sand as I dart back and forth across the tent. I snatch up anything that may be of use, knowing Mikel will already hate me for this.

What's a few stolen supplies?

Hands brimming with pilfered items, I take a quick inventory as my heart hammers wildly and ricochets through my ears. A small canvas tarp. Two tinctures of Mikel's salve. A roll of linen to wrap wounds. I dig around the contents of my pack, making sure everything is accounted for. My map. What's left of my coin. A small amount of food—*I'll have to hunt along the way.* Clothes. Three full canteens. My bedroll is the last thing I need, and I quickly roll it up before strapping it to the bottom of my pack. With everything sorted, I allow myself a full breath. As I find a moment's stillness, I run through the plan one last time.

Hassan and Tariq volunteered to watch the pyre all night; they'll stay out there until the flames burn down to nothing but smoking embers. I'm relying on the others to be too distracted to notice my absence. There's no reason they should think to check on me. Even Malachi—as observant as he is—will be too busy with Quin to think anything amiss.

I grit my teeth as I fling the heavy pack over my shoulder. There's only one person who would notice the empty patch of sand where my bed used to be. My heart beats nervously as I stare at his side of the tent. Mikel is bunking with Kai tonight—

something I insisted on. Luckily, Mikel agreed. Kai can't handle coming back to an empty tent tonight; we both know that. And though it was for my own benefit, I feel no guilt about my deception. At least, that's what I'll be telling myself once I leave this place.

I swallow nervously and steady myself with another deep breath. He's better off without me. They all are.

When the tent's entrance flutters open, my heart drops.

Hassan steps inside and freezes. He takes one look at my pack before his gaze snaps up to my face. Everything I witnessed beside the pyre—his quiet pain, the strength he maintained for the others—it all disappears in a breath.

"What is this?" he seethes.

My eyes flicker to the tent flap behind him, but he quickly steps in closer to block my path.

"*Witch*," he snarls. "What do you think you're doing?"

I swallow thickly, trying to weave a lie onto my tongue, but I know it's pointless. He knows exactly what's going on. "What needs to be done," I offer darkly.

As I move to push past him, he snags my arm.

"And what's that?" he prods. "Running?" Those hazel eyes flare wide, and his grip on me tightens. "I didn't take you for a coward."

I stagger backward as I rip myself free of his touch. "I'm not a coward," I snap. My chest constricts, and I yank the scarves away from my face to find a full breath. "If I was a coward, I would stay here under your protection and pretend everything is fine. I would put my life above all else and be damned to care what happens to the lot of you." I step up to him, and the words pour out in a snarl. "I. Am. *Not*. A. Coward."

He takes a step closer, gaze tightening on me. "You're running away from this because you're afraid," he utters through gritted teeth. "You're making the same mistake you did last time."

My hands shove him roughly before I curl my fingers into his tunic. "This is *nothing* like last time," I stress. My fingers ache from how hard I'm gripping him. "I ran because I thought staying would be the death of me. I ran because I had to."

"And now?" Hassan prods, pressing forward until there's no space between us. His hands cover my own, pining them against his chest. "What's your excuse now?"

I open my mouth to speak, but the words get trapped somewhere along the way. Hassan stares down at me mercilessly—golden eyes flaring like stars. His hands tremble over mine. We're much too close, so close that I can feel the wild thump of his heartbeat beneath my fingertips.

"You're running because it hurts," he states. His jaw ripples with tension before he swallows whatever anger he harbors. "I *know*," he fumes. "I know exactly why you're doing this. So don't pretend. Your lies are wasted on me. They always will be."

My fingers curl into the collar of his tunic, nails scratching skin without remorse. "And what do you think you know?" I sneer.

Though I expect him to, he doesn't return my withering contempt. He merely takes in a heavy breath as he pulls his hands away from mine. "You blame yourself, just as we all do."

I flinch as he gently cups my face. I want to yell—want to shove him away—but something about the way he's looking at me stills my mind. I'm trapped in the orbit of his eyes, lost to the care I see reflected in those hazel hues. All fight leaves me like a dying breath, making me weary. The surrender I find with him scares me more than any foe I've yet to face.

"You think running will rid you of that burden. *It won't*," he rasps. His thumb glides across my skin, and my eyes—now flooding with tears—flutter against the caring touch. "It will only allow it to find its home in you. Trailing you like a shadow for all the days that follow."

His words hit me like a whipping wind, and I sway where I stand. My head falls against Hassan's chest as I let tears slip from beneath closed lids. I clutch his tunic with quivering hands, tugging him toward me for once not in anger, but with need. As the heat of his body presses into me—shields me from the cold breeze that trails into the tent—strangled sobs shake my chest.

"It's my fault," I utter hoarsely, voice lost in a crack of emotion. "He's dead because of me."

"*Shh, shh, shh.*" Hassan tugs my face up gently until our eyes meet. "Riat's death is not a stain on your hands."

As I search his face for any sign of doubt, silent tears stream down my cheeks. "It *is*," I urge. I close my eyes again, shaking my head. "That Turiden. He was my man. I almost had him. If I'd only given in to my gift. If I'd been able to control it, then he wouldn't have— Riat would've..."

The breath quakes in my lungs, snuffing any excuse I hoped to offer. Hassan's fingers drift to the nape of my neck, snaking into my hair with firm care before pulling my focus to him once more.

"It's not your fault." His eyes plead with me, and his fingers knead gently against my scalp. "Whatever happened. Whatever you think you could have done. This is not your burden to bear."

I open my mouth to offer a rebuttal, but he cuts me off.

"You are not the violence you hope to find in the mirror," Hassan asserts. "You are not a blight. Or a curse. Or whatever else this world has convinced you of."

I scoff as I wipe the tears from my face. "And what am I then, if not all those things?"

Hassan's fingers slip from my hair, only to find their place along my jaw. "A witch. A treacherous, conniving woman. A reckless fool. And a devious taunt." My breath hitches as his thumb slides across my mouth, tugging at my bottom lip. "Someone I hope to never stop figuring out."

His eyes lower to my lips, and I watch his gaze fill with heat.

"*Hassan*," I warn. But even then, my body melts into his, called like a desert flower to the comforting rays of the sun.

A thoughtful hum rumbles through his chest before a smirk curls against his mouth. "Yes, Ren?"

My name sounds like a wicked prayer on his lips, a plea to the gods for things that are only for nights as dark as this. I swallow thickly, body all but trembling as he leans in close. His thumb once more tugs at my bottom lip. My breath stutters, and those hazel eyes flicker dangerously as if mesmerized by the way my mouth moves. When that all-consuming gaze drifts higher, my heart leaps in my chest.

"We've waited long enough," he utters. "Don't you think?"

At first, his lips press against mine softly, like he's giving me time to catch up. My eyes flutter closed, and I lose myself to the way his fingers grip my jaw, holding me to him. He's tender—patient in a way that feels wholly *him*—but all too soon, his touch turns hungry.

Hassan kisses me with a force that has me clinging to him. My fingers dig into his tunic, desperate to end all separation between us. He sucks on my bottom lip, teasing it with his teeth and drawing a whimper from my lips that would have me blushing in embarrassment if only I cared. But I don't. My breath is a thrashing mess, and my heart does its best to keep up. Hassan's hands trail down my body with fevered reverence, his touch worshiping me as if I'm worth more than the godsblood in my veins and the death it promises.

I moan as his mouth drops to my neck. Hassan drags his lips across my skin like I'm a meal that might be ripped from his hands at any moment. My hands tug at his tunic, sliding under the fabric to grant me access to the hardened muscles beneath. His skin is warm and flushed under my fingers, and he growls into my ear as I drag my nails down his chest. It's not enough. I need more.

As if hearing my silent plea, rough fingers begin to fumble with my leathers. My hips buck into Hassan's hands, urging him onward. I press a distracting kiss along his jaw. Then another. Muttered curses spill from his lips as he struggles with the lacing of my pants, and just as I lean my head back to loose a breathy laugh at his impatience, voices outside turn my blood cold.

It's Mikel I hear first, then a wounded voice that shudders in its wavering pitch. I wish I didn't recognize its sorrow, but it's all but embedded in my soul now. Kai's muffled cries are an omen, reminding me of what has already passed, and what is inevitably to come. Hassan is still fumbling with my leathers when the voices drift away, but the ghosts of their suffering remain too thick in the air for me to not choke. Just as Hassan unknots my leathers and begins weaving his fingers through the tight lacing, I shove him away.

"*Stop*," I pant.

His brow furrows deeply, eyes still blown wide with desire as his chest heaves. "What's wron—"

"How can we—" I falter. "What are we—"

Guilt spikes panic in my heart, eating every last bit of my breath. Tears flood my eyes once more, but the touch of them against my cheek only strikes rage in me now.

I don't get to feel this ache.

Not when I've caused it for so many others.

Anger swallows anything good I'd momentarily let myself feel—burns through every wanting thought and desperate touch I'd gladly offered the man before me. Riat rests amidst a mass of devouring flames, hole through his chest, and I thought I could simply forget. How foolish of me.

"Ren—"

As Hassan begins to take a step closer, I lurch away.

"*Don't,*" I spit. "Don't try to coax me back to whatever that was."

He glares at me, determination heavy in his eyes. "And what do you think *that* was?" he huffs. "A mistake?"

"A trick," I snarl. "A way to make me forget all I've done. All it is that I am."

Hassan looses a laugh that's anything but friendly as he runs a hand through his hair. "*Gods,*" he mutters. "You just can't admit it, can you? Can't let yourself believe that this thing between us could actually exist. Too scared to see if it does."

"I'm not scared," I argue. "What could I possibly be scared of? A kiss? *You?*" I huff, though my voice wavers in strength. "Don't try to dream up notions of fate just as your cousin does. My path was never meant for us both. The gods carved it in blood and death, and I won't let you be fool enough to walk it willingly."

Hassan's hands clench at his sides. "Do you hear yourself? Condemning fate while rambling on about the curse of yours? You think the gods hate you so, but I find no proof of it when I look at you. I see just how you care for others, how you sacrifice yourself for their benefit time and time again."

"Riat is dead!" I snap. "Dead because of me. Do not forget that!"

Hassan's eyes blaze. "His death is not your—"

"Tell me, how many of your men are you willing to risk? How many deaths will I collect while you keep me around? Waiting to fuck me just to sate your curiosity. Who will you let me take from you next? Kai? *Savi?*"

He snarls, closing the distance between us with angry footfalls. "And what else will you sacrifice in your determination to suffer in this life? Your friends? Your happiness?"

"Don't you understand? I don't deserve happiness!" I shout.

Shadows whip out from me in the blink of an eye, thrashing around the tent like a storm only the dark god could conjure. The darkness culls my rage, churning it into panic. It's with fast hands that I draw my blade and slice it through my palm, crisscrossing the cut I'd already offered in Riat's name. The biting pain twinges, and—as quick as they came—my shadows slip into nothing. I expect to find rage, maybe fear, when I meet Hassan's gaze, but what I see hurts more than anything.

He stands deathly still, no part of him cowering from the darkness I just raised. Hassan watches me with worry in his eyes—like it's concern for my safety that traps him in bated breath. It's compassion, and pain, and a silent petition that fills his gaze, making me waver under its scrutiny. In front of me, I see Hassan for who he's always been: a man who would do anything to keep his people safe. I don't know when that started including me.

"The gods took my happiness from me long ago," I utter softly. "And they rip away whatever I hope to claim with eager hands." I grab my pack from where I dropped it in desire's haste and swallow roughly as I look up at him.

"I'm sorry for Riat and everything I've lead your way since our paths crossed." I bite back the wobbling pitch in my voice, pushing it down into the depths of me. It's numbness I call forth, a chasm within where all unwanted things get buried.

I brush against Hassan's shoulder as I pass, but linger for a breath that nearly shatters my resolve. He tenses next to me, hands twitching at his sides. Part of me yearns for his comforting touch, if only to pretend I deserve it.

I'm unable to look at him as I utter my final words. "Don't follow me. Else the gods spill your blood next."

I push past him before he can stop me, disappearing into the night's suffocating darkness—right where I belong.

CHAPTER 33

My hands ache against the reins as I slow Mirage's pace to a steady walk. We've been riding for days, sprinting southwest across the gods-drenched north with no rest other than a handful of moments every few hours. Any more is a risk I cannot take. Though I'm hopeful Hassan will heed my warning and ignore the trail of hoof prints I'm leaving behind, I'm not fool enough to think Mikel will keep his distance. My friend is no doubt tearing across this desert to find me, and I need to be deep into the mountains before he does.

Mirage huffs beneath me, hot breath chuffing out from overworked lungs. I pat her flank, comforted by the whinny she looses when I scratch my nails against her coat. It almost feels like that time we escaped Denheir—back when fate first intervened. But much has changed since then; I'm reminded of that each time my blood stirs panic in Mirage's eyes.

It's a miracle there have been no incidents during our endless days of travel. When I first strapped my pack to her saddle, I was sure she'd rebel against the thrum of this curse inside me—just as she'd done for weeks. But it was a risk I had to take, and luckily one that panned out in my favor. She's tolerated me thus far, and I can only hope the gods will continue to pity me by bestowing such fortune.

The rising sun is a warm embrace, chasing away the night's chill. I drop the reins from my tired grip and stretch out the cramps from where I've clung too tightly. My right hand is bound with a swathe of fabric, much too snug and tinged with blood. Even the slightest glance reminds me of the crisscrossed cuts beneath the gauze, and I want nothing of the memories of days past. As my eyes scour the land in front of me, I'm met with an uneasy feeling in my gut. Everything looks the same out here, and if not for the silhouette of the Kohe Mountains on the horizon, I fear I'd be going in circles. The last thing I need is to end up returned to the others.

A deep sigh spills from my lungs as I stretch my arms overhead, loosening any kinks that formed while hunkered down against Mirage's sprinting gait. The noise is the first that's left my lips for hours, and it sounds weathered and weary to my ears. I wish fatigue was all I felt.

My scarf came unraveled somewhere amidst the journey, and now my cheeks feel raw and wind-burned. Just touching the tender skin makes me wince. It's with relief that I pull the fabric away, welcoming in fresh air and releasing the trapped heat from my scalp. I've never enjoyed concealing myself in layers of fabrics, and I all but groan at the freedom allowed. This moment feels almost peaceful with the way the sun heats my skin with tender warmth. There's no one out here for miles, so I'll take this comfort while I can.

Another look at the horizon has me grumbling. So much sand. So much further to go. Aside from the mountains looming ahead, my map is the only thing guiding this foolish journey. I yank it from my pack and drag my fingers across the worn parchment like I have so many times over the past few days. I have no idea how far north I truly am—can only pick a point on the map and hope for the best. Though, soon enough, it won't matter much. As long as I keep heading west, I'll reach the mountains eventually. From there, there'll be nothing left to do but climb.

I squint my eyes, trying to decipher anything amidst the map's dense illustrations and faded smudges of ink. There's no path up the mountains—at least, none that I can see. From the looks of it, it's nothing but dense trees until you reach the ridgeline. Good for me, I guess. It'll be easy to lose any tail I've picked up. Hard for someone to track me if they're lost themselves.

Mirage huffs loudly, pulling my focus.

"I know, girl." I pat the side of her neck and earn another huff. "Just a little longer."

I've run her all but ragged, desperate to leave camp behind us. And as much as I don't want to risk anyone catching up, we can't keep going on like this. Mirage needs rest, and so do I.

I massage my fingers into my temple, but it does nothing to temper the ache that's taken root there. Pain is second nature, embedding itself so deep within me that I can't imagine its departure. Squeezing my eyes shut, I loose a shuddering breath and force myself to acknowledge a torment I've been steadily ignoring. There's a violent, splitting ache in my head and an unsettling flicker in my veins. I can feel my blood thrumming with impatience. It's frustrated. My shadows have been locked up for days, leashed behind walls so thick I feel them like steel under my skin. I can't risk spooking Mirage, and—more than that—I'm not ready to face that darkness again. Not after it failed me so greatly.

Looking back at the map, I clench my teeth and pretend the pain isn't there. I have bigger problems—at least, for now. The Kohe is depicted as nothing but a dark blur—an expansive, tree-riddled obstacle that consumes the Continent's western edge. Not many venture there, and those that do don't take the journey lightly. There's no telling what I'll encounter amidst those trees, though I'm certain it won't be anything good.

I use my fingernail to measure the distance I'll have to hike. *Three days? Five?* Again, it's nothing but a guess. My thumb drags past rows of trees marked in ink until it inevitably lands on the one place I must go.

Tol Dena.

A shudder runs along my spine at the thought of that hell deep within Kohe's ominous peaks. It's nothing but a rocky grave buried beneath it all. I've heard stories—more nightmarish tales than facts, but those will have to do. That place is said to be carved from the mountains themselves. A great dwelling in the rock. A tomb for the Continent's most damned. It's rumored to hold over two hundred men and women inside its cavernous pit. Each cell is a dank cave—a hole in the earth. And, if the stories are true, there's only one way in and one way out.

A nervous twinge fills my stomach at the thought.

Mirage whinnies and looks back at me with restless eyes. I toss a glance over my shoulder, a nervous habit I've had for days on end. No shapes blur against the lightening horizon. I spot no horses saddled with riders, no camels laden with supplies. No one is coming for me—*yet.* I might as well take advantage.

I relent and tug on the reins. Mirage stops in record time, and once I slip down from the saddle, I see just how tired she is. She drops her head and lets out a deep chuff. I wish it didn't stoke my guilt, but it does.

I make quick work of getting her watered. From my saddle, I untie one of two large, leather bladders. This one is still full to the brim, though I'll need to find a well soon enough to replenish the other. As I lower it to the sand, the muscles in my arms strain and quiver. The weight is a test of my strength, and I struggle to keep the vessel firmly in my grasp. It would be too great a loss to spill its precious contents, so I take my time.

With a hearty *thud*, I manage to set it on the ground. Mirage perks up as I tug on its thick cord. She nudges me with her fuzzy nose, over and over again. A laugh slips from my lips at her insistence. She huffs right in my face before nudging me some more. As soon as I offer the open vessel to her, she stops badgering me.

I watch her carefully, making sure my horse doesn't drink too much too fast. The more water she guzzles, the more my hands twitch with worry. Though the other bladder still has a little left, I fear the journey ahead will not prove as kind as one across the Jahaer would. Out there, wells are as constant and true as the sun. There was a time before the Rebellion when the Jahaer Desert was brimming with flourishing outposts, and water was a resource well cultivated. Though the remnants of those places have long since been lost to time, the wells remain. But here in the gods-drenched north, there are no such luxuries.

Mirage gives me a whinny and an irritated nuzzle as I drag the water vessel away. It's significantly lighter now, but I still have to flex and strain to hoist it back up the saddle. Once that feat is over, I grab my pack and slump down to the sand.

Every muscle in my body aches from lack of use, and while I know I should be using this time to stretch my legs, I can't find the strength to get up. The growing heat makes me complacent, lulling me toward a sleep I can't allow myself to take. So instead, I tilt my head back and stare up at the sky. Pale, milky blue is all I can see, flecked with bursts of golden yellow that make my eyes water if I stare for too long. The sunbeams warm my face, and, though the day has just begun, I can already feel sweat beading down my back.

Another might find this morning peaceful, but it's too quiet. I've been plagued by this same silence for days, and it holds more horrors than one could imagine. There's nothing to distract me but the *shhh* of sand and the whip of wind. Though, even that does nothing to keep my thoughts at bay. Too often I've found my mind wandering places I beg it not to go. It's worst in moments like this—when everything slows, then stills to a hesitant interlude. It feels like the gods are holding their breath, waiting for the perfect time to resume their wretchedness.

I didn't realize how much it helped to be around others until I faced this stillness alone. There are no voices chattering in the background of my thoughts. No barking laughs and playful yells to pull my focus. There is only the thrum of my restless blood and the nightmarish prod of memories. And though I wish for nothing else, there is no escaping those recollections. They play on repeat, rehashing the worst of what I've left behind.

The ragged shudder of his breath.

Riat's name yelled across oceans of sand.

Those hissing flames that ate skin and chewed bone.

My throat grows drier than the air around me, and I struggle to swallow the emotions that wobble across parched lips. The shudder of my breath makes me clench my teeth. The time for tears has passed, only strength will take me where I need to go.

I choke back the frustrated yell that wishes to break free and turn my attention to my pack.

The canteen is dangerously light when I snatch it with greedy hands, and its weightlessness sends a nervous ripple through my stomach. The warm water tastes heavenly though, and while I could drain the entire thing, I pull the canteen away sooner than I'd like. I give it an appraising shake before I stuff it back into my pack, and the soft swish of liquid feels like a taunt from the gods. Grumbling curses, I quickly distract myself with things that feel less unsettling than my dwindling water supply.

I count my blades, just as I've done each day since I left the others. *Seven.* I've managed to keep every blade I obtained in Hira, and though the notion should warm my heart with pride, I can only worry if it'll be enough for what's to come. My gift flickers in my veins, reminding me that not all weapons rest among sheathes. I banish the less-than-gentle reminder swiftly, biting my nails into skin until the godsblood in me settles.

Too aggressively, I pull an apple from my pack and rip it apart between my palms. It splits with a satisfying *snap*, dripping juices down my fingers. Before I can even offer her a piece, Mirage is nudging my shoulder like a needy child. As soon as I place her half into my open palm, she sucks it up with the funny pucker of her lips. I snort, shaking my head as I munch on my own. The fruit is gone much too quickly, and my stomach rumbles in complaint.

I settle deeper against the sand, once more allowing my focus to drift to things best left untouched. Mirage's chomping all but fades into the background as the Kohe looms before me like a threat.

Gods, what have I gotten myself into?

Knees pulled high, I drop my head into my lap. After all this time, I'm finally alone, but the freedom I've craved since Olen dragged me out of the desert feels bittersweet now. No one guides my hand. No one steers my fate. I can go anywhere I want—but, somehow, I find myself heading for a dead end. A place to be trapped. A place where this all ends.

Am I ready for it to end?

My fingers press into my temple as I try to get my thoughts straight. I'm so tired, so very tired. My soul feels like it's been wrung dry and left limp. I wish for nothing more than to rest here until my bones turn to dust, but the gods aren't done with me yet, and I have things to do.

I raise my gaze, looking beyond heavy lashes to find the dark blur of faraway mountains. Somewhere within the Kohe's dark tangle lies the beginning of the end.

Tol Dena.

Once more, the name echoes through my head like a death toll. As much as the very thought of that place makes my skin crawl, I have no choice but to go there. Vish was certain the only person who knows the Hesha Mol's location resides within those walls, and gods do I need that dagger. That cursed thing is the key to ending this all—to making sure no one else is caught in this deadly web of fate. Without the Hesha Mol, there can be no Born. And without the Born, maybe some of the suffering that's been woven into so many of my visions can end. But, deep down, I know that cutting the prophecy off at its knees isn't enough. Once I've destroyed the Hesha Mol, there's still one last threat to smother.

My stomach clenches, some instinctive part of me rejecting the future I've all but carved in stone. For days I've ignored the weight of this decision—pushed my thoughts far from those steeped in darkness. But neglect will bring no hope. I can no longer ignore the way Veles's gift rages through my veins, nor the blinding pain that acts as punishment for its captivity. And even though my heart quickens at the thought—though it stutters with fear—there is no changing course now. I've seen too much of what the future holds, and every act is carried out by the deathly touch of my hands.

The blood of the Durit must spill, and I will be the one to drain every drop.

My breath stills in my chest like death has already claimed me. I wonder what it will be like. *Will the gods grant me peace in the afterlife? Or is it a rotting, mindless pit that awaits me for eternity?*

I shake my head, pushing away thoughts of that inevitable abyss and instead think of what I'll leave behind. My heart grows tight, painfully so. I swallow quickly before the withered thing can creep up my throat. I've endured so much more in this life than I ever expected to, but still, that time feels minuscule weighed before me now.

Those distant years growing up in Merket. The excitement and danger that befell me in Artolen. Roaming across the Jahaer. Never letting my guard down. Never staying long enough to feel anything but the past nipping at my heels, desperate to draw blood. Always running. And then...

Everything changed.

Denheir. Back into the desert. Off to Letka.

So much has happened in the past month; it feels like a deck of cards spread between unsteady hands. I can't tell how many I hold, can only feel them slipping.

And what else will life grant me in what little time I have left?

I can only stare at the path ahead like the answers are painted in its blank expanse. Death. Destruction. I've seen it all play out behind my eyes—been given too many visions of it to be convinced of anything else. My path was always stained with blood; it's about time I accepted it.

Though I don't want to, I think of the others. *What are they doing now—I wonder—now that I've left them behind?* Hazel eyes flash in my mind, though I'm quick to shake them away. Every memory of what happened in my tent days ago threatens to unravel my resolve. It would only take a moment of weakness to sway me off this path—to sow doubt in my already wayward mind. And that just won't do. However, I do let myself ponder other things, like who Hassan told first.

Was it Mikel? Or did the hunter keep my departure to himself, only deigning to mention it when the others noticed my absence? Did they even care that I was gone?

My heart lurches at the thought. I guess it doesn't matter; but still, something aches in my chest at the reminder that I'll never again wander out of my tent to see them lazing around the campfire. The finality of my decision hits me then. There will be no goodbyes. No final moments. No chance to say I'm sorry.

But would an apology even be enough?

Riat's face plagues me, a taunt that comforts me as much as it guts me clean. *No.* No, it would not. For as much as this guilt seeks to bury me—aims to trap me under its endless weight—I know it will never be penance enough.

The rising sun bakes me where I lounge against my pack. My body feels like a husk, left to dry and wither amidst this cruel, nameless desert. I haven't had true rest in days—stolen nothing more than a few moments atop the saddle despite my best intentions. My eyes flutter closed before I can stop them.

I shudder, then twitch.

A gasp tears into my lungs as I rip awake. My skin throbs—flushed and much too warm. I draw my dagger, clenching it in tight knuckles as panic swallows all sanity. Everything aches, and my mouth feels like it's full of sand. I blink the haze from my eyes, though sleep isn't so quick to leave. I float in that nothing space for much too long, mind swimming in the dreamy way that promises no sense or verity. It's only when Mirage nudges me with her muzzle that I release the breath from my lungs and loosen the grip on my blade.

With a grunt, I let the desert come back into focus through the prickly blink of my eyes. The sun is a harsh glare above me, baking every inch of exposed flesh. It's only when I drag a hand across my cheek and feel the imprint of gritty sand, that awareness hits like a slap.

I fell asleep.

"Fuck!" I shout, jumping to my feet.

As I brush the sand from my leathers, panic takes root once more. I sheathe my blade, retie my pack to the saddle, and make sure to count my stashed weapons before hoisting myself onto Mirage. She huffs with irritation, but there's no time to temper her mood. One quick look at the sun above reveals how fucked I truly am. It's already midday. I've lost hours to sleep. The apprehension that floods my stomach has me quickly checking the horizon.

My eyes flicker across every inch of desert in search of the consequence of my own carelessness.

Who will it be that comes for me?

Mikel? Another band of Turidens?

Maybe the gods will see fit to send a horde of beasts after my inattentive, moronic ass.

My face pales when I see the one thing I should have expected, but didn't.

Shit.

If I wasn't already saddled, fear would have brought me to my knees. As I stare at the horizon, my chest grows so tight I can't catch a breath.

"*Hael save me,*" I whisper.

With a burst of adrenaline flooding my veins, I drive my boot into Mirage's side. She whinnies and rears back before racing across the desert. The wind slaps my face and tugs at the scarves hanging loosely from my neck. There's no time to fix them back into place; I need to run. My hands tremble as I snap the reins and urge Mirage faster.

It doesn't feel fast enough, *but would anything be?*

Dread snakes up my throat. I risk a glance back, and the sight that greets me churns my stomach with a vicious swell. Miles behind me, too close for comfort, is a wall of sand. It billows and bulges like angry clouds called forth by the gods. Its haze of grit blocks out the sky, barreling toward me like an impenetrable wall. The sandstorm floods the horizon with a force that threatens to swallow the day whole. And it's headed this way.

My thighs flex with tension as I hug myself to Mirage's flank and prod her forward. All I can hear as we sprint across the desert is the pounding of hooves and the nervous thump of my own heart. But all too soon, the distant roar of sand finds me.

I yell for the gods to pardon me, fear manifesting in the crack of my voice and the wind-whipped tears that streak across my face. My knuckles turn white as I grip the reins. I prepare to nudge Mirage again—urge her to go faster—until I realize there's no faster pace to meet. She huffs underneath me, lungs heavy and thick muscles straining as she carries us across uneven terrain. Fear clenches my heart as I look back and confirm what I already know.

We're not going to make it.

I swear under my breath and scan the desert ahead. There's nowhere to hide. Nothing but sand and—

Hope lurches in my chest as I spot the faint bulge of rocks. I tug the reins quickly and Mirage breaks left. My eyes burn against the sting of swirling grit as we change course. We're cutting closer to the storm—a fool's choice if there ever was one. But it's our only hope.

The roar is getting louder now. I don't dare look back, for my only chance at a future lies straight ahead. Before me, the desert gives way like an answered prayer from Hael. My eyes lock on the large outcropping of hoodoos, their forms huddled together like a flurry of arms punching the sky. Against the swirling grit that scratches my eyes, I search for shelter within those faraway, rocky crevices. I cough and sputter as sand slips down my throat, but I don't relent. My thighs clench against the saddle, and I kick my heels against Mirage to propel us faster.

The erratic patter of my heart stills as I spot it. A nook, no bigger than Mirage herself, rests in between the strange rock formations. I home in on it like a hunted animal running back to its burrow. It's a beacon of salvation—a blessing from the gods. My left hand drops the reins as I fumble through the contents of my pack. As soon as I tighten my grip around the bundle of canvas, the world lurches.

It's over before I can blink.

Mirage stumbles, crashing to the sand with a mighty splash. I lurch from the saddle and greet the desert face first. Chaos is alive in the whip of wind and the restless churn of sand around me. Mirage's whinny is a shrill burst in my ears, barely cutting through the roar of the storm that'll soon be upon us. She scrambles against the sand as she tries to right herself—panicked legs kicking and flailing. I reel back just as her hoof sails past my face. Heart beating wildly, my eyes search for sense amidst this chaos.

The world comes back much too quickly, and panic has me huffing in a gritty puff of air. I barely manage to roll out of the way as Mirage gets her legs underneath her. Limbs shuddering, she rears against the death that barrels down on us. Her hoof hits the sand beside my head, and she's gone the next moment. I can only watch as she races off, disappearing in a blur, before I finally remember what I was running from in the first place.

My gaze snaps up just in time to see the wall of sand blocking out the sun. The wind howls, barreling across the desert in grating bursts. I blink and cough, but it's too late. It's here. Churning grit leaps out from the storm like devils tugging at chains. It's a great beast, a force of destruction that has come to eat its fill.

Gods help me.

My hands flail against the ground, grasping for the only thing I have left—my only lick of salvation. I tug at the canvas tarp, and it unfurls against the increasing rush of wind. It flaps wildly, snatched by the gale that's eager to rip it from my hands. I grunt, using every ounce of strength I have left to haul it over my shoulders. My fingernails strain against the earth as I dig. All the while, the roar behind me grows, quickening with the thump of my heart.

I dig and dig—burrowing like a beast eager to return to the underworld. My breath is nothing but choked gasps; adrenaline squeezes my lungs too tightly and coats its walls with dust. I clench the tarp with desperate fingers as I nestle down into the sand. Panic seizes my chest, and—like Veles is trapping me in the palm of his hand—the day goes dark.

I steal one last glance at the sandstorm through the canvas's gap before it comes for me.

All is still, until it's not. I bear down, curling underneath the tarp just as I'm swallowed. The wind roars like the gods are screaming, slapping my flimsy shelter against my back. The force rocks me like I'm no more than a pebble, and I grit my teeth as I take on the brunt of the storm that seeks to bury me.

Sand rushes in. I tense and struggle, straining my shoulders to keep the canvas pulled taut. Strained groans spill from my lips as I give this life everything I have left. The storm's muffled roar is now a deafening howl. I can hear every grain of sand, every shriek of the sky as it barrels down on me. The grit tears at my skin and sneaks into my lungs. I cough and hack, desperate for a breath of fresh air, but I'm given no such quarter. My eyelids squeeze shut as I feel the sand reach there, too. I don't dare open my eyes, but I know if I did, there would only be crushing darkness.

It's consuming me. Burying me.

My breath heaves uncontrollably as panic takes root. I'm being entombed—trapped in the very desert that thrums with the likes of my blood. *But where is my gift now?* It's there. Silent. *Waiting.*

But for what? For me to prove how weak I truly am? For me to beg for its forgiveness?

Maybe this is my real punishment—Veles's way of reminding me that my fate rests in the hands of no one but the gods themselves. I open my jaw to scream, only to be met with a mouthful of sand. Choking hacks leave my throat raw and burning. My body shudders and shakes, and I fight every instinct that tells me to dig my way out of this fresh, new hell.

It's better to die in the light, isn't it?

Tears spill from my eyes and drip their awful saltiness over my lips. It's a pitiful thing to die in the dark—alone and left with only your regrets. There's a violent ache in my hands where I'm clenching the tarp, fighting against the storm to keep my illusion of safety. Each increasing press of this desert's weight on my back adds to the knowing ache in my chest—the one that tells me this is finally it. Death has been delivered with swift hands.

I asked for this.

The thought pulls a choked sob from my throat. I dig my teeth into my cheek as the storm rages above.

No, not like this. Never like this.

Not with fear clenching my heart, stoking this pitiful ache inside. Not with so many regrets and nothing to show for it.

I thrash and scream, but there's nowhere to go. The sand pressing down on me only drives my panic further, pushing my exhaustion to its limits. I lose track of time, not knowing if it's been mere seconds or hours. It all feels the same buried in the dark. I drift off, only to come back to the roar of the storm and the heaviness holding me to the earth.

Eventually, everything grows still.

My eyelids flutter open gingerly, cracking against the crust of sand and dried tears. There's nothing but darkness to greet me. Nothing but suffocating silence. I unfurl my clenched hands and stretch them out from under the tarp, but I can't tell where it ends and the sand begins. For a moment, terror overtakes me. I thrash and flail under the weight that pins me, but there's nowhere to go.

My nails claw their way through the sand, desperate to find the surface though I'm unsure which way is up and which is down. Breath tears through my lungs until my body says *enough*.

I still feel it—that feral panic, that overwhelming urge to live—but it's quieter now. Fading. What I feel, now more than ever, is an all-consuming need to rest.

Fear tempers to a dreary lull. Everything feels too heavy. Too still. The darkness calls me into its embrace with the promise of peace. There's a chill snaking through my body, a nipping cold that makes me twitch amidst my tomb. My fingers curl against a handful of sand, feeling a touch of warmth from somewhere far away. It calls me like a memory of things unclaimed.

The rough pad of his thumb against my lips.

The comforting press of his hand on my lower back.

My eyes flutter shut, and I loose a shaky breath.

Hazel eyes find me in the dark, coaxing me toward dreams of a future I know I'll never have. Quiet mornings wrapped in blankets. Stolen kisses in market streets.

As I press my cheek against the sand and offer myself freely to that inevitable abyss so many fear, I realize it's kinder than I thought it would be.

CHAPTER 34

There's a distant tug, and it rips me awake. All at once, I'm returned to this world, but it's just as I'd left it. *Suffocating.*

It closes in around me like a fist, growing tighter every second. The air feels too thin, and dust squeezes my throat at the first intake of breath. I cough and choke, but it gets no easier. The tugging comes back, but this time, I can feel its urgency. Pulling. Yanking. Nails digging into skin.

My wrist strains and flexes under the forceful grip, though I can't see who maneuvers it. I can't see anything. I blink sluggishly, only to find slivers of sunlight where there was once only darkness. Rough, scared fingers tangle around the tendons in my wrist and pull so hard it feels like I may come apart. The sand holds me steady, and I all but scream at the strain. I arch my back and squirm in search of relief, only to realize where I truly am.

Buried. *Entombed.*

Panic pierces my heart. The canvas tarp scratches against my skin as I kick and flail against its blanketed hold. Sand spills under its edges, joining me in my earthen grave. Yet, those faint beams of sunlight hold my focus and urge me toward the sky.

As my mind comes back to me—shaken awake by the promise of a death I thought I'd already met—I realize the only way out is through. I flex my fingers, curling around the unrelenting hand grasping mine. It's then I feel it—the heat in the air. It's like a deep breath forced into waterlogged lungs. A kiss of life on dead lips. It gives me the most dangerous feeling of all. *Hope.*

Before I can reach for more, the tugging resumes. It's rough and hasty. I groan as the sand's unrelenting weight pins me down, fighting that determined pull. I hear heavy, panting breaths and muffled yells. The sun paints warmth across my fingers, and I'm desperate for more. It feels too far away to be real, but gods do I need it to be real.

I stretch my other arm beyond the safety of the tarp, digging out handfuls of sand. Everything shifts around me, and, much too late, I realize my mistake. The pocket of air I'd secured among this hell caves in, and all of a sudden, the sand is moving like water. It ripples and floods the safety of my tarp, consuming me. I choke and gasp, reliving my own burial once more. Though, I know this one will take; the gods don't let you cheat death twice. But suddenly, the crushing weight lessens. The sand grows scarce. My eyes blink rapidly against the increasing light, and only when my other arm breaks through the surface do I understand what it means.

Freedom.

I dig, crawling upward and shedding my tarp's protection like dead skin. Soon enough, I feel hands circling both wrists, and the distant tugging gives way to a merciless pressure that feels like my arms might pop free of their sockets. I gasp and flail, choking on sand and the fresh air I thought I'd never taste again. Muscles burning, I struggle to be free of the death I wasn't ready for, and beg the gods to see another sunrise. For once, they listen.

In a sudden rush, I break through the sand's surface like a child being born. The hands leave me instantly, and panic takes root. I fear I'll slip back under the crushing weight that sought to be my burial. Desperation has me clawing at every gritty grain, digging my way out of that hell. I scramble—lurch forward with every ounce of strength I can muster. Heaving my body like deadweight, I finally drag myself out of death's grip.

For a moment, I'm lost to what it means to live. Every gasping breath. Every shudder of nerves. It's all-consuming and unrelenting. I stifle the urge to vomit, though fading panic settles in my stomach with a sickening ache. Biting back nausea, I heave in heavy breaths that soon turn smothering. I retch up grains of sand, choking against the air I was so desperate for. Finally able to pull in a full breath, I sink to the sand on shaky limbs that have no more use. I'm wrecked. Muscles spent. Adrenaline fried. As I lower my forehead to the ground, silent words tumble from chapped lips.

Thank you. *Thank you.*

The sun's burning rays warm my back as I heave in gaping mouthfuls of air—eyes closed as I revel in the survival the gods have granted me. I'm shaking, still consumed by a terror I thought I'd never be free of. When I finally raise my gaze, daylight sears into my eyes like burning stars. I have to squeeze them shut to be rid of the violent white splotches that pepper my vision. Nausea winds its way back up my throat, but I quickly swallow it down. My body can't suffer anymore agony at present, so I allow it none.

Heartbeat raging in my eardrums, I roll onto my back and stare at the sky I thought I'd never see again. But instead of the cloudless blue, I'm met with a sharp-toothed smile and two mismatched eyes.

"Welcome back to the land of the living."

I reel upright, heavy limbs scrambling through sand. My body screams in protest as I work to find my legs underneath me. Every movement feels forced, every heaving breath a challenge. I thought I'd escaped the horrors that awaited me, but it seems the gods crave my suffering. The fate they've woven here is a testament to their continued cruelty and a singular truth.

Death would have been kinder.

With shaky hands, I rip my daggers from their sheaths.

The man before me cocks his head, amusement flickering in the sheen of his one good eye. "No *thank you?*" He takes a step forward, and I nearly collapse into the sand as I stagger back. "I did save your life after all."

The smile that pulls into the hollows of his face is wide and taunting. He stares me down from under a shadowed brow, stringy black hair falling across his face like a beast risen from infernal depths.

Maybe I did die in that storm.

Roel twirls his wrist in an arrogant flourish, sparking fire in his palm before I can blink. It's deathly hot and violently wild. Though I've found distance between us, the rush of hungry, crackling flames still makes me flinch. My reaction fuels his delight. Roel eats up every bit of panic on my face, stoking it further with each predatory step he takes in my direction.

"You know," he starts, "I was sure I'd lost you."

My hands shake around the daggers I've pulled, so much so that they almost slip.

"Imagine my surprise" —Roel runs a hand over his mouth, sharp nails prodding smiling lips— "when I turned west, absent of all hope I'd track my way through the gods-drenched north, only to find my prize lying in wait."

Fear is the fitful beat of my heart, the sweat coating my skin. My breath is no more than panting gasps, scrapping its way up and down my sand-ravaged throat. As I tighten the grip on my weapons, my knuckles feel like they may split.

"Lucky you," I rasp.

Roel's brows flash in a taunt. "Lucky me."

He raises both hands in another grand gesture, grinning wide as he does so. In an instant, flames burst free, scalding their way across the desert. I'm trapped in a ring of fire, and I realize it much too late. I try to flee, but am quickly halted by the searing heat that licks at my tunic. When I look across the wall of flames, something unwanted and all too familiar slips its way through me.

The heat stokes memory. It flares hot and heavy, choking all moisture from the air until I can't even take a full breath. The flames reach up like vicious tongues—stretching as if they can reach the sky and burn Hael from his throne. An uncanny shiver races up my spine, reminding me this is one of many futures I had hoped to escape. It's just as it was in my vision, though somehow much worse.

Roel stares at me through the flames with sick interest. Predatory. Eager. My gaze darts between his eyes, searching for solace, but I find none. The black decay that fills his left socket makes me shudder. It's much too listless—like a pit of hell that only promises to pull you in deeper. But it's the right eye that has me clenching my blades tighter. It shines with a monstrous glee that promises no quarter, only slow, unyielding pain.

I swallow thickly, eyes darting around the desert in search of salvation. What I find is far from that. Three men linger in the distance, eyes beady and unkind as they watch on with the same amusement alight in Roel's gaze. I search their arms for marks, but find none. All I see are weapons. Blades tucked into holsters. A lone sword resting at a hip. My focus snaps back to Roel as he begins to circle me, and panic spurs my heart to a frantic beat.

"There's nowhere to go, girl." He holds his hands by his sides, and Veles's cursed flames lick the air as he stalks me like the devil he is. "It's just you and me. No place to hide. No Shade to rescue you this time."

My jaw clenches tight as I watch him pace. "I can bleed you myself," I snarl. "I'll make sure to cut deeper this time." My eyes flicker across him in search of the wounds I know are long since healed. "Leave you with a reminder."

"Is that so?" Roel hums thoughtfully. He plays with the fire in his palm, letting it dance across his knuckles as he rolls his wrist. "Tell me, does the great Durit still have to rely on her blades?" His gaze devours mine. "Or are you finally capable of wielding that godsblood inside of you?"

Anger shudders through my chest as I stare him down. I feel it slinking through my veins—that thread of power he dares taunt. It's buzzing. *Fervent.* But it feels heavy—thrashing with that same instability it's harbored for days. Ever since Riat, I've kept that flicker of unruly violence tampered. Locked it down tight, unwilling to fuel it with the anger that's wrapped its way around my heart. That power could have changed everything if only I'd been able to wield it. But now, as I stare at the bastard before me, I wonder if my anger could have use.

I push past the piercing ache in my head and reach for my gift behind walls I've built thick. It thrums and twitches under my skin, slamming against the vein. Uneasy breath huffs through me, and I clench my fingers around the hilts of my blades to curb a familiar pain. I fight to steady myself, then call my gift with every ounce of strength I have left.

It comes slowly, but I feel it—that cool flicker of darkness. It's a chill on my skin as it drifts past my wrist. I can only watch on, mesmerized by how it hovers, then grows stronger. It whips out in a tiny flare as if testing the air. When I raise my gaze to Roel, what I see douses any satisfaction I've found.

His head is cocked to the side, arms crossed over his chest like he's watching a child perform street-magic. "Is that all?"

Rage steals my sense, and my shadows lash without thought. Darkness shoots across the ring of flames, splitting it like the sharpest of blades. I'm overcome with the surge of power that lurches through me, but all too soon it slows—gets stuck like honey in my veins. Before that violent whip of shadow can reach Roel and carve him up like I want it to, its might wanes. Roel's flames burn bright as I stare at the empty space where my gift existed moments before, now gone like fading smoke. Shock gives way to anger. Anger gives way to shame. I quickly try to conjure another, desperate to call that darkness back, but the pain that follows brings me to my knees. I choke and gasp. It's a merciless, splitting ache—worse than ever before. There's a band of immeasurable pressure against my temple, a blinding agony I cannot escape. Nausea churns my stomach and my vision peppers with black. It's a punishment fit for my ignorance.

Roel shakes his head before loosing a deep sigh. "Shame, really. I thought you'd prove more of a challenge this time."

Breath shudders in my lungs as the pain continues to ravage me. My veins feel ready to burst—like Veles himself seeks to claw his way out. A whimper leaves my lips just as I close my eyes, desperate to seek any escape from this torment.

"And to think you have the blood of both brothers swimming through you, yet you can do nothing with it..."

My eyes snap open to find Roel's face through the spitting flames. His shaggy black hair pools around his shoulders like inky muck. The greasy strands stick to his neck and shine against the fire's heat. His markings only seek to taunt me more.

He *tsks*. "It's a wonder you're worth anything."

The Shade's cut scarring his face pulls taut against his lavish grin. Each swathe of black decay makes him out to be the devil he truly is. Suddenly, I can't bear the sight of him—can't stand the thought of his face being the last one I see. Reality clenches my heart with unforgiving hands, squeezing until I feel a fresh bout of adrenaline course through me.

I can't die here, and I won't be taken back to Denheir.

That only leaves one option.

Shaking, I pull myself to my feet. My eyes dart past Roel, sizing up the men I quickly overlooked. If no marks truly rest along their skin, I should be able to take them. I ignore the blinding pain shooting through my head, disregard how my body feels battered and far too weak for such a fight. All I can do is swallow thickly and believe it's possible. I have no other choice. This is the hand the gods have dealt. This is the fate I must face.

As I go to look away, something snags my focus. Horses rest beyond the men, tied to freshly-staked posts. They huff against the heat as their tails swat flies. The sight alone stirs hope, but it's the ghostly white mare amidst those brown stallions that makes my heart beat a little faster. As I watch Mirage stomp against the sand, pulling at the rope confining her, I almost laugh.

Fate, indeed.

Mirage is still here—alive and unharmed—and it feels like a portent. It seems the gods seek to put me on trial one last time, and I daresay they favor me. If I can fight off Roel and his men long enough to get to my horse, I might have a chance. I just might live to see another day.

When my gaze slides back to Roel, his mouth twitches in knowing delight. All around me, the fire flares to new heights, locking me in a prison fit for the underworld. I pay it no mind. My gaze stays on Roel—on the renewed twinkle in his good eye. I know he's enjoying this game we're playing, but I wonder if he knows it's only just beginning.

I widen my stance, twirling the blades in my hands.

Roel laughs. "Don't tell me you think there's a way out of this?" He glances at the horses behind him and hums thoughtfully. When he looks back at me, his wolfish grin pulls high against gaunt cheeks. "Shall we see if you make it?"

My heart patters uneasily as I clench my blades in sweaty hands. Fire rages around me, dancing atop the sand like gleeful devils. Roel watches. He waits. He stands before me: hands relaxed at his sides, hungry grin stretched into place. It's only when the flames behind me flicker and die that I understand what's coming—what I've been too trapped in fear's fog to remember clearly. Roel is a predator, a beast eager to hunt. He takes no pleasure in dealing swift blows. He won't simply command his fire to cut me down. No, that would be much too quick.

I'm left with no other choice but to play his wicked game—to allow him his fill. As Roel takes a step closer, the flames spread for him like a curtain. He grins his vile grin, and his tongue wags against taunting words.

"Run, girl. *Run.*"

So, I run.

CHAPTER 35

The sand sprays behind my boots as I sprint across the desert. I'm running the wrong way, but I need distance to find my footing. My arms pump in tandem with the frantic thrust of my legs. My fingers twitch around the hilt of my daggers. Two blades in my grip. One in my boot. Three sheathed in the harness at my back and tucked under scarves—those will prove the most difficult to draw in a rush. One more resting at my thigh.

Gods, please let it be enough.

My mind spins, weaving plans that only seem more foolish the more I consider them. Breath tears into my lungs. I hear the sound of pounding boots, and it's much too close behind me. Flames lick at my heels, but they're nothing more than a taunt— Roel reminding me he could end this quick if he so chose. My legs almost buckle underneath me as adrenaline collides with the energy my body can't give. I'm in no shape to outrun him, so it's time I stop trying.

I suck in a quick breath before lurching to the left. My legs flex and bend. Muscles scream in overuse, and my hands graze the sand as I pivot on my toes. I'm dashing back toward the horses—and my enemy. With quick reflexes, I chuck a dagger at Roel. Surprise burns his gaze bright, but it's short-lived. He manages to dodge my throw at the last second, sweat beading his brow as he lunges for me as I pass. I shift and lurch from his grasp, and his fingers brush my tunic like claws eager to sink deep. His eyes gleam wide in delight as I slip away; I'm making this fun for him.

I don't waste time with my blade when it falls to the sand with a *thud*, don't glance back to witness Roel's predatory pursuit. I can only push my body harder as manic laughter rips from his lungs. A black dagger sails through the air moments later, missing me by the width of a finger. Panic floods me like a desert hare with only one thought. *Survival.* With the devil nipping at my tail, I find my second wind. Legs weary—yet full of hot, pumping blood—I bolt across the sand. The shifting grains are like tides under my boots, seeking to pull me under. I can't let them. I push harder. *Faster.* My vision is hazy, tunneled on the freedom my ghostly white mare promises. I'm so focused on my escape that I don't notice it at first. Not the hot snap of wind, or the scorching *crackle* that follows. Only when I feel its searing bite do I realize Roel is growing tired of our games.

Fire sizzles against my sleeve, chewing the fabric up until there's nothing left but char. My skin is next. It sears with a vicious heat, destroys my flesh with a god's touch—eternal and unforgiving. A strangled yell tears from my lungs, flooded with agony, but I don't stop running. Stopping now means something worse than death. It means going back to Denheir. It means Rohan wins.

My hand slaps at the flames until they're no more, but the damage is already done. The skin is blistering, every inch violently red and throbbing. I grit my teeth and resign myself to the pain.

Pain means I'm alive.

Pain means I'm still in this fight.

The thought sends a rush of strength through me. I offer Roel a fleeting look over my shoulder before I hurl a blade. It's quick. Efficient, if not a little rushed. I don't wait for my dagger to hit its mark, only trust that it does. Seconds later, a guttural yell proves me right. With great effort, I withdraw two blades from behind my back, knowing the pain I've dealt will only incite Roel further. My boots slap across the sand as I rush forward with everything I've got left. I can only hope it will be enough.

Before me, Mirage is a beacon of hope. Her honey-white mane shines against the setting sun, a touch of heaven amidst this hell. Just a little farther. My heart is beating so heavily I can feel it in my throat. Nausea floods my empty stomach, and exhaustion is the growing weight in my limbs. None of it matters, not when I don't have a choice but to keep going.

Roel's men are ready when I finally reach them—weapons drawn and faces curled into waiting sneers. The sight should unnerve me in my weakened state, but a single thought keeps me sprinting toward my opponents.

They're not allowed to kill me.

I unleash myself upon them before they can mount a strategic attack. The first blade leaves my hands just as I reach for another. It embeds itself into the closest man's chest, and while not a killing blow, it buys me the time I need. The blood is barely pooling from his wound when I begin our dance of death. I lunge, hurling myself at him sideways before wrapping my legs around his waist. I tug at the back of his neck, pulling him off balance.

My weight sends him flying over me, and I roll us through the sand before pinning him. My blade is in his throat before he can think to thrust his own. I feel no guilt as his blood coats my blade.

A choked yell leaves my lips as I'm yanked back by my scarves. I don't have time to glimpse the man who drags me away from the body beneath me; I barely have time to react. My legs flail as he hoists me to my feet like I weigh no more than a bag of grain. Just as I steady my blade to strike, his fist connects with my face. Everything goes black, and I come back to the moment with an unsteady flicker in my eyes.

The man is laughing, gripping me by my clothes like a thieving child. My face aches, pounding worse than the piercing pain that wracks my skull. I feel myself being shoved across the sand, though each step brings the world back to me with savage force. Disorientation wavers, giving way to rage. I stare up at my opponent through one eye—the other quickly growing swollen— and make sure it's death he sees in my gaze. The grin spread across his face is snuffed as soon as he spots my own. He's holding me too close and forgotten my blades. It's a mistake I won't let him forget.

It's with unhinged fury that I tear at him. Blood flows like shuttered rain as I stab, and scream, and thrust—piercing the meaty flesh of his forearm until the pain makes his grip go lax. The dagger is slippery in my grip, though I keep it steady as I drive steel into his sternum. The blade scratches against bone, but I don't pull it free until the last gasping breath leaves my opponent's lips. Though some part of me knows it's wrong, I enjoy the pleasure that shudders through my blood. It feels righteous, but I know its depravity will stain.

I kick the man's body away and remind myself this is far from over. Panting, chest heaving like a wild beast, I turn to face the last of my foes. The final man stares at me like I'm one of Veles's kin, and by the gods that's exactly what I am. Death. Damnation. Even without my shadows, I'll kill anyone who seeks to drag me back to Rohan.

I snarl, clenching two dirtied blades as I let blood drip off me like I've climbed my way out of the deepest hell. My eyes lock onto the man, ignoring everything about him other than where I'll deliver the deathblow. He's no longer a person to me, nothing but an obstacle in my path. By the time I've started running at him, I've forgotten he's not the only enemy lingering amidst these sands.

The man braces himself, but his eyes flash to what lies behind me. I'm too caught up in the hum of my anger and the twitch in my hands to truly clock the gesture for what it is. A fleeting plea. A man asking permission. I advance on him before I can think. Something changes in his eyes as I barrel toward him. Uncertainty shifts to fear, then to anger. He raises his sword just as I meet him, and I know this will be nothing like the others. Something has changed. He's no longer hesitating. He's looking to kill, same as me.

The long blade in his grip slices through the air, just missing my neck as I pitch to the side and roll. I hurl a blade at him, and it lands with a vile *thud* in his calf. He bellows and screams, but the moment only lasts a breath. With the next, he quickly comes at me like pain means nothing. His sword catches the sun as it arches toward me, cutting the air with a violence that promises to spill my blood. I don't give it the chance. I duck and lunge, aiming my blade at the meaty part of his thigh. It'll be the end of him if I succeed.

I don't.

He staggers to avoid my blow, shifting his weight in a way I don't anticipate but should have. His blade comes quicker than I expect it to. I duck under his attack, careening on legs that weren't prepared for the lurching rush. I think I've cleared the blow, think I've avoided the glint of steel, but know I'm wrong when I see it in the corner of my eye. It rushes toward me like a fierce wind; there is no escape. I feel the sword graze my shoulder, feel the blade sink into skin and draw a fresh string of blood. My next move is pure instinct, and though pain sears through me, I don't hesitate. I rip my final blade free of its sheath and let agony fuel my desire to live.

My body slams against the man's as I tackle him to the sand. His breath is hot against my neck. Unforgiving hands claw at my back, free of the sword that's now lost to the sand. I thrust and scream, unleashing all my fury onto this final obstacle. Before we hit the earth, he's screaming, too. A beastly howl rips from his lungs. I can hear the torment in it—the pain. He squirms and thrashes, but I hold him tight, enduring the strain until the inevitable happens. My arms are still wrapped around his body—blades buried deep between his ribs—when he stills.

I collapse onto his chest, breath tearing through my lungs in a way that makes me light-headed. My arms shake as I rip both blades out of his body, releasing him from the embrace that brought him death. I slide off him, tumbling to the sand in a heap. But then I hear it from above the rush of blood in my ears—the voice that ripples chills across my sweat-coated skin. It's a reminder of the mistake I've made. Something I don't doubt I'll pay for with more blood.

One remains.

"The gods must favor me something strong."

I look up to find Roel's mouth curled into a sinister smile.

"I wasn't eager to split the bounty with them" —he gestures toward the lifeless bodies I left in the sand— "and their massacre guarantees I now collect Rohan's payment alone, and in full."

He looms over me, flames dancing across his blackened fingertips. "Because it seems you're all out of fight."

I try to scramble away, but he's right. My body has nothing left to give. He tugs me back by the ankle, rough fingers snatching me in a viper's grip. Adrenaline crashes through me as I rear up like a snared beast—bared teeth and all. My blade slashes through the air, but the shakiness in my arm makes the strike weak and desperate. It's no effort to see it thwarted. Roel slaps the dagger from my grip, sending it spinning through the air. It hits the sand with a damning *thud*, too far away to be of use now. I have only one blade left, but before I can wield it, he's on me.

Roel snatches me by the hair, yanking the strands so viciously that a scream tears from my lips. His other hand grips my arm, digging his talon-like nails into blistering flesh. Another scream rips free, yet it only serves to entice him. I glare as he prods my fire-torched skin further. It's then that I seal my lips, preventing even a whimper from slipping. My suffering will only bring him satisfaction, and he deserves none.

Roel chuckles to himself as he releases my arm and drops me to the sand. Just as I raise my last blade, he stomps his boot on my seared arm. I shriek, fingers spasming as I lose my dagger to the sand. He merely grins.

"So predictable," he chides.

The toe of his boot digs further into my ruined flesh, forcing my teeth into my tongue. I won't scream, won't cry. I steel myself against the rush of pain that blackens the edges of my vision and bear it all. He won't get another sound from me.

Please don't let him get another sound from me.

Tsk. Tsk. Tsk. Roel snaps his tongue against his teeth as he bends down to my level. "Does it hurt, Durit?" he goads. "Are those tears I see in your eyes?"

I quickly blink them away and grit my teeth. "Fuck you," I seethe. My arm thrashes beneath his boot, delicate skin tearing, but he doesn't let up.

"Tell me," Roel coos. "Do you wish I'd left you buried? Wish I'd let the gods take you nice and slow?" He leans down to rest his mouth against the shell of my ear. Wafts of foul breath fill my nose, all but choking me. "I can't promise our travels to Denheir will be nice," he admits. "But I'll make sure every moment is one you remember." He nips my earlobe before loosing a breathy laugh.

I flinch away, cowering like the scared, battered thing I've been reduced to. Roel stands up, stepping on my arm one last time before he relents. The pain is everywhere. I feel it in every heaving breath, in every throb of torched flesh. Black spots pepper my vision, and my body feels too heavy to move. I blink slowly, feeling my swollen eye protest when I try to open it again.

"I don't know what he wants with a worthless thing like you."

I jolt out of pain's haze as Roel once more snatches my hair with rough fingers. My hands shake, curling into fists for a desperate strike when he slaps me across the face.

"Pitiful." He laughs. "Such a waste of your gifts."

Anger shudders through me, sparking one last course of adrenaline. I claw at his arms as he hauls me up, drawing beads of red.

He only grips me harder, yanking strands of hair until my neck aches. "Rohan could spill every drop of your blood, and still, I don't think the gods would grant him any favor."

Pain and fury war inside of me. My veins feel like they could burst, and the splitting ache in my head makes me want to scream. It's too much. *I can't bear this anymore.*

Roel looks me up and down, and his lips twitch into a smirk. Sharp nails dig into my scalp, drawing pricks of blood I'll never see. "Maybe I'll spare him the disappointment and spill it myself. Show the world the ichor flowing through you is godless after all."

Roel drops me, letting my body collapse to the sand like I'm not worth the effort it takes to keep me upright. He kicks and kicks until the fight in me dies. My hands shake against the power choking my veins—the strain of holding back that which I should never have leashed.

What if it's all been for nothing?

I pray and pray. At last, the gods take pity.

A tendril of shadow snakes around my wrist, startling me with its cool touch. It's a fleeting comfort that has tears lining my eyes. It's gone too quickly, and I have no sense of how to call it back. Breath heaves in my lungs. Pain clings to every inch of me. All grows still. For a moment, I think I've endured the worst of this day. How foolish of me.

I feel the blade sink deep, and it takes my mind too long to catch up. The scream gets caught in my throat, choked by tired lungs that have nothing more to give. My eyelids flicker heavily as Roel wiggles the blade in my arm, scorched flesh stabbed through. Nausea heaves up from my stomach, but I swallow it down.

He withdraws the dagger, only to slap the dirtied blade against my face in a vile taunt. "No, I think I'll collect what I'm due," Roel utters to himself. "After all, Rohan promised to pay handsomely, regardless of what a waste you are."

The blade dances across my cheek, slicing gently. Blood trickles down my face. I loose a shuddering breath and close my eyes. The heat bakes me where I lie—a thing left to rot and decay. Roel *tsks*, and, without warning, the blade sinks into my arm once more. I bear down against the earth as he yanks it from my flesh.

As my eyes flutter open, a single, hot tear glides down my cheek. I stare out across the desert, vision hazy against the pain that racks me with shudders. All at once, everything I've endured in this life comes to me like a flickering mirage.

Mother slamming the door in my face.

Begging for scraps a stone's throw from the home I grew up in.

Malachi leaving me for dead.

Narrowing my purpose to a single task: survival.

The first life I took to save my own.

Injuries born from brutal hands.

Rohan carving me up.

Silas shattering the last shard of my heart.

Never truly knowing what power lied within.

Riat's final breath.

And now, this.

I grit my teeth and close my eyes. I've only ever known these pains, only ever faced them to find more on the other side.

But what if the gods desired more for me? From me?

What if I'm fighting the wrong battles? Caging myself only to let others bleed me dry?

My eyes flash open as Roel's boot connects with my stomach. I gasp and sputter, feeling something crack when he does it again, and again. He looses a crazed laugh as he steps back to admire my agony.

"Now, will you behave for our journey to Denheir?" he prods. "Or shall I break a leg next?"

My gift thrums violently under my skin, coursing with a rage that's all my own.

When will I stop letting others dictate my fate?

When will I learn to wield the violence they so willingly inflict?

Roel leans down, and I flinch. His grin is feral with glee as his gaze roams over me. The gleam in his good eye speaks of untold horrors, ones I will surely meet on the journey ahead. I don't need to know what heinous cruelty awaits me; I know I'll never be able to wash the stain from my skin. Roel only confirms my fears when he gathers a slick of my blood on his fingertips, grinning as he raises it into the sunlight to admire his handiwork.

"What do you say, Durit?" he taunts. "Shall we keep playing?"

Roel's smile widens as I push myself upright. Every second is agony, and I grit my teeth through the unsurmountable pain. He backs away, gaze flickering excitedly like he's already imagining what he'll do next.

My head pounds. The godsblood in me thrashes through my veins with a sickening pressure. My heart patters restlessly in my chest, spiked with an inescapable dread. That dire feeling from my vision returns with a force so potent, I wonder if Hael got the timing wrong. I'm far from that dark, raging battle where my blood spilled freely, but I feel just as hopeless as I did then.

This life has been for nothing.

It sounds through my mind like a chiming bell, dragging me back to the truth time and time again. I have wasted so much of this life, fought the gods for too long. I thought I was protecting myself, but the admittance stings like a lie with sharp thorns. It was fear that kept me shackled, me who brought on this suffering.

For how else would the gods treat someone who shunned their gifts so ardently?

I go to stand and immediately collapse.

Roel sneers, shoving his boot against my ribs and drawing a ragged gasp from my lungs. "Such a weak thing," he muses. "It would be kinder to kill you."

He's right. It would be. But a nagging thought has burrowed its way into my chest, hollowed me out and left a place for only darkness to grow. *Yes, this life has been for nothing, but there's still time to remedy that.*

Roel's fingers prod my cut cheekbone, and I gnash my teeth at him like a rabid beast. "*Do it*," I rasp. "I'm done fighting fate. I'm ready."

"Is that so?" Satisfaction stretches across Roel's face. "But what if I'm not done having my fun?" He sneers at me, too caught up in his glee to realize I'm not talking to him.

With a wavering exhale, I finally let go.

The world stills, as if the gods wish to remember this moment for ages to come. And then suddenly, the day turns to night. It's a howling storm of black, a tidal wave that seeks to consume all it greets. The scream that leaves my throat is ragged and cutting, tearing free with a guttural cry. My body twitches, then shudders. The power that floods my veins darkens my vision, though consciousness returns much too quick. I'm lost to the pressure, the feeling of writhing shadows tunneling under my skin only to burst free of the chains I kept so tight.

I don't realize Roel rests in the sand before me until my eyes flicker toward the source of those monstrous sounds. Ripping flesh. Squelching blood. His voice pleads in untold agony. Roel screams as my shadows tear him apart—as my gift takes on a life of its own. It knows what must be done; I don't even need to command it. *Hael above.* The sight should stir my stomach with nausea, rise bile to my throat. But the bloody mess of flesh and decay sprouting across Roel's body only drags a creeping grin across my face, one that has never been less kind, but never so welcome.

"You should have left me the fuck alone," I snarl, breath heaving as I struggle to stand.

My ribs scream in pain. Blood pours down my face. I care for none of it. As I loom over Roel's twitching body, my world narrows to only that of the satisfied thrum in my veins.

The darkness leaves Roel, slinking across the sand to hammer around me like war drums. I'm much too calm as I bear witness to the fear blanching his face. It's the utter panic of someone who is only used to dealing death, never meeting their own. He tries to drag himself away, but it's no use. His legs are sliced deep, a mere cut from being severed cleanly. A wayward shadow obliges my darkest urges. It curls around his ankle, tugging gently only to rip a guttural cry from Roel's lips. Blood drenches the sand. My gaze tightens as I watch him thrash and scream.

How quickly the hare becomes the hunter.

My gift prods me, asking permission for the one thing we both crave, but I deny it. Roel is mine, and mine alone.

A firm pressure in my boot draws a sly smile across my face. I slide my hand down to rip the hidden dagger free. There is no shake in my fingers, no nerves fluttering through the organ in my chest. There is only a certainty that settles over me, a knowing that this is what the gods desire.

I settle next to Roel, blood coating my leathers as I kneel. His good eye widens at the sight of me. That fear of his is palpable, desperate as he tries to drag his broken body out of reach. It's a wasted effort. My gaze darkness like the night itself, and my lips quiver into a wolfish grin.

"Tell the gods who sent you."

The blade sinks into his heart too easily.

There is no resistance. No fight.

As blood seeps into the fabric of his tunic, relief floods my chest. It's the feeling of peace, of no longer fearing you might drown in violent waters. Now there's home in those depths.

Roel coughs and sputters, choking on the life that dribbles down his chin. My gift recoils at the sight, thrashing wildly before slinking back into the vein. I can almost feel the mourning as if it's my own. It seems my shadows don't like the taste of godsblood, nor the death of kin.

Veles doesn't want his own blood returned to the earth?

Pity.

I yank my blade from Roel's chest as I stand, flicking the blood of it with a singular swish of my wrist. The breath in my lungs is tempered, same as my heart as I sheathe the dagger and begin riffling through Roel's pockets. It's a foul thing to strip the dead of their possessions, but I can't find it in me to care.

I step over Roel's body once I've parted him of all his worthy belongings, then do the same to his men. I stalk the sands in search of my daggers, only relenting when they're clean and sheathed in place. The sun sinks lower with each passing moment, and by the time I've finally situated myself atop Mirage's saddle, night has fallen. I expect the darkness to feel different—to send an uneasy shudder through me—but it's all the same.

No suffocating thrum of night.

No inching dark that creeps across my skin as if to bite me.

As I stare out toward the horizon, at the west that's held this journey steady, I realize I've felt the weight of this abyss all along. In silent moments carved by darkness, in those corners of my mind—the ones I dared not touch—the world has always been this still. That pitch black nothing inside me is settled like never before. Content. Relieved it's finally been embraced after waiting with open arms.

It's solace I now find in the shadows—a solace I resisted for too long.

I take a deep breath and sink into the feeling. There is no splitting ache piercing my skull. No gods-cursed consequences shackling me to suffering. There are only the pains man has dealt, and I know those will fade with time. My gift is a warm slink in my veins, a comforting surge of power. Its unguarded presence is a stark reminder—ink on parchment.

There is no coming back from this.

I expect to feel fear, but there's only acceptance filling my chest, chasing away the near-constant ache I've felt for weeks. A soft smile flickers across my face, and, though I wince against the swelling there, I don't let it fade.

With blood coating my hands and quickly drying into flakes, I guide my horse forward with new purpose. The Kohe Mountains are dark blurs on the horizon, but their shadowed peaks no longer provoke dread in me. It's with comfortable resignation that I allow them to draw closer—an almost eagerness that has me prodding Mirage, urging her faster.

Shadows curl around my wrists as I ride, rubbing soothing circles against my skin. I can feel fate like a thread tugging me forward, every step loosening my chest as the tension fades. Too long I fought fate. Too long I allowed others to leave me bloodied and bruised while tempering a violence that could have saved me. I thought I was cursed—a blight that should keep to herself. I let them convince me I was weak—a daemon with no use of her gifts.

My lips twitch at the thought.

If only they could see what they've created.

I kick my heels against Mirage once more, sending us into a gallop that has me tucking my body against hers.

If the gods want me to be the Durit—to be this monster who spills blood and makes her enemies pay in flesh—fine. So be it. I'll be their monster.

I'll be the worst the Continent has ever seen.

EPILOGUE

"Tell me what I need to know."

Walen eyes me from behind his pint, cocking a bushy brow. "*Acht*," he chitters. "Can't a man have a drink before we get to business?"

My lip twitches up into a smirk I know he expects before I wave him off. "Have at it," I offer boredly. "After all, you're much less attached to your secrets once deep in a few pints."

His eyes shine with dull pleasure, and it takes him no time at all to guzzle a throat-full of ale. I can only watch on as my hands strangle the armrests of my chair. I've waited all day to see Walen—already stayed in this godsdamned city for too long—*but what's a few more hours?* I stifle the flare of irritation in my blood and force a deep breath through my lungs.

As Walen drinks, my gaze snaps around the hovel the good people of Sefti consider proper for a tavern. The southern coast's heat muddies the sea breeze that spills in from open windows, making already ripe bodies flush with sweat. Overhead, the wood ceiling creaks and moans, beams too full of damp to stave off sway. The moisture-laden rot wafting through the shack is enough to distract me from its patrons—but not for long. Dress skirts sway while men's heads fall into waiting bosoms. The bard's lute is out of tune, clashing with the off-key ballad that spills from drunken lips. Ale sloshes against the floor as fists raise pints too high in celebration. There was a time when I'd find home in an unsavory place such as this—drink myself full and pay for a pretty face to pass the time—but those days are long behind me. Death changes a man.

The curl of my lip is the only reaction I allow myself as I watch two men arm wrestle, only to have one convinced the other is cheating. The brutal *smack* as the man beats his companion bloody over the tabletop draws little attention from those around me. It seems The Widow's Pearl has witnessed far worse; I doubt this will be the sole fight this tavern sees tonight.

I watch it all from Walen and my darkened corner, but not even the shadows provide me the anonymity I seek. Too many eyes met mine when I walked in, and, even now, I find wary gazes trained on me. They know who I am. They can guess what I'm after. And though they despise my presence here, they take one look at my marks and think better of testing their luck. I almost wish they would be foolish enough to try. It would be nothing for me to leave this tavern in shambles, bodies still and bones shattered. But as much as I crave a little violence—if only to take the edge off—I have no time for pointless brawls. Not tonight. Not with fate knocking on the hourglass with each passing day.

"*Gods and devils.* There's a lot of bastards in here tonight," Walen utters through a laugh. He takes a long swig of ale, only to have much of it seep into the bristled ends of his beard. "They pass through endlessly now. Everyone and their gods-loving mother thinks they have a chance. Desperate enough to go up against the world's foulest brutes just for some coin."

Walen shoots me a fiendish look. "No offense."

I hide my sneer and wave him off again.

He laughs, sighing into his drink before his eyes flash back to me. "You heard about it, right?"

I merely raise a brow at Walen. The pint clenched in his meaty hands is almost drained, and though I know it'll take more than one to loosen his tongue, this surely isn't his first of the night. I can tell by the lazy sheen in his brown eyes that he's been at this all day—taking pints in exchange for the secrets he hordes. If I only hold out a little longer, I'll have what I need. Then I can leave this gods-forsaken city behind me.

So, I play along.

"Heard about what, Walen?" I mutter.

"Don't play smart with me." His mouth stretches wide, showing off rows of rotten teeth. "That bounty." He whistles, and I tense. "20,000 yenti out on a Seer. A woman, at that!" He slaps the table and laughs.

I take a sip of the ale in front of me, the one I hadn't seen fit to touch in the time we've been here. It's as watered-down as I expected—not nearly strong enough to provide the distraction I need.

"Surprised to find you're headed in the opposite direction," Walen muses. "Last I heard she was spotted in Hira, and you were on the job."

My jaw ticks, but I give him no more than that. Crossing my arms over my chest, I shrug, feigning indifference. "All in good time."

I say nothing more, and Walen takes a moment to appraise me—searching for something to use against me, no doubt. He's always been a conniving bastard. If only he had the brains to pose any real threat, then this meeting might be worth the headache.

"Fine. Fine," Walen grumbles. "Keep your secrets."

He goes back to drinking his ale, and around me the tavern's chaos pitches and rolls. Another fight has broken out, this one a little more deadly. My jaw clenches as I watch fists slam into faces. Chairs topple. Drinks spill across tables. A man hits the floor and doesn't get up. The godsblood inside me twitches, eager for a share of that violence.

Walen's voice snaps me away from the tempting thrum of my gift before I can submit to it. "I've seen the posting, you know. Heard the rumors."

He slams his drink down, and it clatters with a hollow *thud*. His eyes sweep from me to the cup expectantly until I give him what he wants. With a grunt, I wave down the bar keep and gesture for another round. It comes quickly, though there's other patrons in need of drink. I don't miss the way the bar keep's gaze darts across the markings on my face before he rushes away, careful not to turn his back on me too soon.

I'd take pride in that if I wasn't in such a shit mood. My notoriety no longer stirs my own amusement, only simmering rage. It's a gnawing reminder of what I've done and what I failed to do. I refuse to name what plagues me, but the foreign feeling has me unsteady nevertheless. My blood itches for carnage. Punches thrown. Bloodied lips. Anything to dispel the weak feeling clenching my chest. But for some reason, I'm holding back.

"I wouldn't mind running into her, see what the fuss is about," Walen rambles on. "Pretty little thing. Heard she's got some fight in her, too." His grin grows foul, leering. "Just how I like 'em."

My stomach churns. Black spreads through my eyes in an all-consuming flood. I lean across the tabletop, head tilting to the side like a devil hungry for blood. "You think you could take her?" I laugh bitterly. Candlelight flickers against my skin, highlighting columns of markings that should have been warning enough not to push me. "She would tear you to shreds."

Walen hums, eyes skating across my chest where my tunic dips low. His mouth quirks into a shit-eating grin when he spots the black scars that are new since the last time he saw me. "Speaking from experience?"

I snatch Walen by the collar quickly, brute strength hauling him out of his chair. It would be easy to break every bone in his face, but when I realize the tavern has gone still, I temper that violence. The room is quiet, dangerously so. It's only when I shove Walen back to his seat and settle against my own that the night resumes its debauchery. Like nothing happened, the gods-awful music picks up again, as does the singing.

"It seems another Shade ran you through..." There's a glint in Walen's eye that tells me he knows too much. "Maybe it's time to retire."

I've fought men for less than the look he's giving me. Though I want to wring his thick neck, I can only offer him a wry grin before taking a sip of ale. Walen is much too pleased with himself, but he should know my patience only goes so far.

"Do you have the information I need, or not?" I demand to know.

He grins into his cup, taking a leisurely sip before addressing me. "Do you have the coin I require, or not?"

I chuck the bag of gold on the table, scowling. Though I try to avoid it, my heartbeat stumbles at the sight of that leather pouch. It's only when Walen snatches it away with greedy hands that I settle. Never have I been so grateful to part ways with coin.

Walen gives me a pleased look as he drains the rest of his pint. He belches into his hand before leaning back in his chair like he has not a care in the world. "You're dealing with eleven guards. Two outside. One patrolling every tunnel. The rest stay deep within, too busy with their... fun."

He rips a hunk of bread off a passing tray before shoving it in his mouth. The bar maiden carrying said tray slaps him upside the head, though Walen merely pats her ass in return. She squeals, then slaps him again. Only when she's out of reach and I've cleared my throat does Walen remember me. He chuckles, then begins again.

"There's three tunnels. Avoid the right one at all costs, unless you wish to meet the gods." He wags his eyebrows, but I'm less than amused. He *tsks* and continues on. "That's where the majority of the guards are. No one heads down there and makes it back alive. They'll strip your skin from your bones if only to find a new way to put it back on. Will carve you up until the ground runs thick with your blood."

The bastard is enjoying this, practically drooling around his chewing as he regales me with tales he thinks will scare me off. If he only knew death and I were close friends.

"And what of the others?" I pry. "What tunnel holds those with debts?"

Walen stops eating and raises a brow. His glassy eyes hold too much focus, and as something wicked sparks in his gaze, I know I've said too much.

"Debts, you say?" Walen's smile grows wide. "*Ah*, don't tell me you're that reckless?"

I grit my teeth, barely holding back my scowl. "Answer the question."

He leans forward, rotten-toothed grin still stretched into place. "He'll most likely be in the left tunnel," Walen offers quietly. "The poor bastards there are said to be held for lesser offenses. Thieving. Debts. Anything not dealt in flesh. At least, until you get to the back cells." His gaze gleams, speaking of secrets he's not willing to share for free.

I roll my eyes and quickly finish my first drink before reaching for the second. "And what of the guards?" I prod. "Are the rumors true?"

Walen stares at me with too much delight on his face; it pulls his grin higher, stretching his sagging jowls. "As much as the rumors of you are true," he taunts. "No one is said to fight them and live."

I scoff, knowing talk of that sort no longer holds weight. I wish it was anger I felt when I think of that day, but it's something far worse.

Walen leans over the table, dampening the sleeve of his tunic in spilled ale. "Are you really going to risk his fury? What if the bastard finds out his favorite daemon has gone rogue?" Walen pats my arm like I'm an ignorant child. "Come now, old friend. Is kin really worth that much to you?"

Though I know I should show restraint, I can't stop the black from bleeding into my eyes. "Keep your mouth shut, *old friend*, and Rohan won't know of such things." I push up from my chair, screeching its legs against the dirty, stone floor. "Don't think I've forgotten what happened in Heshin all those years ago. Nor the way I spared you for that mistake."

I lean over him, teeth bared like a snarling predator. My hands grip the table's edge roughly, splitting the wood with gods-given strength. "I will gladly offer you to the earth if you outlive your usefulness. Don't forget that." Snatching my cup, I drain every last drop of ale. When I'm done, I slam it mere inches from his hand. "You never saw me."

Walen grins, black teeth gleaming against the candlelight. "I never do."

Hope is the folly of weak men.
Snare it before it guts you.

Turn the page for a sneak peek into Book 3.

BORN OF BLOOD

My eyes scan the horizon slowly and meticulously. I fixate on every smudge of shadow, every flicker of movement across these desolate sands. Though my nerves itch under my skin, the only thing I find is the usual quiet. The gods-drenched north is as empty as it's been for weeks. I'm disappointed for a moment, only to realize I'm not as alone as I thought.

Movement to the north sends my heart pounding through my chest. It's the type of unsuspecting prey I beg the gods for every morning. Finally, they've taken pity on me. My smile stretches wide, and my gift flares out from my wrist in thin tendrils, lashing the air. It's as eager as I am.

I hum with quiet delight as my shadows ebb and flow, surrounding me like a moon-drunk tide. Mirage doesn't bother to look up from where she eats. My gift is a constant now—a thing she's learned to tolerate. She chomps and chews with an acquired indifference, but the power within me feels anything but impassive. It's been days since my shadows had any excitement, days since I gave them a true challenge. I can feel them hungering.

Who am I to deny them?

I make quick work of tying up Mirage's feed bag, much to her dismay. Though her irritation is soon quelled by the apple I offer in its place. It's the last one we have, and its bruised flesh reminds me of the few injuries that still linger on my skin. I'm nibbling on my own half as I slink across the sand, leaving Mirage with an open bladder of water and the promise that I'll be back before the sun rises.

The morning is silent, and I keep my footsteps quieter than anything that scurries across this desert. Mirage is a distant blur at my back, and her chuffs have long since faded away. The soft sift of sand is the only thing that threatens to announce my arrival, but, when it comes time, I'll be much too quick to be given away by such things.

My eyes track every step my prey takes, gaze tightening in determination. There's no room for error, no second chance. I have to be smart about this. Each deliberate footfall and carefully concealed breath is fueled by the empty ache in my belly. The rations I stole from Roel and his men ran out a week ago. Dried meats. Hunks of bread. I was greedy in their consumption and now face the consequences. If I want to survive this desert, I'll have to find my own food.

I crouch low, knees brushing the sand. The antelope's large ears twitch, its whole body growing still. The movement steals my breath, but my presence here is no more than a whisper and quickly overlooked. The animal begins eating once more, too busy nibbling bone-dry brush to realize it'll soon be the one sating hunger.

My hands quiver at my sides, eager for the daggers I won't allow them. I curl my fingers into fists and push away the doubt that clings to the rim of my thoughts.

What if I miss?

What if I go another night without the comfort of a meal?

What if I once again cause more harm?

I clench my jaw and force myself to focus. Those thoughts will do nothing to help me, do nothing to ease the ache in my stomach or dispel the weakness from my limbs. There are no guarantees in this life. I could surely miss. This is practice, after all—but practice I desperately need. If I don't take this opportunity, who knows when the next one will come.

Anxiety eases in my chest. The wild patter of my heart turns steady and strong. It comes without me having to call it. That familiar, sludge-like pressure slinks through my veins, taking its time as it floods me with heady power and untold weight. The shadows are barely a tease against my skin, hovering in the air with a patience that's mirrored by the tempo of my steady breath.

I watch the antelope—study how its lanky, white legs bend so that it can reach the scrub that's been baked under the sun for too long. Its antlers reach into the morning gloom like violent spires. The golden-hued bones twist roughly, reminiscent of the jagged rocks that decorate this very land. One of the antlers has fractured at the tip, leaving a grisly crack like a dry riverbed running through a canyon. My shadows twitch across my skin as I drop my gaze to the animal's hooves. Black cloven feet are covered in pale, orange dust—remnants of the terrains this animal has crossed all its life. But it's what rests above the desert's traces that makes my chest clench too tight.

Black, ink-like patterns snake up its front legs, blending into its pale fur like shadows. I've never seen a merov antelope in the flesh, only ever glimpsed one in the Book. It's a regal, gentle thing. Poised. *Ethereal.* It's said they were born of Hael, given to this land by the loving god to sate his children's hunger. But when Veles's blood fell from the skies and drenched the earth, the animal's feet were stained, forever a reminder of the treachery of the youngest brother god.

A shiver runs up my spine; I tell myself it's the lingering chill. I don't let myself think about what my shadows might do once they realize this animal is touched by the gods. I can only rise from my hidden position crouched behind a dune and pray Veles grants me a bit of his favor this morning.

The antelope's ears twitch, detecting its demise, but it's already too late. In a mad rush of darkness, I come for it. The shadows have their task, and as they cut across the desert like a deadly wraith, I know they won't falter. A searing whip of black. A deathly moan. It's over before I loose a full breath from my lungs.

It drops to the sand quickly—torso cleaved through, bright, red blood flowing back into the earth. My shadows swirl around their kill, preening like a child who did their best and now seeks a reward. I roll my eyes as I make my way over but can't deny the flush of pride that hums through me.

A successful kill—one of the few I've had in the weeks I've spent honing this gift. Though I'm eager to, I don't let myself revel in the moment just yet. My eyes scour the antelope as I crouch to its level, checking for any signs of breath—any hint of suffering. There are none. I swallow thickly, trying not to think too hard about the hunts that came before this one.

Desert hares squealing amidst their drawn-out deaths.

A pehmi who evaded the dinner pot but left behind a leg cleaved by shadow.

I press my hands to the earth—fingertips resting in hot blood—and bow my head in reverence. My shadows swirl and sway as I offer gratitude to the god who's allowed me this triumph. That darkness drifts across my back, slinking about like an infernal sentry. It does that now—guards me like a loyal hound whenever a flicker of vulnerability makes my chest tighten. It's a heady thing to have a god watching your blind spots, but it's addicting in a way that can make even the most diligent of warriors negligent.

As I raise my hand to pray, my gaze stalls, then lingers on the black spread across my skin. My marks have grown steadily over the past few weeks. Swirling swathes of ink-like darkness crawl up my right arm—but what started as a mere streak has now bled into a flurry. Not an inch of unmarked skin remains on the inside of my forearm. My fingers trace over the markings delicately, heart lurching with something made of old panic and newfound awe. Veles has staked his claim on me with a heavy hand. There is no denying how much the dark god favors me, nor how much I have taken to him.

I swallow thickly and continue my devotion. My blood-coated thumb glides over my arm, painting my skin red. I utter my thanks before pressing the digit into the earth. After years of contempt, the act no longer stirs resentment in me. It's only peace I feel—an unfamiliar flicker of warmth in my chest.

Would it be so bad, for this to be my life?

My stomach rumbles, reminding me there's still much to be done before I'm sated. I peel my hands from the sand, skin coming away covered in grit and sticky with the life I took. I stare at my fingertips for too long, letting the past, present, and future collide with an unshakable truth. The gods will always desire blood on my hands. There's no use fighting it, so I've stopped trying.

I don't bother wiping clean, knowing what comes after this will only see to more gore on my skin. It all happens with quiet focus and a practiced hand. I drag my blade through fur, slitting flesh open from groin to neck. Heat and ichor floods my nostrils, and I'm quick to gag. I should have brought one of my scarves to shield my face, but some things are more important than comfort.

First, I remove the antelope's organs, chucking them aside for the buzzards to chew. Next, skin rips away from muscle with the delicate force of my blade. It's a mess of putrid stenches and flowing ichor that I force myself to overlook. I'm covered up to my elbows in blood, and sweat beads down my forehead in steady drops. My shadows move before I ask them to, pushing damp hair out of my eyes and tucking it behind my ear. The gesture is almost tender and reminds me too much of another's darkness. I dig my teeth into my cheek and shove those thoughts away. I can't think of Malachi now, not when my stomach is clenched against empty nothing and the flies are already buzzing my face. There will be time later to stew in my enmity—there always is.

I carve meat from bone with a heavy-handedness that would make a butcher cringe, but this is survival; there is nothing pretty about it. Time ticks by steadily, and only when the sun rouses from sleep does weariness find me. My hands ache from strain, cramping as I tie cording around steaming cuts of meat. When I stand on shaky legs—hefting my bounty over my shoulders like a gruesome cloak—dizziness blotches my vision. It's been too many days since I had more than halves of apples and bites of whatever poor creature I managed to snare with shadows. There was a desperate morning where I attempted to eat some of Mirage's feed and promptly lost it all to the sand in a sickening rush.

Yes, this meal is long overdue.

I teeter for a moment, body almost collapsing against the weight I now bear, but as I stumble forward, I find my legs bolstered by a familiar darkness. A heavy breath pulls into my lungs as I regain my balance. One step, then two. My shoulders ache, and it's only moments before I feel the load lighten. My gift is a shadowy sling against my back, hefting the spoils of my hunt higher when my body wavers in strength.

A thought hits me abruptly, churning an irritation that's for no one but myself.

Why did I resist this for so long?

As I walk back to camp, the thrill of my hunt fades. The desert holds a razor-sharp quiet; it can be peaceful, but only if your mind is free of the type of burdens I possess in plenty. I needle my lip heedlessly with my teeth. There's a nervous tick in my gut, one that seeks to overshadow the desperate hunger I've felt for days. I refuse to acknowledge it—just as I refuse to acknowledge so many things that plague me out here in this endless nothing. Though, something tells me that soon I will no longer have the luxury of ignorance. The dreams are getting worse, more frequent. I know who sends them, and I know just what he wants.

My jaw clenches; I'm unwilling to let my thoughts slip to him. Instead, I force my gaze to drift across this vast land, basking in my isolation while it lasts. For a brief, startling moment, it feels lonely. But as shadows wind their way around my wrist, tracing soothing circles on my blood-stained skin, I realize I'm not truly alone. I never will be again. Veles has made sure of that.

Acknowledgments

As always, this book would not have been possible without a handful of amazing people...

First, to my beta readers who continually hold it down for me. I am so grateful for the time and effort you lent to reading the early draft of this story. Your feedback helped make this book the best it could be. Thank you for catching my silly typos and for leaving comments that made me laugh out loud. #TeamHassan reigns supreme.

To my personal cheerleaders: Mom, Karisa, and Haley. Thank you for always being there to listen to my rambles (crash-outs) and for always making time to read "just one more" revision. If I don't say it enough—THANK YOU. You help quiet my inner critic and remind me that I can do whatever I set my mind to.

I would be remiss if I didn't mention all of the friends, family, and readers who make being an author so special. Each DM, shout-out, and conversation means so much to me. Sometimes I forget how many people are truly cheering me on throughout this author journey, and every single comment, book recommendation, and sale hits deep. Thank you for your endless support. I hope this book made you proud.

Last but certainly not least, a massive thank you to my wonderful cover designer—Luísa Dias. You are incredibly talented at what you do. Thank you for yet another amazing book cover.

A final note to my readers: whether you're new to this series or have been here since day 1, thank you for taking a chance on me. As an indie author, it often feels like I'm screaming into the void, and I'm grateful you heard the call and decided to pick up. I promise it only gets better from here. Until next time, happy reading.

About the Author

Angie Caedis is a mood writer with a love for too many genres, but—above all else—fantasy has her heart. When she's not hunkered down at her laptop with a cup of tea, she enjoys hiking, horror movies, solo travel, and reading anything she can get her hands on.

Follow her on all social channels @angiecaedis or visit angiecaedis.com for book news and sneak peeks.

9 798988 868828